Bug Jack Barron

BUG JACK BARRON

NORMAN SPINRAD

WITH AN AFTERWORD BY MICHAEL MOORCOCK

Overlook SF&F Classics

The Overlook Press
Woodstock & New York

This edition first published in paperback in the United States in 2004 by
The Overlook Press, Peter Mayer Publishers, Inc.
Woodstock & New York

WOODSTOCK:
One Overlook Drive
Woodstock, NY 12498
www.overlookpress.com
[for individual orders, bulk and special sales, contact our Woodstock office]

NEW YORK:
141 Wooster Street
New York, NY 10012

Cataloging-in-Publication Data is available from the Library of Congress

Manufactured in the United States of America
ISBN 1-58567-585-7
1 3 5 7 9 8 6 4 2

Dedicated, in gratitude, to

MICHAEL MOORCOCK

and to

THE MILFORD MAFIA

"SPLIT BOYS, will you?" drawled Lukas Greene, waving his black hand (and for that nasty little moment, for some reason, thinking of it as black) at the two men (perversely seeing them for the tired moment as niggers) in the Mississippi State Police (coon to the right) and Mississippi National Guard (schvug to the left) uniforms.

"Yessur, Governor Greene," the two men said in unison. (And Greene's ear, caught in what he could outside viewpoint see as the dumb mindless masochistic moment, heard it as 'Yassah Massah.')

"Tote dat barge," Governor Greene said to the door when it had closed behind them. What the hell's wrong with me today, Greene thought irritably. That damned Shabazz. That dumb trouble-making nig—

There was that word again, and that was where the whole thing was at. Malcolm Shabazz, Prophet of the United Black Muslim Movement, Chairman of the National Council of Black Nationalist Leaders, Recipient of the Mao Peace Prize, and Kingfish of the Mystic Knights of the Sea was neither more nor less than a nigger. He was everything the shades saw when they heard the word nigger: Peking-loving ignorant dick-dragging black-oozing ape-like savage. And that cunning son of a bitch Malcolm knew it and played on it, making himself a focus of mad white hate, the purposeful prime target of garbage-throwing screaming Wallacite loonies, feeding on the hate, growing on it, absorbing it, saying to the shades, "I'm a big black mother, and I hate your fucking guts, and China is the Future, and my dick is bigger than yours, and China is the Future, and my twenty million bucks like me in this country, a billion in People's China and four billion in the world who hate you like I hate you, die you shade mother!"

As the Bohemian Boil-Sucker observed to the chick who farted in his face, Greene thought, it's people like you, Malcolm, who make this job disgusting.

Greene swivelled in his chair, and stared at the little TV perched on the desk across from the in-out basket. Instinctively he reached for the pack of Acapulco Golds sitting on the pristine desktop, then thought better of it. Much as he needed a good lungful of pot at this moment on this day, it was not a smart move for anyone who was where anything was at to be under the influence of anything on a Wednesday night. He glanced surreptitiously at the dead screen of his vidphone. The screen might very well come alive during the next hour with the sardonically smiling face of good old Jack Barron.

"Jack Barron," Lukas Greene sighed aloud. Jack Barron. Even a friend couldn't afford to be stoned if he got a public call from Jack. Not in front of a hundred million people he couldn't.

But then it had never paid, even in the old Jack-and-Sara days, to give an edge to Jack Barron. What's-his-name—whoever remembers anymore?—made the mistake of letting Jack guest on his Birch grill for one night, and Jack grew all over him like a fucking fungus.

And then—no more what's-his-name. Just a camera, a couple vidphones, and good old Jack Barron.

If only... Greene thought, the same old familiar Wednesday night 'if only' thought... if only Jack were still one of us. With Jack on our side the SJC would have a fighting chance to break through and beat the Pretender. If only...

If only Jack weren't such a cop-out. If only he had kept some of what we all seemed to lose in the seventies. But what had Jack said (and oh, was he right; and don't I know it!), "Luke," Jack Barron had said, and Greene remembered every word—Jack could always stick a phrase in your head like a Bester mnemonic jingle—"it sure is a bad moment when you decide to sell out. But a worse moment, the worst moment in the world is when you decide to sell out and nobody's buying."

And how do you answer that? Greene thought. How do you answer that, when you've parlayed a picket sign, a big mouth, and a black skin into the Governor's Mansion in Evers, Mississippi? How do you answer Jack, you black shade you white nigger you?

Lukas Greene laughed a bitter little laugh. The name of the show had to be an inside joke, a real inside joke, inside Jack's hairy little head, is all...

Because (since he had waved bye-bye to Sara) who in hell could really... *bug Jack Barron?*

Not a night to be alone, Sara Westerfeld unwittingly found herself thinking under the sardonic blind gaze of the dead glass eye of the portable TV which suddenly seemed to have infiltrated itself into her consciousness in her living room, where Don and Linda and Mike and the Wolfman stood unknowing guard against loneliness—ghosts of Wednesday nights past, and she against her will realised (and realised against her will that she always realised) that it had been a long time (don't think of the exact date; you know the exact date; don't think of it) since she had spent a Wednesday night with fewer than three people around her.

Better to play games with Don Sime (will I—won't I—is tonight the night—or will I ever?) than to sit alone the way I maybe want to, with the dead glass eye daring me to turn it on. Better still just to sit here and dig the Wolfman rapping with half an ear and let the broken record of his harmless talking-just-to-hear-himself-talk bullshit turn off my mind, turn off memory, and let me drift in the droning not-really-Wednesday now...

"Dig, so I say, man, why ain't there a cheque for me?" the Wolfman was saying, pulling at his scraggly muttonchops. "I'm a human being, ain't I?"

"Know what the fucker says?" the Wolfman whined with a great display of wounded dignity Sara could not tell was put on or not. "Says, 'Jim, you're too young for Social Security, too old for AID, and you ain't never worked ten weeks in a row to qualify for Unemployment. In fact you are a bum in hip clothing, is what *you* are.'"

The Wolfman paused. And now Sara saw a strange thing happen to his face as the supercilious mood left it—revealed as superciliousness by its passing—and she saw what the others in the pseudo-Japanese room also saw, that for once the Wolfman was grotesquely pitiably earnest.

"What kind of shit is that?" the Wolfman asked stridently, and the joint he was holding slid from his fingers and fell unheeded, burning the black-lacquered coffee table.

"Screw it, will you, Wolfman, and pick up that Pall Mall you dropped on the table," Don said, trying to act like the Defender of Hearth and Home in front of Sara, make his dumb little points with her in her own apartment.

"Screw yourself, Sime," the Wolfman said. "I'm talking about like real injustice. People like you, people like me—"

"Aw—" Don began, and the moment stood still for Sara, knowing what he was going to say, the three words, the exact cynical intonation, having been flayed by those words dozens of times a week for years, wincing, dying a little each time she heard those three last words, knowing that Don Sime would now never ball her, not with a billion screaming Chinese holding her down, not ever. Sooner would she make it with a gila monster or Benedict Howards than give herself to a man who said those three words on a Wednesday night between 8 and 9 p.m., and by the little death induce the *grand mal déjà vu,* images on his face on the television screen carefully tousled over his face on the long ago blue-flowered pillow carelessly neat his beard blue and stubbly...

Don Sime, unheeding (and, she saw, an unheeding, rotten swine by his thoughtless reflex reaction), nevertheless said the three magic words, the outsider's inside expression that shrivelled to death for an instant the insides of Sara.

"Aw," said Don Sime, "*bug Jack Barron.*"

Cool was the night breeze in Benedict Howards' throat as he lay easily in the crisp white sheets of the hospital bed, snug and safe in the monolithic citadel that was the Rocky Mountain Freezer Complex. Out beyond the half-strength heat-curtain opening onto the balcony (they had screamed when he demanded to feel the breeze when he came out of it, and they told him it seemed to have worked, but no half-ass gaggle of quacks was going to give any lip to Benedict Howards) the mountains were vague shapes in the heavy darkness, and the stars were washed out by the muzzy twilight glow from the busy lights of the Freezer Complex, *his* Complex, *all* of it now, and...

Forever?

He tasted Forever in the pine breeze that blew in from the mountains and from New York and Dallas and Los Angeles and Vegas and all the places where lesser men scurried for crumbs bug-like in the light; tasted Forever, lying calmed and warmed against the breeze by postoperative weakness in the sheets that he owned in the Complex he owned in the country where Senators and Governors and the President called him *Mr* Howards...

Tasted Forever in the memory of Palacci's smug grin as he had said, "We know that it's taken, Mr Howards, and we know that it should work. Forever, Mr Howards? Forever is a long time. We can't know that it's forever till it's been forever, now, can we, Mr Howards? Five centuries, a millennium... who knows? Maybe you'll have to settle for a million years. Think that will do, Mr Howards?"

And Howards had smiled and allowed the doctor his dumb little death-joke, allowed it, when he had broken bigger men for less because what the hell you couldn't nurse every little dumb grudge like that for a million years, now, could you? Had to take the long view, get rid of excess baggage.

Forever? Howards thought. Really, this time I could smell it on the doctor's sweat, see it in their fat little bonus smiles. The bastards think they've done it this time. Thought they'd done it before. But this time I can taste it, I can feel it; I hurt in the right places.

Forever... Push it back forever, Howards thought. Fading black circle of light, big-eyed night nurses, daytime bitch with her plastic professional cheeriness back in the other sheets in the other hospital in the other year tube, wormlike, up his nose down his throat, in his guts, membranes clinging and sticking to polyethylene like a slug on a rock, with each shallow breath an effort not to choke, not to reach up with whatever left rip-gagging tube from nose-throat rip blood-drip needle from left arm, glucose solution from right; die clean like a man, clean like boyhood Panhandle plains, clear-cut knife-edge between life and death, not this pissing away of life juices in plastic, in glass, in tubes and retches enemas catheters needles nurses faded faggot vases of flowers...

But the circle of black light contracting, son of a bitch, no fading black circle of light snuffs out Benedict Howards! Buy the bastard, bluff him, con him, kill him! No dumb-ass wheel flipping to goddamn Limey limousine gives lip to Benedict Howards. Hate the bastard, fight him, burn him out, buy him, bluff him, con him, kill him, open up the circle of black light... wider, *wider*. Hate tubes hate nurses hate needles sheets flowers. Show 'em! Show 'em all they don't kill Benedict Howards.

"No one kills Benedict Howards!" Howards found himself mouthing the words, the breeze now cold, warm weakness now gone, fight reflexes pounding his arteries, light cold sweat on his cheeks.

With a shudder Howards wrenched himself out of it. This was another hospital another year; life poured into him, sewn into him, nurtured in Deep Sleep, not leaking out in tubes and bottles. Yes, yes, you're in control now. Paid your dues. No man should have to die twice, no man twice watching life leak away youth leak away blood leak away all leak away muscle turn to flab, balls to shrivelled prunes, limbs to broomhandles, not Benedict Howards. Push it back, push it back for a million years. Push it back—*forever*.

Howards sighed, felt glands relaxing, gave himself over again to the pleasant, healthy warm weakness, knowing what it meant, warmth pushing back the cold, light opening the fading black circle, holding it open, pushing it open—*forever*.

Always a fight, thought Benedict Howards. Fight from Texas Panhandle to oil-money-power Dallas, Houston, LA, New York, where it all was action open oil leases land stocks electronics NASA, Lyndon Senators Governors, toadies... *Mr* Howards. Fight from quiet dry plains to quiet air-cooled arenas of power, quiet air-cooled women with skin untouched by sun by wind by armpit-sweat...

Fight from tube up nose down throat fading black circle to Foundation for Human Immortality, bodies frozen in liquid helium, voting assets liquid assets frozen with them in quiet dry helium-cooled vaults of power Foundation power my power money-power fear-power immortality power—power of life against death against fading black circle.

Fight from dry empty Panhandle-seared women lying in wrecked car blood trickling from mouth pain inside fading black circle, to this moment, the first moment of Forever.

Yeah, always a fight, thought Benedict Howards. Fight to escape, get, live. And now the big fight, fight to keep it all: money power, young fine-skinned women, Foundation, whole goddamned country, Senators, Governors, President, air-cooled places of power, *Mr* Howards. Forever, *Mr* Howards, *forever*.

Howards looked out the heat-curtained window, saw the busy lights of the Freezer Complex, Complexes in Colorado, New York, Cicero, Los Angeles, Oakland, Washington... Washington Monument, White House, the Capital, where they lay in wait, men against him, against his citadel against Foundation against Freezer Utility Bill against forever, men on the side of the fading black circle...

Little more than a year, thought Benedict Howards. Little more than a year till Democratic Convention—destroy Teddy the Pretender, Hennering for President, Foundation man, my man my country, Senators, Governors... *President*, Mr Howards. Month, two months, and they vote on the Utility

Bill, win vote with money-power fear-power of life against death—then let the bastards find out how I let 'em choose then. Sell out to life to Foundation to forever—or give themselves to the fading black circle. Power of life against death, and what senator, Governor, President chooses death, *Mr* Howards?

Howards' eyes fell on the wall clock: 9:57, Mountain Time. Reflexively, his attention shifted to the tiny dormant screen of the vidphone (Mr Howards is not to be disturbed by anyone for anything tonight, not even Jack Barron) on the bedside table next to the small TV set. His stomach tightened with fear of the unknown, the random, exposure.

Just reflex action, Howards thought. Wednesday-night conditioned response. Nothing more. Jack Barron can't get to me tonight. Strict orders, lines of retreat, back-up men. ("Mr Howards is on his yacht in the Gulf is in plane to Las Vegas duck hunting fishing in Canada, can't be found, a hundred miles from the nearest vidphone, Mr Barron. Mr De Silva, Dr Bruce, Mr Yarborough will be happy to speak with you, Mr Barron. Fully authorised to speak for the Foundation, actually in more intimate contact with details than Mr Howards, Mr Barron. Mr De Silva, Dr Bruce, Mr Yarborough will tell you anything you want to know, Mr Barron.") Jack Barron could not, would not be permitted to bug him in this first night of forever.

Just a dancing bear anyway, Benedict Howards told himself. Jack Barron, a bone to the masses the reliefers loafers, acid-dope-hux-freaks Mexes niggers. Useful valve on the pressurecooker. Image of power on a hundred million screens, image not reality, not money-power, fear-power, life-against-death power Senators, Governors, President, *Mr* Howards.

Walking tightrope between networks, sponsors, masses, FCC (two commissioners in Foundation's pocket) Jack Barron. Bread-and-circus gladiator, with paper-sword image of power, Bullshit Jack Barron.

Nevertheless, Benedict Howards reached out, turned on the TV set, waited stomach-knotted, through colour images of Dodges, network emblem, Coke bottles dancing, plastic piece of ass starlet smoking Kools Supreme, station emblem, waited frowning tense in the cool night breeze, knowing others waited, bellies rumbling with his in quiet air-cooled vaults of power in New York, Chicago, Dallas, Houston, Los Angeles, Washington waiting for three words (scarlet on midnight-blue background) to begin the hour's ordeal of waiting, glancing at dead vidphones, pustules of Harlem, Watts, Mississippi, trip City, Village niggers, loafers, losers randomly popping—a hundred million cretins, hunched forward, smelling for blood, blue venous blood from circles of power:

"BUG JACK BARRON."

"BUG JACK BARRON" —red letters (purposefully crude imitation of traditional 'Yankee Go Home' sign scrawled on walls in Mexico, Cuba, Cairo, Bangkok, Paris) against flat dark-blue background.

Off-camera gruff barroom voice over shouts: "Bugged?"

And an answering sound-collage as camera holds on the title: students heckling People's America agitator, amens to hardrock Baptist preacher, mothers crying soldiers griping sour losers outside the two-dollar window. Barroom voice in cynically hopeful tone: "then go *bug Jack Barron!*"

Title becomes head and shoulders shot of man against uncomfortable dark background (semisubliminal whirling moiré pattern flashes seem to hang on brink of visibility like black India ink over kinesthop underpattern effect). The man is wearing fawn-yellow collarless sportjacket over tieless open-necked red velour dress shirt. He looks about forty? thirty? twenty-five?—anyway, over twenty-one. His complexion seems to hover between fair and grey, like a harried romantic poet; his face is composed of strangely hard-edged softnesses, tapestry of stalemated battle. His hair is reminiscent of dead men—sandy JFK cut about to grow down the back of his neck, flank his ears, spring wild curls upward, and become Dylan-like unmade-bed halo. His brat-eyes (knowing eyes) smoulder with amused detachment as his full lips smile, making the smile a private in-group, I-know-you-know-I-know thing with latest Brackett Audience Count estimated hundred million people.

Jack Barron smiles, nods, becomes Acapulco Golds commercial:

Mexican peon leading burro up winding trail on jungle-covered volcanic mountain, a fruity-authoritative Encyclopaedia Britannica voice over: "In the high country of Mexico evolved a savoury strain of marijuana which came to be known as Acapulco Gold in the days of the contraband trade."

Cut to same peon cutting a stand of marijuana with a sickle and loading it onto burro: "Prized for its superior flavour and properties, Acapulco Gold was available only to the favoured few due to its rarity and..."

Roll to border patrolman frisking unsavoury Pancho Villa type Mexican: "...the difficulties involved in importation."

Aerial view of huge field of geometrically-rowed marijuana: "But now the finest strain of Mexican seeds, combined with American agricultural skill and carefully controlled growing conditions, produce a pure strain of marijuana unequalled in flavour, mildness... and relaxing properties. Now available in thirty-seven states: (Cut to close-up of red and gold Acapulco Golds pack.) Acapulco Golds, America's premium quality marijuana cigarette—and, of course, totally noncarcinogenic."

Back on screen comes Jack Barron, seated on old school armrest-desk type chair, desk of which holds two standard white Bell vidphones; white chair and white phones against black wash over moiré pattern background make Barron look like knight in front of forms of darkness dancing.

"What's bugging you tonight?" Jack Barron asks in a voice that knows it all—knows Harlem, Alabama, Berkeley, North side, Strip City, knows it all knows clean-painted cement walls of a thousand Golden Age Projects urine inside jail cell knows cheque twice a month just enough to keep on

13

dying (Social Security, AID, Unemployment, Guaranteed Annual wage pale-blue-cyanide Government cheque), knows it all and knows what the fuck but can't stop caring, the outsider's insider.

"What bugs you, bugs Jack Barron." Barron pauses, smiles basilisk smile, dark eyes seem to pick up moving shadows of kinesthop-through-black background, Dylan-JFK-Bobby-punkid-Buddha. "And we all know what happens when you bug Jack Barron. Call collect. The number is Area Code 212 969 6969 (six-month fight with Bell-FCC over special mnemonic number), and we'll take the first call right... now!"

Jack Barron reaches out, thumbs audio of vidphone (vidphone camera and screen face away from studio camera). A hundred million television screens split. Lower left-hand quarter shows standard black and white vidphone image of whiteshirted, white-haired Negro, vague grey vidphone-washed-out background; the remaining three-quarters of the screen is occupied in living colour by Jack Barron.

"This is *Bug Jack Barron*, and you're on the air, friend. It's all yours until I say stop. A hundred million fellow Americans, and all of 'em waiting to hear who you are and where you're from and what's bugging *you*, man. This is your moment in the old spotlight—your turn to bug whoever's bugging *you*. You're plugged into me, and I'm plugged into the whole goofy country. So go ahead, man," high from the image of white-shirted, white-haired Negro, vague grey lip, and damn the torpedoes—"bug Jack Barron." says Jack Barron reeling it off with a big let's-you-and-me-stomp-the-mothers smile.

"My name is Rufus W Johnson, Jack," the old Negro says, "and as you and the rest of the country can see, out there on television, I am *black*. I mean, there's no getting away from it, Jack. *I'm black*. You dig? I'm not coloured, I'm not of dark complexion, not a mulatto, quadroon, octoroon bassoon, or baboon. Rufus W Johnson is a black nig—"

"*Cool it,*" interrupts the voice of Jack Barron, authoritative as a knife; but with a tiny hunch of his shoulders, a little smile, *really* cools it as Rufus W Johnson smiles, hunches back.

"Yeah," says Rufus W Johnson, "we mustn't use that word, man. Uptights all them *Afro*-Americans, coloured folk. American Negroes, what you call 'em? But we know what you call 'em... Not you, Jack. (Rufus W Johnson laughs a little laugh.) You a shade, but you a *black* shade."

"Well, maybe let's make that *sepia*," says Jack Barron. "Wouldn't want to get me cancelled in Bugaloosa. But what's happening, Mr Johnson? I hope you didn't call me just to compare complexions."

"But that's where it's at, ain't it man?" says Rufus W Johnson, no longer smiling. "That's where it's at for me anyway. That's where it's at for all us Afro-Americans. You black, even down here in Mississippi, what's supposed to be black man's country, that's where life is at. Ain't nothing but what you call it—a comparison of complexions. Wish you could vidphone in colour, then I could go to my TV set, screw around with the colour controls, and see myself for once as red or green or purple *coloured* folk, y'know?"

"When do we get to the nitty-gritty, Mr Johnson?" Jack Barron asks, a shade of a degree colder. "Just what *is* bugging you?"

"We *is* at the nitty-gritty," answers Rufus W Johnson, grey-on-grey image of black face—lined, hurt, scowling—expanding to fill three-quarters of the screen, with Jack Barron in upper right-hand catbird-seat corner.

"When you is black only one thing bugging you, and it bugs you twenty-four hours a day, seven days a week, time you're born time you die. Or anyway, once was a time when being black was over when you died. Not no more. Now we got that *medical science*. We got that Foundation for Human Immortality. Freezes them dead bodies like instant pizza till them medical scientists get enough smarts to defrost 'em, fix 'em up and make 'em live till Judgement Day. What they say, that Howards cat and his flunkies, 'Someday all men will live forever through the Foundation for Human Immortality!'

"Yeah, we the leading country in the world, we got ourselves a Foundation for Human Immortality. Make that the Foundation for Shade Immortality. 'Course we got plenty cats around like old George and Bennie Howards think it all amounts to the same thing. Solve the Negro problem the easy way—get rid of the Negroes. Too messy—why, then, just fix it so the shades live forever. Let them black men have their three score and ten, who cares, when a shade can live forever, long as he can pony up that $500,000."

Tiny cold tension lines appear at the corners of Jack Barron's eyes as the screen splits even down the middle, faded black and white image of Rufus W Johnson facing living-colour reality of Jack Barron, as Barron says hard but quiet: "You're talking around something that's bugging you, Mr Johnson. How about letting us in on it? Riff it out. So long as you don't talk about any intimate parts of the human anatomy don't use four-letter words, we're still on the air and plugged in, no matter what you say. That's what *Bug Jack Barron*'s all about. It's hit-back time, worm-turning time, and if you got a real bind on any powers that be, this is the time they gotta sit there and take it while the you-know-what hits the fan."

"Yeah, man," says Rufus W Johnson. "I'm talking about that there Foundation for *Human* Immortality. Hey, man, Rufus W Johnson is like human. Bleach me white, do a plastic job on my nose, and why, every shade looks at me and says, 'There goes that Rufus W Johnson, regular pillar of the community. Got himself a successful trucking business, new car, own house, sent three kids right through college. Regular model citizen.' Was Rufus W Johnson white instead of black, why, that there Benedict Howards'd be more than pleased to give him a contract for a freeze when he flakes out and have the chance to collect the interest on every dime Rufe's got till that Big Defrost Day comes—was Rufus W Johnson a shade, that is. Know what they say down here in Mississippi, Harlem, out there in Watts? They say, 'You a shade, you got forever made, but, baby, if you're black, when you go, you don't come back.'"

Back to the upper right-hand corner catbird-seat goes living-colour Jack Barron. "Are you charging the Foundation for Human Immortality with racial discrimination?" he asks, dancing black semivisible moiré pattern flashes from backdrop off white desk-chair in his slightly downturned eye-hollows turning his face to a mask of smouldering danger, suddenly solemn and sinister.

"I ain't charging them with going through a red light," drawls Rufus W Johnson. "Look at my hair—that's the only white part of me you'll see. I'm sixty-seven years old and I about used up this one life I got. Even if I gotta live it all as a black man in white man's country, I want to live forever. Bad as it may be to be alive and black, when you dead, man, you are like *dead!*

"So I go to them Foundation shades, and I say, 'Hand me one of them Freeze Contracts. Rufus W Johnson is ready to sign up for Forever.' Two weeks go by, and they sniff around my house, my business, my bank account. Then I get a real fancy letter on real fancy paper about three yards long, and what it says is, 'Man, you do not make it.'

"Well, you figure it out, Mr Jack Barron. My house—it costs me $150,000 I got $50,000 in the bank. And, man, my trucks alone cost nearly five hundred big ones. And Bennie Howards can have it all long as I'm on ice. But the Foundation for *Human* Immortality says I got 'insufficient liquid assets for us to offer a Freeze Contract at this time.' My money's the same colour as anyone else's, Mr Barron. Think it's the colour of my *money* they don't like or could it just possibly be the colour of my *something else?*"

The screen snaps to a full close-up of the concerned flashing face of hard-jawed, kick-'em-in-the-ass Jack Barron. "Well, you certainly got something to be bugged at—if you've got your facts straight, Mr Johnson. And you've sure bugged Jack Barron."

Barron rivets the camera with his eyes promising bottomless pools of earnest bad-boy, brick-throwing, thunder-and-lightning. "And how does it grab *you* out there, plugged into the two of us? How's it grab you out there, Benedict Howards? What's the scam from the powers that be? And speaking of the powers that be (abrupt facial shift to sardonic-shrug-inside-joke smile)—it's about time to see what's bugging our sponsor. You hang right on, Mr Johnson, and you too out there, and we'll be right back where it's all happening—right here right now no-time-delay live, after this straight poop from whoever's currently making the mistake of being our sponsor."

2

PRETTY GOOD CURVE you got there, Vince, you smart-ass wop, Jack Barron thought, watching his image on the outside studio monitor become image of new model Chevy.

The moment he was off the air Barron was up on the edge of his chair, thumbing the intercom button on the number one vidphone, "Fun and games tonight, eh, *paisan?*"

Behind the thick glass of the control-booth window, he saw Vince Gelardi smile, smugly cynical, then Vince's voice filled the small spare studio: "Want Bennie Howards in the hotseat slot?"

"Who else?" Jack Barron answered, repositioning himself in the chair. "With Teddy Hennering number two, and Luke Greene in the safety slot." Barron thumbed off the intercom, read '60 seconds' flashing across the bulb grid of the promptboard, and poured his attention into the brief pause.

Smart-ass Vince putting through a six-week dud like that Johnson (but every so often a dud becomes a potato even live one like tonight). Professional spade calls in every damn week new ethnic sob story and probably never got past the first monkey-block screen before. But add the latest dumb beef, against Foundation this time, to Freezer debate on the Hill, and you got a real hot potato (...you shade, you got Forever made... Wonder if Malcolm Shabazz & Co, are spreading that one?) Too hot to handle with Howards' two tame schmucks sitting on the good old FCC. Can't afford to make waves in *that* league for one lousy show, and Vince should've known that, it's his job, that's what I've got him running the monkey block for.

But shit, Barron thought, as the promptboard flashed '30 seconds,' Vince *did* know it but got to give him credit, he saw beyond it, saw that Howards wouldn't be pissed because the Foundation'll freeze any Negro got $500,000 in liquid assets (*liquid's* the kicker; liquid, not rotting old house not decaying trucks—liquid cash bonds negotiable securities negotiable power). Foundation's got enough trouble with Republicans, SJC, Shabazz & Co., without buying race trouble. Foundation cares about only one colour—green money colour, crazy bastard Howards' not *that* far round the bend. Yeah, Vince saw it all, saw Rufus W Johnson full of it, saw whole country's tongues hanging out, slavering over the Freezer Debate, saw good hot show but safe from tigers, with Howards, happy to get free publicity with his big chestnuts in the Congressional fire, saw formula for next forty minutes: Howards squirming a bit in the hotseat, enough to make sparks without making waves because on the race thing (about the *only* thing) Foundation's in the clear. Everyone makes points—Howards pushes his Freezer Bill, the Great Unwashed gets Jack Barron in top fun-and-games form, I look like champ and just flesh wounds, no one gets hurt enough to try to hurt back. Good old Vince knows how to walk that line!

'Open line to Rockies' Freezer' flashed across the promptboard, then, 'Greene on line, Teddy H?' then, 'On Air,' and Barron saw his face and shoulders on the big monitor below the promptboard, saw image of Rufus W Johnson grey on grey in the lower left-hand corner of the monitor and on the number one vidphone screen; hard, prim, good-looking, tough piece of ass-secretary on number two vidphone, and we're off and running at Hialeah, thought Jack Barron.

"Okay, Mr Johnson (you silly fucker you)," Jack Barron said. "We're back on the air. You're plugged into me, plugged into the whole United States and all hundred million of us, plugged right into a direct vidphone line to the headquarters of the Foundation for Human Immortality, the Rocky Mountain Freezer Complex outsider Boulder, Colorado. We're gonna find out whether the Foundation's pushing post-mortem segregation, right here right now no time-delay live from the man himself, the President and Chairman of the Board of the Foundation for Human Immortality, the Barnum of the Bodysnatchers, your friend and mine, Mr Benedict Howards."

Barron made the connection on his number two vidphone, saw the hard-looking (like to get into *that*) secretary chick's image appear under him (ideal position) in lower right on the monitor, gave her a dangerous pussycat (claws behind velvet) smile and said, "This is Jack Barron calling Mr Benedict Howards. A hundred million Americans are digging that gorgeous face of yours right now, baby, but what they really want to see is Bennie Howards. So let's have the bossman." Barron shrugged, grinned. "Sorry about that. But don't worry, baby, you can leave your very own private phone number with my boy Vince Gelardi." (Who knows?)

The secretary stared through the smile like a lemur, her telephone-operator voice said, "Mr Howards is in his private plane flying to Canada for a hunting and fishing vacation and cannot be reached. May I connect you with our Financial Director, Mr De Silva? Or our—"

"This is *Jack Barron* calling Benedict Howards," Barron interrupted (what goes here?). "Of *Bug Jack Barron.* You *do* own a television set, don't you? I have on the line a Mr Rufus W Johnson who's mighty bugged at the Foundation, and I'm bugged, and so are a hundred million Americans, and we all want to talk to Bennie Howards, not some flunky. So I suggest you move that pretty thing of yours and get him on this line *muy pronto*, or I'll just have to bat the breeze about Mr Johnson's public charge that the Foundation refuses to freeze Negroes with some cats who see things a *little* differently from the way the Foundation sees 'em, dig?"

"I'm sorry. Mr Barron, Mr Howards is hundreds of miles from the nearest vidphone," the secretary said. "Mr De Silva, or Dr Bruce, or Mr Yarborough are all in intimate contact with the details of Foundation operation and would be happy to answer any questions."

Set spiel, thought Jack Barron. Chick doesn't know which end's up (like to demonstrate), parroting Howards' bullshit, is all. Show the bastard what happens when he tries to hide from me. Horrible example, Mr Howards. In instantaneous gestalt the rest of the show spread itself out before him: grill Howards' flunky (Yarborough is the biggest foot-in-mouth man), second commercial, riff with Luke, third commercial, then ten minutes with Teddy Hennering to ease up a bit, then go out and get laid.

"Okay," Barron said, turning his smile into a vulpine leer. "If that's the way Bennie wants to play it, that's the way he'll have it. Get me John Yarborough." He crossed his legs, signalling Gelardi to cut the secretary's image off the monitor, and the screen split evenly between Barron and Johnson as Barron tapped the button under his left foot twice. Barron smiled crookedly as he stared dead on at the camera, purposefully building himself up into the galloping nasties, and said, "I hope Bennie Howards catches himself a big one, eh? And I'm sure all hundred million of you out there, who Mr Benedict Howards is too busy to talk to, wish him loads of luck too—and don't you know, out there, that he's gonna need it."

Barron saw the promptboard flash "Open lines to Luke, Teddy." Yessir, he thought, show that goddamned Howards it doesn't pay to mickeymouse me—and really give 'em a show tonight.

"Well, Mr Johnson, we're about to do a little hunting on our own," he said. "Let Mr Howards shoot himself a moose, and we'll shoot ourselves the truth."

"Who's this Yarborough?" asked Rufus W Johnson.

"John Yarborough is Public Relations Director for the Foundation," Barron answered. "We're the public, and we're gonna see what we can get him to like *relate*." Barron's number two vidphone showed a sallow balding man. Barron foot-signalled, and the left side of the monitor screen was shared by Johnson (top) Yarborough (bottom), Barron looming twice their size to the right, living-colour Big Daddy. "And here's Mr John Yarborough now.

"Mr Yarborough, this is Jack Barron calling, and I'd like you to meet Mr Rufus W Johnson. Mr Johnson, to belabour the obvious, is a Negro. He claims that the Foundation refused him a Freeze Contract. (Play that non sequitur gambit, Jack, baby.) A hundred million Americans would like to know if that's true. They'd like to know why the Foundation for Human Immortality, with a Public Charter as a tax-exempt foundation, refused an American citizen his chance at immortality just because that citizen happens to be a Negro." (Have you stopped beating your wife yet, Mr Yarborough?)

"I'm sure there must be some misunderstanding that we can easily clear up," Yarborough said smoothly. "As you know—"

"I don't know anything, Mr Yarborough," Barron cut in. "Nothing but what people tell me. I don't even believe the baloney I see on television. I know what Mr Johnson told me, though, and a hundred million Americans know it too. Mr Johnson, did you apply for a Freeze Contract?"

"I did, Jack."

"Did you agree to assign all your assets to the Foundation upon your clinical death?"

"You know I did."

"Did those assets exceed $500,000?"

"Six or seven hundred grand, easy," said Rufus W Johnson.

"And were you refused a Freeze Contract, Mr Johnson?"

"I sure was."

Barron paused, grimaced, lowered his head to catch reflected ominous flashes from the backdrop off the shiny desk-arm in his eyes. "And you *are* a Negro, I notice, aren't you, Mr Johnson? Now, Mr Yarborough, you were saying something about a misunderstanding—something that can be easily cleared up? Suppose you explain the hard facts. Suppose you explain to the American people why Mr Johnson was refused a Freeze Contract."

Start digging out from under, Dad, Barron thought as he tapped his right foot-button three times, calling for a commercial in three minutes (just a few shovelfuls so I can throw on more).

"But it *is* all quite simple, Mr Barron," Yarborough said, voice and face dead earnest, put visually in the dock, as Gelardi cut out Johnson's image, left Yarborough tiny black and white, surrounded on three sides, all but engulfed by close-up (backdrop darkness shadows swirling behind) of Jack Barron.

"The basic long-range goal of the Foundation is to support research that will lead to a time when all men will live forever. This requires money, a great deal of money. And the more money we have to spend on research, the sooner that day will arrive. The Foundation for Human Immortality has only one source of capital: its National Freezer Program. The bodies of a limited number of Americans are frozen and preserved in liquid helium upon clinical death so that they may be revived when research, *Foundation* research, provides the answers to—"

"Aw, we know all this bull!" exclaimed Rufus W Johnson (still off-screen). "You freeze fat cats, *shade* fat cats, that is, and while they're on ice you get all their money and stocks and whatever they have, and they don't get it back till they're alive again, if they ever are. That's cool, I mean, you can't take it with you, might as well gamble, got nothing to lose but a fancy funeral." (Keeping his face sombre and glowering, Barron let the unseen voice rave on and waited for the pounce-moment.) "Okay, that's what you're selling, that's what Rufus W Johnson is buying. Only you ain't selling to no nig—"

"Watch it, Mr Johnson!" Barron cut in, and Vince, thinking along with him, cut Johnson's audio as the promptboard flashed '2 minutes.' "You see, Mr Yarborough, Mr Johnson is overwrought, and with good reason. He's got a house that cost him $150,000, $50,000 in the bank, and over $500,000 in trucks, and I'm no Einstein, but by my reckoning, $500,000 plus $200,000 is more than $500,000. Is it not true that the minimum net worth that's supposed to be assigned to the Foundation upon clinical death in order for the Foundation to issue a Freeze Contract is $500,000?"

"That's right, Mr Barron. But, you see, the $500,000 must be in liquid—"

"Please, just answer the questions for a moment," Barron cut in loudly. Don't let him explain, keep him bogey-man, he thought, noting wryly that Vince had granted the grey-on-grey image of Yarborough three-quarters of the screen, pale, unreal Goliath versus full-colour David effect. "It all seems simple to me. $500,000 is supposed to buy any American a Freeze. Mr Johnson offered you his total net worth, which exceeds $500,000. Mr Johnson is an American citizen. Mr Johnson was refused a Freeze Contract. Mr Johnson is a Negro. What conclusion can you expect the American people to draw? Facts are facts."

"But race has nothing to do with it!" Yarborough answered shrilly, and Barron frowned publicly, and grinned inwardly as he saw Yarborough finally blow his cool. "The $500,000 must be in liquid assets—cash, stocks, negotiable property. Any man, regardless of race, who has $500,000 in *liquid*—"

Barron, crossed his legs, signal to cut Yarborough off the air, as the promptboard flashed '60 seconds,' said. "And, of course, we all know it's the *Foundation* that decides whether a man's assets are... *liquid* enough. Makes it nice and cosy, eh, folks? The Foundation doesn't want to freeze a man, just tells him his assets are 'frozen', no pun intended. Wonder how many Negroes have frozen *assets*, and how many have frozen *bodies*? Well, maybe we can find out from a man who's got some strong opinions about the current proposal in Congress to grant this—shall we say *whimsical*?—outfit that calls itself the Foundation for Human Immortality a monopoly on all cryogenic freezing in the United States—the Social Justice Governor of Mississippi, Lukas Greene. So hang on, folks, and hang on, Mr Johnson. We'll be talking to the Governor of your home state right after this attempt to... *unfreeze* your pocketbooks by our sponsor."

Hope you're watching this, Howards, you schmuck you, Barron thought as they rolled the commercial. See what happens when you mickeymouse Jack Barron! He thumbed the intercom button said: "Let me have a couple private moments on the line with Luke."

"Hey what you want from this po' black boy, you big bad shade you?" Lukas Greene (one eye on the Acapulco Golds commercial the other on the vidphone image of Jack Barron) said. "Isn't shafting Bennie Howards enough for one night? Gotta pick on us Crusaders for Social Justice too?"

"Relax, Lothar," Jack Barron said. "This is you-and-me-stomp-the-Foundation night. This time good old Jack Barron's playing ball with you, dig?"

Well, that's a relief, provided I can trust Jack, Greene thought. But what's all this race-flak with the Foundation? "Dig," said Greene. "But we both know Bennie'd freeze Chairman Wang himself, if the cat coughed up the bread, let alone some poor buck. Why the knife? You comin' home to the SJC, Claude?"

"Don't hold your breath," Jack Barron told him. "I'm just showing Howards what happens to a vip thinks he can be out to Jack Barron. Observe and learn, Amos, case you ever decide to be away from your vidphone some Wednesday night. But, cool it; we're about to go on the air again."

Same goddamn Jack Barron, Greene thought as Barron made with the introduction. ('...Governor of Mississippi and leading national figure in the Social Justice Coalition...') Sell his mother for three points in the ratings, Howards could be eating babies raw and it'd be no sweat, no heat, too much power for the balless wonder, but don't answer that phone and you get the knife, Bennie boy. ('...your constituent has charged...') Okay, we play Jack's game tonight, both shaft Howards, maybe help kill the Freezer Utility Bill, and so what if Jack has asshole reasons.

"...and it is well-known that the Foundation has been refused permission to build a freezer in Mississippi, Governor Greene," Jack was saying. "Is this because the Mississippi Social Justice Coalition suspects, as Mr Johnson charges, that the Foundation discriminates against Negroes?"

Well, here goes nothing, thought Greene. Let's see how much SJC flak he lets me get away with. "Leaving aside the racial question for a moment, Mr Barron," Greene said into his vidphone, noting that Generous Jack was granting him half the TV screen at the moment, angular black face sharply handsome in black and white, "we would not permit the Foundation to build a Freezer in Mississippi if Mr Howards and every single one of his employees were as black as the proverbial ace of spades. The Social Justice Coalition stands firmly for a free Public Freezer Policy. We believe that no individual, corporation, or so-called non-profit foundation should have the right to decide who will have a chance to live again and who will not. We believe that all freezers should be publicly owned and financed, and that the choice of who is to be Frozen and who is not should be determined by the drawing of lots. We believe—"

"Your position on the Freezer Utility Bill versus the Public Freezer proposal is all too well known," Jack Barron interrupted dryly, and Greene's TV screen now showed him scrunched down in the lower left-hand corner (gentle reminder as to who was running things from old Berkeley buddy Jack Barron).

22

"What's bugging Mr Johnson, what's bugging me, what's bugging a hundred million viewers tonight is not the theoretical question of private versus public Freezing, but the practical question: does the Foundation discriminate against Negroes? Is Benedict Howards abusing his economic and social power?"

Old college try, thought Greene. "That's what I was getting at, *Mr* Barron," he said, deliberately great-man-testy. "When a private company or foundation acquires the enormous power that the Foundation for Human Immortality has, abuses of one kind or another become inevitable. Should the Foundation succeed in getting its Utility Bill through Congress, and should the President sign it, this life-and-death power will be written into law, backed by the Federal Government, and at that point the Foundation can discriminate against Negroes, Republicans, sha—er, *Caucasians* or anyone else who refuses to play Howards' game with impunity. That's why—"

"Please, Governor Greene," Jack Barron said with a put-on jaded grimace. "We're all on the side of the angels. But you know the equal-time laws as well as I do, and you can't make political speeches on this show." Jack paused and smiled a just-for-him for-chrissakes-Luke smile, Greene saw. "I'd ruin this groovy sportjac if I got cancelled and had to go out and dig ditches. The question is, is the Foundation *now* discriminating against Negroes?"

Well, that's where it's at, Greene thought. I want to make points on Howards, all I can do is help make it look like he's playing the Wallacite game, Jack's hobbyhorse for the night, and we both know he's not that loopy. But those hundred million voters Jack mentions every other sentence maybe don't, maybe can bug enough Congressmen to get them to vote the other way, kill Howards' bill if we make the right waves. So, Bennie Howards, yo' is a big, bad nigger-hating shade for the duration, sorry about that, chief.

"Well," Greene replied, "the record shows that although Negroes are roughly twenty per cent of the population, less than two per cent of the bodies in the Foundation's Freezers are Negroes... "

"And the Foundation has never explained this discrepancy?" Jack asked, and gave Greene back full half-screen for playing ball.

You know the reason you sly shade mother, Greene thought. How many of us in the good old U S of A buzz off worth five hundred thou? Foundation don't discriminate more than everyone else. Why should it be different when a black man dies than when he's alive—'You a shade, you got forever made, but if you're black, when you go you don't come back.' Even though Malcolm planted that one don't stop it from being gut-truth, shade-buddy Jack. Foundation's cleaner than GM, unions, bossman vip bastards—only colour Howards digs is green-money colour—but gotta squash the mother like a bug any way you can...

"Never heard of one," Greene said. "I mean, what *can* they say, those are the figures in black and white (he smiled wanly)—*sorry about that*. Even if there's no conscious racial bias, the Foundation, set up as it is on the basis of who can pay, must in fact discriminate because everyone knows that the average income of a black man in this country is about half that of the average white. The Foundation, by its very existence, helps perpetuate the inferior position of the Negro—even beyond the grave. In fact it's getting so's a gravestone instead of a Freeze's gonna become a black thing, like nappy hair, before too long.

"I'm not accusing any man of anything. But I do accuse the society—and the Foundation swings an awful lot of weight in the society. And if Howards isn't exercising the social responsibility that should go with social power... well, then, he's copping-out. And we both know, Mr Barron (sickly-sweet smile for cop-out Jack), that a cop-out's just as guilty as the Wallacites and Withers' that his irresponsible indifference allows to flourish." Two points on Howards, Greene thought, and two points on you, Jack.

Jack Barron smiled what Greene recognised as his words-in-your-mouth smile. And sure enough, he saw that Jack had now given him three quarters of the screen. Prols see Luke Greene while hearing words of Jack Barron schtick and why don't you use that sly shade brain of yours for something that counts, you cop-out you.

"Then what you're saying in essence, Governor Greene," Jack said, in what Greene recognised as the sum-up-kiss-good-bye-here-comes-the-commercial pounce, "is that the very character of the Foundation for Human Immortality itself creates a de facto policy of racial discrimination, whether this is *official* Foundation policy or not, right? That whether Mr Johnson was refused a Freeze Contract because he was a Negro, or whether his assets are actually insufficient by Foundation standards, those very financial standards arbitrarily set by Mr Benedict Howards himself are actually a form of built-in racial discrimination? That—"

"One hundred per cent right!" Lukas Greene said loudly. (You may get the last word, but you don't put it in *this* black boy's mouth, Jack!) "So far as you've gone (and fence-sitting Jack cuts me down to quarter screen but lets me babble got extra brains where his balls should be). But not only discrimination against Negroes. The existence of a private, high-priced Freezing Company discriminates against black men, white men, the poor, the indigent, six million unemployed and twenty million underemployed Americans. It places a dollar value on immortality, on human life, as if Saint Peter suddenly put up a toll booth in front of those Pearly Gates. What right does anyone have to look into a man's finances and say, 'You, sir, may have life eternal But you, you pauper, when you die, you die forever?' Every American—"

Abruptly, Greene saw that his face and voice were no longer on the air. His TV screen was now filled with a close-up of earnest-lipped, sly-eyed Jack

Barron. (Oh, well, thought Greene, at least we made *some* points.)

"Thank you, Governor Greene," said Jack Barron. "We sure know what's bugging *you* now. And you've given us all food for thought. And speaking of food, it's that time again for a few words from them that pay for my groceries. But hang on, America, 'cause we'll be right back with the other side in the hotseat—Senator Theodore Hennering, co-author of the Hennering-Bernstein Freezer Utility Bill, who's on record as thinking that the Foundation for Human Immortality's just fine and dandy as it is, and would like to see the Foundation granted a legal monopoly. We'll try to see where the good Senator's head is at, after this word from our sponsor."

Hey, Greene thought excitedly as a Chevy commercial came on, if he knifes Hennering on the bill that could be it! Jack could cut Hopeful Henny to dog meat he wanted to, shift ten votes in the Senate, or in the House and the Bill's dead.

"What in hell you trying to do, Luke?" Jack Barron's vidphone image said. "Screw me good with the FCC? Howards's got two commissioners in his hip pocket; we both know that."

"I'm trying to kill the Freezer Utility Bill, and we both know *that* too, Percy," Greene told him. "*You* the cat decided to knife Bennie, remember? And you can do it, Jack You can kill the bill right now by slaughtering Teddy Hennering. Nail him to the wall, mm, and put in a few extra spikes for me."

"Nail him to the wall?" Jack Barron shouted. "You're out of your gourd, Rastus! I want Howards to bleed a little, teach him a lesson, but not in the gut, Kingfish, just a couple flesh wounds. Howards can murder me if I hit him too hard where he lives. I gotta play pussycat with Hennering, let him make up some points the Foundation's lost, or I'm in goddamned *politics*. Better I should get a dose of clap than a dose of *that*."

"Don't you ever remember what you were, Jack?" Greene sighed.

"Every time my gut rumbles, man."

"Win one, lose one, eh, Jack? Back then you had balls but no power. Now you got power and no—"

"Screw you, Luke," said Jack Barron. "You got your nice little bag down there in coon country, let me keep mine."

"Fuck you too, Jack," Greene said, breaking the vidphone connection. Fuck you, Jack Barron good old Jack Barron, what in hell happened to the good old Berkeley-Jack-and-Sara Montgomery Meridian sign-waving caring, black shade committed Jack Barron?

Greene sighed, knowing what happened... what happened to all no-more-war nigger-loving peace-loving happy got nothing need nothing love-truth-and-beauty against the night Baby Bolshevik Galahads. Years happened, hunger happened, Lyndon happened, and one day, age-thirty happened, no more kids, time-to-get-ours happened and them that could, went and got.

Jack got *Bug Jack Barron* (losing Sara, poor-couldn't-cut-it good-heart good fuck Peter Pan living relic of what we all lost making it all a silly-ass-lie Sara), and you got this gig in Evers, Mississippi, you white nigger you. Schmuck you are to think anyone could bring it all back, bring back youth truth don't give a shit close to the blood happy balling days when we *knew* we could do it all if only we had the power. Now we got the power, I got the power, Jack got the power, and to get it he paid our balls, is all.

Who are you to expect Jack to play hero, lay it on the line, lose it all for some dumb dream? Would you, man, would *you*?

I would if I could, thought Lukas Greene. Was I white and it could matter. And, masochistically he left the TV on, sat back to watch and hope in the man who *could* matter, if he got it back, the man playing his cop-out game with Howards' stooge Hennering—good old Jack Barron.

Cop-out, eh, Kingfish? thought Jack Barron as he waited for to the commercial to end. Just trying to get me to blow my cool, eat dumb bastard Hennering on the half-shell, fry *your* fish, Luke, while Howards gets blood in his eyes for my scalp—kill Freezer Bill all right, but among the fatalities TV career of kick 'em-in-the-ass Jack Barron. Or do you still really believe in the old Berkeley truth-justice-bravery damn-the-torpedoes days bull kamikaze attack? Schmuck either way, Lothar. No one hands hara-kiri knife to Jack Barron. Paid my dues many long years ago name of my game's no longer Don Quixote.

The commercial ended and the too-fiftyish, too-true-blue, too 1930s-FDR-handsome loser face of Senator Theodore Hennering (D-Ill.) split the screen even with Jack Barron. Looks like he's holding in a year's worth of cream-rubber-chicken-plastic-peas fart, Barron thought. To think this dum-dum has eyes for the White House. Teddy and his ghosts'll eat him alive… Make nice, Jack, baby, he warned himself grimly.

"I hope I may make the assumption that you've been watching the show tonight, Senator Hennering," Barron said, giving little fey false-modest, watch-yourself-Teddy-boy smile.

"Uh, yes, uh, Mr Barron. Most interesting, uh, quite fascinating," Hennering said hesitatingly in his fruity-hearty voice. Jeez, thought Barron, I gotta feed this lox *his* lines too? He looks like who-did-it-and-ran tonight.

"Well, then, I'm sure that after hearing Governor Greene you have a few things you'd like to tell the American people, Senator, seeing as you're the cosponsor of the Freezer Utility Bill which would grant the Foundation a Freezing Monopoly, I mean, Mr Johnson and Governor Greene have made some pretty serious charges against the Foundation…?"

"I… uh… cannot speak for the Foundation for Human Immortality." Hennering said, his eyes peculiarly and uncharacteristically furtive. "I will say that I do not believe that the Foundation practices racial discrimination. My... uh record on Civil Rights, I think, speaks for itself and I would er... dissociate myself immediately from any individual, organisation, or cause that would perpetuate racial... ah... policies."

Shit, the old blimp looks like he's scared stiff. Barron thought. What gives? He saw that Gelardi had wisely cut down the now ashen face of Hennering to a quarter-screen inset. I could cut him up and feed him to the fishes and wouldn't Luke love *that*, Barron thought with reflective combativeness. Watch yourself, man, you've got too many knives in Bennie Howards' back as it is...

"You *are* cosponsor of the Freezer Utility Bill?" Barron asked, straining to be gentle. "You do still support the bill? You do still feel it will pass?"

"I'm against discussing the chances of pending legislation," Hennering said, fingering his collar.

Mo-*ther!* Barron thought. He looks like he's ready to croak. I've got to get this boob to say some nice things about Bennie Howards or I'll have the Foundation all over me. Lead the creep by the nose, Jack, baby.

"Well, since you are one of the authors of the bill, surely you can tell us *why* you believe that the Foundation for Human Immortality should be the only organisation permitted to Freeze bodies in this country?"

"Why... ah, yes, Mr Barron. It's a matter of responsibility, responsibility to... uh... those in the Freezers and to the general public. The Foundation must be kept financially sound so that they can continue to care for the Frozen bodies, and continue their... uh... immortality research so that the promise of eternal life that cryogenic Freezing holds will not become a... cruel deception... cruel deception... (Hennering's mind seemed to wander; he caught himself, grimaced, continued.) The Foundation stipulates that all income not required to maintain the Freezers will go into research while the... ah... fly-by-night outfits that attempt to compete with it do not.

"Safety for those in the Freezers, financial soundness, the ability to channel sums of money into immortality research, those are the reasons why I believed... uh, believe that the Foundation for Human Immortality must have a Freezer Monopoly. It is fitting, sound moral and economic policy that those in the Freezers pay for their upkeep and for the research that will eventually revive them. Yes... uh, that's why I sponsored the bill."

"Wouldn't a Federal Freezer Program do the same things?" Barron shot back unthinkingly, wincing even as the words left his mouth. (Cool it, man, *cool it!*)

"Ah... I suppose so," Hennering said. "But... ah... the cost, yes, the cost. To duplicate the Foundation facilities or buy them out would cost the taxpayers billions, and more billions on research. Not practical fiscally, you see. The Soviet Union and China have no Freezer programs at all because only in a free enterprise system can the cost be borne."

You forgot God, motherhood, and apple pie, Barron thought. Is this cretin in some kind of shock? I knew he was dumb, but not this dumb. Howards has him in his hip pocket—this is Bennie's Presidential candidate. Howards must be chewing the rug by now. And son of a bitch Luke must be having an orgasm. Gotta do *something* to cool it; I need Bennie Howards on my back like an extra anus.

"Then you contend, Senator Hennering, that the Foundation for Human Immortality performs an essential service, a service which simply could not be provided by any other organisation, including the Federal Government?" Barron asked as the promptboard flashed '3 minutes,' frantically signalling for Gelardi to give Hennering three-quarters of the screen, my words in his mouth (even if he does look like a week-dead codfish) schtick.

"Uh… yes," said Hennering fuzzily. (His head's farther from here than the Mars Expedition, thought Barron) "I think it's fair to say that without the Foundation there would simply be no Freezer program in the United States of any scope or stability. Already well over a million people have a chance at immortality who would otherwise be… uh… decomposed and buried and dead and gone forever thanks to the Foundation. Uh… of course, there are millions dying each year who cannot be accommodated, who are dead for all time… But… uh… don't you think that it's better for some people to have some chance at living again, even if it means that most people in the foreseeable future won't, than for every American to die permanently until all can be Frozen, the way the Public Freezer people would have it…? Don't you think that's reasonable, Mr Barron…? Don't you…?"

The last was almost a whine, a piteous plea for some kind of absolution. What the hell's got into Hennering? wondered Jack Barron. The SJC couldn't have got to him—or could they? He's not only scared shitless, he's wallowing in guilt. Why do these things have to happen to *me*? He keeps this up, and Howards'll stomp me with high-heeled hobnailed Jackboots!

"It sounds reasonable, when you state it so cogently," Barron replied. (At least as coherent as the Gettysburg Address backwards in Albanian, anyway.) "Quite obviously, *everyone* can't be Frozen. The question is, is the basis upon which the Foundation chooses who will be Frozen fair or not? Is it free from racial—"

"*Fair*?" Hennering practically shrieked as the promptboard flashed '2 minutes.' "*Fair*? Look, of course it can't be fair! What's fair about death? Some men can live forever and others die and are gone forever, and there can't be anything *fair* about that. The nation is attacked, and some men are drafted to fight and die while others stay home and make money off it. That's not a fair choice either. But it has to be made, because if it *isn't*, then the whole country goes under. Life isn't fair. If you try to be fair to everyone, then everyone dies and no one lives—that's being strictly *fair*, but it's also being crazy… Should we turn back the clock and make it that way again…? Does *that* make sense to you, Mr Barron?"

Barron reeled for a moment. The man's flipping, he thought. He's in shock, what's he babbling about? Ask the fucker a simple question he can say a simple no to and cool things and get back Sartre existential nausea why can't he puke his being and nothingness on some shrink? He saw the promptboard flash '60 seconds.' Christ, just a minute to cool it!

"The point's well taken," Barron said, "but the question at hand's not all that philosophical, Senator. Does the Foundation for Human Immortality avoid Freezing financially qualified Negroes?"

"Negroes?" Hennering muttered; then, like a fuzzy picture suddenly clicking back into focus, he became earnest, firm, authoritative. "Of course not. The Foundation isn't interested in a client's race—couldn't care less. One thing about the Foundation that America can be sure of is that it does not practice racial discrimination. I stand behind that statement with my thirty-year record on Civil Rights, a record that some men may have equalled but that no man has bettered. The Foundation is colour-blind." Hennering's eyes seemed to go vague again. "If *that's* what you mean by fair..." he said. "But—"

Barron crossed his legs as the promptboard flashed '30 seconds,' and his face filled the entire screen. Enough of that shit, Teddy-boy, you finally spat it out, saved the bacon, balanced show for God, Motherhood, and the FCC (not to mention Bennie Howards) can put their switchblades back in their pockets, tell the rest to your shrink.

"Thank you, Senator Hennering," Barron said. "Well, America, you've heard all sides of it, and now you've got to make up your own minds, not me or the Governor, or the Senator can do that for you. Take it from there, folks, and plug yourself in next Wednesday night for a new disaster, history made, no time-delay live before your eyes, history made by you and for you every week of the year when you... *Bug Jack Barron.*"

3

JACK BARRON emerged from the closed environment of the studio—with its camera, set, vidphones, promptboard, foot-buttons, monitor, all compressed into a twenty by fifteen by eight foot pocket universe—like a man suddenly brought down from a drunk or a high or an adrenaline-stress situation into a different, and, for the moment of adjustment, not quite as vivid reality.

Barron knew this; knew it so well that he had constructed a fantasy-image to concretise the essentially nonverbal Wednesday night psychedelic moment into the normal stream of memory: The inside of the studio *was* actually the inside of a hundred million television sets. There was a creature bearing his name that lived in there (seeing out through monitor eyes, hearing with vidphone ears, monitoring its internal condition through promptboard kinaesthetic senses, shifting image-gears with the foot-buttons, ordering, threatening, granting grace all through the circuitry and satellites of that great gestalt of electronic integration, the network, into which he was wired, the masterswitch in the circuit) for one hour a week, a *creature* indeed, designed and built by him like a Frankenstein android, a creature of his will but only a segment of his total personality.

Emerging from the studio was a birth and a death: kick-'em-in-the-ass, plugged-in-image-of-power, phosphor-dot Jack Barron died then, cut off from his electronic senses and circuitries of power; and soft-flesh, bellyhunger, woman-hunger, scratch-itch Jack Barron, the kid, the Boy Desperado, Jack-and-Sara (cool it!) Jack was born again.

Barron left the studio, walked up the corridor, opened a door, and entered the monkey block directly behind the control booth. He nodded to the boys who were stretching their muscles and swapping horror stories behind the three tiers of vidphone-packed desks, and was about to open the control booth door when Vince Gelardi stepped through it himself.

"Right in the old groove tonight, baby," Gelardi said. "They loved it in Peoria and other traditional show biz flak."

"In the old groove?" Barton snapped with put-on uprightness, knowing it had gone, over like gangbusters while avoiding the kamikaze plunge off the cliff. "In the old groove? You crazy guinea, you almost got me knocked off the air, is all! If I weren't brilliant twinkletoes boy wonder Jack Barron, you and me and this whole silly monkey block would be out pounding the pavement tomorrow."

"I was under the impression I was working *Bug Jack Barron*, the show with something to offend everyone, not old *Parish Priest* reruns," Gelardi drawled. "We're supposed to be like controversial, aren't we?"

"You said the word, Vince, and the word is *like* controversial," Barron said, now at least half-serious, he realised. "We pick on cripples, heartless bullies with feet of clay, if we feel real fancy we take on some big-mouthed dum-dum like Shabazz or Withers. We do not stick flaming swords into the tender hides of tigers with big FCC network-sponsor teeth like Bennie Howards. We tweak the tigers' tails every once in a while to collect merit badges, but we don't tie their tails around our waists and beat said tigers with bull-whips."

"Aw, horseshit. I knew how you'd play it, knew how it'd come out, and you know I knew," Gelardi said goodnaturedly. "Which is to say, with Bennie Howards getting no worse than a mild ulcer twinge, and that's why I fed you Johnson. I knew you'd make points, but not belly-wound points. You're my idol, Jack you know that."

Barron laughed. "And I suppose you knew that Teddy Hennering had suddenly contracted brain-rot, I suppose?" he said, immensely pleased with his fancy footwork in retrospect.

Gelardi shrugged. "So even the great Vince Gelardi's not perfect," he said. "Seemed more like an attack of conscience, though, to me."

"There's a difference?" Barron asked archly. "If there is, it doesn't matter, cause the results are always the same. And speaking of results, did Howards' secretary leave her number with you?"

"You've gotta be kidding," Gelardi replied, and Barron saw (ah, well!) that he meant it.

"Vince, m'boy," he said, WC Fieldswise, "an esteemed acquaintance of mine, upon reading in a learned journal that one out of fifty women propositioned cold on street corners was willing, tested this theory on the corner of 42nd Street and Fifth Avenue. He received a severe battering with umbrellas, purses, and other painfully rigid objects for his trouble. However, m'boy, he also got laid."

Sycophant laughter drifted to Barron's ears from the boys in the monkey block. "What?" he huffed, still in the Fields bag. "I hear them mocking my words of wisdom? For shame, for shame. No doubt 'twas louts such as these who forced Socrates to quaff the hemlock."

"I see, as per your usual Wednesday night bag, you're feeling randy," Gelardi said.

"Randy?" Barron replied, unable-unwilling to shuck the Fields schtick. "Who is the wench, and is she *worth* feeling?" Dropping Fields, Barron said, "And so saying, he exits stage left and is off into the night." He nodded to Gelardi, bowed to the boys in the monkey block, and was—off into the night.

"You really *are* Jack Barron," she said, cool honey-blonde, Upper-East-Side-27ish executive secretary with hippy *Lower*-East-Side-past hard-edged style. "I recognised your utter arrogance immediately, Mr Barron."

"Call me Jack," he said, flashing her a great travelling-salesman false smile. "All my enemies do." He saw her grimace, badpun-wise, on cue, saw uplift hemibra holding boobs not quite all *that* good, espied little hairs peeping out from shiny black kini (this one wears underwear) telltale phony-blonde *black* hairs, felt hard hungry legs, and knew instantly that living-colour Jack Barron had it made.

He leaned on one elbow on the bartop, offered her his pack of Acapulco Golds, clocked the tiny little-girl conspiratorial grin as she took one and quickly lighted it with her own lighter meaning she was pothead from years past way back prohibition days, when shit had spice of danger from manila-envelope furtive earnest small-time neighbourhood dealer. Why, he wondered, do all old-time heads prefer Acapulco (my sponsor) Golds?

"I'll bet you have all kinds of enemies... Jack" (two points), she said, inhaling the offering, breathing out sweet smoke sweet breath off the bartop teasing his nostrils. "Powerful enemies, important enemies... like Benedict Howards."

"Ah," he said, "gotcha! You caught the show tonight. (Sharp chick, but not *that* sharp.) Don't tell me, you're an old and loyal fan of mine."

Tiny flicker of annoyance told him (would never admit it) that she was, as she said, taking another drag, "I'm no fan of yours. I just dig..."

"The smell of blood?" he suggested. She favoured him With a wee bit feral smile as the grass began to hit, began to loosen thighs, loosen centres of hunger reality hunger make it hunger grab a piece of the action hunger ersatz power hunger fuck me into mystic circle of power where it's all at hunger make me real with your living-colour prick hunger.

"Yeah, we all dig the smell of blood," Barron said, glancing around the carefully musk-dusky room, clean Upper East Side shuck barroom, filled with tightly casual ageing young we made it we're only one step from the top next thing to being real crowd, chicks no longer girls and never to be women. "I like a chick with the balls to admit it. (Dig verbal possession of male organs, don't you, baby?) As you may've noticed, I'm a wee bit savage myself." He cocked his head, caught chandelier lights off slick bartop in the hollows of his eyes, opened his mouth showing glimpse of lazy tongue behind teeth—conscious *Bug Jack Barron* image-trick.

Caught by his eyes, her eyes glistening flashed moment of girl-caught-looking embarrassment, big brown eyes pools of open hole hunger, she shrugged a can't-fool-this-cat shrug, her shoulders slumped, elbows fell to the bartop, hands came up to cup her face, eyes still locked on his, she smiled pink-tongue wetlips smile.

"I think you're probably a rotten swine," she said softly. "You like to play with people's heads, and you're playing with mine, and I'd go take a walk if you weren't so damned good at it."

Knowing now he had her definitely made, Jack Barron said, "That's the way I keep food on my table. Want me to split? Or would you rather I told you I loved your mind? Or would you rather let me play with your... head? It's not all that bad, if you lean back and enjoy it."

"I don't like you at all, Jack Barron," she said. But as she said it, he felt her fingernails through his pants on his thigh.

"But you're pretty sure you're gonna like what I'm gonna do to you, eh?"

"I'm queer for the smell of blood, just like you said," she answered, (feral, lost little-girl smile sending a pang through him, *déjà vu* pang *déjà vu* smile *déjà vu* honey-haired girl, hip-brittle carapace over sweet sigh loser softness; "even if it is my own. A man like you can smell that on a girl, can't he? Okay, monster, lead me to the slaughter."

Easy as that, thought Jack Barron. Better be if you want a piece of the action, baby dozen others in here hungry as you, dozen other bars, dozen other honey-haired... (Cool it!)

"Let's split for you-know-where," he said, taking her dry, cool hand. "I'll give you something to tell your grandchildren about."

Picking instant pussy up off the rack was a sometime thing with Jack Barron, specifically a Wednesday night after the show ritual and Claude, the ordinarily wise-ass doorman didn't even crack a small behind-the-chick's-back smile as he ushered the honey-blonde through the door, across the lobby, and into the penthouse elevator and that bugged Jack Barron.

Fucker Claude's used to this, not even an in-joke between us anymore, Barron thought as the elevator swept them silently upward. Makes me feel like some goddamned fetishist. How long's this Wednesday night thing been going on, how many Wednesday night Saras...? (Cool it—too late to cool it, man, who you shucking?)

As the elevator stopped, Barron looked at the nameless girl clutching his hand, saw honey-blonde-dyed hair big brown eyes slightly-prosthetic made-for-balling body, saw the latest in interminable line of honey-blonde big-eyed not-Saras, felt pattern enmeshing him like fate, like creature plugged into Kismet-relay circuitry, felt stronger-than-lust weaker-than-love thing for the nameless girl, girl hungry for living-colour image-prick of world-famous Jack Barron. Fair deal, he thought, value given for value received, like Howards' Freeze Contract: ball me with your image, baby, and I'll ball you with mine.

The elevator door opened and Barron led the girl out into his private entrance foyer with its bearskin carpeting, kinesthop mural (great humming retina-reversing, image-after-image calculated instability, yellow-on-blue spirals) facing the elevator, and shepherded her silently forward into the narrow dark hall wombtunnel between the closed doors to the office and kitchen and into the inevitable living room stupefaction.

On the twenty-third floor of a New York apartment house in the East Sixties, Jack Barron lived in Southern California. The hall opened onto a narrow breakfast-bar deck that overlooked a vast red-carpeted sunken living room, with the entire far wall great glass sliding doors that opened out onto a palmettoed, rubber-plant-festooned patio. Backdrop was the East River lights haze, ever-dusk of Brooklyn. The ceiling of the penthouse living room was an enormous, clear plexiglass, faceted geodesic-dome-skylight. Living room furnishings: an entire wall of built-in electronic bric-a-brac—TV screens, video-recorder, DVD-recorder, stereo rig, colour organ complex, blipper, vidphones, yards of interlocking control consoles couches in orange, rust, blue upholstery, black-leather hassocks, redwood benches with half a dozen assorted matching tables, camel saddles, six mounds of varicoloured pillows, oriental style, all arranged around a ten-foot square sunken open-flame tiled firepit (sidedraft automatic gas type) casting tall, flickering, orange-red shadows from the already-kindled-by-switch-in-foyer ersatz bonfire.

Barron switched on a remote-control console by the bar (remote-control switches to all gizmos scattered throughout the apartment) and Barron-edited music-collage droned electricity into the air and the colour organ scintillated the skylight facets with ever-shifting spectrum-flashes modulated to the music.

The honey-blonde gasped, eyes turned big (Berkeley eyes for hipstyle-campus hero Baby Bolshevik crusader adore worship eyes always those eyes before she blew him) with wonder on him, on him surprise-synapses whited out, and said dumbly, *"Mr Barron..."*

Barron blinked away *déjà vu* tenderness-images, hardened, picked up colour organ flickers, firepit warmth, in hair, in halfopened mouth, eye-hollows, said, measuredly sardonic, "And you haven't seen the *bedroom* yet."

"I think I'd like to," she said with hard-little-girl sweetness. "I have the feeling it's going to be quite an experience."

Barron laughed, found himself suddenly with *this* girl, right here right now, whatever her name was, smell of her stronger than lingering image-odour of Sara. Just a good simple fuck, he thought as he led her down the redwood stairs, across the carpet to the bedroom door. Make it with *her*, not with Sara.

Feeling like a horny, healthy, mindless phallic animal, he opened the door and they stepped inside to outside.

A balmy late New York May night, and the far wall of the bedroom was open, ceiling to floor, side to side, to the open-air rubber trees of the patio against the city-twilight dusky blackness ceiling was a single continuous clear-glass sky-light-bubble starless city-sky blackness wall-to-wall carpet was sensuous green plastigrass undulating in the breeze off the patio big circular bed elevated on stage centre illuminated in gilded light projected from the semicircular living-ivy-covered, weathered-wood headboard (built-in bookshelves, control console) that half encircled it. Distant surf-roar, quiet insect-sounds tropical night sounds filled the room, replacing the music as Barron adjusted a wall console.

"It's... why, it's..." the girl stammered, looking at him with new eyes no longer sure eyes looking down into depths she knew (he knew she knew) she could never fathom, knowing flash-fashion that *this* (not luck, not accident, not trick) was why she was a reality-hungry executive secretary and he was Jack Barron.

Barron smiled a warm, proud, little-boy Berkeley smile, took both her hands in his, paused in ye olde bedroom routine to savour a moment of genuine non-seduction-oriented pride in the way the bedroom softened her eyes, softened his image, her image, made them two simple human beings holding hands before a bed on a warm spring night. The living room was a purposeful tour de force extension of living-colour Jack Barron, but the bedroom was Jack, was Berkeley Jack-and-Sara pad up on the hill was little Los Angeles house in the Canyon warm summer night plant-scent balling was beachhouse in Acapulco Sara smelling from surf-body-sweat was outdoors-indoors-outdoors wistful double (New York-California-New York) expatriate image happy science-fiction California of the mind.

She broke the moment, fell forward against him, flung arms around his neck; he could see her mouth open tongue already hungrily extended in the instant before her lips touched his mouth—open, waiting, but sardonically compliant role-reversal.

Her tongue live desperation live wanting live make-me-real live in his mouth, she pressed her body undulating from shoulders down breast first belly finally hard angular pelvis totally against him pressed hard body hard tongue hard mouth hard his jaws aching stretching against him on all points of him her interface pathetic frantic attempt to breach interface merge her vague body-image-self with the hard-edged living-colour Coast-to-Coast electric reality of Jack Barron.

Through his open eyes light-years removed, he saw her tightly shut, felt yawning sucking energy-reality-life vacuum of her leaching hungry against him, mouth inhaling his magic breath reality-breath in total desire to be filled, engulfed, permeated, transfigured (in his skin body image, inside looking out, to share electric-circuit-satellite network, public-property hyperexistence) by him.

Repulsion-attraction oscillating, he pressed against her, began to move his tongue drifting her back to the bed, felt her go soft-sigh totally yielding live-limp as she felt him at last as an active principal—softwomanflesh feast wanting only to be devoured, digested, incorporated in his flesh-image-power.

Slipping off his sportjac, he eased she drew him down on the bed nailed fingers clawing away his shirt digging into bare back flesh as he unzipped she slid out snakewise from discarded-skin sheath-dress fumbling his pants as he pulled-kicked them away with his loafers onto the plastigrass floor reached down left-handed flipped off socks unhooked uplift hemibra glided down black silk kini (curled hairs dyed-blonde-black, as predicted) and they were naked together, breeze moving over skin.

Suddenly a strange moment of pause (full beat) as bedroom ripping clothes passion image hungers shifted by flesh-to-flesh in virgin breeze to new style of perception-reality: naked bodies elemental reality. Barron looked down, eyes slow, hands soft and still, saw nipples-breasts-belly-navel-crotch simple right-here-right-now woman's body, warm, soft, well-turned woman-body, is all. The girl held her breath, smiled simple human smile up at him, eyes smouldering pure ball-me eyes simple you-Tarzan-me-Jane anygirl smile. He smiled back at *her*. Happy, sweet, shift-gears moment's pause before...

She clamped legs-vice around him moved under him sucked him welcome in her eyes closed little grunts fingernails in buttocks he moaned moved over her into around with hands chest-muscles mouth organ, his consciousness in skin in hands in muscles in slowly-thrusting organ, tactile kinaesthetic rhythmic he-she pleasure interface rippling itself wildly, independent of either of them.

He closed his eyes opened himself, felt pleasure-waves crescendoeing through organs skin thighs of perception muscles in cresting rhythm-wave rising rising rising felt her riding half-beat ahead of him—*me*-you *me*-you—with each other meshing liquid-smoothly-functioning pleasure-pump organic mechanism to one beat from his own pain-pleasure her-him synapse-whiteout reversal spasm and she —

Came. Moaned screamed dug nails "Jack, Jack, Jack" cries mouth enveloped his ear tongue inside flicked him over the edge into timeless moment rushing orgasm: pleasure whiting out into reversal unbearable delicious *déjà vu* harmonic spasm, touch-see-hear-remember ecstasy-images—

Tongue in ear "Jack, Jack, Jack" cries of Berkeley LA California houses Acapulco beach her hair lips body sea-salty wet, moving Sara-tongue of Jack-and-Sara ears bodies, shared breath sighs smells sweats coming face to face (he opened eyes saw big blonde brown eyes ecstasy grimace) together, coming together, coming coming coming... together.

"Sara, Sara, Sara," he cried, spending himself spending seed pleasure-images flashing through him leaving him moment of reflex-warm tenderness-emptiness; lips tender, he moved toward her mouth, stopped all at once, was back New York Wednesday night back, revulsion-remorse, and the wind blowing in from the patio turned cool, real cool cool.

"The name is Elaine," said the blonde from continental long-distance operator hip-hard carapace 27ish executive secretary pick-up distance.

"No shit?" said Jack Barron.

4

"BENEDICT HOWARDS?" Jack Barron repeated into his office intercom, as if disbelief might make the wraith vanish in a puff of ectoplasm. Oughta stay away from this goddamned office, he thought, let network have me for one hour a week then lie doggo in the pad the rest of the time, trouble like Howards comes looking for me, at least it'd be on my own turf. But the powers that be, are, insist I warm dumb chair under network noses on Fridays to deal with screams of anguish after cooling-off Thursdays, Mondays to plot new Wednesday screams of wounded vips to soothe again next Friday—sadomasochistic daisy chain.

"Send Howards in," Barron half-groaned, hoping Carrie had the intercom volume up so Bennie would know how pleased he was to see him, but knowing she ran tight ship under network orders (try to keep Barron from devouring vips for chrissakes, Miss Donaldson) cool, competent Carrie, efficient and distant even in bed. (Network orders there too? he often wondered.)

The office door opened, held by willowy, dark, suppressing-her-distaste-for-sloth's-den (I sit here on sufferance) decor of inner office Carrie, as '70s-elegant (black buttonless silk suit, white ascot over red ruff-collared shirt), tall, pink-skinned, thin-hair-worn-long, semichubby Benedict Howards bustled by her to stand wordlessly in front of the randomly-littered desk.

"Split, Carrie," Barron said, knowing it would bug Howards, who wouldn't publicly first-name secretary he had been balling for five years. (Wonder if he *is* balling that iceberg of his?) As Carrie left, Barron motioned Howards to the mouldy ancient leather-covered chair in front of the desk, and grinned as Howards gingerly planted his ass on the edge of the chair like a man thoroughly convinced you *could too* get clap from a toilet seat.

"Well, Howards," Barron said, "to what do I owe the somewhat dubious pleasure of your company?"

"You're not on camera, Barron, so you're wasting your smartass cleverness on me," Howards said. "And you know goddamned well why I'm here. I don't like knives in my back, and I warn you, no one does it three times to Benedict Howards. First time you get a warning, second time you get squashed like a bug—"

"If you weren't so fucking charming, Howards, I'd take that as a threat," Barron said. "Fortunately for you, I've got an easy-going disposition. Because I don't like threats, man: they bug me. And this Wednesday you got a small taste of what happens when you bug Jack Barron. But it was just a taste, Howards, nobody got really hurt, and we both know it. I made some points because that's the name of the game, but I gave you a chance to get out

37

from under. It wasn't my fault you didn't take me up on it. I hope you got yourself a big one."

Barron smiled as he saw Howards' face go blank for a moment. (Mr Howards is on a hunting and fishing trip in Canada, Mr Barron.) "I thought so," Barron said. "I don't know why you thought it was a smart move to be out to me when I was on the air, but I didn't like it. You got cut up, it was strictly your own fault. You had your chance to make points for your goddamned Freezer Bill, and you blew it. I run a simple show, Howards. You make me look dumb. I return the favour. Which is why I cut up Yarborough and gave Luke Greene the floor."

"I seem to remember that you and Greene were pretty tight at one time," Howards said. "For all I know, you're still involved with the Social Justice Coalition. The way you made Yarborough look like an asshole, and then let that goddamned coon spout his Communistic—"

"Let's get a couple things straight," Barron snapped. "One, John Yarborough is a *self-made* asshole. Two, I'm in show business, Howards, I'm not a politician. I kissed the SJC good-bye when I got this show, and I consider it good riddance. I'm interested in my ratings, and selling cars and dope and nothing else. You don't like me, fine, but give me credit for being a cut above an imbecile. I use the show to roll any party's little red wagon, I get stomped by the FCC quicker than you can pass the word to your two tame commissioners and then I can *really* go back to waving picket-signs. But there's mighty little bread in that line of work, and I like the way I'm living now a lot better than I liked scrounging around Berkeley and Los Angeles.

"And, finally, Howards, while I don't give a shit about Luke's politics, he *is* an old friend of mine, and if you call him a coon or a nigger to my face again, I'll kick your ass all around this office."

"Do you know who you're talking to?" Howards shouted. "No one gives lip to Benedict Howards! I'll squeeze your sponsors and the network and put pressure on the FCC, and I've got more than enough muscle to do it. Cross me, and I'll cut you to dogmeat and feed you to the fishes."

"And how long do you think that'd take?" Barron asked mildly.

"I can have you off the air in a month, and you'd better believe it."

"Four weeks, four shows," said Jack Barron. "Think about that. Think about what I could do to you if I had nothing to lose because you were killing my show anyway. Four weeks worth of sheer spite. Four hours in front of a hundred million people, and me with nothing better left to do than take revenge on you and your Foundation.

"Sure, you can destroy me if you want to commit hara-kiri and, for that matter, I can always kamikaze you. We're both big boys, Bennie, too big for either of us to do the other in without making it a Samson-smash. I don't like you, and you don't like me, but you've got nothing to worry about from me unless you back me into a corner. But if I go, you go too, and don't you forget it."

Suddenly, unpredictably, Howards went smooth. "Look," he said, with jarring reasonableness, "I don't come here to trade threats with you. You hurt my Freezer Bill, cost me a few votes, but—"

"Don't blame me," Barron said. "Blame that schmuck Hennering. He's your boy, and that's why I put him on, to let your side make points and even things out. It's not my fault if the dum-dum—"

"That's all ancient history, Barron," Howards said. "I'm interested in the future. Man like me's gotta take the long view. (Howards smiled a weird beatific smile. What the hell's *that*? Barron thought.) The *real* long view... And the Freezer Utility Bill's mighty important to my future, to the future of the human—"

"Aw, spare me that crap, will you..." Barron drawled. "You want a bill passed to give you a Freezer Monopoly, that's your bag, but don't try to bullshit me about the future of the human race. You're looking out for Number One, period. Keep it on that level, and maybe I'll listen."

"All right, Barron, I'll lay it on the line. You've got something I need—*Bug Jack Barron*. You've got a pipeline to a hundred million Americans, and what they think about the bill can swing some votes in Congress, not as many votes as they'd like to think, maybe, but some. I want those votes. I want you to do the kind of shows that will get me those votes—not every week, we can't be too obvious, but just the right touches here and there. You've got the following and the know-how to pull it off. That's what you can do for me, Barron, and in return—"

"You're crazy, you know that?" said Jack Barron. "You expect me to risk the show by grinding your private axe? Where's the percentage, Howards? I knock down four hundred thou in a good year, and I got a lot of years left with *Bug Jack Barron*. Show biz gives me enough money to let me live exactly the way I want to, and I *dig* it. Forget it man, you can't buy me the way you buy loxes like Teddy Hennering. You just don't have anything I want that bad."

Benedict Howards smiled a smug smile. "Don't I?" he said. "I've got something everyone wants, something you can't buy with money—*life*, Barron, life itself. Immortality. Think about it, man, a life that goes on and on, not for a lousy century but millennium after millennium, young and strong and healthy forever. Think about what that means every morning when you wake up, knowing it's all there forever—the way food tastes, the way a woman's body feels, the smell of the air—all of it yours, and all of it forever. Wouldn't you sell your soul for that? Wouldn't anyone? Because you wouldn't need a soul to go somewhere and play a harp when you croak. You'd have it all, right here on terra firma. Forever... Forever..."

"You sound like you're about to breathe fire and brimstone and ask me to sign a contract in blood," Barron remarked dryly.

Howards seemed to start; his hot eyes suddenly contracted to cold boar-shrewdness as if he were talking about something he suddenly realised he shouldn't—or, Barron thought, as if old Bennie just realised how loopy he sounds.

"I'm talking about a Freeze Contract," Howards said. "A *free* Freeze. No assignment of assets. I got tentacles, Barron, and I know you spend money as fast as you make it. You'll never hold on to enough to buy a Freeze. And just between you and me, even if you did, I'd never let you buy it now. Because I don't want your money when you die, I want *you*, Barron, live, right now. That's the deal—you play ball with me and have your chance at immortality, or when you die you're wormfood. Forever is a long time to be dead, Barron."

What goes? thought Barron. Bennie's bill's a ten votes to spare in the Senate thirty in the House shoo-in, all over but the shouting. Why's he so hot for *my* bod? Free Freeze is fat-cat Senator-Cabinet-Supreme-Court-Justice level bribe, and way out of line for purchasing kick-em-in-the-ass Jack Barron. He's popping cookies all over the lot—admitting to me Freezes can be bought or withheld for other than money. What's the schtick, what's he know I don't, why's got-it-in-the-bag Bennie Howards running so scared? Scared of *me* ...

But shit, a Freeze beats a fancy funeral anyday. Immortality... who knows what the next century can bring? Live forever, young, healthy, strong...? Nothing to lose in a free Freeze, worst thing can happen it's all a shuck, and, baby, you're dead then either way. Could I pull it off? Play Howards' game, but subtly enough to keep the show? No sweat anyway, once Freeze Contract is signed in triplicate, Bennie can't welch... But honest Jack Barron'd have nothing to hold legal water on paper, could cop-out on Bennie any time. Got Bennie by the balls, it seems. But why? Why? Fun and games out *of my league?* Play it cool, Jack, baby!

"I can smell the wood burning," Howards said. "You can taste it, can't you, Barron? Forever, a million years of life, for at most a few months of playing ball. Every man's got his price, old saying, eh? But I'm something new; the coin I can pay, *everyone's* selling."

"Not so fast, Bennie-boy," said Barron. "This smells like a dead flounder. Okay, so I admit that a Freeze Contract sounds interesting, buying my flesh at top dollar, and maybe, just *maybe*, I might like to take you up on it. But why're you going so high to get me? You've got your Freezer Bill in the bag; you've got the muscle and grease to put it over in Congress, and we both know it. And besides, if you're willing to offer Freezes as bribes, why bribe *me*, why not deal with the Foghorns direct? Jeez, I'm only thirty-eight, and the idea of a Freeze interests me, Senator or Congressman carrying around another thirty years should *really* be interested. It *appears* that I need you more than you need me, and you're just being generous. But I just don't figure you for the philanthropist type. Beware of Greeks and freaks bearing gifts, I always say, 'cause *gift* means poison in German.

"You're holding out on me, Howards, and you're playing in the big leagues. I find that a paranoid situation. You're scared, don't try to *con* me. You're uptight about your Freezer Bill's chances, and from what I know you shouldn't be. Therefore I don't know everything, but I damn well will before I even think about talking turkey."

"It's the race angle your goddamned show stirred up," Howards told him with an obviously-put-on vehemence that put Barron uptight on guard. "All that crap from Greene and the rest of it turning every coon in the country against—"

"Hold it, Howards!" Barron snapped, bugged, but at the same time coldly calculating. "For openers, I told you I don't like the word 'coon', and besides, that's all bullshit. Eighty per cent of the Negroes in the country vote SJC anyway, and the SJC is dead set against your bill, so how can you claim I cost you votes you never had in the first place? So you got the SJC and the Republicans against you for separate reasons, but that shouldn't be uptighting you with Teddy Hennering your front-man and even Teddy the Pretender forced to cool it with the weight you swing in the Democratic party. Democrats control what—nearly two-thirds of Congress? And you got the other factions too spooked to make waves, and Hennering & Co. is in your hip pocket. So what's—"

"You mean you haven't heard?" Howards asked.

"Heard what?"

"About Hennering." Howards reached into his inside breast-pocket, then tossed a ragged clipping across the desk. Barron read:

TED HENNERING DIES IN AIR DISASTER
Private plane destroyed in mid-air explosion.

"Happened late last night," Howards said. "Now you see why I'm a little nervous. Hennering was our big front-man on the bill. With him dead, we're not exactly in trouble but we've lost a piece of the edge we had and I don't believe in taking chances. You can get that edge back for me and cool it with the coo—er, Negroes. That's why I'm offering you a Freeze, Barron. Without you, the bill is still almost certain to pass. But I don't like *almosts*. I want it locked up. I want certainty."

Hennering dead, thought Barron, so that's it, Bennie-boy, you lost your chief presidential-puppet stooge means next President is Teddy the Pretender for sure, and he's not quite in the old hip pocket. Yeah, that sure would uptight you, but…

But not about the Freezer Bill, he suddenly realised. Nothing really lost there but Hennering's one lousy vote, and you got plenty of votes to spare. So why—?

Chill danger signals from somewhere from years of reflex-reaction to gambits of men of power flashed to Barron's mind from gut-nerve endings saying: Big! Big! Big! All too pat too many loose ends *not* loose ends. Hennering acting like walking corpse Wednesday night dead for real Friday morning, prepared clipping, prepared chain of answers from Howards each one more nitty-gritty *seeming* as if extracted under pressure. Buy Jack Barron to make shoo-in triple certain? Don't add up, adds up to something bigger offstage that scares even Howards...

Play your cards right, Jack, baby! Gambler's instinct: you're holding the high ones, Bennie knows it, knows what they are, you don't, so raise, raise, don't call till you know how many aces you're holding.

"Look Howards," he said. "I haven't had lunch yet, and I'm getting tired of being waltzed around the block. You're holding out on me. I don't know what you're sitting on, but you're sure as hell sitting on *something*. Hennering or no Hennering, you've got that Freezer Bill locked up, and don't waste both our time by telling me otherwise. Let's say I'm interested in playing ball with you—why not?—a free freeze you don't throw away because your heart is pure. But I don't go into *anything* blind, and that's what you're asking."

Howards hesitated, pursed his lips, breathed heavily, picked his nose, opened his mouth, closed it, paused, opened it again, and said, "I want you to do a job for me, I don't want a goddamn partner. You're asking partner-type questions that're none of your business. I'm paying you more than the job deserves, and I'm doing it only because I can easily afford it. Make it something other than easy, and you've blown it. I'm way out of your league, Barron, don't push your luck."

That's exactly where it's at, thought Barron. Bennie wants to buy himself another flunky, wants it real bad. Too bad. So I'm out of your league, Bennie-boy? Breadwise, powerwise, maybe. Keep thinking that way, Howards, and you go home in a barrel. Maybe I'm in the wrong league, but you're in the wrong game. Too much power too long to play bluff with me. Three yards and a cloud of dust's where you're at, can't match fancy footwork with good old Jack Barron's been thinking immelmanns around fatter cats too long, Mr Howards.

"Don't push *yours*, Howards," he said. "You can't *buy* me, only maybe rent me as a free agent. You don't buy me as a flunky or no deal. You tell me the truth, the whole truth and maybe you rent yourself an ally. You mickeymouse me much longer, and you've got yourself an enemy. I don't think you can afford me as an enemy—if you could you wouldn't be so hot for my bod."

"Take my word for it, you don't want to know what you think you do,"

Howards said. "I'm not peddling cars or dope, and I'm not an entertainer. I play for the... for blood. Let it go, Barron, you're out of your depth. This is so big... it's none of your business. You got a chance to live forever, don't blow it by trying to stick your nose in a meatgrinder. Yes or no, Barron, right here, right now. No more fencing."

"You've had my final word," Barron said, "and *you* can take it or leave it."

"Look, let's not be nasty," Howards said, again with a weird shift of verbal gears to incomprehensible sweet reason. "I'll give you a week. Think about it. Think about wormfood—and think about living forever."

Schmuck! Barron thought. Bennie-boy, you blew it. Bennie Howards doesn't back down from take-it-or-leave-it unless he thinks the answer will be leave it, and knows he can't afford a leave it from Jack Barron. You're hot for my bod, baby, and before you get it, do I put you through changes!

"Okay," he said. "A week. For both of us to think about it." And will you get something to think about next Wednesday, Mr Benedict Howards!

"That's what I want, Vince," Jack Barron said as Gelardi's grey basilisk image did a double take on the vidphone screen. "That's what I want, and it's my show, and that's what I'll get."

"I don't get it," Gelardi said. "This week you give me static for feeding you a call that just played footsie too hard with Howards, and now you want to aim a boot at his testes. What happened between Wednesday and today, man?"

Barron paused, considered, felt vidphone-camera circuitry carrying his image-words to Gelardi camera-to-camera, screen-to-screen-phosphor-dot patterns talking to each other, in control cool, keep it cool. Big stakes, Jack, baby, with free Freeze maybe just for openers, got to see what Howards has in the hole, how many cards he takes on draw. Play your own hand in *this* game, sorry, Vince, no kibitzers allowed.

"Bennie Howards happened," Barron said. "He happened all over this office about an hour ago."

"So the show *did* put him uptight?"

"Uptight!" said Barron. "Bennie was uptight like Shabazz is black. I'm going to have to have the rug replaced, and there are still toothmarks on my throat. Howards blew his gourd. He threatened to strong-arm the network, lean on the sponsors, and get his flunkies on the FCC to put me on the shitlist, is all."

"Did you cool him?" Gelardi asked nervously. Directing show and monkey block's best gravy train you ever rode, eh, Vince? Barron thought. Get conniptions when I make waves.

"Cool him?" Barron said. "*Cool him?* I cooled him, all right, I told him to go take a flying fuck."

Gelardi made a rude headshaking bellynoise, rolled his eyes upward. Barron smiled calculatingly inward. Need a good wrong reason to do the right thing, he thought, make Vince think highest all-time stakes still the show. Need *Bug Jack Barron*-oriented reason to knee Bennie in the groin.

"You're crazy, you know that, Jack?" Gelardi said in dead earnest. "You keep telling me we don't twist tigers' tails, and now what do you do, you get Bennie Howards uptight, and then instead of cooling it you tell him to go fuck himself. And now we don't have enough tsouris, you want a whole show aimed at Howards' jugular, You on something stronger than our sponsor's grass?"

"In words of one syllable, Vince," Barron said, "we are in trouble. Howards was convinced I'm out to get him, and I couldn't unconvince him. Therefore he informed me that he was going to get *me*, and we both know he can do it, given the time. At which point, knowing sweet reason would do no good, I told Bennie to fuck off, and I threatened *him*. I told him that what happened this week was just good clean fun compared to what would happen to him if he got fancy with me. Which is why we go after his ass on the next show—to give proof positive that I mean what I say, that there's no percentage in *really* bugging Jack Barron even if you've got the muscle Howards' got. We give Howards a taste of the fire next time, and he'll back off. He thinks he's got his Freezer Bill all locked up; I want to show him I can put it in doubt if he gives me reason enough to run the risk. We show him our claws, and he'll suck in his, *comprende, paisan?*"

"Oh, my bleeding ulcer!" Gelardi said. "I dig the necessity now, but the network will have a shitfit."

"Screw the network," Barron said. "There's three other networks would love to have *Bug Jack Barron*, and they know it. As long as we scare Howards off our backs they'll rant and rave, but they won't do squat. And that goes in spades for the sponsors. For the bread the show makes for all concerned, they can afford the milk to baby their ulcers. Question is, what kind of call can we count on getting next week that I can use against Howards? We can concoct a put-up job if we have to, but I don't like that idea very much. If Howards or the network or the FCC found out we were faking calls…"

"How about a deathbed scene?" Gelardi suggested instantly. Good old Vince, Barron thought, give him an angle he can buy and he's off to the races.

"Deathbed scene?" Barron asked.

"Sure," said Gelardi. "We get at least half a dozen every week, crank stuff, I got standing orders with the monkey block not to let 'em past the first screen. Some cat's croaking from something slow, usually cancer, usually on Social Security or Guaranteed Annual Wage, you know, like broke, and the whole goddamn family gathers round the vidphone with the prospective corpse as a prop and wants you to get the Foundation to give the old man a free Freeze. Tear-jerker stuff. Chances are we'll even get one where the dying man does some of the talking. And it's a safe bet we can add on the race angle again if we want to."

Yeah, thought Barron, just the right touch. Milk it for maybe ten, fifteen minutes worth of hot angry tears, then put Bennie on (you *know* he'll be answering his phone this time) for the rest of the show. Give him a taste of the whip, then it's his option, then the knife again, then he makes more points, then another kick in the balls—cat and mouse, show him just where it's at. Show him you can kill him stone-cold-dead, but back off the coup de grace, leaving the goose bleeding but with one more chance to give with the golden egg—and a fucking good show in the bargain!

"I like, I like," Barron said. "But let's lay off the race schtick this time round. He'll be ready for that, and we want to hit him where he ain't. Have the first screen boys feed all deathbed calls directly to you, and give me the best lily-white one you get."

"You're the boss, Jack," Gelardi said. "But personally the whole schtick has me shaking. You hurt Howards *too* bad and you won't scare him off, you'll goad him into a kamikaze. You're gonna really have to walk that line, man—and with both our jobs riding on it."

"That's the name of the game, Vince," Barron told him. "You shove me out on the high wire, and I walk it. Trust old Uncle Jack."

"Trust you like my brother," Gelardi said.

"I didn't know you had a brother."

"Yeah," Gelardi said, grinning. "He's doing five to ten in Sing Sing for fraud. See you in the frying pan, Jack."

5

"CLEAN?" said Benedict Howards, looking past the head of the faceless, bookkeeperish man, out the picture window at the soothing white walls of the main Freezer of the Long Island Freezer Complex, monolith of immortality power, safe from crawling maggots of incompetence like this Wintergreen, random servants of the fading black circle of death like Jack Barron.

"No man's clean, Wintergreen, and certainly not a man with a past as rank as Jack Barron's—a founder of the Social Justice Coalition, ex-Berkeley rabble-rouser, boyhood buddy of every Peking-loving Commie son of a bitch in the country, and you tell me Barron's *clean*? He's about as clean as an open cesspool."

Wintergreen fondled the fat manila folder he kept shuffling from his lap to the desk and back, worried it like a goddamned nervous kangaroo. "Well, of course, not *that* way, he's not, Mr Howards," he said. (Rabbity yes-man bastard! Howards thought.) "But this is a complete dossier on Barron, and there's nothing in here we can use against him, nothing. I stake my reputation on that, sir."

"You're staking a hell of a lot more than your non-existent reputation on it," Howards told him. "Your job's on the line, and your place in a Freezer too. I don't keep a head of 'Personnel Research' to produce a shitload of useless paper on a man I want nailed to the wall, I pay you to find me a handle I can grab on a man. Every man's got a handle, and you're paid to find it."

"But I can't manufacture something that isn't there," Wintergreen whined. "Barron was never a member of any organisation on the old Attorney General's list even though plenty of his friends were. There's nothing to link him to anything more damaging than technically-illegal demonstrations, and these days that kind of thing makes a man a hero, not a criminal. He isn't even a member of the SJC anymore, hasn't been since a year after he got his TV show. He makes large amounts of money, spends it freely, but keeps out of debt. He sleeps with large numbers of unattached women, engages in no illegal perversions, and takes no illegal drugs. There's nothing in any of it we can use against him, and in that sense, which I trust is the sense you're interested in, sir, he's totally clean." Wintergreen picked up the folder again, began bending down the edges.

"Stop playing with that damned thing!" Howards snapped. (Goddamn cretin, whole country's full of cretins who can't find their asses without a roadmap.) "So we can't blackmail Barron," he said, and saw Wintergreen wince at plain truth-word *blackmail*. Imagine *him* living forever, clerk forever, rabbity coward forever. Immortality's for men with the balls to grab it, fight for it, fight from dry windy Panhandle to circles of power circles of forever, toss the rest to the fading black circle garbage disposal, only what they deserve—like damn fool coward Hennering.

"So some men can't be blackmailed," Howards said. "But every man can be bought, once you know his price. So we buy Jack Barron."

"But you've already offered him the biggest possible bribe, a place in a Freezer," Wintergreen said, "and he hasn't taken it."

"He hasn't turned it down either," said Howard. "I know men, which means I got a nose for their prices. That's why I'm where I am today. Way I know *your* price down to the dollar—more money than you can spend, and a place in the Freezers when you croak, and you're mine simply because I know the price you set on yourself and I can afford to meet it fully. Barron's no different from you or anybody else; he wants that Freeze Contract, you can make book on that. He wants it just enough to let me use him on his terms. With that coin, I can buy his services just until he thinks he can double-cross me and get away with it. And once those contracts are signed, we *will* be able to get away with it. And a man like Barron, he won't play ball till I *do* sign. You don't screw around with a man like that; you've got to own him down to the soles of his shoes. And a free Freeze just won't buy that. For that fee, he'll play ball so long as I answer all his questions and he likes the answers.

"But that's not the way Benedict Howards does business. It's easier to buy a Jack Barron than to destroy him, good business too. What I need from you is something that will let me meet the rest of the price he sets on himself. There's got to be *something* the man's hungry for and can't get for himself."

"Well... there's his ex-wife," Wintergreen said hesitantly. "But there's no way we can deliver *her*."

"*Ex-wife?*" Howards hissed. (You dumb puffed-up threescore-and-ten errand-boy bastard, sitting right in front of you all the time, egomaniac like Barron's got to have some woman means something more to him than a good lay. What they call it, mindfucker, yeah, hippie Bolshevik mindfucker's got to have some woman's mind to play with, means *she's* got to be able to screw around with his.)

"Well what about his ex-wife, idiot? What's her name? Why'd they break up, if Barron still wants her? This is what I was looking for from the beginning, man! Do I have to do *all* the thinking around here?"

"I'm afraid it's hopeless, Mr Howards," Wintergreen answered, again toying with the folder. Howards started to bark, then thought—what the hell, forget it, take the long view, patience, patience, easy when you got all the time in creation.

"Her name's Sara Westerfeld. She lives right here in New York, in the

Village. Does kinesthop interior effects. Barron met her when he was still a student at Berkeley. They lived together for a couple of years before they were married, and were divorced about two years after he got the show. I anticipated this coming up, Mr Howards, and had her investigated. It's all bad, sir. She holds a membership card in the Social Justice Coalition, and she's a loud supporter of the Public Freezer League, and you know how *that* kind feels about us. And from what we've been able to learn, she seems to hate Barron as much as she hates us. Seems to have something to do with his being a television star; she actually moved out on him only six months after he got the show."

"Sounds like the last of the red-hot hippies," Howards said. Dammit, he thought, figures Barron would have the hots for a Foundation-hating artsy-fartsy, hair-halfway-down-her-ass Berkeley Bolshevik loser-bitch! But she hates him, good, means he can't get her himself, buy her, you've bought Jack Barron. Question is how you buy screwball kook Sara Westerfeld...?

"And who's she sleeping with?" Howards asked on sudden shrewd impulse.

"An easier question to answer," Wintergreen said primly, "would be who *isn't* she sleeping with. She seems to have gone to bed with every social misfit in the Village at one time or another—and without too many repeat performances. Obviously a nymphomaniac."

Click! Howards felt pieces of the pattern come together in his mind: Jack Barron screwing everyone in creation, ex-wife doing likewise but they were together a long time not likely they both go for one-night stands for no reason, no one does nothing for no reason. Probably both for the *same* reason. Barron's got the itch for her, can't scratch, is why he tries so hard, so she...

"Wintergreen," he said, "it's obvious that you don't know a damn thing about women. She's obviously still got an itch for Barron whether she hates his guts or not, and that's why she's working overtime trying to scratch it because she can't scratch it without Barron—and she wants no part of him. And that's the easiest kind of woman to buy, because she's half bought already. Half loves Barron, half hates him. Give her an extra reason to go back to him and she'll do it in a minute, because she *wants* an excuse to crawl back into bed with Barron. It means she wants to be bought, even if she doesn't know it yet."

Howards smiled because best part is once I get her into bed with Barron I've bought her all the way because then the worst thing in the world for Miss Sara Westerfeld is for Barron to find out I've bought her, she's a whore, my whore, she'll do as she's told, buy her, and you've bought Jack Barron.

"I want Sara Westerfeld in this office within five hours," Howards said. "And I don't care how you do it. Grab her, if you have to. Don't worry.

She won't open her mouth, and won't be pressing any charges after I get through with her."

"But, Mr Howards, a woman like that, how can you..."

"You let me worry about that. Obviously this is a girl with worms where her brains should be, and that kind you can always buy in the bargain basement. Get to it, man—and stop playing with that goddamned folder!"

Christ, I'm tired, Benedict Howards thought. Tired of having to do it all myself tired of dumb-ass politicians with qualms of conscience like Hennering tired of fighting from cold empty plains to oilfields stocks Houston, Los Angeles, New York, Washington circles of power, fighting doctors' heads nodding nurses' needles plastic tube up nose down throat life leaking away in plastic bottles, fighting fading black circle with money-fear power of life against death, fighting, fighting all the way alone idiots all the way incompetent phony sycophants useless fumbling fools lunatics stupidity lies all on the side of death, side of the fading black circle of nothingness closing in, smaller, smaller...

Won't get Benedict Howards! Push you back, open you up, got you now, damn you! Palacci, Bruce, doctors, endocrinologists, surgeons, internists, Foundation flunkies, all against you, all owned by Benedict Howards, say I've got you this time, it works, endocrine balance stabilised Homeostatic Endocrine Balance, young, strong, healthy—feel it when I get up eat piss touch woman hot strong quick like in Dallas Los Angeles oilfield days, all night long, and hungry and strong in the morning, forever, Mr Howards, anabolism balances catabolism, Mr Howards, immortality, Mr Howards.

Fight, fight, fight, and now I've got it all. Got money-power, life-versus-death power, Senators (damn Hennering!), Governors, President...? (Goddamn bastard Hennering!), Mr Howards, got forever, Mr Howards.

And nobody takes forever away from Benedict Howards!

Not Teddy Hennering not Teddy the Pretender not nigger bastard Bolshevik Greene not smart-ass organ-grinder-monkey Jack Barron... Buy 'em, kill 'em, own 'em all, men on the side of death, till only two kinds of men left: Foundation men and dead men, wormfood men, Mr Howards.

One last fight to keep forever safe forever mine forever. Pass Utility Bill, find new flunky (son of a bitch Hennering), make him President, control it all, control Congress, White House, Freezers, power of life against death, immortality-power, all power against fading black circle, hold it back, push it back, open it up forever...

Then rest, rest ten thousand years of smooth cool women in air-cooled arenas of power, young, quick, strong, ten million years, rest spoils of battle forever, my women, my power my country my forever...

Smart-ass Bolshevik con-artist Jack Barron thinks he can stand against me, con me, milk me, play power-games, threat-games, death-games with

Benedict Howards no one plays games with Benedict Howards. Out of his league, squash him like a bug, buy him, own him, use him to pass Utility Bill despite coward Hennering. Own Barron own private pipeline to hundred million loser-slobs own them own fears minds votes bodies Congress White House country, safe when they find out safe, forever, safe…

Last piece in pattern of power, Jack Barron, that's all you are, smart-ass. Just last little piece to fit into pattern of Foundation life against death Senators, Governors, President, safety-power, little gear in big forever machine, little tin gear, Barron.

Stomp me, I stomp you, eh, Barron? *Clean* Jack Barron, nosy question-man bastard, Jack Barron. Think Foundation-power money-power life-against-death-power can't touch you? No one says no to Benedict Howards. I got the handle on you, Barron, find the handle on everyone, sooner or later.

Sara Westerfeld. Howards savoured the name, tasted the syllables with his tongue. Dumb loser kook whore, but she's got you by the balls, hasn't she Barron? Think you're strong, Barron, strong enough to play games with Benedict Howards…

Howards smiled, leaned back in his chair, waited, waited for Sara Westerfeld, Sara Westerfeld, the handle on Jack Barron. No man's strong who's weak for someone weak, he knew. Chain of command: Benedict Howards to Sara Westerfeld to Jack Barron to hundred million dumb slobs to Senators, Congressmen, President…

And all the links were already in place except the first one, the easiest one—Sara Westerfeld. Sara Westerfeld—bargain-basement stuff. Hates the Foundation, eh? Member of Public Freezer League…?

"Yeah," Howards breathed aloud. That was it, that had to be it! Public freezer kooks want Federal Freezer Program so *they* (deadbeat-loser-slobs) can have place in a Freezer. Offer kook free Freeze, and she'll sell out faster than you can buy. Price-tag on Sara Westerfeld: Jack Barron and Forever. And one's her excuse to go get the other!

Barron's in my pocket, good as bought, Howards thought. Sara Westerfeld, price of Jack Barron—lucky Sara Westerfeld!

Curiosity, fear, fascination, and contempt were a knot in her stomach… lightheadedness sense of vision bursting out of her head instead of coming in, stoned-electric-scalp-tingling, as Sara Westerfeld stepped out of the car, stood before the evil white dying-place-blankness of the main Freezer of the Long Island Freezer Complex.

Temple, she thought, it's like an Aztec-Egyptian temple, with priests sacrificing to gods of ugliness and praying for alliances with snake-headed idols to ward off the god with no face, and all the time worshipping him with their fear. No-faced death-god, like a big white building without windows; and inside mummies in cold cold swaddling, sleeping in liquid helium amnion, waiting to be reborn.

She shivered as the balding man touched her elbow silently, priestlike, shivered as if she could feel the liquid helium space-cold sympathetic magic of the Foundation itself in his touch, the decayed-lizard death-touch of Benedict Howards, waiting for her, there in his bone-white windowless lair... Why? Why?

She, followed the man who had come to her apartment with his all-too-polite invitation—politeness of dictators of Los Angeles cops Berkeley cops sinister Peter Lorre-secret-police politeness with paddy wagons riot cops cells guns booted feet waiting behind the crocodile smile—across a wide, green, somehow-plastic-seeming lawn, thinking it can't happen here, we've got rights, writ of *habeas corpus*...

Sara shuddered. A corpus abducted into the Freezer could not be freed by all the court writs since the beginning of time, Not until the Foundation found a way to unfreeze bodies...

Get hold of yourself! No one's going to Freeze you, just a little talk, the slimy creature said. With Benedict Howards. A little talk between an ant and an elephant. I'm afraid, she admitted, I don't know of what, but oh, oh, I'm afraid. Power, that's what *he'd* say, the arena, where it's really at, nitty-gritty market-place of power baby.

That's what *he'd* say, the cop-out bastard. Two of a kind, Jack and Howards. Jack'd know what to say, what not to say in fifteen different ways to tie that slimy lizard in knots. Just Jack's bag.

Jack...

Across the lawn, down a path by the side of the Freezer, and into a smaller, windowed, outbuilding; cold, blue pastel halls with plush red carpeting, walnut doors, smells of secretaries, coffee, soft clickings of muted typewriters, human voices—an office building, no operating theatres, gurgling pumps bottled-blood chemical smells of Freezer building feel of layer on layer of Frozen dead waiting bodies bulging cold graveyard (colder than any graveyard) weight into the air of the corridor. Just an office building, lousy-décor office building, Texan industrially-designed tastelessness of Benedict Howards' office building.

But it made her more afraid. Faceless building like windowless faceless Freezer faceless death-god Howards' faceless polite message faceless polite messenger facelessness of Jack's damned *real* world, power-world where people are faceless images to each other pawns on chessboard faceless game of life and death.

Never my world, she thought. Like overdose bummer-style reality, bad acid freakout, A-head world, all sharp cutting edges paranoia. Feel like soft-flesh creature in metal forest world of knives, cocks like steel pistons.

Jack... Jack, you son of a bitch, why aren't you here with me? Jack'd give you yours, Benedict Howards! Warm loving courage to light up the world, gauntlets thrown in faces of cops Berkeley cops Los Angeles cops Alabama cops rednecks' fists judges, me and my man against all corners balling in open airy spaces feel of his body beside me in bed on one elbow on the phone with Luke setting the world straight our friends listening faces shining to the voice of hope in my bed making it all seem possible. A *man* is all, Benedict Howards, not perambulating lizard-creature, sweet cylinder of flesh, stronger, more enduring than oiled steel piston.

Oh, Jack, where did you lose it where is it where are you I need you now my knight in soft-flesh armour arms around my waist, facing down, shaming, howling mob with only your voice for a sword, our love for armour...

She shuddered as the bald man opened a door, led her through a deserted outer office—half-cup of coffee still on empty secretary's desk, as if witness suddenly cleared away from scene of ghastly lizard-human flesh-steel assignation. And she remembered how alone, how totally alone, how separated in time and space she was from her one and only knight in rusty armour—all that was left of the Jack that was the pain of the memory.

And she remembered his last words to her, sad, lorn words, with not even the warmth of anger: 'The time of the Children's Crusade is over, baby. Find yourself a nice idealistic *boy* with a nice big dick, and maybe you'll be happy. You can't cut it with my world, you can't cut it with me. I've got my piece of the action, and I don't go back to being a loser even for you, Sara.' And he hadn't even kissed her good-bye.

The chill of the memory forged a kind of steel within her. Holding the memory of the Jack that had been to her for warmth, and the image of the Jack that was for anger. She stepped into the inner office as the bald man stepped aside, holding the door for her, said: "Mr Howards, this is Sara Westerfeld." And closed the door behind her.

The man behind the ultra-stark, bare, teakwood desk (not *his* desk, she thought, he doesn't use this office often, desk hasn't been lived on) looked more like someone's rich Uncle Bill—pink, square-dressed, loosely-pudgy in old-time-'70s maroon suit and ascot—than Benedict Howards, swimming sharklike in currents of death-madness-power.

He motioned her to an expensive, badly-designed, uncomfortable teak-and horsehide chair in front of the desk with a soft heavy hand, said: "Miss Westerfeld, I'm Benedict Howards." And looked at her with eyes like black holes feral rodent eyes kinesthop eyes shiny shifting flashes of power-fear eyes junkie-intensity eyes that said here there be tigers.

"What do you want from *me*?" she asked, sinking onto the chair which she suddenly realised was purposely uncomfortable, cunningly designed to uptight asses, hotseat-interrogation chair, focus of paranoid A-head pattern of power.

Howards smiled a crocodile smile of false-uncle geniality, snapping pink face into a basilisk dead-flesh pattern around his shrewd mad eyes, said: "What I want from you, Miss Westerfeld, is nothing beside what I'm prepared to offer."

"There's nothing I could ever want from you," she said, "and I can't imagine what you could want from me. Unless (could it be as silly-safe as that?) you'd like some kinesthop pieces for this office. Maybe designs for the whole building? I've done office buildings before, and this place could certainly use—"

Howards cut her off with a pseudo-chuckle sound. "I'm much more interested in life than in art, aren't *you*, Sara?" he asked "Isn't everyone?"

"I don't know what you're talking about." she said. Then, with little-girl prim petulance: "And I never said you could call me Sara."

Howards ignored it all as if speaking into a one-way vidphone connection. "You're in the kinesthop business," he said, "and I'm in the life business. The business of eternal life. Don't you find that the least bit interesting?"

"I don't find you or your horrid Foundation interesting at all," she said. "You're a loathsome man, and what you do is sickening and disgusting, setting a price on... on life itself. The only interesting thing about you, Mr Howards, is how you manage to look into a mirror without puking. What do you want from me, why did you drag me here?"

"No one dragged you here," Howards said smoothly. "You came of your own free will. You weren't... abducted."

"And if I hadn't come of my own free will, I *would've* been abducted, wouldn't I?" She said, feeling anger burning away fear. "You can go fuck yourself with your stainless-steel cock, Benedict Howards!"

"I'll tell you why you came here of your own free will," said Benedict Howards. "You can't con me with that purity crap; no one cons Benedict Howards. You came here because you're fascinated, like everyone else, you came here to get a whiff of forever. Forget about conning me, I've seen it all, isn't a man or woman on Earth wouldn't like a place in a Freezer ready and waiting when they die, wouldn't want to know that when that black circle closes in, snuffs you out like a candle, it's not forever, blackness isn't forever they don't fill you with formaldehyde and feed you to the worms, and no more Sara Westerfeld, not ever. Better to close your eyes that last time knowing it's *not* the last time, doesn't have to be a last time, in a century or a millennium doesn't matter 'cause all you feel is a good night's sleep—they'll thaw you out, fix you better than new, and you're young and healthy and beautiful forever. That's why you came here, and no one's twisting your arm, you can leave any time you want to. Go ahead, turn your back on immortality, I dare you."

And all the while his eyes were measuring her like a sausage, cold weasel-eyes sulphur-Satan eyes, watching his own words bounce back to him off her face, feeding back to his calm, sure, basilisk smile that said he knew it all, knew next words she would say why she would say them knew her insides knew her buttons better than she did, and for reasons of his own which she could never encompass, was about to push them.

"I... I don't suppose you brought me here to discuss existential philosophy," she said, wanly.

"Philosophy?" Benedict Howards said, making the word shit in his mouth. "I'm not giving you some Berkeley academic bullshit, I'm talking hard reality, woman—death, hardest reality there is. You know anything harder? I don't, and I've looked death square in his ugly face, and you'd better believe that, fading closing circle of black with your life leaking away in tubes and bottles, is the ugliest face there is. And that's going to happen to *you*, Sara Westerfeld, and there's nothing you can do about it. Next week, or next year, or sixty years from now you're gonna be looking down into that pit with no bottom, and the last thing you'll ever think is that you're never gonna think anything again. You took *that* in Philosophy at Berkeley, Miss Westerfeld?"

"What are you trying to do to me?" Sara screamed from the rim of a dark ugly crater bottomless hole being nothingness spume of evil festering lizardman scrawling unspeakable terminal fear-images on the shithouse walls of her mind.

"I'm trying to buy you, Miss Westerfeld," he said softly. "And, believe me, you'll be selling. No one says *no* to Benedict Howards. Because I pay good coin; I buy you totally, but I pay totally too. I buy with what everyone wants."

"You're insane!" Sara said. "I don't want any part of you at any price for any reason at anytime."

"Think what it's like to be dead," Benedict Howards almost cooed hypnotically. "Dead... nothing but a pile of worm-eaten flesh rotting underground. That's the end of you, Sara, the end of all your goddamned principles, the end of everything you ever were or wanted to be. You don't beat death, Miss Westerfeld; everything else you ever do or don't do adds up to nothing but a pile of garbage sooner or later. And it's always sooner."

"Why... why..." Sara mumbled. No one talks about things like that, she thought. You live with it by ignoring it, whiting it out, or they peel you screaming off walls. Why don't you scream when you hear yourself, Benedict Howards?

"I'm telling you about death so you'll value your life," Howards continued, "your immortal life. Because you don't have to die, Miss Westerfeld, not permanently, nor ever. A place in a Freezer, secure, yours when you die—but you'll never really die. You'll just go to sleep old one day and wake up young the next. Doesn't that beat being dead, Miss Westerfeld?"

"A place in the Freezer—in return for what? I don't have that kind of money. Besides, it's not fair—a few people who have something you want going on and on, and everyone else dying and gone forever. That's what's so horrid about you and your Foundation—people dying by the thousands and a couple million rich bastards like you living forever! A Public Freezer Program would—"

"Now who's a goddamned philosopher?" sneered Benedict Howards. "Sure, no one should die. But since I can't Freeze everyone, I Freeze those who have something to offer in return. I'm a monster because I can't do favours for everyone? Public Freezer horseshit! I've got the only viable Freezer system that exists or ever'll be; you do business with me, or you're eaten by the worms. You'll feel goddamned virtuous when you die, but it won't make you any less dead. What do you say, you can get up and leave and never hear from me again?"

Aware only of her flesh, lips, blood-filled tongue, as she shaped the words, saliva-taste, tooth-feel of mortality, Sara said, "All right, so I'm still sitting here. Sure, I don't want to die, but you don't have me yet. There are still a few things I'd never do, not even to live forever."

She flashed horror-images of fates worse than death on the screen of her mind: mutilating Jack's crotch with her teeth devouring living puppy whole rotting in ordure for a thousand years murdering her mother fucking Howards... Hungry hoping search for prices too high to pay to smug, ferret-eyed, all-knowing A-head Satan, she felt powerless in cutting-edge monster reality, knowing truth unbearable—death *is* the end what crime too terrible to make her embrace it? *Please*, she prayed to her mind, let it be something too terrible to stomach!

"Relax," said Benedict Howards. "I don't want you to murder anyone, and I'm not hot for your body. You want to live forever you gotta do just one little thing. You gotta go get your ass in the sack with Jack Barron."

It hit her where she wasn't through no defences at all to the soft woman-flesh of her mind. No unspeakable blood-crime, just Jack's mouth on mine again body hard angles filling me tearing me apart with sweetness laughing tongues together in our secret places mingling of juices—Jack! Jack!

But she saw the cold measuring eyes of Benedict Howards and it all made hard-edged power-sense. How much does this slimy thing know? she thought and knew that Howards must know everything, everything that factored into his pattern of power. Jack's an important power-creature now, a measurable quantity of A-head reality-power, measured by Howards, wanted by Howards, maybe feared by Howards too, and I'm just the price Jack sets on delivery: Sara Westerfeld, back in bed, in love like Berkeley days, but on now-Jack cop-out terms. Go back to Jack, and then live forever with lying ghost of years-dead Jack slunk so low he sends lizard-man Howards to pimp for him...

"So Jack's *slunk* this low?" she asked cynically. "And what's he supposed to do for you when you deliver my body?"

Benedict Howards laughed. "You've got it all wrong. Barron knows nothing at all about this, and he never will. Not from me... and not from you either, eh? I'm not selling *you* to Barron. You're going to get Barron to sell something to *me*. I want Jack Barron to sign a free Freeze Contract just like the one I'm offering you. And that's the deal. The day you get Barron to sign a freeze Contract with the Foundation, I sign yours. And that's all you'll ever have to do with me, after that you and me are even. You can leave Barron or stay with him or even tell him the whole truth, it's no skin off my teeth then. What do you say, isn't it the bargain of a lifetime? A long, long lifetime…?"

"But I don't love Jack," she insisted. "I despise him almost as much as I despise you."

"Your love life doesn't concern me," Howards said, " even though I'm reasonably sure you're lying. Let's not kid around, you're not Little Mary Sunshine. You're humping everyone in creation. Tell me you're in love with all of *them*. So make it with one more man who means… *nothing* to you for a couple weeks, long enough to get him to sign that contract, and you've got immortality, and that's more than you get for screwing half the Village. And we both know you can get him to sign, we both know *he* still loves *you*, eh? And who knows, you may find yourself liking it, we both know that too, don't we, Miss Westerfeld?"

"You're a foul, slimy man," Sara whined. "I hate you! I hate you!" Turn your back on it, she told herself. Walk away walk away from forever forever walk away from horrid power-reality walk away from Jack from Howards let two lizard-men tear each other to pieces, they deserve each other.

But Jack… Jack's in danger; sleepwalking through a forest of hard steel knives poor blind Jack surrounded by—*blind* Yes! Yes! Blind! Oh, you fool, Benedict Howards, you horrid blind fool! And it spread itself out before her like a kinesthop gestalt vision in her mind: Jack, poor blind, cop-out Jack, sleepwalking dream of plastic success, faceless death-god Howards' spiderweb trap spun from bone-white lair around him. Me, last thread in web of evil; love, my love, Jack's love, used like spider-spit cable in pattern of power.

Could it really be Benedict Howards is such a fool? Fool, yes! Blind to love, tuned out from love's power—the fatal flaw in the bone-white lizard-plan. Because turned-on Jack, angry Jack, love filled Berkeley Jack-and-Sara Jack would become apocalyptic angel to destroy Howards destroy Foundation lovers strong against the night against which no faceless lizard-man death-god could stand, against the old Jack Barron that was meant to awaken…

I'll give you Jack Barron! she thought, but I'll give you *my* Jack Barron. Be brave. Yes, yes, take the deal, go to Jack, love him, get him to sign the contract…

"Those contracts," she said, tightly-contained, shrewd, "they'll be the usual contracts, public irreversible? We both get to keep the legal copies?"

Howards smiled a knowing smile. "I'd hardly expect either of you to trust me," he said. "You'll both get standard contracts, in triplicate."

"You're a shrewd, ruthless, ugly man," Sara said. "You knew you'd win in the end, and you have. It's a deal."

Yes, she thought, a deal. Dance to your tune till the contracts are signed, Jack and me together again, this time forever. *Forever!* And not the new-style cop-out Jack, but the old Berkeley Jack-and-Sara Jack. Yes! Drag Jack down, rub his nose in lizardman shit, then tell him, tell him every dirty word, how Howards used me, used him, uses everyone, made me his whore…

Then an angry Jack, apocalyptic angel to destroy you, Benedict Howards, Jack, my Jack, awake and alive again, Jack and Sara back together again the way it was meant to be. And this time, forever. *Forever!*

"A pleasure doing business with a girl like you," said Benedict Howards with a sly smile, flashing ferret-eyes seeing into her belly, sending a cold fear-tremor through her secure have-cake-and-eat-it-too plans—how much does the lizard-man know, how deeply do his weasel-eyes see?

Be brave, be brave! she told herself. Lizard-man death-god's blind to power of love colour wavelength he just can't see, can't factor love into spiderweb of power. What kind of man could suppose he could turn warm soft love into cold steel-edged weapon of paranoid power?

6

"MARRY ME, Carrie baby," Jack Barron said in the warm, naked afterglow of all night long as the morning sun shone through the bubble-skylight of the bedroom on the plastigrass greenery ivy-covered bedstead rubber-plant patio off-pink flesh of Carrie Donaldson and wrote an Adam-and-Eve scenario for the penthouse bedroom set.

Carrie Donaldson muttered unintelligible sarcasm into the pillow beside him. She always wakes up hard, Barron thought, can't stand a woman does the whole bleary, bruised, wilted-orchid schtick the morning after; Sara used to wake up on the bounce, on me, all over, bang-bang, wake me up, not vice-versa. You asked for it, Miss Donaldson, keep an eye-body-lock-on-kook-Jack-Barron network orders smart-ass chick.

He reached behind, fumbling through reptile-warm bedstead ivy, flipped a switch on the control console, waited for reaction as the glass wall-door to the patio slid aside and a naked May morning twenty-third floor breeze rippled plastigrass, tingled his toes, goosefleshed the trim uncovered ass of Carrie Donaldson. She squealed, reflex-foetaled against him, and looked up from the pillow hard-awake, said: "Fuck you, you goddamned sadist. I'm freezing!"

Barron turned a rheostat on the console to an intermediate position; electric heating coils built into the mattress began to send warmth up through their bodies, blood-temperature bed in crisp outdoor breezes. "I hope you don't mean that literally; that was quite a night, and I don't feel up to it. Let me catch my breath, anyway."

"About as serious as your proposal," she said, rolling over on her back away from him, small breasts foreshortened mounds bellyskin drumtight from protruding ribcage, juncture of long muscular legs still suffused with redness, Barron noted with masculine me-Tarzan satisfaction. "I think I know how Benedict Howards must feel."

Barron arched an interrogative eyebrow.

"Thoroughly screwed," Carrie Donaldson said with punchline deadpan flash-smile timing.

Barron uttered a short, pro forma laugh. Good old Carrie, he thought, favourite all-business no-bullshit network watch-dog All-American lay. He stared at her tight cool face, hard-edged, composed even under rat's nest morning-after long black hair, wondered what went on in that network-flunky head of hers. Too good a fuck to fake it, he thought, but where's the connection between her cunt and her head at, anyway? What's she really getting off me? No better balling than she'd get from anyone else who could keep up with her one for one, and all the emotion of an anaconda. Head filled with open-secret network orders, box with plenty of heat for anyone who can cut it, and no gut-connection at all between. Just once, Miss Carrie Donaldson, I'd like to *really* fuck with you, fuck with that so-called mind of yours, that is. But how do you mindfuck network-programmed electric-circuitry-computer with sexy long black hair?

You bug me, Carrie, he thought, ball you week after week, lots of body action, and nothing going on with your head at all. Network calculation that fine? Are powers that be aware good old Jack Barron digs perpetual cool-head challenge without gut-involvement, stasis spice of sex-life, or too much smarts for network bigwig monkeys?

"What's going on in that furry head of yours?" Carrie said, flicking at hairs dribbling around his ears with fingers cool against his earshells.

"Now *there's* a turn-around question if ever I—" Barron was interrupted by the chime of the bedroom vidphone extension. He twisted over on his back on one elbow to face the control console, punched the hold button, transferred the call to the living room complex, remote-activated the gas jets of the living room firepit, jumped out of bed, walked bare-ass into the living room, noted with wry amusement that Carrie, alerted to possible business function of call by network head-programming, was trailing, just as mother-naked, a few steps behind him.

Barron went to the wall complex, took the standard vidphone out of its niche next to the automatic vidphone recorder, sprawled on the deep-pile red carpeting, positioned the vidphone camera to show only his face, made the connection, impulsively turned on the recorder and said, "Jack Barron here," as Carrie squatted down to his left, judiciously out of range of the vidphone camera.

Barron started as the vidphone screen showed the egg-bald skull, broad neoslavic face of Gregory Morris, Republican fluke (squeaking in between powerful SJC, and Democratic candidates) Governor of California, de facto head of the semivestigial Republican Party, saw that Carrie recognised Morris—cool secretary-eyes a shade wider—he recovered his cool as he added up the points Morris had just made for him with Carrie.

"Good morning, Mr Barron," Morris said, confident voice-of-power, fake-power, thought Barron, without a hell, of a lot to back it up. "And congratulations."

What the hell's this? Barron thought, sneaking a glance at Carrie, eyes ever wider, wet lips open, digging boss-man spoiled-brat network-charge lover flapping jaws with real live Governor in the altogether, knowing that whatever the fuck Morris wanted, what he meant to Jack Barron was a way to play with Carrie's head at last, knowing just how and for what he would play this call, with Brackett Audience Count of exactly one, namely Carrie Donaldson.

"Congratulations for what, *Morris?*" He said, flunky-accenting the name, and yes, now Carrie's eyes were strictly eating him up.

"For your last show," Morris said. "A first-rate hatchet-job. You must've cost Howards' Freezer Bill five votes in the Senate, maybe a dozen in the House. You're about to make history, Mr Barron. That show impressed a lot of people, important people. I know that the Republican Party opposes the Utility Bill because it would stifle free enterprise in the—"

"*Horseshit,*" Barron said, digging effect of word on notorious prude Morris, effect of effect on Carrie as Morris pretended the breech of fartsy gentleman etiquette hadn't happened. "You oppose the Freezer Bill because there's big Foundation money behind various Democrats, and you know you're permanently off Howards' gravy train, and you'd love to sell out too except Howards ain't buying. It's a little early in the day for mickeymousing, Morris. What's on your mind?"

"Very well, Mr Barron," Morris said, seeming to swallow enormous distaste according to some prearranged plan. "I'll come right to the point. How would you like to be President of the United States?"

Barron froze around a smart-ass wisecrack reply that wouldn't take form behind his eyes, froze in *déjà vu* Berkeley attic other girl seated on other floor big eyes honey-blonde hair digging him watching Luke Greene, Woody Kaplan, Markowitz, the girl with the pigtail, dark roomful of other eyes glowing, looking at him birthplace of the Social Justice Coalition now controlled two Southern states, twenty-eight Congressmen, pivotal must-buy force in New York, every Southern state, Illinois, California. Full circle from Baby Bolshevik messiah dreaming of power in Berkeley attic Sara worshipfully staring to leader of screwball third party to Jack Barron plugged into electronic-circuitry-hundred-million-Americans to listening to pathetic relic gibber impossible desperation-dreams of returning expiring (now kook third party itself) GOP to power.

"Do I get to choose Luke Greene for my running mate?" Barron shot back a matching improbability.

"Conceivably," said Morris. Barron's turn to be jarred again at incomprehensible answer; the SJC and the Republicans were at opposite extremes of *everything* except for a mutual loathing for the monolithic centre-dominating Democratic one-party government Party. Morris must really be around the bend, or… *what?*

Barron clocked Carrie, now totally absorbed in the dialogue he saw she saw as jockeying between two men of power, not private, for-her-benefit-only performance of *Bug Jack Barron*—at last a scene to swallow up network programming in that head of hers, blow secretary-network-watchdog cool. At least *Carrie's* buying Morris' load of bull, hook, line, and sinker.

"Okay, Morris," said Barron, "so you've got a pitch to make; go ahead and make it."

"It's simple, Barron," Morris said. (Barron could sense him shifting into set-spiel pattern.) "The Republican Party has elected only two Presidents since Roosevelt, and we've *got* to win next year to continue to be taken seriously. And we can't afford to be choosy as to how. The only way we can conceivably win the election is as part of a coalition with the SJC behind a common presidential candidate and on an overriding common issue.

"The only common ground we have with the Social Justice Coalition is opposition to the Freezer Utility Bill. They want public Freezing and we want competitive private Freezing. But we can both agree on opposing the Democratic position, which amounts to the Foundation position. The only man we can nominate who could also get the SJC nomination is you. You're a founder of the SJC, you've just knifed Benedict Howards, you're a close friend of Luke Greene, and you've got *Bug Jack Barron*.

"A hundred million people will see you every week from now till Election Day. We can do with you what we did with Reagan, and do it in spades, using the programme, and by the time you're nominated you'll already have a bigger following than any possible Democratic candidate. I'm dead serious. Barron. Play our game, and we'll make you President of the United States."

President of the United States. The words made weird acid music ('Hail to the Chief,' with electric guitar beat, natch) even coming from a pathetic lunatic. Barron was vastly amused at the reflex-response in his own gut, recalling aural memories of the Inauguration of JFK, more amused pleased at pole-axed Carrie Donaldson staring at him, eyes as bright with little-girl wonder as Sara's had ever been in Berkeley days. Didn't know you were balling the next President of the United States, eh, baby? Jesus H Christ on a Harley-Davidson!

Barron leaned back accidentally on purpose, kicked the vidphone, tilting it sideways and up, giving Morris a nice shot of Carrie's boobs, fumbled it enough, smiling, to show Morris he was speaking to totally bare-ass Jack Barron, watched Morris blanch.

"Come on man," Barron said, scratching his balls ostentatiously, "even the next President's gotta get laid once in a while." (Let's just see how much crap this stuff-shirt fruitcake will really take.)

"Well," Morris said through miser-purse drawstring-lips, "What do you say, Barron?"

"What do I say?" exclaimed Jack Barron. "I say you're out of your fucking mind, is all. For openers... *openers?* This is all so loopy there ain't no openers, gotta hand it to you, you're a nut, but at least you're a nut with style. First of all, I loathe everything you stand for. The Republican Party these days is nothing but a collection of Little Old Ladies from Pasadena, Wallacite screwballs and paranoid fat-cat misers whose idea of a good President is someone about ten light-years to the right of Adolph Hitler. You couldn't win a Presidential election with Jesus Christ and John Fitzgerald Kennedy on the ticket. Why don't you crawl back under your wet rock where you belong? Way I see it, a Republican label is a dose of political tertiary syphilis. Do you get the impression I don't care for your Party, Governor Morris?"

"I didn't think you were all that naive, Barron," said Morris, and now Barron saw the naked, ugly, raw, no-bullshit nitty-gritty in his face, in his voice, remembered that fluke or not, this was the Governor of the largest state in the Union, that hopeless, kook, perpetual-loser party that it was, the GOP still had great gobs of industrialist Madison Avenue Wall Street insurance company banking money behind it, and now Morris was reminding him of it with face, voice, bearing. "You think we don't know exactly what you are, what you've been, and what you think of us? You really believe we're all that stupid, Barron?"

"And you're still trying to sell me the Republican nomination." Barron said, sudden *déjà vu* of Morris' face becoming Howards' face, Morris' deal becoming Howards' deal, intimations of wheels within wheels within wheels of power meshing, clashing, one invisible Frankenstein Monster, with Howards and Morris but two visible aspects of the same unseen iceberg.

"Yes," said Morris, "but not because we like your smell. I loathe you as much as you loathe me, but we both know that when you reach the upper levels of power there are times when you've got to set all that aside for strategic reasons. You're a marketable commodity, Barron, like a nice ripe Limburger, an image behind which we can unite with the SJC to win the Presidency, the *only* image that can create a Republican-SJC fusion against the Democrats and Howards. *Image*, Barron, image is what counts—like Eisenhower or Reagan—not the man. We need your image, and *Bug Jack Barron* to sell it, and never mind what the real man behind the image is like. That doesn't win elections. All the voters ever see is the *image.*"

For a hot moment Jack Barron forgot Carrie, wide-eyed, naked, power-adoring beside him; forgot economic sponsor-network squeezing-power of GOP, forgot *Bug Jack Barron*, was back in Berkeley Los Angeles red-hot Baby-Bolshevik Sara beside him close to the blood-innocent-fury days.

"And if I accept—and if I'm elected," he said coldly, "think I'd really make a good little Republican President?"

"That's our problem," Morris said. "We both know you're no politician, but neither was Eisenhower. You'll have plenty of the right advisors, men of substance and experience to run the government for you. You won't have to worry about—"

"I'm nobody's whore, and don't you forget it!" Barron shouted. "You don't sell Jack Barron like soap, then toss him aside like a used condom when you've got what you came for. You can take your goddamn nomination and shove it up your ass! You're right, I'm no politician, and if you want the reason, look in a mirror sometime if you've got a strong enough stomach. You're lower than a Mexican bordertown pimp; you'd have to stand on top the Empire State Building to reach a cockroach's balls. You and your kind are vermin, lice, clots in the bloodstream of humanity. You're not fit to clean my toilet bowl. I'm an entertainer, not a whore. Value given for value received. You're the last of the dinosaurs, Morris, and it'll be a pleasure to watch you sink screaming into the tarpits where you belong."

"Who the hell do you think you are?" Morris practically snakehissed. "You don't talk to *me* like that, and get away with it! You play my game, or I'll destroy you, lean on your sponsors, pressure the—"

Jack Barron laughed a harsh, false, tension-release laugh. Every schmuck in the country thinks he's got more going than poor old Jack Barron, he thought. Howards, Morris—matched pair of cretins.

"You're pathetic, you know that, Morris?" he said. "Know why? Because I've got this whole call on tape, that's why. Your fat face and your big mouth, all ready to run on *Bug Jack Barron* any time I find you—shall we say, *tiresome?* You've taken your cock out in front of cameras, and I can play it back to a hundred million people any time I want to. You're naked, Morris, bare-ass naked! I get a hint, or even just a vibration that you're making waves in my direction, and, baby, I lower the boom. Go stick your tongue out at babies, Morris, you're wasting your time trying to scare *me.*"

"Think it over," Morris said, suddenly forcing himself back into a tone of sweet-pimp reason. "You're letting the chance of a lifetime go—"

"Ah, fuck off!" Barron said, he broke the connection, shut off the recorder.

"*Jack...*" Carrie Donaldson sighed, throwing arms around his waist, wilting to her knees, lips sucking him in naked-lap wish-fulfilment fantasy Carrie blowing him, her mind blown network orders blown cool blown going down on boss-man mind-fucker, raped by simple *Bug Jack Barron* style vip putdown session. But now Barron saw it for the silly-ass goddamned inverted Sara-fantasy it was: Carrie-Sara turned on all the way by *Bug Jack Barron* scene, turned off the genuine article. Last thing I want now, he thought, pulling away from her, is to be blown by a wetdream ghost.

"Later, baby," he said, "that lox just turned me off." And on impulse (*Bug Jack Barron* subliminal walk-that-line balancing act impulse, he thought wryly even as he dialled) he dialled the unlisted home vidphone number of Lukas Greene.

Greene's angular black face bleered at him on the vidphone screen over a coffee cup, the master bedroom of the Governor's Mansion vaguely opulent in the background. "It's you, eh, Claude," Greene said, glancing at something off-camera. "Jack Barron—at *this* hour?"

"Come on, Lothar," said Barron, "you know I'm a clean liver."

"Percy," Greene said, "I've seen cleaner livers smothered in onions in Harlem greasy-spoons. Speaking of which—where the hell's my breakfast?" And almost immediately a white-clad Negro flitted briefly across the screen carrying a breakfast tray, set it down on the bed, and disappeared silently into the woodwork.

"Beauregard," Barron said grinning, "gotta hand it to you Southern gentleman types. Really got them darkies trained right, don't you?"

Greene nibbled a slice of bacon, dabbed at egg yolk with a roll, said: "You Commie nigger-loving Northern Liberal faggots is just jealous of Southern-style gracious living. We loves our darkies down here. We just loves 'em, and they loves us; any that don't, why we just hang 'em from a sour-apple tree. Hey, why you bugging an important man like me at this hour, shade? It ain't Wednesday night, and we're not on the air—*I hope.*"

"Guess who I just got a call from?" Barron said, clocking how Carrie was even more zonked out at the nitty-gritty race-humour between shade Jack Barron and the black Governor of Mississippi.

"The ghost of Dylan? Teddy the Pretender?"

"Would you believe Daddy Warbucks?" said Jack Barron.

"Huh?"

"Greg Morris," said Barron. "Amounts to the same thing, doesn't it? Would you believe you're talking to the next President of the United States?"

Greene took a long drink of coffee. "A little early for you to be stoned, isn't it?" he said seriously.

"Straight poop, Kingfish," Barron answered. "Morris offered me the Republican Presidential nomination."

"Come on, man, stop putting me on, and come to the punchline already."

"I'm not kidding," said Barron, "it's for real, Luke. The schmuck thinks I could get the SJC to nominate me too, put together a fusion ticket, and we could all go out and zap the pretender."

"I still think you're putting me on," said Greene. "You, a Republican and the SJC in bed with those Neanderthals? Either you're putting me on, or the good Governor of California's finally gone around the bend. How could the Republicans and the SJC possibly get together on *anything?*"

"Morris seems to think opposition to the Freezer Bill's a big enough common issue to brush everything else under the rug." Barron said. "The fusion ticket doesn't run on any common platform, way he sees it, just runs against Bennie Howards. Loopy, eh, Rastus?"

Barron felt a long loud silence as Greene sipped coffee, eyes becoming cold, hard, calculating, saw Carrie, still looking at him hungrily, shift her eyes to stare at the vidphone image of Luke, smelt flesh-wood of Carrie, image-wood of Luke burning. Doesn't anyone have a sense of humour left but me?

"This *is* for real, isn't it, Jack?" Lukas Greene at last said quietly.

"For chrissakes, Luke—"

"Hold on, Vladimir," said Greene. "I'm getting a flash. You. *Bug Jack*

Barron. Republican bread—and they are still flush. You know, it could work. It just might work. Bennie Howards as bogey-man, we wouldn't really have to run you against Teddy. Yeah, we just *ignore* the Pretender, link the Democrats with the Foundation, and we've got your show to do it with. A Social Justice President…"

"Come on, man, what planet did you say you came from?" Barron said, the joke no longer funny. Crazy Luke thinks he's back in Berkeley wet-dream power-fantasy delusion of grandeur. "You can't be that dumb, Morris just wants to use the SJC to elect a Republican President, and if he does, he'll feed all you overgrown Baby Bolsheviks to the fishes. He just wants a fusion figurehead image to lurk behind, is all."

"Sure," agreed Greene, "but that figurehead is good old Jack Barron. Even Morris knows what a cop-out you are, so he thinks you'd be a tame flunky. But I know you better, Adolph. Comes nitty-gritty time, I think you'll remember who you once were. I may be crazy, but I'd be willing to trust you that far. I think the National Council would too, after I got through working on their heads. You get that Republican nomination, and I can get you the SJC nomination. Maybe I *am* talking to the next President. What did you tell Morris?"

"What do you think I told him?" Barron snapped. "I told him to go fuck himself. You gone around the bend too, Rastus?"

Greene frowned. "You and your big mouth," he said. "Hmmm… Morris has got to know where you're at for openers, so maybe you haven't gone and blown it. You got that call on tape?" Greene smiled knowingly. "Sure you have. Claude, I know how your head works. How about blipping me the audio?"

"Forget it, Luke." Barron said. "This is your line of evil, not mine, not anymore. I'm not selling out to Morris or to you either. I sell out to anyone it's to—" Barron caught himself short; name he was about to say was Bennie Howards. Yeah, he thought, you sell out at all, risk blowing the show, you damn well do it for the big forever boodle and not a half-assed pipedream… Hey wait… All these silly-ass politicians can maybe give me an extra ace up my sleeve in a poker game with Howards. Why not?

"Come on man," Greene cajoled, "humour me. Blip me the call. You got your jollies out of it, let me get mine. Nothing else, maybe we can use it against whoever the Republicans *do* come up with. That doesn't hurt you, does it, oh, noble hero Jack Barron? Might even boost your ratings."

"Since you're twisting my arm, I'll blip it to you on one condition," said Barron. "Unless I give you the go-ahead—and I won't—you keep it strictly private. Just between you and me, okay?"

"Beggars can't be choosy," Greene said. "I'll set my recorder for the blip." He did something off camera. "Fire when ready, Gridley."

Barron took the tape from his recorder, placed it in the blipper built into his wall complex. "Ready at this end," he said.

"Blip away," said Lukas Greene.

Barron pressed the blip button; the blipper compressed the sound of the phone conversation into about ninety seconds of high-pitched chipmunk gabble over the vidphone circuit to Greene's recorder in Mississippi, to be fed into a deblipping circuit, give Luke his Machiavellian eat-your-heart-out-baby jollies.

"Got it," Greene said. "Unless you have any more Earth-shaking revelations, Claude, I think I better tend to the business of the state of Mississippi. Later."

That hot to hear it, eh, Rastus? Barron thought. "I never deprive a maroon of his simple-minded pleasures. Later, Lothar," he said, broke the connection.

"Jack..." Carrie snaked across the rug arms around his chest wide eyes visions of larger than life sugar-plums of power tickets to circles where it's at, magic image-musk goddamned eyes why always those goddamned fever-coated eyes same eyes every bitch knows my name sees my dick, gets eyes like fucking vacuum cleaners suck-me-dry eyes for living-colour latest Brackett Count hundred million Americans Jack Barron. Now you too, Carrie Donaldson, cool network-programmed secretary-robot with red-hot cunt don't buy bargain-basement *Bug Jack Barron* image-bullshit too close to home, but let schmuck Morris, crazy Luke whistle "Hail to the Chief," and it's welcome to the club, Carrie, baby.

Hey what's with you man? Barron asked himself as Carrie Donaldson worried his lips with her moist, frantic tongue. Ten minutes ago you wanted action you're getting right now—Carrie's mind totally blown fucked out whited out overscrewed in all mental orifices—and you played it for this, is why you riffed with Morris in the first place. Well, isn't it?

A sudden flash of insight as Carrie directed her demands to nitty-gritty limp and pouting organ, bugged ego-extension of him in her smooth cool hands cradling, wheedling, finally stimulating cold reflex hard-on as he felt blood, attention, desire flow mechanically into it—no chick since Sara had done as much time in the sack as Carrie Donaldson, steady couple-times-a-week cool detached lay for months and months, static strictly belly-to-belly nonrelationship had bugged him with network-orders, head unattached to warm-flesh cunt. But now, with Carrie's cool blown the way he thought he had wanted it, Barron saw that the cool itself was why he kept screwing Carrie—sanity-contrast to an endless string of image-fucking Wednesday-night honey-haired Saras. And now she was a member of *Bug Jack Barron* goddamned vacuum-eyed fan club, giving him Wednesday-night-style-*déjà vu* head wet-dream Sara dream on-her-knees dream eating-kick-'em-in-the-ass world-famous Presidential timber so dumb bitch thinks Jack Barron wet-dream wish-fulfilment *déjà vu* Carrie, like all the others *déjà vu* masturbation-ghosts, not the real thing, one more flesh-and-hair ersatz, not Sara, no longer Carrie. And not Sara. Not ever Sara.

His betraying organ stiff and hard, his mind cold, cold light-years distant and nothing but nothing in-between, Barron rose to his feet, haughty-ironic Great Man hands-on-hips statue, held the immobile mock-heroic posture as warm undulating lips, caressing tongue, frantic rolling half-closed eyes sent waves of hot thick pleasure through thighs, balls, mindless pulsing independent organ: pleasure-waves that stopped stone-cold dead at his waist.

Enjoy, enjoy, Carrie baby, he thought, feeling the spasm building through ten thousand miles of electric circuit insulation. Make it good, old hot-mouthed Carrie, 'cause it's the last action *you'll* ever get from Jack Barron.

Staring into the naked orange flames of the firepit, naked flesh, naked Carrie Donaldson on the bare rug in exhausted, sated semisleep beside him, Jack Barron felt a carapace of image-history-skin encysting him like steel walls of a TV set, a creature imprisoned in the electronic circuitry of his own head perceiving through promptboard vidphone fleshless electronic speed of light ersatz senses, separated from the girl beside him by the phosphor-dot impenetrable glass TV screen Great Wall of China of his own image.

First time I remember being blown feeling like wet put-down ugliness, he brooded. Ugly, he told himself, is a thing you feel—truth is ugly when it's a weapon, lie is beautiful when an act of love ugly when it's one-sided fuck is beautiful when it's simple, mutual, nobullshit balling, ugly when chick gets her kicks off you that really isn't there, is why you feel like a rotten lump of shit, man. Getting blown Sara go down being dug by woman's a pure gas; being sucked off, image-statue living lie, someone else's lie being *eaten* (Let me eat you, let me eat you, baby!) is a dirty act of plastic cannibalism, *her* dirtiness, not mine.

Whole world's full of plastic cannibals feeding their own little bags off meals of my goddamned image-flesh, eating Jack Barron ghost that isn't there. And now Morris and my so-called friend Luke are hot to package my living-colour bod into TV dinners, sell to hundred million viewer-voter cannibals for thirty pieces of power silver.

Anyone sells my body, he thought, it'll be me, the real thing to Howards for life eternal in the flesh, not to Luke or Morris for an asterisk losing candidate gravemarker in a history book nobody reads. But something's happening there too, and you don't quite know what it is, do you, Mr Jones? Howards-Morris-Luke daisychain of power-wheeler-dealers at each other's throats, all with eyes for Jack Barron as a spare set of false fangs. Too much action in too scary a league to be pure coincidence, something's up, big glob of shit about to hit National fan, and no one ready to give the straight scam to Jack Barron.

Well, we'll see about that on Wednesday night, Bennie Howards, see how much cool you keep in *Bug Jack Barron* hotseat, after all, man, you're now playing poker with goddamned Presidential timber hotshot, gonna have to lay all your cards on the table to stay in that bullshit game, Bennie-baby. Yeah, you're in the catbird-seat man, like top trick in a high-class whorehouse, you are—

The vidphone chime interrupted his Germanic self-pity petulance, and good riddance, Jack Barron thought as the familiar stimulus triggered ironic Jack digging vidphone Jack Barron conditioned cynical response. Even money it's Teddy the Pretender himself, he thought wryly, every other power-junkie around's tried to score off dealer Jack Barron already.

But the honey-blonde, big dark-brown-eyed (mind's eye supplying living colour to black and white vidphone image) face on the vidphone screen blew his cool to the far side of the moon as he made the connection and the best he could do was to stammer: "Sara…"

"Hello, Jack," said Sara Westerfeld.

Barron felt a moment of empty, aware-of-his-bare-ass-nakedness blank numbness, sensed the same helpless vacuum behind Sara's frightened-deer eyes, searched for cue to a reaction-pattern on the blank promptboard in his mind, heard his irony-armoured voice saying. "Sadism or masochism, what's on your acid-soaked mind, baby?"

"It's been a long time," Sara began, and Barron, frantically scrabbling for a protocol-reaction-pattern to the ghost of a thousand body-to-body aching memory nights, fell on the inanity like a starving man on a slice of mouldy bread.

"No shit?" he said. "I thought you went out to cop some pot six years ago. Get stuck in traffic, Sara?"

"Do you have to, Jack?" she pleaded helplessly with her eyes. "Do we have to chop each other to pieces?"

"We don't *have* to do anything," he said, felt bitterness rising. "You called me, I didn't call you. I'd never call you. What in hell can I possibly say to you? What can you say to me? You stoned? You freaking out? Whose head are you playing with now, yours or mine?"

"I'm sorry," she said. "I'm sorry for everything. Hang up if you want to. Who could blame you? I… I want to see you, Jack, I want to talk to you. I…"

"You got a TV, turn it on Wednesday night, and you can see me. Pick up a vidphone and call the monkey block, make it good, and Vince'll put you on the air. What's this all about? It's been, six years, Sara, six fucking years, and now you say 'Hello, Jack,' and expect me to come running? Where did you leave your head, Sara?"

"Please…" she said, with the iron defence of soft-woman defencelessness. "You think this is easy for me? I—" (A blankness, a panic seemed to move like a cloud across the sky of her eyes; she hesitated, then began to talk faster and faster.) "I saw your last show, by accident, I admit, but I saw something there I thought was dead. Saw flashes, just flashes in all that bullshit, but they were flashes of *you*. I mean the *real* you, like flickering, but it was there, and it was you, and every time it flashed through it went through me like a knife. And, God help me, I couldn't help loving you, all alone there inside that TV set, all alone inside, flashing between the real Jack and the cop-out Jack, not knowing which was real, and I didn't know which was real—the Jack I loved, or the Jack I hated and I loved you, and I hated you, and I knew I still had a piece of you inside me, couldn't get rid of it, and... and..."

"You were stoned, weren't you?" Barron said with intentional cynical cruelty. "Acid, wasn't it?"

Again that hesitation, like a slot-machine mechanism behind her eyes, before she spoke. "I... yes, it *was* a trip. Maybe... maybe that was it, seeing your show with new eyes, old eyes, like old-new eyes, I mean part of me was back in Berkeley, and part of me was with you that last time, and part of me was inside that TV set with you, and... I've got to see you, got to know whether it was the acid or..."

"So now I'm a goddamned zonk!" Barron snapped. "Like a kaleidoscope or one of your old Dylan records, something to freak out to. Did you bring yourself off? See coloured lights? I don't want to be any part of your bum trips—not even by proxy. You're turning my stomach, calling me up like this, stoned out of your mind. Forget it, baby. Go ride the Staten Island Ferry and pick up a horny sailor and fuck with *his* head, because I'm not about to let you play acid games with mine, not any more. Not ever again."

"I'm not stoned now, Jack," she said quietly. "I'm straight, maybe straighter than I've ever been in my life. We all go through changes. I watched you go through yours, and I couldn't take it. Now I think I've gone through one of my own, a big one. It happens like that sometimes, six years of things just happening to you but not really getting through to your head, and then something, acid plus something, maybe something silly and meaningless triggers the big flash, and suddenly all those six years come through all the way at once and you *feel* them, feel the years before too, and all the possible futures, all in a moment, and nothing's happened in that moment that anyone else can see, but you're just not the same *you* anymore. There's a gap, a discontinuity, and you know you can't go back to being what you've been but you don't yet know what you are.

"And only you can tell me, Jack. I've got no present now, and you're my past, and maybe—if I'm not just finally flipping out—if you still want me, my future too. I see another side of you now. I see that you can see things I don't, and now I'm not so certain that they're all bad. Help me, Jack. If you ever loved me, please help me now."

"Sara—" Sara, you crazy bitch, don't do this to me, put me on, stretch me out like piano wire, play arpeggios on my skull, Ping-Pong with my balls, Barron thought, trying desperately to hug his cynicism-shield to him against the tide washing over him tide of Berkeley cool love-stained sheets tongue in his car hourglass comfort-shape unseen by his side to lean on warm breezes cool bougainvillaea-fragrant California nights in Los Angeles, Berkeley, Acapulco breathing pot-smoke-musk mouth to mouth in rumpled snuggle-beds close to the blood years innocent tomorrow the world years lost years, six years lost and gone and buried in the bodies of Wednesday-night image-balling blondes, and the song of those years that she sang with her off-key beautiful girl-voices sad, wistful, in happy laughing times, prescient sadness of Christmas future song:

> "Where have all the flowers gone, long time passing...?
> When will they ever learn? When will they ever learn...?"

And when will *you* ever learn, Jack Barron? In your guts, you know she's nuts; but in your heart... In your heart is an empty Sara-sized hole, not Carrie, not Wednesday-night *déjà vu*, not anyone but Sara can ever fill if you live million years geological ages promise of Benedict Howards... You're a Sara-junkie, nothing you can do about it, baby, she's the only dealer in town.

"Jack... say something, Jack..."

"Do I have to?" he said—soft surrender to the ghost of hope that would not die. I can do it. *I can do it*, he told himself. I'm kick-'em-in-the-ass Jack Barron can handle Senators, vips, Howards, Morris, Luke, big-league curve-ball artists; Jack Barron afraid to play the big game, love game (game is all!) for only woman I ever love? I'll help you, baby, give you the boost to nitty-gritty reality. You and me in *Bug Jack Barron* twenty-third story penthouse catbird-seat home, fill the rooms with your taste-smell-feel song of home. All for you, Sara, where you should've been all these years. And if it was really acid that opened your eyes, then three big ones for Crazy Tim Leary.

"When can I see you?" he asked.

"As soon as you can get here."

"I'll be down in forty-five minutes," Jack Barron said. "God, oh, God, how I've missed you!"

"I missed you too," she said, and he thought he could see her eyes misting.

"Forty-five minutes," he said, then broke the connection, rose, turning for bedroom clothes and shoes and car keys.

And stood there nose to nose with naked, white-faced Carrie Donaldson, her breasts limp and drooping like wilted hospital flowers.

"Don't say it," she said in her office-secretary voice. "Don't say anything, Mr Barron. It's all been said, hasn't it? All explained nice and neat. And I thought it was just because you were too... too big and important and filled with your work to have room to care about... I thought if I made you comfortable, made it easy, no hang-ups, no bullshit, call me when you want me, warm your bed whenever it got cold, then someday maybe you'd wake up nice and easy, slowlike and see that... that... But I was wrong, I misjudged you... I wonder what it's like to be loved the way you love her? Way the world is, I wonder if I'll ever get to know..."

"Carrie, I didn't... I couldn't... I thought the network..."

"The network! I may be a lot of nasty things, Jack Barron, but, as I just heard someone else say, I'm nobody's whore!" she shouted. "Sure I was supposed to keep an eye on you, but you don't think that..." She began to tremble, tears formed in her eyes and she tilted her head back to hide them, making her look proud, gutsy.

Oh, Christ, what a blind shit you are, Jack Barron! he thought as she stood there, taller in his eyes than she had ever been, and yet he still felt nothing for her, never had, couldn't even fake a moment of it now.

"Why didn't you say something?" was all he could say.

"Would it have mattered? You know it wouldn't. You've always been too hung on her to look at me or any other woman and see anyone that counted. And at least this way... you've been a good lay, Jack Barron. Too bad... Too bad I'll never be able to bring myself to touch you again."

And all he could throw to her was a tiny morsel as he went to the bedroom to dress and allowed her the dignity of crying alone.

7

CROSSING FOURTEENTH STREET is like crossing the panel-dividers between different style comic strips, Jack Barron thought as he inched the Jag down Saturday-jammed Seventh Avenue. Like going from *Mary Worth Rex Morgan Man Against Fear* style reality into *Terry and the Pirates* (old-style pre-Mao Chopstick Joe, Dragon Lady, Chinese-river-pirate schtick) *Krazy Kat Captain Cool* freak-out, surreal Dali comic strip of the Village, sprawling Istanbul-involuted (river to river, Fourteenth to Canal) Barbary Coast ghetto of the mind.

Reaching Fourth Street, Barron impulsively made a left across traffic, then a right into the turgid river of cars clogging MacDougal—Money Street, Anything Goes Sin City Tourist Vacuum Cleaner Street, chief cloaca for outside square-type bread, lifeline of economic sewage into the closed river to river ghetto that the powers that be had carrot-and-sticked the Village into becoming.

And once again we see the sweaty palm of the '70s still heavy on the land, thought Barron as the traffic inched at a foot a second toward Bleecker, past souvenir stands, bare-box strip joints, state-licensed acid parlours, furtive street-corner schmeck dealers local action fading Slum Goddess tourist trade whores, through a solid miasma of grease-fried-sausage smells, pot-musk, drunken-sailor piss, open air toilet aroma of packaged disaster—The pathetic, faded Grand Old Lady Greenwich Village reduced to peddling her twat to passing strangers.

If you can't beat 'em, eat 'em (unspoken, motto of the days after Lyndon). Nice cooled reservation for every tribe in America: give them niggers Mississippi and them pothead long-haired acid freaks the Village and Fulton and Strip City, and the old fuckers Sun-City-St.-Petersburg-subsidised graveyard waiting rooms. All on the reservation, safe in their own bags, and out of the way. And a nice little tourist-trade we can cash in on on the side: See Niggerland, Stoneland, Senior-Citizenland see America First, see America and die.

Turning left onto Bleecker, Barron found himself overwhelmed by sadness—meeting a love of his youth in a Mexican whorehouse blowing for wooden nickels, and brother can you spare a dime.

"Where have all the flowers gone
Long time passing..."

Sara... Sara... Another hooker on the string of image-pimp vampires, a prop in the streets of an open-air cathouse Disneyland-Hippyland turnstile madness...

"It's Jack Barron."

"Hey, Jack."

Shit, I've been spotted! Barron thought, picking up on the ironic paradox of disgust-satisfaction inside him, as a red-headed nicely-stacked chick in kinesthop-patterned leotards (electric blue snakes slithering-flashing ever twatward—Sara design?) shouted his name with banally-worshipful eyes, and eyes turned, faces turned, street traffic momentarily clotted in a small eddy of rubberneck stares.

"Yeah, *it is!* It's Jack Barron!"

A moment of panic, as sidewalks on both sides of Bleecker bulged gutterward with realos and touristas, arms waving, shouting, ripples spreading toward the corner of MacDougal behind him up Bleecker ahead of him, as locals and tourists, come there for the action, seized on the shouting in their desperate boredom, joined in the waving, harmonised in the shouting, indifferent, oblivious to the source of it all—just hungry for the centre of where whatever was at.

But as the Jag inched eastward through the frozen traffic, Barron saw buttons above boobs on jackets under beards—red-on-blue kinesthop flash patterns like hot-vacuum eyes of Wednesday-night Saras on his body like hands waking images of Berkeley, Los Angeles, Meridian marches Baby Bolshevik eyes that no longer were young, staring at him like some plastiglow Jesus, hero to something he no longer believed. His own name mocked him from a freak-show marquee: 'Bug Jack Barron' the kinesthop buttons said.

Yeah, baby, dig your ever-loving public! "Bug Jack Barron" rating-vitamin saying started right here in home to which there's no returning; streets of the past, youth-dream yours for the taking, but all of it bullshit and none of it real.

But caught by the rhythm, heat of warm bodies, sound-smell of his own name in the air, Barron waved, smiled, copped out on himself like a fucking Hollywood premier.

The traffic finally sped up as the Jag passed Thompson faces became phosphor-dot blurs on a TV screen, sounds became just dopplered background noises. And when he turned onto West Broadway, headed to Houston, the main east-west thoroughfare out of the scene, he found he was sweating—like bolt upright in bed at the end of a crazy wet dream.

What made me do *that?* Jack Barron thought as he felt the motion-breeze of the open Jag cool him as he headed east toward First Avenue. *Now* who's playing with Jack Barron's head—the master mind-fucker himself, is all. Who you putting on, man? Should've been straight down Seventh to Houston and nowhere near Clown Alley with all that idiot traffic, knew they would spot you, is all. Jack Barron fan club: every loser in Village, junkies in San Fran, hard-luck chicks wherever you are Berkeley, Strip City, street scene stretching block after block, one big where it all was at from Commercial Street to MacDougal to Haight to Sunset, wallowing in bullshit ghosts of glory, Wednesday-night-digging the boy who made good from the bag.

Barron made a left onto First Avenue, and his mood changed with the street: First Avenue, nitty-gritty insiders' main drag. Ricky-ticky bars, coffee-houses, discos, galleries, zonk shops in lower stories of renovated Ukrainian Polack buildings, street and street-mood where ghosts of the future rubbed tight neon-asses with uptight descendants of Slav-Jew-PR ghetto-spectres of the past.

Yeah, Barron thought, this is where the action is; border-town paranoiasville, semicheap apartments, folk-shops of the new stoned ghetto in building by building guerrilla warfare with the dregs of old-style rent-control slumlord Great Society slum scene of the dying past—Flower People pushing as hard to get in as wave of immigrants since God-knows-when pushed to get out.

The ass is aways greener, Barron thought. Village days, Berkeley was the place; Berkeley days, Strip City, and back to here in goddamned Coast-to-Coast incestuous daisy-chain, Hey, which way to the action, man? And, baby, when you're a loser the action's always somewhere else. So why not the other side of the glass-tit, *Bug-Jack-Barron*-land in electric-circuit contact with places of power, acid dreams of revolution, hundred million Brackett Count insiders' secret: kick-'em-in-the-ass Jack Barron cutting up vips' one of us, man. *That* cat's on *our* side.

Truth, isn't it? Barron thought. Reasons of my own, rating-type reasons, I *am* on their side, the side of every hung-up person in the whole wide universe, phosphor-dot image of the sounds of freedom flashing 'Enemy to those who make him an enemy; friend to those who have no friend.' Boston Blackie, is all.

So what bugs you so much about them buttons?

Who, why, where do they come from? is the nitty-gritty question. Luke or Morris or both already screwing around with trial-balloon free samples of prospective image-meat TV dinners, or just harmless zonk?

Shit, man, you *know* why you're bugged. Sara dragging your million-dollar ass down onto her turf. One lousy phone call, and into the car into the Village into past fast as fat little Michelins will carry you; pearl-diving in sewage, dumb '60s song, but right where it's at:

> *"Slum Goddess from the Lower East Side*
> *Slum Goddess, gonna make her my bride…*
> *The first time that I balled her I went outa my mind…"*

Oh, you *so* right, baby! So here I am, dragging my dick along First

Avenue, right back in the whole dumb scene I kissed goodbye six years ago. Sara, you stoned when I get there, I'm gonna beat the piss out of you, so help me.

But as he parked the Jag on the corner of First Avenue and Ninth Street he wondered who was really gonna beat the piss out of whom.

Sara's apartment was on the third story of a five-story renovated walk-up (like progress; in the old days anyone you went to see in the East Village *always* lived on the fifth floor), and you could tell it was hers by the door: it and the surrounding wall area were painted in a continuous door-outline-blurring kinesthop pattern—undulating free-form black and chartreuse concentric bullseye striping that created the illusion of a tunnel expanding past the doorframe, converging circle-in-circle in uneven circle on a weirdly off-centre yellow doorknob-buzzer, the focus of the pattern strangely placed near the top of the door.

Barron paused, staring at the gold doorknob, feeling himself caught in the pattern, humming hoops of bright-green leaping out from the flat black background like an electric charge neon tunnel around him, sucking him inward like Sara's smooth legs around his waist extended into the environment, pulling attention to gilded goody—open me! Open me! Let me suck you in, baby!—the kinesthop pattern said.

Barron couldn't help smiling, knowing it wasn't his wish-fulfilment bag at all, but goddamn Sara knows exactly what she's doing with stuff like this—making entrance to her pad a cunt to the world. Dig the paint, man, it's old, starting to flake at the edges; this thing was here long before she called you. Remember where *that's* at, and don't blow your cool.

He reached out, pressed the ivory bellybutton in the centre of the doorknob, heard taped Chinese J Arthur Rank gong from within, footsteps on muted carpet—and Sara opened the door. She stood in the doorway, framed by a single wine-coloured spotlight, dark hallway behind her long loose hair bloody-gold to her shoulders, in a black silk kimono flowing over her naked breasts, hips, like oil, nipples low and taut through the cloth, stomach-legs convergence, imagined soft-flesh triangle hinted by heavy folds of black sheen.

Déjà vu irony of entrance to his penthouse, remembering own come-into-my-parlour come-on, his own seduction-environment and from *who* he had learned the kinesthop hypnotic technique, Barron laughed, said: "Way to a man's heart is through his stomach, way to the crotch is through the eyeballs, eh, Sara?"

"Same old Jack," she said, with an unexpected sly smile that caught him off balance, sucked him into brittle-laughing-sad-pathetic-brave eyes, through levels of illusions, inside joke on the universe between them, spark of old love Jack-and-Sara destiny's darlings hard-edged Berkeley Los Angeles mystics, their innocent cynicism a sword against the night. "Magic's lost on you; I forgot that rune you wear against necromancy."

"Thank you, JRR Tolkien," he said, stepping inside and closing the door behind him in a protocol-control gesture. "Some place we can sit in this cave of the winds?" he said, suppressing gland-reaction images battering his cool, wanting to grab her as she hung there before him. Keep your cool, he told himself.

She smiled, led him through the velvet hall-blackness-shadows dancing (black wash over kinesthop patterns, he thought, image of *Bug Jack Barron* set backdrop; we play the same games, only stakes are different), into a straw-mat-floored studio room, low primary-coloured geometric-precision Japanese furniture hard-edged in the neutral, off-white pseudolantern overhead light, thousand-years-distant in cool squares and rectangles from ricky-ticky neon-baroque Village streets. He squatted on a red plush pillow before a black-lacquered table, smiled at the TV sitting arrogantly on it like a Yankee Imperialismo in oriental sheets.

She sat down beside him, opened a blue box on the table, took out two cigarettes, handed him one. He dug the trademark, snapped, "No grass baby. Straight talk, and I mean *straight*, both of us, or I leave."

"Your sponsor, Acapulco Golds," she said fingering the joint coyly. "What would the network think?"

"Cut the shit, Sara."

"All right, Jack," she said, suddenly empty in open little-girl confusion (as if *I'm* the one that started this). "I was hoping you'd... you'd write the script for this scene. That was always your bag, not mine."

"*My* bag? Look, baby, this has been your orbit straight from ground zero. You called me, remember? You asked me to see you, I didn't drag my dick down here to..."

"Didn't you, Jack?" she said quietly.

And he looked into her pool-dark eyes that knew holes with no bottoms inside, his locked on hers locked on his like X-Ray cameras facing each other in feedback circuitry between them gut to gut belly to belly big dark eyes eating him up saying: I know you know I know we know we know we know—endless feedback of pitiless scalpels of knowledge.

"All right, Sara," he said in soft surrender to grammar of mutually understood feedback truth. "I forgot who I was talking to. Been a long time; I forgot that anyone was ever that deep inside of me. Wanted to. Wanted to forget I knew you knew how I still feel about you. It's a bum trip to remember that you walked out on me—and me still loving you when you went."

"What kind of bullshit is that?" she snapped with a defensive pout, but with a hurt-eyes reality behind it. "I didn't leave, you threw me out."

"*I threw you out...?*" Barron started to shout, heard his voice rising into ancient traditional six-years-buried argument she never understood, into pointless, useless brick-wall noncommunication… endless, endless hassle. And called his cool back. "You never understood, Sara, you could never get it through your head. No one threw you out. You kept issuing ultimatums, and I finally got pissed enough to call you on one of them, and you split."

"You made me go," she insisted. "You made it impossible for me to stay. I couldn't take it, and you wouldn't change. You threw me out like a used condom."

"Now we get to the nitty-gritty," he said, "and straight from your own mouth. You didn't want the real me, the way I really was. And when I refused to play Baby Bolshevik games and started living in the real world, you couldn't cut the action and come out of your grass-lined hole, and when I wouldn't crawl back in with you, you split. And this by you is being thrown out?" Waiting for the expected endless-replay snapback, Barron saw the familiar breaking-up-days hurt eyes quivering-lips mask form on her face… and dissolve suddenly into open near-tears.

"No," she said, as if reminding herself of some New Year's resolution. "This is *now* not six years ago. And I don't want to fight, don't want to win any arguments. Last time out I thought I won, and you thought you won… and we both really lost. Can't you see that, Jack? You threw me out I left you… words, words words. When did we stop trying to dig each other and start making points? That's what I felt when…"

She hesitated strangely, something weirdly cold seemed to flicker across her eyes before she went on: "When I saw your show on acid, the you that I loved was still there, was always there. But this other you—making points, always making points—with Hennering and Luke and Yarborough same as you were always making points on me at the end… That's you too, Jack. It always was, always will be, and once I loved that too in you, when your enemies were our enemies… remember? Remember Berkeley and the night *you* put together the SJC? Not Luke, not the others but *you* bringing it all together, making points *for a reason,* and the way you stopped that riot with just your face and your voice? And watching you pick the Foundation to pieces, the way you used to pick me to pieces but the way you picked that fascist bastard to pieces, and got the show in the first place too, oh, that was Jack Barron, all Jack Barron, the Jack Barron that was meant to be. And I thought that maybe you hadn't changed maybe it was me, that I stopped trying to understand, somehow, afraid of power, afraid of safe dreams becoming reality, afraid of the responsibility of being a winner's woman, afraid of the real sharks in the real ocean. If you were a cop-out, I was a coward, putting you down instead of trying to understand.

"Oh, Jack, you're the only man I ever really loved, only man I ever respected, and I still don't understand you, maybe I never will. But if you'll have me, I'll spend the rest of my life trying. I love you, I love you. Don't say a word, fuck me, fuck me, darling, fuck my brains out, I'm tired of thinking, I just want to *feel*." And she fell against him, arms around him, breasts warm and wriggling, thrust her tongue to the hilt unbidden through his stiff-tight lips.

He shuddered in quivering, helpless he-she role reversal as inverted *déjà vu* flashes mocked him, her eyes bottomless, open as she kissed him, Wednesday-night-vacuum-leaching-eyes of endless string of surrogate Saras becoming real Jack-and-Sara Sara, Berkeley, Los Angeles, Acapulco, night-breezes Sara becoming wet-dream California of the mind Sara becoming every Sara that never was in false memory banks of forlorn longing becoming Saras past, Saras future, flashing positive-negative white-out black-out reality-fantasy in and out of past and wet-dream-future time with the rhythm of her liquid thrusting tongue.

Vacuum in the personality-centre behind the windows of his eyes, his hands moved like disbelieving robots pulling aside the black kimono sheen, and her body naked against him—brown freckle in contact with left nipple mole above border of red-gold triangle secret second navel, tongue moving sweet spittle in long-remembered trail along the curve of his cheekbone, hot wetness moving in ear encircled by lips of bougainvillea musk breathing fingers dancing down belly smoothing his thigh in primeval rhythm—filled the void with Sara-flesh reality, image-ghosts fleeing down timelines as his hands closed on the massive breast present. Sara! Sara! It's *you*, and it's real!

I'm Jack and you're Sara, is all that matters—and he pulled her face to him as she rolled him off the pillow, naked under him on the straw-matted floor. Moaning into him as he kissed her tongue on tongue mouths moving in slow pelvic rhythm her hands at his ass kneading and urging, shoving him down between legs spread-eagled encircling caressing, mouth free now and screaming orgasmic rhythm: "*Fuck* me, *fuck* me, *fuck* me..." And...

And...

And it just wasn't there. Spent totally in the night filled with Carrie, in morning-after image-eyed return event—six years of desire-images come to a moment of reality, and in that moment of all moments it just wasn't there!

He felt the cold moment of super-Freudian disaster spiralling around him—then Jack seeing Jack with maniac laughter. What the fuck does it matter, it's me that counts, not my dick, got nothing to prove cockwise in *this* arena. I love her, is all and she's here.

He slid his face down her belly, skin to chin-stubble, buried it in musky coarse-haired dampness, lips to wet lips tasting her body as her thighs gripped his cheeks his tongue went inside her rolling and coaxing with love and wry self-frustration, thrusting and moving in pelvic simulation as she rocked against him in asymptotic rhythm and went off in great groaning spasms.

Resting his chin on the bone of her pelvis, he smiled at her face across the luffing sail of her belly, breasts awry, like puppy-dog mountains, her eyes met his across pink continents of skin-to-skin pleasure...

"Jack..." she sighed. "Oh, thank you, thank you..." Then she looked down at him with a fey knowing smile "that's the best you could do this early in the day? Just out of curiosity, what was her name?"

"Whose name?" he grinned in mock innocence.

"Miss Last Night. I sure hope there *was* one, wouldn't want to think you were..."

"Give me about an hour to recuperate, and I'll answer your question," he said, moving up her body to face to face languor.

She laughed and kissed him quick, dry lips sated, but he felt the hunger there still his to command, taste of her still in him, and he felt it stirring through cotton layers of fatigue as she reached down to stroke it.

"Still in there fighting, just where I left it," she said. And years, melted away, and he knew she was back. "Take it slow and easy, we've got time," she said, hugging him to her. And with a strange-style shudder he had never felt before, said: "All the time in the world."

Haven't done this since they made grass legal, Jack Barron mused as the hand-rolled as in days of street-comer dealer yore joint passed around the mystic circle—himself, Sara, some cat named Sime who was obviously after Sara's ass, a chick calling herself Leeta or something (ironed-blonde Psychedelic Church acolyte), and a hairy type known only as the Wolfman. Barron sucked deep, getting into the anachronistic nostalgia bag, husbanding whiffs of smoke as if the stuff still cost twenty bucks an ounce, still was illegal.

"Wow," he said, drawing out the word in approved early '60s style. "Don't let the word get out, but this stuff has a bigger kick to it than Acapulco Golds."

Sara laughed, "It should; there's some opium in it." Barron smiled, felt a sardonic detachment from the others squatting on the straw-matted floor. From old head days, he knew there couldn't be more than a taste of opium in the shit; you'd have to smoke about a pound of the grass to even get a buzz off O. But that's not where it's at, he thought, kick's in the *idea* of opium because the stuff's still illegal; you can buy pot in any candy store. So bring back images of danger with a couple pinches of O—pushers in the streets pay-envelopes police lock fuzz in the hall, Good Old Bad Old Days, where spice of the opium's at. And maybe there *isn't* any opium, just bullshit, what's the difference, charge is the same.

"Hey," said the Wolfman, "you hung on Acapulco Golds too? Funny how any old head that's really been around a while digs Acapulco Golds. And we all know how long *you've* been around, Jack." The last walking a thin line between genuine innocent affection and sycophant put-on.

Hearing the Wolfman voice the question he was always asking himself, Barron suddenly dug why Acapulco Golds were overwhelming best-seller in the Village, Fulton, Strip City ghettos, among old-time nostalgia-head potheads: *my sponsor,* is all. They're sure getting their money's worth out of *Bug Jack Barron;* smoke Acapulco Golds and you're smoking Jack Barron, act of patriotism for Wolfman, for psychedelic-ghetto types, True Believers in Dylan-haired (gotta get a haircut, starting to itch) Berkeley bad boy, *our* boy kick-'em-in-the-ass myth.

He passed the joint to Sara, saw her drag a deep tight bread times drag, wondered why he hadn't bitched about this pot-party scene, so patently a show-the-flag Jack Barron-returns-to-the-people schtick, had looked forward to it, need for... need for...?

"Hey, man," the Wolfman said, "those stories going round about you and the Foundation true?"

"What stories?" Barron asked, and the whiff of a very professional rumour-mill (Luke's rumour-mill *already*) hung in the air.

The Wolfman took the joint from Sara, dragged, held smoke in his lungs and talked through it in old-time pothead screen-door croak. "Say you're out for Bennie Howards. For blood. Last show a real gas. Public freezer. Man you—" The Wolfman spasmed, coughed smoke in talk-inhale conflict resolution, then immediately continued, loud, and gesticulating in new-found lung-freedom. "Yeah the word is that you're in with the Public Freezer cats, playing it real cool till you got the Foundation set up for the kill, and then Pow! down on the fuckers with both feet, split things wide open, and then everyone's got a chance at living forever not just the usual fat-cat fascist bastards, but like *people,* dig? Like we're all—*people,* dig? One thing you glom onto when you're born, no matter what you do later, like whether you pile up bread or not, or how long you wear your hair, or whether you got a nine-to-fiver or just like *make it,* whether you're white or black or purple dig? Yeah like this death-kick is laid on *everyone* soon as they're born. I mean, one boat we're all in together *people,* see? Like they got Medicare for everyone cause they finally dug that you shouldn't die just because you're wasted. Well, ain't Freezing just one more medical-type thing to beat the death-kick? So it should be free for everyone, like the rest of it. Like people. I'm people, you're people, Bennie Howards' people. We're all people, and we all should have the same odds to live, dig?"

Barron felt the wheels turning. Cat's riffing out straight SJC party line, with a neat little Jack Barron tie-in, *too* neat. Got put in his head real professional-like, but he doesn't know it, thinks it's his own scam, in the air, is all. Rumour-mill stuff, all right: whispers in drunken barroom voices, on street corners, discos real-spontaneous-looking, just stuff everyone hears around. And ten to one it all comes from Evers, Mississippi... And I oughta know, I invented the schtick way back when.

Yeah, Barron thought, as he picked up on the moment hanging in the air, the four of them looking to him with life-death desperation in their eyes, vacuum-eyes of Brackett Audience Count estimated hundred million people, planted story, but a good one 'cause it hit a nerve. Luke and Morris are right, death is like *the* issue. Face of death, we're all just people, do anything (lie, kill, form Foundation for Human Immortality, sell out to Bennie Howards) to stay alive just one more second, 'cause when you're dead, mortality bullshit dies with you. Only two-party system on issue of life and death: Death Party and Life Party. Gut-level Presidential campaign: SJC-Republican-Jack Barron Party of life eternal versus Howards-Democratic Party of death by the numbers.

Jesus H Christ on a Harley! Barron thought as it hit his gut-reality for the very first time—I actually *could* make the old college try for President!

"Well, like I'm with you in principle," Barron said, with horrid awareness of his words as possible projected instrument of history (stuff history!) public statement from the Man Who thrust unwillingly into electric-contact reality social-conscience reality (goddamned silly-ass Berkeley bullshit is all!) he needed like an extra rectum. "But from where I sit, the whole Public Freezer schtick's nowheresville. Don't you see what you're bucking? Bucking Benedict Howards and like billions in frozen assets bucking the Democratic Party that's elected every president but two for over half a century bucking Teddy the Pretender and his ghosts and bucking the Republicans too—they don't want Public Freezing, just a piece of the action for their own fat cats, is all, and they're still rolling in bread. So what's that leave on the other side, the SJC and my big mouth, and a few hundred fruitcakes parading around with picket signs? Big fucking deal!"

"Hey, you're beautiful, man!" the Wolfman said sincerely. "You got more people listen to you than any cat in the country, and you don't dig your own power, so groovy. You're the coolest head around, is what you are, sitting up there with those sons of bitches, bigger than any of 'em and not playing *that* game, still keeping your cool. Cat we can *trust*. Shit, you're beautiful, man."

"He's right," the blonde chick said. "Don't you dig? You got the power like the rest of the bastards, but you're the only one didn't get it on a pile of dead bodies, so you can use it the way it should be used, for *people*..."

"Don't you see, Jack?" Sara asked, staring hungrily at him with those old Berkeley eyes. "Power... Remember how we talked in the old days about power, what we'd do when we got it? Sure you remember all that bullshit. But don't you see, it doesn't have to be bullshit anymore. We've got you, and *you've* got the power. You weren't afraid to lay yourself on the line in the old days, when it accomplished nothing, and now you can do it again, but this time it'll *matter*."

"Power!" Barron snapped. "None of you know shit from shinola about power! Look around you, take a good look, and you'll see Howards and Teddy and Morris—*that's* power. They're people, dig, *people*, is all, but, baby, they're *junkies*. All of 'em power-junkies. That's what power does to you, a fucking monkey on your back—just like junk. First shot's free, kiddies, but after that you've gotta go out and cop more and more and more to feed the monkey. I'm a beautiful cat, eh? I'll take you outside and show you fifty former beautiful cats you wouldn't piss on because, baby, they're *junkies*. And a junkie don't give a shit about anything but junk. Power and smack—it's all the same junk."

"Luke Greene's a junkie?" Sara said quietly.

"Bet your sweet ass he is! There he is, stuck in the Mississippi boonies, the poor lonely fucker, surrounded by sycophants and plain ordinary schmucks, hating every minute of it, hating himself, hating manipulating people... All that race-put-down come-on—only it's real. He hates himself for being a nigger, thinks of himself as a nigger surrounded by niggers. Luke Greene—*there* was a beautiful cat, my best friend, and now look at him, hating himself, hating everything, nothing but a big throbbing vein to feed the power-monkey on his back. You wanna see *me* like that, Sara?"

The silence was so thick you could cut it with a knife. What brought that on? Barron wondered. Jeez, what's in this grass, maybe it *is* loaded with opium junk... Junk... Yeah, maybe that's it, man, once you really were a power-junkie, in the old days, just a bag now and then to keep the monkey quiet. Wasn't that why you got yourself the show in the first place, biggest jolt of power-junk you ever had? Worked funny, didn't it, OD'd you, got you off it? And now you got everyone shaking the stuff under your nose, feel that hunger so hot you can taste it, and everyone telling you go ahead, shoot up, *you* can't get hooked again sonny, you're a *beautiful cat!*

And that's where all this is at, he knew. Whole Village is a power-junk supermarket for old Jack Barron, and that's why you dug this party idea, baby, you smelled the shit like an old junkie, couldn't keep away. One fix, and you're hooked.

Not this time, Sara. Too much to lose, *Bug Jack Barron,* maybe a free shot at forever. Throw *that* away for a surge of Presidential bullshit Samson-smash junk? Would you? Would anyone? Gonna be a junkie, be an immortality-junkie—at least *that* monkey gives as good as it gets.

Screw this whole scene! Barron thought bitterly. Truth, justice, you a beautiful cat bullshit—no different from the rest, all want my bod for your own bags.

I'm tired of it all, Machiavellian motherfuckers, Howards, Luke, Morris, all losers; maybe you too, Sara, who knows? Goddamn paranoid nightmare!

Show you all Jack Barron's his own man, nobody's flunky. I'll get what I want, one way or another, and on my own fucking terms!

Wonder who did this stuff? Sara Westerfeld thought behind her shield of purposeful cynicism against Jack-reality as the elevator door opened, revealing the entrance foyer to his little-boy treehouse-penthouse and the crude, not-quite-making-it kinesthop mural on the wall (should be whole kinesthop *wall* around the hallway entrance, really suck in all those chicks he's supposed to be balling, she thought professionally).

Jack smiled a little-boy smile, hair all curls like fresh from pillow years flaking away dig my pad baby smile of first meeting first love first lay in dingy Berkeley attic. She reached out and pinched his ass—still firm cute ass-flesh felt the about-to-be-fucked-for-the-first-time thrill of the unfolding unknown.

He put his arm around her waist, led her past doors down a dark hallway toward a vast space she could kinaesthetically sense beyond, paused suddenly, yanked her off her feet into arms around shoulder hand firm under her ass caressing divide, and she went with it, arms around him, face muzzled into wild curls roughness around his neck as he laughed, said: "I never got to carry you over any threshold, baby, so better late than never."

She giggled with semi-sincere, go-with-it-it's-his-bag pleasure, said: "Darling, there are times when you're so beautifully square." He carried her forward (she could feel muscles deliciously tight straining against her), paused at the brink of something (she could see stars, night-treeshapes across bulking distance), fiddled with some panel on the wall and…

Flames leapt up billowing orange from huge firepit in the centre of a vast scarlet-carpeted room, dancing ruby shadows across chairs, pillow-piles, furniture, huge gizmo electronic wall consoles to a California patio beyond, rubber-trees against the naked sky scintillating firelight glow from the faceted-dome skylight-ceiling reflecting sparks into the dead New York sky, and she saw they were on a deck-balcony above the huge living room as rock-montage music began to play from somewhere and colour-organ spectral flashes swirling with the music spun acid-reality magic in the air, and she felt him quiver against her, waiting for a reaction to his externalised head like a cornucopia before her—or just as like some silly-ass Hollywood set.

She hugged him silently, unsure of the truth of her reactions: so like Jack, magic, cop-out, phony, extravagant, bullshit, and yet… and yet…

Yet it's *real*, real fantasy playpen, no interior-decorated-calculated baloney, straight from Jack's head to reality, with nothing inbetween. It's *him*, it's his dream—Berkeley, Los Angeles, California candy-store window, unafraid naked garish conscious-subconscious Jack Barron day-dream, sugar-plum reality that money had made real.

Sara felt herself teetering on the brink of a dangerous truth: Who was really the cop-out, Jack who went and got what he needed to make his dream real, moulding a Jack Barron reality to the shape of his dreams, or *me*, shaping dreams to the size of mundane reality (takes balls to be garish 'cause garishness is your bag)? A hero's a man with the courage to live in his dreams.

"How's *that* grab you, baby?" he said, carrying her down to the lush-carpeted surface, setting her on her feet, staring into her eyes, giving the question pregnant ego-involvement intensity.

I don't know how it grabs me she thought vertiginously. Your bag, not mine, little-boy stuff, like tin soldiers, silly Hollywood crap. But you dig it, I dig you, and, Jack darling, it's *real*. "It's *you*, Jack," she said quite truthfully.

"You think it's a lot of silly bullshit," he said. "I can see it in your eyes."

"No!" she said loudly, impulsively, aware that she meant it only after she said it. "It's just... I've never seen anything like it before. It's like... like seeing your head, I mean, the inside of your head, out *there*. It's so... *naked*, I mean it's the nakedest room I've ever seen. Like you had a magic wand and just waved it and everything that you wanted in your head suddenly *was*. I won't con you, Jack, you know it's not my bag out there, it's yours, and if I was waving the wand, it'd be all different. But the idea of waving the wand in the first place—that's such a pure groove! I dig this place because it's *you*, exactly what you wanted to make it. It's a whole new bag, a whole new idea to me—wanting something like this, a dream, and having the power to make it reality. I... I... I'm not sure what I feel."

He smiled a knowing smile, kissed her lightly, and said, "There's hope for you after all. Sara. You're getting a taste of it, Sara, a taste of where the world's really at. It's all out there, every dream, everything anyone wants. But you don't get it by talking about it or dropping acid and wishing. You gotta get out there in the nitty-gritty and grab it, take as much of what's out there as what's inside you can get you. *That's* reality. Not what's inside or what's outside, but how much of what's inside you can make *real*. If that's copping out—getting your hands dirty—well, then I'd rather be a cop-out than a one-eyed cat forever peeping in a seafood store. Wouldn't you? Is being hungry all your life *really* being true to yourself?"

Jack Barron, she thought. Jack Barron. Jack Barron. JACK BARRON. Christ, it's hard to think of him as anything but JACK BARRON in great big red capital letters. Hate him, love him, cop-out comic-book-monster hero lover, whatever he is, it's impossible to keep your cool around him. Jack's Jack, makes his own rules no one else can even follow, lies become truth becomes cop-out becomes psychedelic vision-reality becomes lover becomes power becomes rock-bottom honesty, comes on like acid-flash white-out reversal-images; foreground-background indeterminate interface of dynamic instability, and what he is is the paradox interface itself—not figure, not ground, but the standing-wave-pattern between. JACK BARRON.

And she knew fear, knowing he was something greater than herself, something hyperreal, encompassing her reality as a facet of himself, only *one* facet; knew fear that he saw through her like through glass, saw lizard-man Howards pushing them together in chessboard gambit from bone-white windowless temple of power. And she knew guilt at her own cop-out, holding within her Howards' plan within her plan, playing the very same game she put Howards down for. But Jack himself had given her the path from guilt to resolution—reality, truth—is how much of what's inside you that you can make real. And she knew hunger for him, for his body-reality love, for inside-head dreams made real, not for a moment or a year or a century, but forever. Forever. She knew hunger, and knew she had never hungered like this before.

But she also knew a feeling that filled her with soul-jeopardy dread: *guile*. She felt the serpent-shaped slithering word within her, holding a piece of her back in cool rock lairs coil in reptile coil, waiting basilisk cold centuries ready to pounce; knew she was faced with an order of decision-reality she had not believed existed—life eternal with Jack forever knight in soft-flesh armour against a million years of wormeaten nothingness. Knew in her hands was the darkness-power of life versus death for her, for Jack... for how many millions? And she knew with infinite sadness that at age thirty-five she was no longer girl Sara Westerfeld, but woman Sara Westerfeld, playing adult-deadly game with man Jack Barron for the highest stakes of all, for the right to think of herself *really* as Sara Barron in great big red capital letters forever. Sara BARRON. SARA BARRON.

"Let me show you something that's *us*," he said, taking her hand. "A dream made real we can both dig together." And led her across the red carpet to a small door. "Remember, Sara?" He opened the door to the bedroom, and she stepped inside—and saw and felt. And remembered.

Oh, she remembered! She remembered sun-warmed grass against her back pushed to rich wet earth by him open sighing flash of stars glowing blue-black skylight above bed open to the stars tropical night-smells heard Acapulco breakers in the surfsounds that came on at the touch of his hand; patio foliage outlined against the dusk-glow of Brooklyn against sunset clawing through leaf-frond windows of Los Angeles bedroom his face blue and stubbly arms sleeping around her. Ivy-walled bedstead of Berkeley attic first-time thrill grey wood texture of college-fuck walls. Saw plastigrass carpet, console in bedstead, surfsound recording, sliding panels, scenery, props—the backside of a dream.

Her dream.

She turned toward him, and he was smiling, fey, knowing buddha-eyes like scalpels, the conscious creator of her midnight-tears dream.

Do I love him, or hate him? She wondered if she'd ever know, if it mattered, for no other man so knew her, no other man gave off that dangerous heat. She could hate him and love him in her innermost being (where love and hate might be the same thing)—beside JACK BARRON (in flaming capital letters) who else could be real?

"Jack..." she croaked, crying and laughing, flinging herself at him, her *self*—bundle of hate, love, thirty-five years of girlhood—open, reservations forgotten. Poor fool lizardman Howards, thinking he can use me against Jack Barron—a handful of sand thrown against the sea.

She was on the bed under him without remembering moving, swimming in tides of total sensation, a balloon of diffused nerve-endings living the moment on her sentient skin. And he was ...

Exploding within her, imploding around her, filling her, gorging her with electrical being, blunt lance of pleasure around which she surrounded, caressing it, feeling it, digging it, taking it in. Feeling him gasping in spiralling spasms, feeling molecule by molecule wet scorching osmosis, him-her symbiotic flashing interface where skin touched skin, she screamed with his throat as he flashed through her, and time jumped a long beat of unbearable pleasure and she soared in a dream of Islamic heaven—slow-grinding orgasm for ten million years.

Opening her eyes, she saw his closed and dreaming. Jack! Jack! she thought. I'm a phony, a liar. I came here like some damned Mexican whore. And she teetered on the edge of telling him all—Benedict Howards using her, and she using him.

But she felt his weight on her, the touch of his skin, his hair tickling her nipples, and the thought of his body lying in humus, dead, gone and forgotten, tied her belly and tongue in constricted knots. She remembered that she stood between him and oblivion. If she were brave a little longer, held it back for a while, all that was Jack, all that was between them, never had to die.

Oh, Jack, Jack! she wanted to shout but didn't, someone like you should never die!

8

'DEATHBED AT GO' the promptboard flashed, and Jack Barron, clocking Vince's smart-ass Sicilian-type grin, was sure Gelardi had to have Mafiosa blood in him somewhere even though he claimed to be strictly Neapolitan. The promptboard flashed '45 seconds,' and Barron shuddered as the last seconds of the opening commercial reeled by—schtick was a bunch of diplomats relaxing around the old conference table with good old Acapulco Golds. Ain't as funny as it looks, he thought, vips run the world like they're stoned half the time anyway, and for the other half things are *worse*. Wonder what Bennie Howards would be like high? Well, maybe tonight all hundred million Brackett Count chilluns gonna see—they say adrenaline's like a psychedelic, and before I'm through tonight, Bennie's gonna go on an adrenaline bummer he won't believe.

Watching the commercial fade into his own face on the monitor, Barron felt a weird psychedelic flash go through him, the reality of the last week compressed into an instantaneous image flashed on the promptboard of his mind: Sitting in the studio chair, electronic feedback-circuitry connecting him with subsystems of power—Foundation power SJC-Democrat-Republican power, hundred million Brackett Count power—he was like the master transistor in a massive satellite network confluence circuit of power, gigantic input of others' power feeding into his head through vidphone circuits, none of it his, but all feeding through him, his to control by microcosmic adjustment; for one hour, 8-9 p.m. Eastern Standard Time, that power was de facto *his*.

He felt his subjective head-time speeding up, like an alien drug in his bloodstream, at the focus of forces far beyond him yet at his command as letters crawled across the promptboard an electric-dot message that seemed to take ten million years: 'On the Air.'

"And what's bugging you out there tonight?" Jack Barron asked, playing to the kinesthop-darkness shapes double-reflected (backdrop off desktop) in his eye hollows ominous with foreknowledge of the shape of the show to come. "What bugs you, bugs Jack Barron," he said, digging his own image on the monitor, eyes picking up flashes as never before. "And we'll soon see what happens when YOU bug Jack Barron. The number is Area Code 212, 969-6969, and we'll take our first call right... *now*."

Now, he thought, making the vidphone connection, nitty-gritty time, Bennie-baby, better be good and ready, here it comes *now*. And the screen split down the middle; left half a pallid grey on grey image of a dough-faced middle-aged woman with deep lines of defeat-tension etched around her hollow-bagged eyes like dry kernels of mortal disaster, a hag-grey ghost begging her living-colour image for alms from the gods.

"This is *Bug Jack Barron,* and you're on the air, plugged into me, plugged into one hundred million Americans (drawing out the words for special audience of one, one hundred million, count 'em Bennie, 100,000,000) and this is your chance to let 'em all know what's bugging you and get some action, 'cause action's the name of the game when you bug Jack Barron. So let's hear it all, the right here right now live no time-delay nitty-gritty; what's bugging *you*?"

"My... my name is Dolores Pulaski," the woman said, "and I've been trying to talk to you for three weeks, Mr Barron, but I know it's not your fault. (Vince gave her three-quarters screen, put Barron in upper right-hand corner catbird-seat, living-colour Crusader dwarfed by yawning grey need. Just the right touch, Barron thought.) I'm calling for my father, Harold Lopat. He... he can't speak for himself." Her lips quivered on the edge of sob.

Jesus Christ, Barron thought, hope Vince didn't feed me a crier, gotta underplay this schtick or I'll push Howards too far. "Take it easy, Mrs Pulaski," he soothed, "you're talking to friends. We're all on your side."

"I'm sorry," the woman said, "it's just so hard to..." Her eyes frightened and furtive, her jaw hardened to numbness, the tension came across beautifully as she forced herself calm. "I'm calling from the Kennedy Hospital for Chronic Diseases in Chicago. My father, he's been here ten weeks... die... die... he's got cancer, cancer of the stomach, and it's spread to the lym... *lymphatics,* and the doctors all say... we've had four specialists... He's dying! He's dying! They say they can't do anything. My father, Mr Barron. My father... he's going to *die!*" She began sobbing; then her face went off-camera, and a huge pale hand obscured the vidphone image as she picked her vidphone up, turned its camera on the room. Trembling, disjointed, out of focus pieces of hospital room stumbled across the monitor screen: Walls, wilted flowers, transfusion stands, bed, blankets, the thousand deathhead's wrinkled ether-smell shrivelled face of a ruined old man, and her voice— "Look! Look! Look at him!"

Jeez, Barron thought, pumping his screen-control foot-button even as Vince changed the monitor-mix to three quarters Jack Barron the lower left-hand quadrant still a jumble of sliding images, old man's face fingers vased flowers trays of needles bedpan—hideous grey montage of death by inches now muted at least, surrounded by full-colour embracing image of concerned Big Brother Jack Barron, and Dolores Pulaski's screaming sobs were a far-away tinny unreality as Vince bled her audio and Barron's voice reestablished control.

"Take it easy, Mrs Pulaski." Barron stopped just short of harshness. "We'll want to help you, but you'll have to stay calm. Now put the vidphone down in front of you, and just try to remember you'll have all the time you need to say what you want to. And if you can't find the words, I'm here to help you. Try to relax. A hundred million Americans are on your side and *want* to understand."

The woman's face reappeared in the lower left quadrant, eyes dull, jaw slack, a spent, pale-flesh robot-image, and Barron knew he was back in control. After a little hair-tearing, she's got nothing left in her, you can make her say anything, she won't make more waves. And he foot-signalled Vince to give her three-quarters screen, her schtick to the next commercial, as long as she stayed tame.

"I'm sorry I had to be so short with you, Mrs Pulaski," Barron said softly. "Believe me, we all understand how you must feel."

"I'm sorry too, Mr Barron," she said in a loud stage whisper. (Vince, Barron thought, on the ball as usual, turning up her volume.) "It's just that I feel so… you know, helpless, and now when I can finally *do* something about it, it all just came out, everything I've been holding in… I don't know what to do, what to say, but I've got to make everyone understand…" Here it comes, Barron thought. Sitting on the edge of your sweaty little seat, Bennie? Not yet, eh? Keep cool, Bennie-baby, cause now you get yours!

"Of course we all sympathise, Mrs Pulaski, but I'm not quite sure what anyone can do. If the doctors say…" Give, baby! Shit, don't make me fish for it.

"The doctors say… they say there's no hope for my father. Surgery, radiation, drugs—nothing can save him. My father's dying, Mr Barron. They give him only weeks. Within a month… within a month he'll be dead."

"I still don't see—"

"Dead!" she whispered. "In a few weeks, my father will be dead forever. Oh, he's a *good* man, Mr Barron! He's got children and grandchildren who love him, and he's worked hard for us all his life, and he loves us. He's as good a man as anyone who ever lived! Why, *why* should he be dead and gone forever while other men, bad men, Mr Barron, men who've got rich on good men's sweat, they can live forever just by buying their way into a Freezer with the money they've stolen and cheated people like us to get? It's not fair, it's… *evil*. A man like my father, an honest, kind man, works all his life for his family, and when he dies he's buried and gone like he had never existed, while a man like Benedict Howards holds… holds immortal lives in his filthy hands like he was God…"

Dolores Pulaski blanched at the weight of the word that hung from her lips. "I didn't mean …" she stammered. "I mean, forgive me, to mention a man like that in the same sentence with God…"

Jeez, spare me the Hail Marys! Barron thought. "Of course you didn't," he said, picturing Howards sweating somewhere in the bowels of his Colorado Freezer with no place to hide. He tapped his right foot-button twice, signalling Vince to give him a two-minute count to the next commercial as he paused, casually kind, before continuing. "But tell me, Mrs Pulaski, what are you asking *me* to do?" he said, all earnest choir-boy innocence.

"Get my father a place in a Freezer!" Dolores Pulaski shot back. (Beautiful, thought Barron. Couldn't be better if we were working from a script; you're show biz all the way, Dolores Pulaski.)

"I'm afraid I don't swing much weight at the Foundation for Human Immortality," Barron said archly as Vince now split the screen evenly between them, "as I'm sure you'll remember if you, saw the last show." The promptboard flashed '90 seconds.' (Don't fail me now, Mrs Pulaski, come out with the right line and I make you a star.)

"I know that, Mr Barron. It's that Benedict Howards... one man in the whole world who can save my father, and he sells immortality like the devil buys souls. God forgive me for saying it, but I mean it—like Satan! Who else but Satan and Benedict Howards are evil enough to put a price on a man's immortal life? Talk to him, Mr Barron, show the world what he's like. Make him explain to poor people dying everywhere without a hope of living again how he can set a price on human life. And if he can't explain, I mean in front of millions of people, well, then he'll have to do something about my father, won't he? He can't afford to look like a monster in public. I mean, an important man like that...?" The promptboard flashed '60 seconds.'

"You've got a point, Mrs Pulaski," Barron said, cutting her off quickly before too much more peasant shrewdness could come through. (Such a thing as *too* show biz, Dolores Pulaski—can't stand a straight man steps on *my* lines.)

Vince expanded his image to three-quarters screen, cut Dolores Pulaski to a prefadeout inset, cut her audio too, and a good thing, the chick's getting a wee bit naked, Barron thought as the promptboard flashed '30 seconds.'

"Yeah, Mrs Pulaski sure has a point, doesn't she?" Barron said, staring straight into the camera as his living-colour image filled the monitor screen in extreme close-up, darkness-shadows, bruised sullen hollows framing his eyes. "If there's a reason to set a dollar value on a man's chance at immortality, there's sure as hell a reason to hear what it is, with all America watching, with a bill pending in Congress to make this monopoly on freezing into Federal law. And we'll get the answer from Mr Benedict Howards right after this word from our sponsor—or a hundred million Americans will know the reason why."

What a lead-in! Barron thought as they rolled the commercial. Dolores Pulaski, you're beautiful, baby! So long as you don't flip out again while I'm playing chicken with Bennie...

He punched the intercom button on his number one vidphone "Hey Vince," he said, "keep your finger on that audio dial. It's me and Bennie all the way from here on in. I want Mrs Pulaski seen but not heard. Keep her audio down, unless I ask her a direct question. And if you gotta cut her off, then fade it—make it look like a bad vidphone connection not the old axe. Got Bennie on the line yet?"

Gelardi grinned from behind the control booth glass. "Been on the line for the last three minutes, and by now he's foaming at the mouth. Wants to talk to you right now, before you go back on the air. Still got 45 seconds...?"

"Tell him to get stuffed," Barron answered. "He'll have more time than he can handle to talk to me when he's on the air. And, baby, when I get my hooks into him, he won't be in any position to hang up."

Poor Bennie! Barron thought. Two strikes already. He's playing the master's game on the master's turf, and he's gibbering mad to boot. And as the promptboard flashed '30 seconds.' Barron suddenly realised that for the rest of the show he held Benedict Howards, the most powerful man in the United States, right there in his hot little hand, to play with like a cat plays with a wounded mouse. Can kill his Freezer Bill just for openers if I get that feeling; do him in all the way any time I want to close my fist just gotta twitch and he's had it, is all. Cat and mouse. And Luke and Morris out there now, wondering just what the hell game I'm playing... maybe theirs? It's what they're both hot for, ain't it—Jack Barron down on the Foundation with high-heeled hobnails and off to the races...? So hung on 'Hail to the Chief' the poor bastards could never dream there could be *bigger* game in town...

'On the Air' the promptboard said.

Barron made the number two vidphone connection and Dolores Pulaski appeared in a small lower-right inset, with Howards seemingly glowering down from the upper left quadrant at her across the colour image of larger-than-either-adversary Jack Barron. Groovy, Barron thought as he said, "This is *Bug Jack Barron*, and the man on the screen with me and Mrs Pulaski is Mr Benedict Howards himself, President, Chairman of the Board, and founder of the Foundation for Human Immortality. Mr Howards. Mrs Pulaski has—"

"I've been watching the show, *Mr Barron*," Howards interrupted, and Barron could see him fighting for control, eyes hot in the cool and earnest mask of his face. (But he still can't keep from dripping acid, Barron thought gleefully.) "It's one of my favourites and I rarely miss it—it's sure long on excitement; you know how to create heat. Too bad you're so short in the light department."

Tsk, tsk! Watch it Bennie, your fly's open and your id's hanging out, Barron thought as he smiled nastily into the camera. "That's my job after all, Mr Howards," he said blandly. "I'm just here to turn the spotlight on things that need seeing, like... turning over a lot of wet rocks to see what crawls out. I'm not here to tell anyone anything; I just ask questions America thinks need answering. Enlightenment's gotta come from the other end of the vidphone, *your* end, Mr Howards. So since you've been watching the show, let's not bore a hundred million Americans with repetition. Let's get right down to the nitty-gritty. There's a man dying in a hospital in Chicago—fact. There's one of your Freezers in Cicero, isn't there—that's a hard fact too. Mrs Pulaski and her family want a place for Mr Lopat in that Freezer. If he isn't Frozen, he dies and never lives again. If he is Frozen, he's got the same chance at immortality as anyone else in a Freezer. You hold Harold Lopat's life in your hands, Mr, Howards, you say whether he lives or he dies. So you see, it all boils down to one simple question, Mr Howards, and a hundred million Americans know that you and only you have the answer: does Harold Lopat live or die?"

Howards' mouth snapped open, and time stopped for a beat; he seemed to think twice, and closed it. (Got you right on the knife edge, Bennie—the Nero schtick: thumbs up, the cat lives, thumbs down, he dies. Thumbs down, you're a murderer in front of a hundred million people. Thumbs up, and you've opened the floodgates and the dam's busted for every deadbeat dying everywhere, people, Mr Howards, people, is all, free Freeze for everyone on Emperor Howards... Whatever you say next, Bennie, it's gotta be *wrong.*)

"Neither you nor Mrs Pulaski understands the situation," Howards finally said. "I don't have the power to say who's to be Frozen and who isn't. Nobody does. It's sheer economics, just like who can afford a new Cadillac and who has to drive an old '81 Ford. Five hundred thousand dollars or more must be assigned to the Foundation for every man Frozen. I assure you that if Mr Lopat or his family have the requisite assets, he will be Frozen, if that's what they want."

"Mrs Pulaski...?" Barron said, foot-signalling Gelardi to cut in her audio.

"Five hundred thousand dollars!" Dolores Pulaski shouted. "A man like you doesn't know how much money that is—more than my husband makes in eight years, and he's got a wife and a family to support! Even with Medicare, the specialists, the extra doctors, aren't covered, and our savings, my father's and my husband's and my brother's, are all gone. Why don't you just make it a million dollars or a billion; what's the difference, when ordinary people can't afford it, what kind of filthy..." Her voice trailed off in crackles, fading simulated hisses as Gelardi cut her off.

"Seems to be a bug in Mrs Pulaski's connection," Barron said as Vince rearranged the images, giving Howards' naked discomfort half the screen alongside him, Dolores Pulaski reduced to a tiny inset-creature looking on. "But I think she's made her point. Five hundred thousand dollars is a hell of a lot of bread to hold onto, taxes and cost of living being what they are. You know, I knock down a pretty nice piece of change for this show, I probably make more money than ninety per cent of the people in the country, and even I can't squirrel that kind of bread away. So when you set the price of a Freeze at five hundred big ones you're really saying that ninety per cent of all living Americans gonna be food for the worms when they die, while a few million fat cats get the chance to live forever. Hardly seems right that money can buy life. Maybe the people who're yelling for Public Freezers—"

"Commies!" shouted Howards. "Can't you see that? They're all Communists or dupes of the Reds. Look at the Soviet Union, look at Red China—they got any Freezer Programs *at all*? Of course not, because a Freezer Program can only be supported by a healthy free enterprise system. Socialised Freezing means no Freezing at all. The Commies would love—"

"But aren't you the best friend the Communists have in America?" Barron cut in, signalling for a commercial in three minutes.

"*You* calling *me* a Communist!" Howards said, forcing his face into a soundless parody of a laugh. "That's good, Barron, the whole country knows the kind of people *you've* been involved with."

"Let's skip the name-calling, shall we? I didn't call you a Communist... just, shall we say, an unwitting dupe of the Reds? I mean, the fact that less than ten per cent of the population—shall we say, the exploiters of the working class, as they put—it has a chance to live forever, while everyone else has to die and like it... is there a *better* argument against a pure capitalistic system that the Reds can dream up? Isn't your Foundation the best piece of propaganda the Reds have?"

"I'm sure your audience isn't swallowing that crap," Howards said (knowing it damn well is, Barron thought smugly). "Nevertheless, I'll try to explain it so that even *you* can understand it, Mr Barron. Maintaining Freezers costs lots of money, and so does research on restoring and extending life. It costs billions each year, so much money that, for instance, the Soviet government simply can't afford it—and neither can the government of the United States. But an effort like ours must be financed somehow, and the only way is for the people who are Frozen to pay their own way. If the government tried to Freeze everyone who died it'd go bankrupt, it'd cost hundreds of billions a year. The Foundation, by seeing to it that those who are Frozen pay for it, and pay for the research, at least keeps the dream of human immortality alive. It may not be perfect, but it's the only thing that can work. Surely a man of your... *vast intelligence* should be able to see *that*."

Five points for you, Bennie, Barron conceded. Thing is that the fucker's essentially *right*. Letting the few that are Frozen now feed the worms won't get anyone else into a Freezer, and if you got a thousand people dying for every slot open, well baby, that's where life's always been at—the winners win, and the losers lose. But you're too right for your own good, Bennie, muscle talks, and muscle's what you'll get from good old Jack Barron.

"Of course I understand the hard economic realities," Barron said as the promptboard flashed '2 minutes.' "I mean, sitting here, fat and healthy and thirty-eight years old. Dollars and sense and all that crap, on paper your Foundation looks real good. Yeah, *I* understand, Mr Howards. But I wonder if I'd feel so damn philosophical if I were dying. Would you, Mr Howards? How'd you like to die like Harold Lopat—broke, and the life leaking out of you drop by drop, while some cat in a two-and-a-half thousand dollar suit explains real logical-like how it's economically impractical to give you the chance to live again some day?"

To Barron's surprise, Howards seemed genuinely stricken: a mist of what seemed like sheer madness drifted behind his eyes, his jaw trembling, Howards muttered something unintelligible and then froze entirely. The basilisk himself turned to stone? Bennie Howards with an attack of conscience? Barron wondered. More likely something he ate. Well, it's an ill wind, he thought as the promptboard flashed '90 seconds.'

"What's the matter, Mr Howards," Barron asked, "can't you identify with the situation? Okay, Mrs Pulaski, let's give Mr Howards some help. Please turn the camera of your vidphone on your father and hold it there."

Vince's right on the ball, Barron thought as Vince blew up Dolores Pulaski's small inset to virtually fill the entire monitor screen as the image danced fragments of walls, vase, ceiling, then became a huge close-up black and white newspaper photo-image of the wasted old man's face, a long rubber tube trailing from one nostril and taped to his forehead; the grey deathbed photo tilted at a crazy home-videotape angle, and made the closed blind eyes of Harold Lopat seem to stare down at the image of Benedict Howards in the lower left-quadrant like an avenging ghost of death looking down at a scuttling insect after kicking over a wet rock, as the promptboard flashed '60 seconds.'

And Jack Barron, in a once-in-a-blue-moon off-camera spectral-voice gambit, etched Howards' face into a mask of terror and fury with precise scalpel-words: "Look, Howards, you're looking at death. That's not $500,000 on your balance sheet, that's a human being, and he's dying. Go ahead, look at that face, look at the pain, look at the disease eating it up behind the mask. Only it's not a mask, Howards, it's a human being—a human life in the process of being snuffed out forever. We all come down to that in the end, don't we, Mr Howards? You, and me, and Harold Lopat, all of us, sooner or later, fighting for just another breath, another moment of life before the Big Nothing closes in. And there, but for $500,000, go you or I. What's so holy about five hundred grand that it buys a man's life? How much is $500,000 in pieces of silver, Mr Howards? A thousand? Two thousand? Once a man's life was sold for thirty pieces of silver, Mr Howards, just *thirty*, and *he* was Jesus Christ. How many lives you got in your Freezers worth more than His? You think any man's life is worth more money than was the life of Jesus Christ?"

And Gelardi filled the screen with the face of Benedict Howards, ghost-white in an extreme close-up that showed every razor nick, every pimple, network of coarse open pores, the eyes of a maddened trapped carnivore as Jack Barron's voice said, "And maybe we'll have some answers from Benedict Howards after this word from our sponsor."

Jesus H himself on a bicycle! Barron thought gleefully as they rolled the commercial. Days like this, I scare *myself!*

"Oooh, does *he* want to talk to *you!*" Vince Gelardi's voice said over the intercom circuit the moment the commercial was rolling. "Sounds like he's down with hydrophobia." Barron saw Gelardi grin, give him the highsign, start the count with '90 seconds' on the promptboard as Benedict Howard's face appeared on the tiny number two vidphone screen and his voice came on in the middle of a tirade:

"...to the fucking fishes! No one plays games like *that* with Benedict Howards. You lay off me, you crazy bastard, or I'll have you off the air and in jail for libel before—"

"Fuck off, Howards!" Barron said. "And before you shoot your big mouth off again, just remember that this call goes through the control booth, it's not a private line. (He shot Howards a cool-it, we're-still-fencing, don't-spill-the-beans look) You know where all this is at, and you've got about sixty seconds before we go on the air again to give me a reason to lay off—and I *don't* mean a lot of dumb threats. I don't like threats. Tell you just what's gonna happen in the next segment. I'm gonna tear you to pieces, is all, but I'm gonna leave just enough left so you can throw in the towel during the next commercial and save what's left of your ass. Unless you wanna be smart, meet my terms *now*—and we both know what those terms are."

"Don't threaten me, you goddamned clown!" Howards roared. "You lay off, or I'll just hang up, and when I get through with you, you won't be able to get a job cleaning cesspools in—"

"Go ahead, hang up," Barron said as the promptboard flashed '30 seconds.' "I've got five calls just like the first one—only seedier—lined up to fill the rest of the show. I don't need you on the air to do you in. One way or the other you're gonna learn it doesn't pay to screw around with me, 'cause unless you come around by the next commercial your Freezer Bill has had it, and your whole fucking Foundation will stink so bad you'll think Judas Iscariot was your press agent. How's that grab you, bigshot?"

"You filthy fuck—" And Gelardi cut Howards off just in time as the promptboard flashed 'On the Air'.

Jack Barron grinned at his own image filling the monitor—flesh-eyes digging phosphor-dot-eyes in adrenaline-feedback reaction—and he felt a strange light-headed exhilaration, a psychic erection. More than anticipation of the coming catbird-seat five-aces-in-the-hole poker game for the bit chips with Howards blood humming behind his ears, Barron felt the primal sap rising, the hot beserker joy ghost of Berkeley Baby Bolshevik jugular thrill of the hunt, amplified by electronic satellite network hundred million Brackett Count living-colour image-power shooting sparks out of his phosphor-dot eyes, and for the first time felt himself giving the show over to the gyroscope of his endocrine system and didn't know what would happen next. And didn't care.

Gelardi gave Howards a lower left-quadrant inquisition dock inset— Dolores Pulaski having finished her schtick—as Barron said: "Okay, we're back on the air, Mr Howards, and we're gonna talk about your favourite subject for a change. Let's talk about money. How many... er, clients you figure you got in your Freezers?"

"There are over a million people already in Foundation Freezers," Howards answered (and Barron could sense him fighting for purchase, trying to anticipate the line of the jugular thrust he knew was coming). "So you see, Freezing is not really just for the few at all. A million human beings with hope for eternal life someday is quite a large—"

"You ain't just whistling Dixie," Barron interrupted. "A million's a nice round number. Let's continue with our little arithmetic lesson, shall we? How much would you say it costs to maintain one body in a cryogenic Freezer for one year?"

"It's impossible to come up with an average figure just like that," said Howards. "You've got to figure in the cost of preparation for Freezing, the cost of the Freezing itself, amortisation on the Freezer facilities, the cost of replacing evaporated coolant, power to run the pumps, salaries, taxes, insurance..."

"Yeah, we know you run a real complicated show," Barron replied. "But let's take a generous average figure no one can say is stingy..." Lay the trap right, he thought. True figure can't be more than thirty thou per stiff per year, and he's gotta know it, so give him more than enough rope... "Let's say $50,000 will cover it, fifty thou per client per year. Sound reasonable?—or am I way too high? I don't have much of a head for business, as my accountant keeps telling me every year around April fifteenth."

"I suppose that's about right," Howards admitted grudgingly, and Barron could see the fear showing through his eyes. (Scared shitless, eh, Bennie? 'cause you don't see where all this is going, 'cause you know there's something happening and you don't know what it is, do you Mr Jones?) "And in order to be Frozen, you've gotta sign over a minimum of $500,000 in liquid assets to the Foundation in order to cover costs, right?"

"We've gone through all that," Howards muttered, obviously uncertain as to what was going to happen next.

"All rightie..." Barron drawled, foot-signalling to Vince to kill Howards' audio. He stared straight into the camera, tilted his head forward, picking up darkness-shadows reflected off the desk-arm of the chair from the kinesthop background in the hollows of his dead-end-kid innocent eyes, gave a little bemused inside-joke grin. "Okay, out there, we've got the figures, now let's all do a little arithmetic. Check me, out there, will you? I've got a lousy head for figures—at least the *numerical* kind. Lessee... multiply how many bodies in the Freezers by $500,000 per body... That comes to... ah... ten zeros and... why, that's five hundred billion dollars, isn't that right folks? Foundation's got at least five hundred billion bucks in assets. Now *there's* cigarette money! About half the defence budget of the United States, is all. Okay, students, now one more problem in multiplication—$50,000 for each body for a year times a million bodies in the freezers... in nice round numbers it comes to... *fifty billion dollars*. Now, let's see—if I had five hundred billion bucks to play around with I ought to be able to make—oh, say ten per cent a year on it. Couldn't you, out there?—and wouldn't you like to try? That comes to... why, it's about fifty billion dollars, isn't it? What a coincidence! Same as Foundation expenses—one tenth, count it folks, ten per cent of the Foundation's total assets. Boy, numbers are fun!"

Visualising the path to the punchline, Barron signalled Gelardi to give him a two-minute count to the next commercial and to cut in Howards' audio.

"What the hell is this?" Howards snapped. "Who do you think you are, the Internal Revenue Service?"

"Patience, Mr Howards, patience," Barron drawled with purposefully irritating slowness. "Jack Barron, great swami-knows all, sees all, tells all. Now let's try some simple subtraction. Subtract fifty billion in expenses from fifty billion a year in interest on your assets. That leaves a big fat zero, doesn't it? That's exactly how much maintaining those million bodies in the freezers cuts into that five hundred billion bucks in assets you got squirreled away—*zero!* Not at all. How neat! And that's how you hold on to your non-profit, tax-exempt status, isn't it? Expenses balance income. And that $500,000 each client chucks in—why, that's not nasty old income at all, is it? Technically it's not even yours, and that keeps the Income Tax boys' hot little hands out of your till. Boy, I'd like to borrow your accountant!"

"What're you gibbering about?" Howards said, with a totally unconvincing show of incomprehension.

"I'm gibbering about the small matter of five hundred billion dollars," Barron told him as the promptboard flashed '60 seconds.' "Five hundred billion dollars free and clear that you've got to play around with *above* Freezer expenses, a five-hundred-billion dollar slush fund. Who do you think you're putting on, Howards? That's enough bread to provide a free Freeze for every man, woman, and child who dies every year in the United States, and in Canada too, for that matter, *isn't it?* Five hundred billion bucks sitting there, while Harold Lopat and millions like him die and are gone forever while you poormouth us! What *does* happen to that five hundred billion, Howards? You must have mighty big holes in your pockets or else—"

"Research!" Howards croaked frantically. "Without research—"

Gelardi, anticipating even as Barron foot-signalled, flashed '30 seconds' on the promptboard and cut his audio off.

"Research!" Barron mimicked, his image now filling the entire monitor screen, a mask of righteous indignation scowling into Brackett Audience Count estimated hundred million pairs of eyes.

"Yeah, sure, *research*, but research in *what?* Research in how to buy votes in Congress to get this cosy little set-up written into law? Research into how to own Governors and Senators and... who knows, maybe your very own Presidential candidate? I don't like to speak ill of the dead—the conveniently *permanent* dead—but you were awfully tight with a certain late Senator who was putting on a rather well-financed campaign for the Democratic Presidential nomination, weren't you? That come under 'research' too? Five hundred billion bucks worth of *research*—with people like Harold Lopat dying all around you every day. Research. Yeah, let's talk about research! And we'll have plenty of time to discuss five hundred billion dollars worth of scientific—or is it *political*—research after this word from our relatively impoverished sponsor."

As they rolled the final commercial Barron felt a weird manic exhilaration, knowing that he had set up a focus of forces which in the next few minutes could squash the five-hundred-billion-dollar Foundation for Human Immortality like a bug if Bennie proved dumb enough to not holler 'Uncle.' Five hundred billion bucks! Never added it up before, Barron thought. What the fuck *is* he really doing with all that bread? Shit, he could buy the Congress, the President, and the Supreme Court out of petty cash, if it came down to it. Talk about big-league action! Bennie Howards is bigger than the whole fucking country!

Yeah, but right here right now no time-delay live, he's nothing but a punk I can dribble like a basketball. And what's that make me? Luke and Morris maybe not as crazy as they sound...?

He made the connection on the number two vidphone and Howards, his eyes now reptile-cold gimlets, stared up at him from the oh-so-tiny vidphone screen like a bug trapped in amber.

"All right, Barron," Howards said in a dead-flat, money-talk voice, "you've made your point. We've been playing your game, and we both know I'm no match for you at it. You, hurt me, and you hurt me bad. Maybe you can do more damage to me than I thought possible, but I warn you, you play ball and get me out of this mess or I'll *really* finish you and quick. And don't con me, you know damn well I can do it. You keep this up, and you'll find out just how much muscle five hundred billion dollars is—I'll use every penny of it, if I have to, to pound you to a pulp. You'll lose more than your show, I can have your tax returns for the last ten years investigated, sue you for libel and buy the judge, and that's just off the top of my head. Play ball, remember what you've got to lose—*and what you've got to gain.*"

And it brought Barron down like a bucket of ice water smack in the face. Sure, I can finish the hatchet-job, he thought, but good-bye *Bug Jack Barron,* and good-bye free Freeze, and Christ knows what else the bastard can do to me—kamikaze's the name of that game. An old Dylan lyric ran through his head:

> *"I wish I could give Brother Bill his big thrill;*
> *I would tie him in chains at the top of the hill,*
> *Then send out for some pillars and Cecil B De Mille..."*

Yeah, I can do him in and he can do me in if we both want to do that Samson schtick. Bluff's the name of the *real* game.

And the promptboard told him he had sixty seconds to play his hand.

"Look Howards," he said, "we can do each other in, or play ball and cool it. *Your* choice, Bennie-baby. You know what I want, the straight poop plus that *other thing.* I don't change my mind—matter of principle. So maybe I'm bluffing, so call me on it, I dare you. But before you do, ask yourself what you've got to gain by calling me that's worth the risk of losing what *you've* got to lose. I'm a dangerous lunatic, Howards, I'm not afraid of you. You *that* sure you're not afraid of me?"

Howards was silent for a long moment, bit his lip, then said, "All right, you win. It's all negotiable. You get me out of this, and we'll talk turkey on your terms. Good enough?"

The promptboard flashed '30 seconds' for instant decision on the course of the rest of the show and all that was riding on it. As close to 'Uncle' as you'll hear from Bennie, Barron knew. He'll say anything now to get off the hook, thinks he can maybe welch later, those five-hundred-billion-bucks Foundation aces, but he doesn't know all the ace I got—Luke and Morris' fun and games up my sleeve, enough to bluff him out for good, comes nitty-gritty time, no matter what he's holding. So okay Bennie, you get off the hook or anyway I don't give the *descabello,* leave your bod bleeding but alive.

"All right, Howards, things don't get any worse tonight, but don't expect to make any big points in the next ten minutes either. All I'm gonna do is make things kinda fuzzy in all those heads out there."

"But you've got me backed into a corner," Howards whined. "How you gonna get me out of this with a whole skin?"

"That's my line of evil, Bennie," Barron said. He flashed Howards an ironic man-in-control smirk. "What's the matter, Bennie, don't you trust me?"

And the promptboard flashed 'On the Air,' and Gelardi gave Howards the same lower left-quadrant inquisition seat as before.

"Now what were we talking about?" Barron said. (Gotta back off real gradual-like, and not too far.) "Ah, yes, *research.* Five hundred billion dollars worth of research. Since by some fancy slight of hand the Foundation is tax-exempt, I think that the American people have a right to know just what kind of... research that money is being spent on. Now, we can always check this with the tax boys, Mr Howards, so let's have the straight poop—just what *is* your annual research budget?"

"Somewhere between thirty and forty billion dollars," Howards said. Barron foot-signalled Gelardi to give him a half-screen, ease him out of the hotseat.

"That's a far cry from five hundred billion dollars, isn't it?" Barron said, but with the cutting edge eased out of his voice (come on schmuck, he telepathed, pick up on it, don't expect me to make your points for you). "What's the story on that five hundred billion?"

Howards seemed to relax a bit, catching on that the lead was being passed over to him. "You've been tossing that figure around pretty freely," he said, "but you obviously don't understand what it represents. If you'd studied a Freeze Contract you'd know that the $500,000 per client is *not* a fee turned over free and clear to the Foundation. Upon clinical death, the total assets of the client go into a *trust-fund* administered by the Foundation for as long as the client is biologically and legally dead. But on revival all assets originally placed in the trust fund revert to the client, and only the interest and capital appreciation during the time the client is in the Freezer actually become the property of the Foundation. So you see, that five hundred billion dollars is simply not ours to spend. It certainly is an enormous amount of money, but the fact is that we must maintain *all of it* as a reserve against the day when we can revive our clients and return it to them. The fund works essentially the way a bank works—a bank can't go around spending its deposits, and we can't spend that five hundred billion dollars. It's not really ours."

Can't make *me* look bad, Barron thought. Can't make it too easy; gotta back off slow. "But a chunk of capital that big grows awfully fast unless you're some kind of idiot or you're blowing it on the horses," he said. "And you've just admitted that all increases in the original capital *do* belong to the Foundation, so you've gotta have billions in assets that *are* yours free and clear. What about that?"

Howards pounced quickly. (Now he sees daylight! Barron thought.) "Quite true. But our expenses are enormous... something like fifty billion a year for maintenance, and that eats up all the interest on the original capital. So the forty billion for research must come from profits on the investment on our *own* capital. After all, if we started spending *capital* on research we'd quickly go bankrupt."

Suddenly, almost unwillingly, Barron realised that Howards had handed him a weapon that could make the rest of the show look like a love-pat. Shit, he thought, Bennie's got a vested interest in keeping all those quick-frozen stiffs dead! The day he can thaw 'em out and revive 'em he loses that five-hundred-billion-dollar trust fund. Hit him with *that* baby, and you'll stomp him into the ground! Why Cool it! Cool it! he reminded himself. You're supposed to be pulling the lox out of the hole, not digging it deeper!

"So it all comes down to *research*," Barron said, reluctantly leading away from the jugular. "Forty billion bucks is still one hell of a research budget, more than enough to hide… all kinds of interesting things. Suppose you explain what kind of research you're spending all that bread on?"

Howards shot him a dirty look.

Jeez, what you expect, Bennie? Barron thought. I still gotta look like kick-'em-in-the-ass Jack Barron, don't I?

"First off, you've got to understand that all those people in our Freezers are *dead*. Dead as anyone in a cemetery. All cryogenic freezing does is preserve the bodies from decay—those bodies are simply corpses. The problem of bringing a corpse back to life is enormous. I'm no scientist and neither are you, Barron, but you can imagine how much research and experimentation must be done before we can actually bring a dead man back to life—and it's all very expensive. And even then, cures must be developed for whatever killed the clients in the first place—and most of the time, it's old age. And that's the toughest nut of all to crack, a cure for ageing. I mean, so you revive a ninety-year-old client, but if you haven't licked ageing, he dies again almost immediately. See what we're up against? All this will cost billions a year for decades, maybe centuries. Man in my position's gotta take the long view, the real long view…" And for a moment, Howards' eyes seemed to be staring off into some unimaginable future.

And Barron got a flash: Could it be that the whole Freezer schtick's a shuck? Way to raise money for something else? Pie in the sky, in the great bye and bye? The whole Freezer Program's useless unless they lick ageing. (And how much is that free freeze *really* worth? Maybe I'm selling myself awful cheap …) But the way Bennie babbled in my office about living forever, *that* was no shuck, he was really zonked on it! Yeah, it all adds up he doesn't want to lick the revival problem 'cause that'd cost him that five hundred billion. But he's sure hot to live forever. Five'll get you ten the Foundation scientists are just pissing around with revival research, big bread's gotta be behind immortality research. And if *that* gets out, how many more suckers gonna spring for that five hundred thou? Bennie-baby, we gonna have a long long talk. Let's see if we can hit a little nerve, he thought, what they call an exploratory operation, as the promptboard flashed '3 minutes.'

"Someday all men will live forever through the Foundation for Human Immortality," said Barron.

"What?" Howards grunted, his eyes snapping back into sharp focus like a man called back from a trance.

"Just quoting a Foundation slogan," Barron said. "Isn't that where it's really at? I mean all that bread spent on Freezing is money down a rathole unless it really leads to immortality, right? Some old coot signs over five hundred thou so you can revive him a hundred years later so he can die again of old age in a year or two, that doesn't make much sense to me. The Freezer Program is a way to preserve a few people who die now so they can have immortality in the future, whenever you lick *that* one. I mean young cats like me, the country in general, main stake we've got in letting the Foundation do business is like that slogan of yours about *all* people living forever someday through the Foundation for Human Immortality, right? So either you're going hot-and-heavy on immortality research, or the whole thing's just a con. You follow me, Mr Howards?"

"Wh... wh... why, of course we are!" Howards stammered, and his eyes went reptile-uptight cold. "It's called 'The Foundation for Human Immortality,' not 'the Freezing Foundation,' after all. Immortality is our goal and we're spending billions on it, and in fact..."

Howards hesitated as the promptboard flashed '2 minutes.' That hit a nerve, all right, Barron thought, but *which* nerve? Seemed like he was on the edge of blowing something he didn't want to... 120 seconds to try to find out what.

"Well, it seems to me," said Barron, "that with you having tax-exempt status and by your own admission spending billions on immortality research and some of that bread being indirectly public money, you owe the American people a progress report. Just how is all this expensive research going?"

Howards shot him a look of pure poison. Lay off! his eyes screamed.

"Foundation scientists are following many paths to immortality," Howards said slowly. (He must be watching the clock too, Barron realised.) "Some, of course, are more promising than others... Nevertheless, we feel that all possibilities should be explored..."

Barron tapped his left foot-button three times, and Vince gave him three-quarters of the screen, with Howards in the inquisition slot again, as the promptboard flashed '90 seconds.' "How about some specifics?" he asked. "Tell us what the most promising line of research seems to be, and how far along you are."

"I don't think it would be right to raise any false hopes this early," Howards said blandly, but Barron's teeth sensed something tense?—fearful?—threatening?—behind it. "Discussing specifics would be a mistake at this time..." But false hopes are your stock in trade, Barron thought. Why don't you want to give a nice sales spiel, Bennie...? Unless...

"You mean to tell me you've spent all those billions and you're right back where you started?" Barron snapped in a tone of cynical disbelief. "That can only mean one of two things: the so-called scientists you've got working for you are all quacks or idiots, or... or the money you've got budgeted for immortality research is going for something else—like pushing your Freezer Bill through Congress, like backing political campaigns..."

"That's a lie!" Howards shrieked, and suddenly he seemed back in that strange trance state. "You don't know what you're talking about! (The promptboard flashed '30 seconds.') Progress *is* being made. More progress than anyone drea—" Howards shuddered, as if he had suddenly found himself blowing his cool, caught himself short.

Barron foot-signalled Gelardi to give him the full screen wind-up. Something's going on here, he thought. Something bigger than... bigger than...? Anyway, too big to thrash out on the air. Good timing, as usual.

"Well that's about it, folks," he said, "we're out of time. Been quite an hour, eh? And if this whole thing's still bugging you, then next Wednesday night you just pick up that vidphone and dial Area Code 212, 969-6969, and we'll be off to the races again with another hour of *Bug Jack Barron.*"

And they were rolling the wrap-up commercial, and he was off the air.

"He wants to—"

"No!" Jack Barron said even as Gelardi's voice spoke over the intercom circuit. "I don't talk to Howards now for no reasons under no conditions."

Gelardi made hair-pulling motions behind the glass wall of the control booth. "I've never heard any of your victims this pissed," he said. "You've gotta get this fruitcake off the line before he melts every circuit in the joint. Such language!"

Barron felt the old talked-out satisfying fatigue come over him as he got up out of the hotseat and thought, as usual, about going somewhere and picking up a chick and fucking her brains—and then, like a new burst of energy, he remembered. Them days is gone forever! Home to Sara, and Sara there! Changes, changes, and good ones for a change *this* time round.

"Come on, Jack, for chrissakes, cool Howards already!" Gelardi whined.

Who the fuck wants him cooled? Barron thought. Something happened during those last few minutes, I hit something real tender, and he almost spilled some mighty important beans—and not because he kept his cool. Let him stew a while. I want him hot and raving when we get down to nitty-gritty—and no witnesses, Vince, baby.

"Give him my home phone number," Barron said. "If that doesn't cool him, tell him to fuck off. In fact why don't you give him my number and tell him to fuck off anyway? Tell him... tell him Mohammed can damn well come to the mountain."

"But man, all we need is Howards.—"

"Let me do the worrying, Vince. Boy Wonder Jack Barron's still in the catbird-seat."

As vip Bennie Howards will soon find out.

9

JACK... JACK, maybe I never understood, Sara Westerfeld thought as she stood on the breakfast deck overlooking the penthouse living room, listening to the May shower rattle against the skylight facets and to the faint hum of the elevator rising to the entrance foyer. How long's it been like *this*, she wondered. This sure wasn't what he was doing with *Bug Jack Barron* when he threw me out... or when I left him. Maybe he's been right all along, maybe I *did* leave him by copping-out, refusing to dig where his head was really at?

As she heard the elevator door open, his footsteps down the hall, the pressure of his being moving like a shock wave down the narrow passage impinging on unknown kinaesthetic senses, Sara felt on the edge of a new-style awareness of man-woman contrast that cut far deeper than what was revealed when pants came down.

Power's a man's bag, she realised. Any chick that digs power, really feels where it's at, almost always turns out to be some kind of dyke in the end. Power's somehow cock-connected; woman's hung-up on power, she's hung-up on not having a cock, understands power only if she's thinking like someone who does. Power's even got its own man-style time-sense: man can wait, scheme, plan years-ahead-guile-waiting games, accumulate power on the sly, then use it for good—if the man's good deep inside like Jack—like a good fuck good cat can bring a frigid chick along, cooling himself, holding back when he has to, until he's finally got her ready to come. Man kind of love, man kind of delayed-timing thinking, calculated quanta of emotion and only when the time's right, and not like woman, needs to feel everything totally the moment it happens—good, evil, love, hate, prick inside her. Like a man digs fucking a woman, woman digs *being* fucked. Is that all that came between us, Jack? Me thinking like an always-now woman, you thinking future time manthoughts?

And then he was standing before her, wet curls framing eyes glistening with afterglow-fatigue of a hundred remembered battles in Berkeley, Los Angeles, now at last *New York*, the lines in his face like time-lines from past dreams to present-planned reality, mosaic of love in four-dimensional space-time man-flesh, she saw the boy still living behind the face of the man, saw in memory's eye the man that had grown behind the soft-flesh shining armour of the boy she had tasted in action-swirling streets and bedrooms, loved the boy and his dream, and the man and his past, and the JACK BARRON (in flaming capital letters) of past-present-future mortal lovers-against-the-night combats oh, this is a man!

She kissed him quick but deep with her tongue; bubbling over, she pulled away from his mouth, still in an arm-on-shoulders mutual embrace, said: "Jack, Jack I watched you on television, I mean *really* watched you, *really* saw for the very first time what you were doing. You were magnificent, you were everything I always knew you would be the first day I met you in Berkeley, but better—better than anything I could've imagined—because then I was a girl, and you were a boy, and today you were a man, and I... Well, maybe at the advanced age of thirty-five I'm leaving adolescence and I'm ready to try loving you the way a *woman* should love a man."

"That's... uh... groovy," he said, and now she thrilled even at the way he was preoccupied, the old Berkeley distant focus preoccupation, thinking through her, above her, warm exciting man-thoughts enveloping her in him were the moments she had always loved him most.

"Groovy, and I dig what you're saying—I mean about us. But the show... look, Sara, there are things I've got to tell you. I mean, don't think I'm back in the silly old Baby Bolshevik bag. I suppose it looked that way to a lot of people, and there were moments when I... but I don't do things without a reason, and there are things going on that—"

"I know, Jack," she said. "You don't even have to tell me. It stands out all over you. You're involved in something big, something important, the kind of thing you were always meant to do. Something real like you used to—"

"It's not what you think, not what anyone thinks," he muttered, brows furrowed at some hidden contrapuntal train of thought. "I don't even know the whole story myself. But I feel something, can smell it... something so big, so... I'm afraid to even think about it until I—"

The vidphone chime interrupted. "Already...?" Jack muttered, and he bolted down the stairs, across the carpet to the wall consoles, made the vidphone connection, and sprawled on the floor, as she followed a few steps behind.

"What's shaking with you, Rastus?" he was saying as she sat down beside him, saw that the face on the vidphone screen was good old Luke Greene, and remembered good days screwing around with Luke before she met Jack.

"Never mind me, Huey," Luke said. "What's shaking with you, lot of people are asking?"

Jack picked up the vidphone, pointed the camera at Sara. "Hello, Luke," she said, "it's been a long time."

He smiled back at her, long-gone no-hang-ups ancient-history-lover pure friendship smile. "Well hello Sara," he said "you and Jack...?"

"You know it, Kingfish," Jack said, turning the vidphone camera back on himself. "We're back together, and this time it's for keeps."

The thrill of being owned by her fated man went through Sara as he goosed her off-camera.

"Well, congratulations, mah chillun," Luke said. "Sara, maybe you can keep this schmuck off the streets, give him some of dat ole time religion, good for old Jack Barron, and good for the SJC."

Sara saw a flicker of annoyance cross Jack's face, wondered why as Jack said, "I get the ugly feeling that that plug for Baby Bolsheviks, Inc. is what the nitty-gritty of this call's about, Luke. Or are you just using the tax money of the good people of Mississippi to make long-distance vidphone calls strictly for kicks? What's going on in that twisted excuse for a mind of yours?"

"It's *your* head that seems to be going through changes," said Luke. "You're back with Sara... and after tonight it looks mighty like you're back with us. Welcome back to the human race, Jack."

"Uh... what race you say that was?" Jack said archly. "Rat race, you say, Lothar? Race from nowhere straight to oblivion? Race, shit—you don't even catch me near that *track*."

"Cut the crap, you shade mother you," Luke said, "you're not bullshitting with Bennie Howards now. You got the bug, Claude, knew you would. Could taste it, couldn't you, and when you got on the air with Bennie, you just couldn't help it... Well, you made your point, Jack. You made it with me, and with a whole lot of others, including those fat-cat Republican dinosaurs."

"What in hell are you babbling about?" Jack asked and Sara sensed he meant it, was as confused about what Luke was saying as she was about Jack, and wondered if he too felt the shadow of something big and important about to come on.

"I'm talking about the show you just did, what else?" Luke said. "I never saw any vip *that* cut up; Bennie must be leaving a trail of blood from here to his digs in Colorado. Shit, man, you *know* what I'm talking about, you said it all, and you said it perfect. Something for everyone. Morris flipped over the economic angle; it's a tie-in to their whole damn Adam Smith Platform—fat cats who want a piece of the Freezer action for themselves are ready to shell out big. Oh, man, like I always say, a man that's got the instinct for politics just can't shake it! You let Bennie off a little too easy at the end maybe, but you know, I begin to think that was the right come-on too. Like Morris says, we gotta develop your position slow and easy before you come out into the open next year."

"In words of one syllable for us ignorant shades, please," Sara heard Jack say, still feigning confusion. But, you *are* faking it now, aren't you, Jack? she thought. Putting on *Luke*... Wow, what's going on? And she felt as she did when she was eleven, peeking in between wooden shack slats and watching naked boy-flesh shapes doing exciting dirty-little-boy things. Like the old Jack in bed beside her, talking big-world phone-talk over her quiet listening-flesh with Luke, and how good, oh how good to be Sara *Barron* again, watching my man doing his man-things.

"How's *yes* for a word of one syllable?" Luke said. "I just got off the phone with Morris, and, baby, the word is *yes*. You pulled it off, you made up all the points with the Republican vips you lost by bad-mouthing Morris. After the way you stomped Howards tonight—and they loved the way you linked him with Hennering—they are like hot for your living-colour bod. You know what a tight little cabal that bunch is, so when Greg Morris says he can personally guarantee you the nomination if I can deliver the SJC, you *know* that means that all their vips have spoken. And with that word in old Luke's hip pocket, don't you worry, we're home free with the SJC Council.

"You know what this means, Clive? You dig? We're gonna do it! We're really gonna do it, not another Berkeley pipe dream, not a little piece of the action like I have here, but the whole schmear, Jack, *all* the way, an SJC National Administration, just like you told us in that dirty old attic. It took one hell of a long time for you to remember who you were, but, Claude, it was worth the wait 'cause when you returned to the fold, prodigal baby, you brought more than the bacon back, you brought the whole fucking hog."

"For chrissakes, Jack, tell me!" Sara said excitedly. "What's this all about?"

Jack grimaced, handed her the vidphone. "Go ahead, Machiavelli," he said with a peculiar weariness. "You do it, at least you'll be able to keep a straight face. Tell the little lady what it's all about."

"You mean you haven't told...?" Luke said incredulously. "Sara, us movers and shapers gonna make this cretin you're balling the next President of the United States, is all."

Jack snatched back the vidphone before she could answer, before she could do anything but gape at him as if he were some mystical avatar suddenly revealed in his full glory by a flash of psychedelic light. Yes! Yes! she thought, where in the world is there a bigger man than Jack, and who can stand against him if he stands naked, the whole total Berkeley-knight-in-soft-flesh-armour JACK BARRON in front of those hundred million people? They've *got* to want him; all he's gotta do is show the world *Jack*.

"I got a one-syllable word for you too, Luke, and it's even shorter," Jack said. "The word is *no*. If nominated, I shall not run, if elected, I shall not serve, and all that Sherman jazz. Okay, let's say you can get me a Republican and SJC nomination. Let's say the Pretender gets himself killed, like Hennering, and I end up running against some obvious Howards stooge and everyone is stoned on Election Day, so I win. What then? I don't know shit from shinola about being President and what's more I've got no eyes to learn. It's just *not* my bag."

"No sweat," Luke said smoothly. "You'll have plenty of political geniuses like yours truly to run things for—"

"Look Svengali, I'm nobody's front-man, not even yours, and I never will be, and don't you forget it! Think I'm so stupid I don't know where it's at? You and Morris want an image-candidate, an Eisenhower, a Reagan, a fucking-mindless-celebrity mouthpiece, is all, someone you can package and sell like soap. And the answer is *no*. You so buddy-buddy with Morris, why don't you run yourself?"

"This is a *vidphone*, isn't it?" Luke said bitterly. "Take a good look at the colour of my face and say that again, *shade*."

"Sorry, Luke, I'm *really* sorry," Jack said with that instant belly-radar reflex-reaction that always seemed to tell him when he had drawn blood, intentional or otherwise, with that inner vulnerable little-boy empathy Sara had always loved behind the kick-'em-in-the-ass exterior, drawing immediately back.

"You know me, man," Jack said earnestly. "I really don't notice your colour until it smacks me in the face. I'm not giving you some bullshit come-on. Anyway, I really meant it—you're the man should be President, not me. It's your bag, not mine. You've worked all these years in that direction even though you knew... *what you were up against*, and I've been off in an entirely different bag, the show biz scene... Which is yet another good reason for my saying no. Who am I to waltz onto your turf and make like top dog? You try and get yourself a phone-in show, and I'll be out to stomp you dead. Let's be friends, but let's each of us stick to his own line of evil."

Sara caught a glimpse of poor wounded Luke (hung up over it even in Berkeley days, she thought. Number one type cat always number two, being black and too hip not to know it was where it would always be at), smiling it away (how brave to be black and still be a man she remembered how contained, hard-edged he had been, even in bed), and saying real cool like Luke-cool:

"You know you're right, Clyde. I always knowed I was a better man than you, never thought you'd finally up and admit it. (And Sara, through body-remembered senses knew the triple-level—reality-put-on-reality—of Luke's sarcasm). But the hard fact is that you can do it and I can't, because you're a shade and I'm a nigger—it's as simple as that, and I don't hold it against *you*. But that's why I have to do it through you, why we all have to do it through you. What's the SJC but a collection of coons, Flower People, Baby Bolsheviks, and just plain losers, think I kid myself? You're the only big-league shade we got going, only cat that can ring in that Republican bread and support. You could be a fucking chimpanzee and we'd have to go with—'cause you're the only ape can win."

Sara felt a pang of the old remembered thing for Luke with the balls to say the truth and the brains to say it right, and though anyone paled beside Jack, for her, she felt a warm snug satisfaction at the memory of how once she had been able to give Lukas Greene some small balm for that ever-open black wound.

"Sorry Luke," Jack said. "The answer's still no. And you can tell Morris to forget it too. There's no point in even thinking about it any more. N.O. No!"

"Okay, B'rer Rabbit, I won't throw you into the briar patch," said Luke. "Not today. But I'm telling you right now, I'm gonna stall Morris as long as I can till I can get you to change your mind."

"You won't," Jack said flatly.

"Sara," Luke said, "you tell this prick where it's at. Maybe you can get in through that concrete skull of his. I'm tired, chillun, gonna go lynch me a brace of rednecks or something, y'know, relax. You listen to that chick of yours, Jack. She knows you better than you know yourself, knows the best part of you part you still seem to be strangers to. Listen to her, will you, stupid? Later."

And he broke the connection, and Jack put away the vidphone, and they were staring at each other the old contest of silence game; who would yell first?

"Jack I—"

"Do I have to hear it from you too, Sara? Does everyone have to tell me what a fucking cop-out I am? Goddamned broken record! You and Luke… you think Luke *really* knows what's coming off? You so sure you do?"

"But, Jack, *President* …" The word was an enormity in her mouth, choking off the impossible thoughts of what it implied.

"President, horseshit! A fucking pipe dream! You saw the show. Howards got a five-hundred-billion-dollar slush fund, and whether he can legally spend it or not the muscle's still there. Bennie Howards is gonna pick the next President, and you better believe it. I let them talk me into that crap, and I have the privilege of losing—not only the Presidency, but the show too… and maybe a whole lot more. For what, a chance to shoot my mouth off? They *pay* me to do that every week as it is."

"But, Jack (Can't he see himself as I see him?), you *could* do it. You're—"

"It's groovy to know your chick thinks you're a little tin god. That, and fifty thousand bucks'll pay the rent for a month on this pad. What'll we do if I blow everything by kamikazeing into Howards, open a cat-house, with you as door prize?"

"But—"

Again the vidphone chime interrupted. "If this is Morris, I'm gonna tell him to go—"

She saw his face change abruptly to a mask of cold calculation, and a cold chill came over her as she looked at the vidphone screen over his shoulder and found herself staring at the grey lizardman deathmask, fear-mask of life-and-death power of the man who had brought them together again for reasons of his own, the terrible windowless white face of Benedict Howards.

"You imbecile! You double-crossing smart ass—" Howards was screaming; Sara could feel hot-leather reptile-stench emotions of fear, rage, hate, carrion teeth all but reaching out of the screen, windowless white teeth around a forked rattlesnake tongue spitting venom at Jack's throat. The sight of a man of such hideous power, a man who held the secret that could destroy her, destroy Jack and Sara *Barron* again and forever, in such a black mindless rage, terrified her and she felt like a bird before a cobra indeed.

But the moment Jack spoke, the spell was broken. "Look Bennie," he said in what Sara recognised as his put-on lazy-indifferent style, calculated to infuriate and intimidate those with actual power by an illusion of cooler-than-thou calm, "I've had a rough day and I'm in no mood to listen to you gibber. This is an unlisted number for obvious reasons, and I didn't let Vince give it to you so you could scream at me like a red-assed baboon with bleeding piles. You got something to say to me, you take a deep breath, count to ten, light up an Acapulco Gold, and come on real cool-like, or I'm gonna hang right up on you and put my vidphone on 'reject,' dig?"

And in the long moment of silence that followed Sara felt the weight of it heavy upon her. *Bennie?* Jack called him *Bennie!* Double-cross? Howards had said 'double-cross'! She sensed the electric conflict of wills humming in the silence between Jack and Benedict Howards across the vidphone circuit; sensed that silence operating on multiple levels of power-guile combat; could read from the tiny image of Howards—reptile rage seeming to contract in on itself into a patchwork facade of iron-control—that Jack was somehow the stronger, and that both of them knew it.

"All right, Barron," Howards finally said in a voice like steel, "I'll assume that I'm talking to a rational human being and not a raving lunatic. A rational human being should know what happens when you double-cross Benedict Howards. I thought we had reached an understanding. You were going to get me off the hook, and then you turn around and—"

"Hey, what's all this double-cross scam?" Jack said (And Sara sensed *this* was no put-on. But what's going on between Jack and Howards?). "I wasn't gonna get you off anything. I just wasn't gonna ram the knife home in the last segment, way I could've. I gave you the chance to talk about research and make points, didn't I? Not my fault if you're not a pro like me. I gave you the perfect lead-in to tell the world how great your immortality research is going, and you blew your big chance to make good in show biz. Come to think of it, you acted pretty funny—almost as if you had something to hide…"

"Never mind all that," Howards said coldly. "We've got some business to transact, remember? You've already cost me Christ knows how many votes in Congress with this last disaster, and it's about time—"

"Not on the phone," Jack broke in. "My office. Two o'clock tomorrow."

"Look, Barron, you've mickeymoused me long enough. No one plays games with Benedict How—"

Jack laughed what Sara recognised as a calculated laugh. "If you insist, Bennie. Of course I better tell you I'm not alone." Jack stared at her; she could sense worlds behind those eyes, alien worlds of guile and power, Jack-Howards clandestine-combat worlds. And with a pang of fear she wondered if Jack saw the worlds behind *her* eyes—Howards working on her, twisting her, sending her to him for reasons of his own, (Was that the business they were talking about? Sell-out to Benedict Howards? Am I just a piece of lizardman sure-thing insurance?) and her own plan within Howards' plan...

"What?" Howards shouted. "Are you crazy? You want to screw us both? Who—"

"Relax, Bennie," Jack said. "Just my once-and-future wife, Sara... Sara Westerfeld née Barron née Westerfeld. You don't keep secrets from your chick for very long." He laughed falsely. "Not as long as your chick can keep secrets from you anyway," he said.

Sara felt a moment of pure panic. Does Jack *know*? About me and Howards? Has the lizardman told him? Or will Howards tell him now, use me against Jack? Should I tell Jack everything now, is it time? Too soon! Too soon!

But Howards laughed a cold-reptile laugh she knew was for her, knew he was as good as reading her mind. "Far be it from me to interfere in your love life, Barron," Howards said, and Sara could feel daggers of sarcasm nibble at her as Howards toyed with her, reminded her of his power to destroy her through Jack—and Jack through her.

"Okay, tomorrow at your office. I'll fly tonight. And... and give my regards to Sara Westerfeld." And Howards broke the connection.

Jack turned to her, and she felt the hesitation in his eyes matched by her own. Building within her, she felt the tension of subterfuge, a bubble demanding to be burst. Tell him! Tell him everything! But... but is this the time? Will he play *our* game if...? Or will it be the end of everything that ever was between us forever? Forever, a huge word—and a bigger stake.

She decided that the decision would be Jack's, not hers. If he would tell her, tell her all, tell her that Howards was offering him a place in the Freezers, she would know he was as ready as he'd ever be, and she'd tell him what Howards really was, and together they'd destroy him...

"What was that all about?" she asked blandly, felt the moment, the shadow of his next words, hanging like a dagger above their lives, above all that had been, all that might be... forever.

Jack hesitated, and she felt the decision-turmoil behind his eyes too, but when he spoke, she felt the pregnant moment shoved aside, a trip to the dentist postponed, as she saw the shield go up behind his eyes, universes of danger sheering off from the mutual moment of mortal truth they both individually knew must soon come.

"I don't know yet," he said. "But tomorrow I'm going to find out. And… trust me till then, Sara. I just can't tell you now."

Deep within her, she sighed in relief, felt the pattern of lies, cop-outs, evasions as a kind of ironic bond between them. But she knew that that bond of falsehood would not last past tomorrow—that after Jack met with Howards there would either be truth between them… or nothing.

"Yessir, Mr Barron, no sir, Mr Barron, you stink, sir, Mr Barron," Jack Barron muttered toying with the pack of Acapulco Golds, a sardonic invitation amid the clutter of his desk, his day, his head. Goddamn Carrie, he thought. Could understand if she quit her job or got the network to transfer her, who could blame her? Not my fault, not hers. But, no, the bitch's gotta go on with the show, baby, sit out there with that yes, sir no, sir crap, and that big eat-shit-you-bastard office-smile. Still hung-up on me or just being a sadist…? Or maybe it's fun-and-games time, I gotta fire her before she passes 'go' or she don't collect two hundred dollars. Well, screw you, Carrie, you can stew in your own bile till your tushy's mushy before I play your game and can you.

Barron pawed out a cigarette, stuck it in his mouth, lit it, then played tease-games with the potsmoke, sucking it in to the back of his throat, dribbling it out without inhaling, wondering whether it would be smart to have the big showdown with Howards loaded.

The sweet smoke promised an out from the Lukes and Saras and Carries, all playing their dumb little games for dumb little stakes and expecting Jack Barron to lay his whole bod on the line to back their dumb little action.

But *something* held him back, and the fact that he could only sniff a faint aroma (like a week-dead codfish across the street) of that something *really* uptighted him. What's bigger than the Presidency of the United States? he wondered. What's bigger than five hundred billion dollars? What the fuck *could* be that big? *Something* is, I can smell it, feel it, like a junkie feels heat coming at him in a squad car fifty blocks away. Man, it's out there, whatever it is, else Bennie Howards is just plain flipped acting the way he is. And come to think of it, that might be interesting right there, with the cards I'm holding.

But he wondered if the cards he held were really as unbeatable as they looked, too damn good for the league I'm playing in, is Bennie really that bad? Am I really that good? Goddamn, Bennie knows something I don't, is what I'm playing this game for in the first place, and you know that whatever that something is it's the ace in the hole for somebody, and how the fuck can I know whose ace it is until I know *what* it is?

And whatever it is, baby, it's big, big enough to make Howards blow bubbles with his tongue when he had the opening to make points on the show I gave him; big enough to scare him shitless when he caught himself almost blowing it—and big enough to make him blow his cool in the first place, and with a reptile like Howards, *that* is like *big*.

Barron snubbed out the joint in an ashtray. No grass today, he told himself. Today Riverboat Jack's in the big game for the big pot, and you better be sure your head's all here when Bennie—

"*Mr* Barron, *Mr* Benedict Howards is here to see you," Carrie's tinny voice said, dry-icewise, over the intercom.

"Send Howards in, *Miss* Donaldson. Thank you, *Miss* Donaldson, go fuck yourself, *Miss* Donaldson," Barron said, the last without breaking rhythm but after he had snapped off the intercom.

As Howards half-stormed half-slunk in through the door, slamming a prop-attaché case stuffed no doubt with prop-documents down on the desk top and sitting down immediately without speaking like a Russian diplomat arriving at the umpteen-hundredth session of the Geneva Disarmament Conference, Barron felt a flash go through him as he looked at a Benedict Howards he had never seen before—a stone-seat-grim efficient Texas speculator, who had come from the Panhandle with holes in his pockets and who had fought and connived his way to the five-hundred-billion-dollar point where he held life versus death power over two hundred and thirty million people, would own the next President of the United States like a deaf Smith County judge. It was the big leagues, all right, and Barron knew it.

But Bennie knows it too, he thought as Howards stared at him like a stone basilisk, waiting for the man whose turf he was on to make the first move. Seeing Howards, Mr Big League Action himself looking at him with not anger, not quite fear in his eyes but cold and, for the first time shrewdly-calculating appraisal, Jack Barron dug the image of power mirroring genuine near-fear of the living-colour image of himself—and, in Howards' cold eyes granting him the ultimate compliment of emotionless scrutiny got a heady musk-whiff of his own power.

"All right, Howards," Barron said in a cold voice he saw caught Howards half off-balance, "no bullshit, no pyrotechnics. You're here to do business, I'm here to do business, and we both know it. Give. Make your pitch, and in words of one syllable."

Howards opened his attaché case, placed three copies of a contract on the desk. "There it is, Barron. A standard Freeze Contract, in triplicate, signed by me, the assets clause marked 'Assigned by Anonymous Donor' and made out to Jack Barron, effective immediately. That's what you throw away if you don't play ball, a Freeze, free and clear, and no-one can take it away from you."

"And of course, that 'anonymous donor' would reveal himself as Benedict

Howards, along with a copy of the contract to the press, if I sign it and then don't play ball," Barron said, feeling the calculus of power filling the air with the gold-stench of necromancy.

Howards smiled professionally. "I've got to have *some* insurance. All right, Barron, just sign on the dotted lines, and we can get down to the business of repairing the damage your big mouth has done to the Freezer Utility Bill."

"That wasn't the deal we made, and you know it," Barron told him. "You're not hiring a flunky, you're leasing my specific services as, shall we say, a public relations counsellor? That's freelance work, and it means I gotta know everything about the product I'm supposed to peddle. *Everything*, Howards. And, for openers, I gotta know exactly why *you're* so hot for my body."

"After last night, you ask me *that*?" Howards snarled. (But Barron saw that the snarl was calculated.) "Thanks to you, the Freezer Bill's in real trouble. I need that bill, which means I need votes in Congress, which means I need public pressure on *my* side, which means I need your pipeline to a hundred million votes, which means, unfortunately, that I need you. But don't misunderstand me, you say 'no' to me, then I need your scalp nailed to the barn door—and I'll get it. You're in too deep, Barron. You either play my game, or you don't play any game at all."

"You're lying," Barron said neutrally. "Your Freezer Bill was a shoo-in till I started making waves, and I didn't make waves till you started playing footsie with me. So it couldn't have been to save the Freezer Bill that you were after my ass in the first place. Had to be something else, something bigger, and I don't screw around with anything that big till I know exactly what it is."

"I've had enough of you!" Howards snapped and now Barron was sure he had finally pierced Bennie's cool. "You spend so much time trying to convince me how dangerous you are, all right, all right, I'm convinced. You know what that gets you? It gets you pounded to a pulp same as I'd smash a scorpion, unless you play ball. Scorpion's deadly, could kill me if I gave it a chance, but that doesn't mean that the moment I see it's really become dangerous I can't squash it like a bug. 'Cause it *is* a bug, and so are you."

"Don't threaten me," Barron said, half-calculatedly, half-responding to adrenaline-signals. "Don't give me the idea I've got my back to the wall. 'Cause if I get to having an itchy back, I'll do a show on the Foundation that'll make the last one seem like a Foundation commercial. And the next will be worse than that, and worse, and worse every week till you can get me off the air. And by then, Bennie, it'll be way too late."

"You're bluffing, Barron," said Howards. "You don't have the guts to blow your whole career just to get me. And you're not stupid enough either to throw yourself out in the cold, a ruined nobody, with no place to go."

Jack Barron smiled. Bennie, he thought, you've walked right into it. You're out of your league after all, bigshot, here comes them four aces in the hole. "Funny you should say that, Bennie," he drawled, "'cause the fact is I got all kind of people telling me there's someplace else I *ought* to go."

"*That* I can believe," Howards said dryly.

"Good to see you've still got a sense of humour, 'cause you're gonna need it. Because if you force me to blow the show by knifing the Foundation, it won't just be crazy revenge, y'know, I got people asking me to do just that, *powerful* people like Gregory Morris and Lukas Greene begging me to play *their* game, and do you in, and to hell with *Bug Jack Barron*. And they're offering me something bigger than anything you've laid on the table so far to do it, too." Barron said and waited for the straight line.

"You're bluffing again," said Howards, "and this time it's really obvious. What could anyone offer you that's bigger than a place in a Freezer, a chance at living forever?"

You're beautiful, Bennie, show biz all the way, Barron thought as he made with the tailor-made punchline:

"Would you believe the Presidency of the United States?"

"Would I believe *what*?" Howards goggled, seemed about to say something cute, then Barron sensed him backing off, putting one and one and one together in his head and getting only two and a half, not knowing how to react, whether it was a gag or pure bluff or some weird new equation of power. He sensed that Howards was waiting for him to speak—and sensed status-relationships in a state of uncertain flux.

"Well, would you believe a Presidential nomination?" Barron said, still not quite able to bring himself to use the whole silly schtick seriously. "You know how tight I've always been with the SJC, Founding Father and all that crap; well, when Luke Greene saw me dig my spurs into you he figured I could use the show to build myself up as The Hero of the People at your expense, and run for President on the SJC ticket next year. And without my giving him the go-ahead he nosed around, and now he tells me he really can deliver the Social Justice nomination." Hold the last ace for the showdown, he told himself. Let Bennie walk into it with his jaw.

"So *that's* what you mean by a Presidential nomination," Howards said, smiling easily. "The SJC nomination and a first-class plane ticket just *might* get you to Washington with a good tailwind, and you know it. I don't get it, Barron, you're not dumb enough to throw away a free Freeze over a chance to lose your show and make a public joke of yourself. That's not even a decent bluff. You're slipping, Barron, you're slipping."

Barron smiled. This is it, he thought. Now I knock you right on your ass, Howards. "You know, Bennie," he said, "that's just about what I told Luke at the time. (He saw Howards relax some more and plunged straight through the hole in the line.) Yeah, I told him kamikaze's not the name of my game… but, of course, that was before Greg Morris offered me the *Republican* nomination."

Howards started, went a trifle pale. "That's a lie," he said, but without too much conviction. "You a Republican? With *your* background? Who they supposed to run on the ticket with you, Joe Stalin? You've gotta be stoned to think I'd believe that."

Barron pushed his vidphone across the desk. "You don't have to believe anything," he said. "Call Greene. Call Morris. You're a big boy, Bennie; I'm surprised no one's told you the facts of life yet. Add it up. The Republicans have been sliding down the drain since Herbert Hoover, they're desperate, they've gotta win, and, as Morris so flatteringly indicated, they'd run Adolf Hitler if that's what a victory would take. The only Chinaman's chance they have of winning is on a fusion ticket with the SJC, and the only man they can run who could get the SJC nomination is yours truly, Jack Barron."

"Ridiculous," Howards said, his voice thin and unconvincing. "The Republicans and the SJC hate each other worse than either of 'em hate the Democrats. They don't agree on anything. They could never get in bed together."

"Ah, but they do agree on one thing," Barron said. "They agree on *you*. They're both against the Freezer Utility Bill and the Foundation for Human Immortality—and there's your fusion platform. They don't run me against the Pretender or any stooge you may still be able to ram down the Democrats' throats. I run against *you*, Howards. I use *Bug Jack Barron* to hang you around the Democratic candidate's neck like a rotten albatross stinking from coast to coast, and I run against *that*. Get the picture? Win or lose, the Foundation gets cut to pieces in the process. And win or lose, it'd mean you couldn't muscle me off the air because even though the Republicans can't deliver votes anymore, most of the fat cats in the country are still behind 'em. Pressure my sponsors, and the GOP can line up ten others. Republican-type bread still controls two out of four networks, still has as much leverage with the FCC as you do."

"It's… it's absurd," Howards said weakly. "You could never win. The Democrats can't lose, and you know it."

"You're probably right," Barron agreed. "But that's not the point; I've got no eyes to be President. Point is, in a campaign like that *you* lose no matter who wins. By the time I'm finished working on you, you'll stink so bad the Democratic candidate even if he is your stooge—will have to jump up and down on your bleeding bod to win. And who really knows…? Tom Dewey was a sure winner in '48…"

"You're turning my stomach," said Howards. "A Commie cretin like you even thinking about being President…"

Barron shrugged it off. "So do your patriotic duty, and save your own skin while you're at it. I don't have eyes for the White House. Buy me. I'm sitting here, waiting to be bought. My cards are all on the table. Let's see what *your* hole card is. And it better be good, 'cause if you don't come clean now you won't have another chance."

Barron felt the moment hanging high and cool in thin air between them like the Continental Divide; like being high on Big Stuff, he thought as he studied the gears meshing, tumblers falling into place behind Howards' cold rodent eyes. He's bought it, he thought, or anyway he's not laughing it off, shit the whole schtick's *real*. Look at the cat measuring me, measuring himself against me, measuring five hundred billion bucks life-and-death power against nothing but a fancy pyramid of bullshit, and, baby, you got him going, got your hot little hands around his throat. How's it feel, Bennie, to finally meet a cat who looks like he's your size?

What the fuck, Barron suddenly realised, it's no shuck, I *am* his size—smarter, trickier, thinking circles around him, Jack Barron's *anyone's* size. Who's a better man—Luke, Morris, Teddy, Howards...? just bigger muscles, is all, you really be afraid of any of 'em in a fair fight? Just men like you, is all, and probably not even as well hung. Crazy to imagine myself as President. Know damn well the job's too big... but maybe it's too big for *anyone*, and deep inside anyone who's ever looked across that Rubicon's gotta think he's getting flippy. It's all a game of bluff, money, power, President—life is all—and who wrote *that* book but good old Jack Barron? Anybody's got the openers can play to win in any game. Is *that* what Sara sees?

He almost half-hoped that Howards would call him, tell him to get stuffed, push him off the cliff into unknown waters; felt like a power-junkie sitting on top the Mother Lode, the Last Big High sitting in his spike, and who knows how it would come out, who really knows? Whee, he thought, brat-wise, that hole card of yours had better be good, Bennie!

"Look at me, Barron," Howards finally said. "What do you see?"

"Let's not get into..." Barron began to snap back, then stopped when he saw the strange, strange manic-junkie look creeping like a plague into Howards' glistening eyes.

"Yeah, Barron," Howards said, smiling a mirthless reptile smile. "Take a good look. You see a man in his fifties, in pretty good shape, right? Take another look ten years from now, twenty, a century, a million years from now, and you know what you'll see? You'll see a man in his fifties, in pretty good shape, is what you'll see. A decade from now, a century from now, a thousand years from now—forever, Barron, *forever*.

"I'm not just a man now, I'm something more. You said it yourself, forty billion dollars a year is a lot of money to spend on immortality research without getting results. Well, my boys finally *got* results, and you're looking right at 'em. I'm immortal, Barron, *immortal!* You know what that means? I'll never get older. I'll never die. Can you feel it? Can you taste it? To wake up every morning and smell that air and know you'll be smelling it every morning for the next million years... maybe forever. Dumb joke the doctors made—they won't know if I'll live forever till I've lived forever. No data, see? But Benedict Howards is gonna give 'em their data, gonna live forever, *forever*... You see what you're up against, Barron? An immortal—like a god! Think I'd let *anything* stand between me and that? Would you?"

"No..." Barron whispered, for the look on Howards' face told him in flaming letters a mile high that it was true. True!

Immortality he thought. Even the word doesn't sound real. *Forever!* To really live forever. Never to die, to be young and strong and healthy for a million years. Explains where Bennie's head's at, shit for that a man would do just about anything. *Just about...?* And to think this perambulating pile of shit's got it! Immortality! This motherfucker lives for the next million years, he'll still stink like the pile of shit he is, laughing for a million years while I rot in the ground we all rot and shit-eating Bennie goes on and on and on...

"I'm gonna buy you, Barron," Howards said, reaching into his attaché case. "Down to the soles of your feet, right now." He pushed another Freeze Contract in triplicate across the desk at Barron. "That's a very special contract," he said, "first one of its kind, just like the other one, but with one important difference—there's a clause in there entitling you to any immortality treatment the Foundation shall develop at your own discretion. And we've *got* an immortality treatment now. Forever, Barron, *forever*. You give me a couple lousy years out of your life to put over my bill, elect me a President, and... sew things up, and I give you the next million years. Take it from the only man in the world who really knows, eight years ain't even worth thinking about; it's less than the blinking of an eye from where I stand. From where *you* can stand..."

"Who do you think you are, Howards, the Devil?" And even as he said them, the words filled him with mortal dread he had never believed would ever be possible for him to feel. Funny word, he thought, *devil*. Cat with a long spiked tail knows the secret, *the* secret, everybody's secret, everybody's price, and got the bread to meet it too no matter what it is, and what you give him in return is a thing called a soul, *immortal* soul, ain't it, supposed to be the biggest thing a man's got to give. Immortal soul means like young and healthy and alive in paradise forever—price the Devil *gets* is the fee Howards *gives*. Devil, shit he's just a busher; Bennie can outbid him anytime. Satan, watch out the Foundation don't foreclose the mortgage!

"I take it back, Howards," he said. "Beside you, the Devil's on welfare. Just my name in ink on the dotted line? I don't have to sign it in blood? Copies for me that I can keep in a very safe place? Not subject to cancellation or exorcism?"

"A thousand copies if you want 'em, Barron, an iron-clad contract even I couldn't break. Yours, forever. All you gotta do is sign."

Sara! Barron suddenly thought. "Sara?" he said. "My wife… same deal in her name too?"

Benedict Howards smiled a sulphur smile. "Why not? I can afford to be generous, in fact I can afford just about anything. Secret of my success, Barron: I can afford to destroy an enemy, and I can afford to give any man I want to buy anything he wants, including—if he comes that high and he's worth it—eternal life. Come on, Barron, we both know you're gonna do it. Sign on the dotted line."

Barron fingered the contracts; his eyes fell on the pen sitting on his desk. He's right, he thought. Immortality with Sara, forever, I'd be an idiot not to sign. He picked up the pen, and his eyes met the eyes of Benedict Howards. And saw Howards staring greedily at him like some monstrous mad toad. But behind the egomaniacal madness, he saw fear—fear as naked as Howards' megalomania, an unguessable feral fear feeding his madness, giving it strength; he realised that Howards' whole crazy power-drive was fuelled on fear. And Benedict Howards was afraid of *him*.

Something's rotten in Colorado, Barron knew for certain. With this in his pocket and five hundred billion dollars, Bennie can buy anyone and everyone he needs. So why's he need *me* so bad to pass some lousy bill when he can buy Congress, the President and the fucking Supreme Court? And he *does* think he needs me, look at that hunger in those eyes! He's after my bod because somehow he *really* needs it to fight whatever he's afraid of. And if *he's* afraid of it, and I'm supposed to be some kind of sacrificial front man, where's that leave *me*?

"Before I sign," Barron said (conceding to himself that he would), "would you mind telling me why, with *this* kind of action going, you think you need me?"

"I need public support," Howards said, frantically earnest. "It's the one thing I can't buy directly. That's why I need you, to sell immortality to that goddamned public of yours."

"To sell immortality? You crazy? You need a salesman for immortality like you need a salesman for money."

"That's the point," Howards said. "You see, we do have an immortality treatment, but it's… it's… *very* expensive. Maybe we can treat a thousand people a year at about twenty-five million a throw, but that's *it*, and it'll be it for years, decades, maybe always. That's what you've gotta sell, Barron—not immortality for everyone but immortality for a few, a select few—a few *I* select."

Barron's instant reaction was disgust, at Howards, at himself, even as he felt his second reaction—all questions now answered and the game was worth the candle. But his third reaction was caution—this was the biggest thing there ever was, and more dangerous than the H-bomb, get involved in *that?*

"This treatment," he asked, "what is it?"

"That's none of your business, and that's final. It's a Foundation secret, and it stays a Foundation secret no matter what," Howards told him, and Barron was sure he had hit bottom, pushed Howards as far as he would ever go. "If… if *that* got out …" Howards mumbled, then caught Barron catching him and clamped his mouth tight shut.

But you don't put one over on Jack Barron, Bennie! Shit, he's willing to let out that immortality's gonna be only for a few fat cats, and he thinks I can shove *that* down people's throats, but he's afraid to let anyone know what the treatment is. Must be some treatment! That's what he's scared of, and if it scares him.

…What the hell could it be… his immortals all end up as Transylvanian vampires? Hell… maybe that's not so funny. Immortality, sure, but what the hell's he getting me into? But… but is there *anything* so rank it isn't worth doing if you have to do it to live forever?

"I need time, Howards," he said. "You can see that…"

"Jack Barron turning chicken?" Howards sneered. "I'll give you time, I'll give you twenty-four hours, not a minute more. I'm tired of talking; the only words I'll listen to from you from here on in are 'yes' or 'no.'"

And Jack Barron knew that the game was played out, the time for negotiation was over. And he had no idea of what his answer could possibly be.

10

THE VIDPHONE CHIME began to sound again. Sara Westerfeld walked barefooted over to the wall complex, reached for the phone, hesitated, then once again let it lapse into silence without answering it.

Still feels like this is strictly Jack's pad, with me just hanging around, she thought, not *our* place, with me having as much right to move things around or answer the phone as he does. Phone keeps ringing, but would Jack want me to answer it? Who knows, might be more of this President thing… or even Howards. (No, Jack's supposed to be seeing Howards himself now.)

Truth is, she thought, I still can't start thinking again like Sara Barron. Sara *Barron'd* answer the phone if Jack wasn't here, 'cause she'd know who she was, where she stood, where Jack stood, be able to react to anything. But Sara Westerfeld was still someone from the past, someone who didn't know where she stood in Jack's present world, didn't even know the shape or limits of that world, and when she did, might or might not accept them, might or might not be able to make the quantum-jump back to being Sara *Barron*.

And might or might not be able to cut it with Jack, she knew. It was easy to let the lizardman bulldoze me into going back to a Jack I thought I hated—Howards' high-paid whore was all I started out to be—had nothing to lose, either be able to bring back the Jack I once loved or walk away with no regrets from cop-out *Bug Jack Barron* Jack.

But how could I know I'd start seeing for real the Jack I thought I'd have to fake seeing? Is it real? Is the old Jack back already, *my* Jack Berkeley boy now a man playing real man-game to make the old boy-dreams real, destroy Howards, Social Justice President of the United States, attic dream becoming a reality in ways we never imagined? Wouldn't *that* Jack hate me, knowing I thought so little of him that I could use him to get us Frozen, gamble like a cold-blooded windowless white lizard that I could shock him into becoming what he really was all along? And if Jack's really involved in some dirty deal with Howards, wouldn't it just help the lizardman get Jack for whatever filth he wants him for, if he knew that Howards was able to buy and use even me? Could… could that be what Howards was planning all along? Seeing through me seeing through him, letting me think *I* was putting one over, and *that* setting me up as his secret weapon against Jack…? *Wanting* me to tell Jack everything?

But if it's half one thing, half the other, plans in conflict, neither Jack nor Howards is in control, and Jack on the knife-edge between being the old Berkeley Jack or taking the biggest copout of all, then I've *got* to tell him. It's all up to me…

The unbearable choice weighed heavy on her; existential choice holding past and future time-lines in mortal balance, a *woman*-choice, she knew, and it was still hard not to think of herself as a *girl*, helpless in a larger-than-life man's world.

The vidphone began chiming again.

Maybe it's Jack? Maybe that's why it keeps ringing, anyone else'd figure no one's here, but Jack knows I'm here, knows I might not answer till I knew it was him ringing again and again...

Pissed at herself for being unable to make even such a piddling decision, she forced herself to the vidphone and made the connection.

And felt abysmal regret, cold numb terror clean through her, as the windowless white face of Benedict Howards stared out at her with knowing rodent eyes from the vidphone screen.

"It's about time you decided to answer the phone," he said. "I've been trying to get you for half an hour. What's the matter with you?"

"You... you were calling *me*?" Sara stammered, feeling serpent-coils winding themselves around her.

"I wouldn't be calling Barron, would I? Not since I just spoke to him in the flesh. Of course I'm calling you. We're... *business associates*. Remember?" And Howards smiled an awful I-own-you crocodile smile.

"Now you listen, and you listen good," he said. "Barron is on his way home, far as I know. I've made my final offer to him, and he's got about twenty-three hours to accept. Which means you've got about twenty-three hours to complete your end of our little bargain—or no Freeze for either of you. So you start working on him the moment he gets there, and you better make it good."

From the greater fear of losing the Jack she had found again, Sara mustered the courage to face the lesser fear, held up her head in her mind's eye, said: "I don't care about that anymore. I've got *Jack* now, and nothing's as important to me as that. You brought us together for your own dirty reasons, but you didn't understand that we love each other, always have, always will. And that's all that matters now."

"Have it your way," Howards said. "But just remember, all I have to do is tell Barron what you are, my whore, Miss Westerfeld, and where's your great love then?"

"Jack will understand..."

"Will he? Will he want to? Will he believe you or me? He'll believe *me* because he'll want to, after what I've offered him."

"You think you're so smart," Sara said, "but you're a fool. You don't understand what love is, stronger than anything you can use to buy people..."

Howards leered at her, and she realised he had anticipated her every action in the serpent-lair of his mind. "You think so?" he said. "But there's something stronger than any... *mortal* love—immortal love. Barron loves you, eh? Would a man who loves you be willing to let you die, when instead he could give you the greatest gift a man can give a woman? Greatest gift a man can give himself?"

Sara felt something foul and gigantic in Howards' voice that spoke of things she didn't want to know, things that might really be stronger than love, monstrous jungle truths with great gleaming fangs of bone leering from lipless reptile mouths; but she felt herself fascinated, drawn on by the primal dawn-marsh stink that seemed to hover over Howards' image on the vidphone screen.

"What... what could be stronger than love?" she asked.

"Life," said Benedict Howards. "Without life, you got nothing—no love, no taste of good food in your mouth, no nothing. Whatever anyone wants the most, he loses it all when he's dead."

"You call that life—a body lying stiff and cold in a Freezer? You think Jack'd give up what really mattered to him for that, thirty or forty years from now?"

"He might," said Howards. "He just might. But that's not what I'm talking about. I'm talking about the real thing, Miss Westerfeld, *immortality.* Look at me! I'm immortal now, my scientists have made the breakthrough. Immortal! I'll never get older. I'll never die. Words, just words to you, what else can they be? But there are no words for what it's really like to wake up in the morning knowing you're gonna live for centuries—*forever.*

"*That's* what I'm offering Barron, the next million years, immortality. Think he'd rather have *you?* Would you rather have *him* if the choice were yours? Immortality, Miss Westerfeld. Can you imagine what it's like to know you're not like ordinary men—don't have to die? Can you imagine anyone turning his back on it? Can you imagine anything Barron wouldn't do to live forever? Can you imagine anything *you* wouldn't do? *Love?* How much is love worth when you're dead?"

"It's not true!" she cried. "You can't be able to do it, not *you.* ...." Not you, you bloodless reptile, not with your plastic frozen money, not buying it like you buy everyone and everything, not Benedict Howards with power over death forever, on and on and on, webs of hate and power spinning on and on, forever, from your bone-white lizard-lair, it just isn't *right.*

But Howards' cold eyes stared straight through her, his lips parted in a thin smile, and she felt him digging her thoughts, sucking up her hate, fear, sense of wrongness, letting her know he knew the loathing she felt. And letting her know he found it amusing.

"It *is* true, isn't it?" she said quietly. "You really can make Jack immortal...?" And she imagined Jack, knowing what could be his, loving her, being Jack Barron and... and *what?* Can he love me enough to die with me in forty or fifty years, when he can have forever? And I thought *I* had an impossible

decision to make! But Jack... to choose between love and immortality...
And it struck her like a sledgehammer: Howards has to be working on me
because he knows Jack *hasn't* decided. He wants *me* to make Jack choose
immortality. And... and maybe he's right, how can I want anything less than
immortality for Jack, sell him on... on death, even though I die and Jack
has to go on alone forever...? Oh, you miserable shit, Howards! Why is a
bastard like you so damn clever?

"Not only Barron," Howards said. "Anyone I choose. You, for instance.
You're right about one thing: Barron loves you. First thing he asked when I
made the offer was for immortality for you too. And..."

The cruelty in Howards' eyes raped her as he smirked, waited for her
to ask the question, sucking pleasure like a junkie from watching her
squirm.

"And?"

Howards laughed. "Why not?" he said, "I can afford it. It's a nice little
daisy-chain this way—I buy Barron with immortality for the both of you, and
I buy you with the same thing, and I buy your help in making sure he sells.
Three for the price of one. You can have love and life, both forever. Think
about that, you and Barron, forever. And if you don't deliver, I tell Barron
everything and you've blown it all—him and immortality. That's not such a
hard choice, is it, Miss Westerfeld? You've got twenty-three hours. I won't
be talking to you again. I don't really have to, do I?"

And he broke the connection.

Sara knew how right he was, how right he had been every step of the way,
Eternal life with Jack or... *nothing*. She thought of Jack, young and strong
beside her, together for a million years, growing and growing together in the
innocent strength of adolescence—the strength that comes from not really
believing you'll ever have to die—but based now on truth, not self-delusion,
giving the courage to do anything, dare anything, soft-flesh knight in the
armour of immortality, and the world what they could make it forever
and ever... Growing without growing older, like that ocean sunfish that
keeps getting bigger and bigger, never ages, never dies... Jack like *that*,
and me with him forever!

And Benedict Howards forever, a small sly voice reminded her. Feeding
forever on power and fear and death and Jack... Jack his flunky, keeping
him there in his bone-white temple of death while aeons and billions of
people are born and die and are gone forever like smoke, while Howards
and those who fawn on him like on some awful death-god live forever
at the price of their souls... With a pang of despair she realised that this
was the world that was coming, Jack or no Jack, with his help or despite
him, inexorable as Judgement Day, and no one could stand against it,
against Foundation power of money and life eternal against death. Benedict
Howards was right. He *was* almost a god, god of life and death. God on

the side of evil and nothingness; the Black Christ, and no one his size to stand against him.

No one but... but Jack Barron! she thought. Oh, yes! yes! Jack's smarter than Howards, stronger than me. If Howards makes us immortal, what hold can he have over Jack then? If Jack's already got all that Howards has to give, and if he hates Howards the way I hate him... Not even Benedict Howards could stand Jack Barron then—the full, true Jack Barron, fighting for me and for himself and for hate and for everything we ever believed in, armoured in immortality!

She felt both proud and afraid, realising what lay in her hands, and hers alone. Billions of immortal lives, and hers, and Jack's. Jack was strong, clever; he would know how to keep immortality, and destroy Howards too, bring immortality to the whole world. President, maybe...? Luke thinks so... What could Howards do *then?* Yes! Yes! It was all in her hands, she could make Jack immortal, make him hate, wake him up to what was always meant to be. She could do it; she only had to be brave alone for one moment in a life that could be endless.

And I will, she vowed. And as she waited for Jack to arrive she savoured what it was to at last think of herself as a woman—as Sara *Barron.*

Catching him preoccupied, the stomach-drop of the elevator was just one more jolt in a day of jolts for Jack Barron. He stubbed out the butt of his Acapulco Gold in the elevator ashtray, caught up with his belly tried to catch up with his head as the elevator sucked up the sealed shaft to his slice of California twenty-three stories away from New York's stinking paranoid gutters. And he got a flash of what the penthouse playpen (with genuine authentic Sara Westerfeld at last installed) really meant to him.

Time machine is all, he thought. California science-fiction time machine to a past that never was, pot-dream California of the mind that never could be, big league action image through the eyes of Baby Bolshevik kid didn't know where the big leagues were really at, dream made real by *Bug Jack Barron* bread—but making it real changed the dreamer. What Sara just can't understand—got the balls to do it, sure you can make dreams real, but getting out in the nitty-gritty's *gotta* change the dreamer, 'cause he ain't dreaming anymore; he's *real,* doing real things, fighting real enemies, and when he's cut he bleeds real blood, not ectoplasm. Which is why I'm a winner, and all the old Baby Bolsheviks except maybe Luke are all losers Too hung-up on big beautiful acidhead dreams to risk losing it, risk losing Peter-Pan selves by getting their hands dirty making it real. Stay a dreamer, and you'll never have your dream; get down in the nitty-gritty, and when you get your dream you see what horseshit it was in the first place.

Game of life's run by an ex-con cardshark, he thought morosely as the elevator came to a stop and the door opened. Deck's marked, dice loaded, and the only way you don't go home in a barrel is to play by the house rules, namely no holds barred.

He crossed the foyer, entered the dark hall, heard a Beatles album playing, picked up on the subliminal presence of Sara. And he remembered that he had to decide for her too; her immortality was in the big pot too. Feeling her presence filling the apartment with Saraness, making the joint at last a home, it was impossible to believe that the gestalt that was the total Sara could ever cease to be, become nothing more than a random pattern of inert food for the worms.

But it *can,* he thought. Doesn't have to now, but it can, and the cat who can do it is Jack Barron. Say 'no' to Howards, and you're not only coming on with the kamikaze schtick, you're murdering the only woman you ever love, and so what if it's forty years from now? So what if she never knows it? It's still murder, is all. Ugliest word there is, *murder.* No holds barred is the name of the game, but don't put yourself on, Barron, at murder even you draw the line. Only crime that's always wrong no matter what the circumstances, murder. Blowing Bennie's brains out'd just be *killing,* and that's cool, but letting Sara die when you can save her just by signing your name, that's murder.

Yeah, sure, but how do you know what you're getting into if you *do* sign that contract? Could be things worse than murder. Like genocide—and isn't that Bennie's bag, save the winners and let the losers die, and wouldn't *Sara* be a loser on her own if Howards didn't want me, to the worm-ovens with the rest of the untermenschen losers...? Choose one from column A, or one from column B (eggroll and won-ton included in the dinner): genocide or murder.

He knew it was not a decision he had the right to make alone. Sara's life too, not just mine. I've gotta tell her the whole thing, what a woman's for, isn't it, someone in the whole shit-eating world you can be up front with, take it or leave it? Got enough trouble playing footsie with Howards, at least I can have truth between me and Sara.

She was out on the patio, leaning against the parapet, staring out over the East River at Brooklyn, long dusk-shadows twilighting the rush-hour traffic in the street far below.

"Jack..." she said, turning as he stepped out on the patio; and he saw a strange manic desperation in her eyes, glazed over pool-deep darknesses, and something grim and fragile in the lines of her face, and she seemed to be looking into him and at the same time through him. In a weird way, he almost recognised that look... yes, look of some vip on the show about to parrot a memorised set-spiel.

"I've got something I've gotta tell you," Barron said, crossing the terrace, leaning against the parapet close enough to taste her breath but unable to bring himself to touch her.

"And I've got something I have to tell you," she said, and he saw her jawline go white, a pulse twitch in-her left temple.

"Later, baby," Barron said, knowing it was now or never. Whatever's uptighting you can wait, Sara, he thought. Either you'll forget all about it, or you'll *really* be uptight after I lay it all on you.

"It's about me and Howards," he began. "I suppose by now you know there's some hanky-panky going on there, and I owe it to you to let you in on what's shaking. And big things are shaking, bigger than you could ever imagine, bigger than all this President bullshit, bigger than... bigger than anything's ever been, bigger than anything you can even think of. Bennie Howards is hot for my bod, Sara. He needs me. He needs *Bug Jack Barron* to push through his Freezer Bill, to... to put over something... well, something people just won't stomach. He's desperate, he's hotter for my bod than Luke or Morris or—"

"I know," she said in a tiny voice all but drowned out by the rush-hour traffic-roar from the street below, and he sensed a huge electric-potential-tension charge building between them, reached out for her hand gripping the cement lip of the parapet to bleed off the electric hum in the air between them; and her skin was rubber, cold and dry, as if she were a thousand miles away talking through vidphone circuit-insulation, and he found with a kind of relief that he was slipping into the *Bug Jack Barron* cool Wednesday-night-feedback game, hating himself for doing it, hating himself worse for being thankful. And what the fuck does she mean she knows?

"Yeah," he said, "I suppose it's been pretty obvious. (But *has* it, he wondered, feeling danger-signals of future-shock precognition surging down time lines toward him.) But before you do the whole cop-out number, you better hear the coin he's paying. Immortality, Sara, *immortality*. Bennie's boys have licked ageing. He's keeping it real quiet 'cause there's a big catch—it's real expensive, like he's talking about twenty-five million bucks per treatment, and even with that kind of bread, he claims he can only treat about a thousand people a year. But it's no shuck; it's the real thing. He says he's had the treatment himself, and when you listen to him gibbering about it you *know* he's not bullshitting. That's where it's at, immortality for maybe a thousand people a year, people who can get up twenty-five million, people who Bennie chooses, and everyone else is stuck with three score and ten, is all. And that's why he's so hot for me—he wants me to help him shove *that* down the throat of the Great Unwashed: immortality for the few, and death for everyone else. A lot harder to peddle than Chevys or dope. But..."

He stared into the unreadable vacuum of her eyes that seemed to mock him, accuse him, and he sensed his words going straight through her like a commercial out across the city to Brooklyn and beyond, and she seemed to be waiting for something, and he waited for her to speak, scream, yell, jump up and down, do something, anything, react. But she just stood there, and even the pressure of her hand in his didn't change, and Barron felt cold and afraid and didn't know why.

"Twenty-five million dollars," he said. "But for us, free. That's the deal, Sara. I agree to play ball with Howards, and we both get ironclad contracts out in front. That's the decision I've gotta make by tomorrow—sign the contracts, and we both have immortality, or tell Howards to fuck off and throw it all away. And not just immortality—he'll cream me, try to cost me the show, and I'll have to play games with Greg Morris & Co. just to keep our heads above water. Some choice! But it's got to be *our* choice, not just mine."

"I know, Jack," Sara said, "I know it all."

"Come on, will you?" Barron snapped, bugged at the deep unreadable pools behind her eyes (damn big soulful brown eyes, Christ knows what's really behind them, Christ knows if *anything's* behind 'em but Peter-Pan acid bullshit—where is your head at Sara?). "Okay, so it's hard to get down, but don't just stand there gaping at me. And what the hell you mean you know it all?"

She pulled her hand away from his, touched his cheek, then let her hand fall to her side, and when she spoke, she looked away from him, down, down at the brawling honking streets of rush-hour Manhattan, and from the set of her jaw and the quaver in her voice, Barron knew she was staring down, deep down, into some private freak-out snakepit.

"You're not the only person Benedict Howards's used," she said, "that... that monster can buy anyone—*anyone*, Jack. He's the most thoroughly evil man in the world, and now he can go on buying people and using people and holding life-and-death power over people forever... He's evil, and clever, and totally amoral, and he can give anyone anything they want. Everyone's got his price, and Howards can afford anyone he needs to buy, that's what he told me, and I didn't believe it. But now... now... oh, Jack, is it wrong to want to live forever? Everyone wants to live forever, and I want you to live forever, does that make me so rotten, so...? *Jack!*"

And she whirled, flung herself into his arms, not sobbing but clutching him to her with manic strength. But even as his reflexes passed soothing hands over her back, Barron went steel-cold as he struggled with her words, rejected them, felt them stinging back like dry-ice bees.

He pushed her away, holding her shoulders at arms' length, stared into her stricken face, muttered: "You...? Howards...?"

"You've got to, Jack..." she said. (Her lips began to quiver, her eyes were wet, she was shaking in his rough hands.) "Don't you see? If you sign the contracts, then we're immortal, we've got all that Howards can give and no one can take it away from us. Don't you see? You're the only man in the world can stop him, destroy him. You're the only man big enough to stand up to Benedict Howards and his loathsome Foundation. You've *got* to! There's no one else! But I don't want to die, I don't want you to die... Sign the contracts, and then... then we can fight him together, and he can't do anything to hurt us..."

Barron shook her, shaking himself "What the fuck is this? Stop gibbering, damn you, Sara, and tell me what all this is about!" But he knew with dread certainty what it was all about. Bennie got to her, he thought. Somehow, somewhere, the slimy motherfucker got to her, found the handle... The—

"I love you," she sobbed. "You've gotta believe I love you. I did it because I love you. I love you, Jack, I've always loved you, I'll always—"

Barron slammed her body up against the parapet. "Cut the shit," he said cruelly, feeling the cruelty cut into her, cut into him, grim razor of reality and way down below he heard the sounds of metal and rubber and concrete abrading synthetic world of steel cutting edges way down there below him. "In words of one syllable—what's the scam with you and Benedict Howards?" And he felt himself coming on like living-colour Jack Barron backing a vip into a corner. And knew no other way to react.

He saw Sara stare blankly into his eyes with numb wet eyes like those of a mindless parrot as she spat it out, spat it all out like pieces of rotten meat.

"He... he had me dragged to his Long Island Freezer. He promised me a free Freeze Contract if I got you to sign one. I told him to go to hell. But... but that man sees right into your guts, sees what he wants to see, and he knows how to use it, knows more about the dirty places inside you than you do yourself. He knew... knew deep down that I still loved you... before I knew it myself, and when he offered me a chance to live forever, and all I had to do to get it was go back to you... Don't you see I wanted you, I never stopped wanting you, just stopped *knowing it,* and when Howards gave me an *excuse* to go back to you, a good excuse... He conned me into conning myself into thinking I could con you. I thought I hated you, but I thought maybe I could change you back to the Jack you were meant to be if I went back to you and got you to sign the contracts and then... then did just what I'm doing now, tell you everything, show you what a swine Howards is, kind of man you're involved with stops at nothing, and how a man like that can make *anyone* climb right down there in his sewer with him... Oh, Jack, how you must hate me now!"

Barron let her go, smiled crookedly as he saw her crying big wet tears like a cocker spaniel just shit on the rug waiting to be kicked. Hate you? he thought. Hate you for playing games with Howards, where does that leave *me?* Don't have enough hate for you, too much hate for that cocksucker Howards playing with my silly chick's head—chick with no defences at all against big-league Foundation action—shit, who *wouldn't* play footsie for a free Freeze chance to live forever, wouldn't you? Didn't you? Aren't you? Where it's at, is all.

He looked past her at the dusk-lights of Brooklyn, past the East River murk, over the roaring, cursing New York traffic, steel-jungle-carnivore noises clashing twenty-four hours a day, and even in his little California twenty-three stories above it all, he knew there was no escaping the gutter-reality, daisy-chain power-reality that made the world go round chasing its tail up its asshole—not for Sara or Luke or Brackett Audience Count estimated hundred million people.

Or Jack Barron.

Either you grow teeth, or you end up fed to the fishes.

"I'm too pissed to hate you," he said. "Maybe I even owe Bennie a favour for growing you up, way I never could. Maybe you won't yell cop-out so loud now, 'cause Bennie's right, we all got a price. Cat thinks he don't, just hasn't been offered *his* price yet. Hate you, I gotta hate myself, and you came back to me, did it to have a chance to live forever, play Baby Bolshevik games with my head on the side. In a funny way, I respect dart—what I would've done in your place, after all. Question is, do you really love me now?"

"I've never loved you more in my whole life," she said, and he saw the funky worship-look in her eyes, and warmth went through him from the tip of his toes, curled around his ears as he clocked the hot hungry love for *him*, not for living-colour image-Jack-Barron, not Baby Bolshevik Galahad cheap-talk bullshit hero… *Me*, he thought. Maybe she finally digs *me*, where I'm really at—wherever the fuck *that* is!

"Likewise," he said, and he kissed her a soft and tender first-kiss type kiss, mouths open tasting each other like for the first time, but tongues apart, love-kiss without passion, and he never remembered kissing her quite like this before.

"You'll do it?" she asked, arms around his waist, face inches from his, earnest little-girl conspiracy face, playing games even now, and how can I put it down when it's so like me?

"Do what?" he said, smiling a vidphone gambit put-on smile.

"Sign the contracts."

"I'd be a schmuck not to, wouldn't I?" Jack Barron said. And that's where it *is* at, isn't it? he thought. Who's a big enough schmuck to choose death? You know that real good, don't you Bennie?

"But you won't… you won't play that horrible reptile's game…?" she said (and he saw that damned old Berkeley look creep back into her eyes, Jack and Sara versus the Forces of Evil, won't she ever grow up all the way? Do you really want her to?). "All those people out there who trust you, whether you like it or not… You *can't* sell out all those people who believe in you, let them die just because we've got ours. I mean, once we've got immortality for ourselves you've gotta fight Howards. You're the only man can stop him, the man a hundred million people believe in, the only man Howards is afraid of, you're… you're *Jack Barron*, and sometimes I think you're the only one doesn't know what Jack Barron is. You can't be Howards' flunky, a stooge, a... You're *Jack Barron*."

Barron hugged her to him, looked out over the teeming streets, the lights of Brooklyn stretching from coast to coast, as she buried her face in his neck, a hundred million TV-antenna Wednesday-night-eyes all on him and what would *they* say, those image-vampires, if they knew it all?

Play *our* game, is what they'd say, he knew. Lay your ass on the line for us, boy, you owe it to us. No different from Luke or Morris or Bennie, all thinking they own my bod—except they don't have the stake to play the game.

Yeah, just like Bennie. Everybody wants to own poor old Jack Barron, and nobody's got the word that Jack Barron owns *himself,* is all.

Jack Barron pulled the warmth of his woman to him. "Don't worry Sara," he said, "I don't play Howards' game." (Or anyone else's.)

Fuck you, Bennie, he thought, fuck you all! None of you, not Bennie, not Luke, not the Great Unwashed losers down there, not even you, Sara—is gonna own Jack Barron!

11

BETTER BE IT, or I feed you right to the fishes, enough crapping around Barron, and I gotta come to this crazy joint too? Benedict Howards thought as he sat down on some screwy iron-and-leather kite of a chair, stared across at Jack Barron perched like some oily Arab oil trader on a silly-ass camel saddle, framed by the open terrace behind him palm trees or whatever you call the dumb things look like cheap-hotel phony rubberplants hot and cold running whores in Tulsa or San Jose or some other nowhere boom town with plenty of money and no class—yeah, it figures Jack Barron would go for that kind of California horseshit.

Howards opened his attaché case, took out two contracts in triplicate, handed them across to Barron along with his old-fashioned 14-carat-gold felt-tip pen. "There they are, Barron," he said. "Contract for you, contract for Sara Westerfeld or Barron or whatever her last name is—made out to Sara Westerfeld, since that's her legal name at the moment. All signed by me, paid up by 'anonymous donor,' and standard Freeze Contracts except for the immortality option clause. Just sign all the copies, and we can get down to *your* end of the bargain."

Barron leafed through one of the copies, looked up, measured Howards with those goddamned smirking eyes of his, said: "Let's get this straight, Bennie, once I sign these contracts, you can't welch, I send one of my copies to a very safe place, with instructions to release it to the press with the whole scam on your having an immortality treatment, in case anything should happen to me, dig?"

Howards smiled. You're so smart, Barron, think you're two steps ahead of Benedict Howards, think I don't know what you're thinking—Jack Barron's got *his* insurance, where's yours, Howards, smells too easy? Chase your own tail, Barron, never figure out *your* insurance is really *my* insurance till it's way too late and I own you down to the soles of your feet, and you're too far in to ever back out till it's your immortal life million years strong young cool-skinned women, air-conditioned arenas of power forever to lose same as mine, and then you're my man all the way, like Senators, Governors, and, goddamn it, President too, Mr Howards, despite goddamn idiot Hennering.

"You don't even have to trust me that far," Howards said with carefully-guarded casualness. "You and your wife can exercise the immortality option the moment you sign, if you want to. In fact you can fly back to Colorado with me tonight, have the treatment, and be back better than new in time for your next show. With Deep Sleep recovery, it's all over in two days. You don't have to trust me at all; you can collect your payoff before you have to deliver anything."

Barron's eyes narrowed even as Howards anticipated his suspicion. "That smells like a dead flounder to me. I don't figure you for the trusting type, Bennie, and it looks like you're trusting *me*, and *that*, baby, I don't trust at all."

Keep on thinking that way sucker, Howards thought. Go home in a barrel thinking you can out-con Benedict Howards.

"Who trusts you?" Howards replied smoothly. "I got it set up so neither of us has to trust the other, and you better believe it. I can play the press-release game too, and where would that leave you, Mr Champion of the Underdog? On public record, selling out to the Foundation. How long you think you keep your show *then*? You may be a lot of things, but I don't think you're stupid enough to blow everything just to double-cross me. We both got our names on dangerous paper, and neither of us can afford to make it public. It's a double insurance policy, Barron." And once you have the treatment, it'll be more than your silly career, it'll be your life, your million-year-life in my hands, if you think about pulling a fast one.

Howards felt Barron measuring him, trying to think holes in his position, knew that he wouldn't find any because there's only one hole, and it gives me the big edge, Barron, and you'll never find *that* one till you're in way over your head. Go ahead, smart-ass, try and out-think Benedict Howards won't be the first man's tried, won't be the last to go home in a barrel oil leases Lyndon, Senators Governors doctors nurses tube up nose down throat fading black circle all thought they could get Benedict Howards, and I beat 'em all, conned 'em, bought 'em, destroyed 'em, owned 'em, really think you can get the best of the only man bigger than death, winner over all forces of the fading black circle?

Barron looked at him blankly for a long moment; not an inch of flesh moved, but something changed behind his eyes that Howards could sense from long experience with big men in air-cooled vaults of power to surrender, flunky, Mr Howards, and Howards knew he had him bought even before Barron said: "Okay, Howards. Deal." And signed his contract in triplicate.

"That's real smart," Howards said. "Now you get a hold of Sara Westerfeld by tonight, get her signature, and I'll fly you both to Colorado in my plane for the treatment, save you the air fare, show you even little things go better when you play ball with Benedict Howards."

Barron smiled a nasty *Bug-Jack-Barron* smile Howards couldn't read, and he felt a small pang of uneasiness, still playing games, what now, Barron? Take it easy, he told himself, once you get him to take the treatment, you got him hog-tied same as any other beef.

"Hey, Sara!" Barron yelled. "Come on in here, got something for you to sign."

Barron smiled so blandly as Sara Westerfeld stepped out of a doorway and crossed the living room toward them with a nervous blank face, slowly so damned slow, that Howards felt a real moment of fear, felt the possibility of his control of the situation maybe about to slip away, the irrational fear that Barron was playing with him—has that goddamned crazy whore spilled the whole thing? He saw that Barron was holding all six contracts tightly... about to rip 'em up, go ape? Damn him, how much does he know? That dumb bitch tell him and screw everything up?

Jack Barron toyed with the contracts as Sara Westerfeld stood by the camel saddle he was sitting on like some Saudi Arabian slave dealer, and Howards felt as if it were his neck being fingered as she shot him a look of studied non-recognition, then looked at Barron with sickeningly worshipful eyes as if to tell Howards that if she was anyone's whore, she was Jack Barron's. But how much does he know? Howards wondered frantically, fighting to keep his face blank. She got the brains to keep her mouth shut now?

Barron looked at him with eyes lowered to catch shadows in the deep hollows, what Howards recognised as a calculated *Bug Jack Barron* cheap trick, and Barron seemed to be reading every knot and convolution in his gut. This prick could be dangerous, Howards realised, more dangerous than I thought, he's smart, real smart, and he's crazy as a coot and that's a bad, bad combination unless I got him bought all the way. *Got* to get him to fly back with me and take the treatment tonight!

Jack Barron laughed a laugh that increased the tension said: "Don't get so uptight, Bennie. Sara already knows everything. She's my chick all the way." He paused (or am I imagining things?), Howards thought, seemed to be emphasising the words for his benefit (or the girl's?). "We don't keep secrets from each other."

Barron handed three contracts to Sara Westerfeld, along with the pen. "Go ahead, sign 'em, Sara," he said. "You know what you're signing, don't you?"

Sara Westerfeld looked straight at Howards as she signed the contracts, smiled a thin smile that could've been acknowledgement of the deal completed between them or could've been an inside smile between her and Barron, said: "Sure I do. I know just what we're getting into. Immortality. Jack's told me everything, Mr Howards. Like he says, we don't keep secrets from each other."

This dumb bitch playing games with me too? Howards wondered. But it doesn't matter, he told himself as she handed the contracts back to Barron, who sorted them, handed Howards a copy of each. Signed, sealed, and delivered. Got 'em both now, right here in my hand, in black and white. And by the time you go on the air again, Barron, it'll be in flesh and blood, yours and hers, and who gives a shit whether you know how I used her? She's done the job one way or the other, is what counts. I got you, I own you, Jack

Barron, clean through to your bones.

Howards tucked the contracts safely into his attaché case. "Okay," he said, "so then I suppose I can talk freely in front of her. (Time for the spurs, Barron, you'll have to get used to 'em anyway, and your woman might as well get the message, right at the beginning, see who's boss, how's *that* grab you, smart-ass?) I'll send a car for you about seven tonight, take you to the airport. We'll have plenty of time to put your next show together on the way to Colorado.

"I figure first order of business is to get back those votes in Congress for the Freezer Bill you lost me with your big mouth. What you'll do is get some jerk on the line who was taken by one of those fly-by-night freezer outfits, maybe a surviving relative of someone who did business with them and had his body rot when they went bankrupt. And don't worry, I'll dig someone like that up by Wednesday, or, if I can't, I'll get someone to fake it. Then you put a couple of these phony operators on the hotseat—I got a whole list of the worst of 'em—and show what crooks they are, get it? Safety's the pitch, only a Foundation Freeze is safe and Congress gotta pass—"

"Hold it, Howards," said Barron. "For openers, you don't tell me how to run my line of evil. It'd smell like an open sewer if I did an about-face on the Foundation right after the last two shows. We gotta cool it first. I'll do a couple shows got nothing at all to do with the Foundation, take the heat off. Then three or four weeks from now, I do maybe ten minutes on a victim of your so-called competition at the *end* of the show, and that'll set things up for grilling a couple of those schmucks the week after that. *Bug Jack Barron's* supposed to be spontaneous, unrehearsed, audience-controlled. Remember? You want me to do you any good, it's gotta keep looking that way."

"Like you say, it's your line of evil," Howards agreed.

This prick's gonna be *real* useful, he thought. Knows his own business just fine, he's right, gotta be subtle, and Barron knows just how to do it. Let him run his own little piece of the action and he'll do just fine. Tell him *what* to do, and let him handle the *how.*

That's the best kind of flunky, after all—flunky with brains enough to take orders and carry 'em out better than you could if you had to spell out every word. What they call a specialist, wind 'em up, and watch 'em work.

"Well play it your way," Howards said. "You've been at it a long time, and should know what you're doing." He got up, feeling a day's work well done. "Car'll pick you up at seven, and about two days from now you'll have had the big payoff. Think about it, getting up every morning for the next million—"

"Not so fast," Jack Barron said. "I think we'll pass on the immortality treatment for now, see how things go. We're both young, there's no rush, contract says we can exercise the option any time we want, after all."

"What's the matter with you?" Howards said shrilly. Then, as he saw

Barron's eyes measuring him, realised he *did* sound shrill, was treading very thin ice (Gotta get him to take the treatment soon, can't scare him off, make him any more suspicious than he is), lowered his voice, feigned indifference. "Don't you want to be immortal?"

"Wouldn't have signed the contract, if I didn't, now, would I?" Barron said. (Howards sensed the shrewd, electric danger in his sly voice. Watch it! Watch it! He's playing that *Bug Jack Barron* game again.) "Question is, why are you so hot to make me immortal so damned quick?"

Benedict Howards felt the scalpel in the question probing for what the bastard's been probing for all along—the secret of the treatment. And you're not gonna find that out no-how, Barron, not till it's too late. Can't push him now, gotta back off, damn it, or... *Can't let him get suspicious about the treatment!*

"Tell you the truth, Barron," he said, "I get carried away. Just thinking about it reminds me I'm immortal, really immortal, and I just can't see why anyone would wait five minutes longer than they had to. But I suppose you can't feel that now—just wait till you stand where I stand, you'll understand then. But you do what you want. I don't give a damn. It's your life, Barron, your immortal life; I've got mine, and that's all I really care about."

"Never figured you for a True Believer, Bennie," said Barron, smiling. (But the smile was guarded, a put-on?) "Don't worry, I'll be there to collect when I'm good and ready."

And I'll be there to collect you, you smart-ass bastard, Howards thought as he turned to leave. Save your bullshit tricks for Wednesday nights, Barron, we're both gonna need 'em. You'll go to Colorado, and you'll do it soon, or else. No flunky holds out on Benedict Howards!

"For the last time, Sara, we play this my way—not yours," Jack Barron said, seeing her naked body stiff, half-foetaled, and about as sexy as an old inner tube, lying uptight and pale in the sickly city moonlight that filtered through the bedroom skylight, framing them both, curled face to face untouching like bleached tadpoles on the electrically-warmed bed, like the spotlight of some cheap-Jack off-off-Broadway two-hundred-seat playhouse.

"But what the hell *is* your way?" she said, that old six-years-dead whine creeping back into her voice, ghost of breaking-up days, and her eyes were glassy mirrors in the darkness, mirroring depths beyond depths—or just an illusion about as deep as a phosphor-dot pattern on a TV screen?

Half the time I think I know this chick through to where she lives, he thought, and the rest of the time I wonder if she lives *anywhere* or do I just see illusions of depths, my self-projected Sara of the mind on the vidphone screen of her face? And his naked body next to hers felt at this moment like a piece of meat connected to his mind only by the most novocained of sensory circuits.

"Why didn't we go to Colorado with Howards?" she was saying. "Why don't we take the treatment right away? Then that slimy Howards'd have nothing left to hold over our heads, and you could start right in on him again next Wednesday. And why did you want to play that stupid game with him, leave him guessing whether I told you everything or not? Why...?"

Why? Why? Why? thought Jack Barron. Jesus H Christ on a bicycle! Go explain to her; you can't even explain it to yourself—belly-message is all, smell of danger behind everything, reality behind reality behind reality slippery feel of uncertainty like driving through traffic in rain fogged wind-shield stoned on acid; impossible to know where objective stone-wall reality's at, but knowing for sure you don't see it yet, gotta inch along real slow by the seat of your pants or get run over by Howards' Mack Truck Chinese box lie within lie within lie puzzle ...

"Because it's just what Bennie wants me to do," he said, if only to cut off the nagging sound of her voice with his own. "He wanted us to have the treatment now, he wanted it real bad, so bad that when I let him know that I knew how hot he was for us to do it, he backed off. And that's just not Bennie's pattern, that cat's gotta be *real* uptight about blowing *something* to back water..."

Just don't add up, Barron thought. Bennie's too paranoid, and not dumb enough to trust me. Makes no sense, one thing he really has on me now is immortality, I was him, I'd withhold the treatment until I delivered the goods, got the Freezer Bill through at least, only real insurance Bennie's got. And *that* he's hot to throw away! Stick the ace he holds right up my sleeve, put me in the catbird-seat. So, somehow, that immortality treatment's gotta be his real insurance—*his* ace in the hole, not mine. But how? It just doesn't add up. And until it does, Jack Barron doesn't come within a thousand miles of that damned Rocky Mountain Freezer.

Sara reached out, touched the inner curve of his upper thigh. But it felt mechanical and far away; he just wasn't in the mood, didn't think she really was either. "What're you thinking about?" she asked. "You're a million miles away."

"I wish to hell I knew," Barron said. "I just got the feeling I'm in over my head, is why I don't want to take that treatment now, got the feeling it'd get me in too deep in something I don't dig. Everything that's happened since I got involved in this daisy-chain with Howards seems unreal—this President bullshit... immortality... they're just *words*, Sara, words out of some comic book or science fiction magazine, can't taste 'em, feel 'em, smell 'em, make 'em add up to anything that feels real. But that fucker Howards, he's real, no doubt about it, he smells real. And there's something oozing out of him that's real too, something big and scary, and I'm in it up to the eyeballs and I just don't know what it is..."

"I think I understand," Sara said, and her hand tightened on his thigh; she inched closer to him on the bed and he began, almost against his will, to pick up on the warmth of her beside him.

"But isn't it just because you're letting things happen, not making them happen? You're looking at it backwards—you should say to yourself, I've *gotta* stop Benedict Howards, and I've gotta keep immortality, and I've gotta do whatever I have to to do it. You can't wait for Howards to give you an opening, and you can't wait for someone else to do it, and you shouldn't worry about what Howards could do to us. Believe in yourself, Jack. Believe you can beat Howards no matter what he does; I believe it, and it's *my* life too. Oh, Jack, it's just too big... immortality for the whole world, or that lizard Howards going on and on and on... You *can't* cop-out now!"

"Cop-out?" Barron snarled in an instant lash-out defensive reaction. "Who the fuck are *you* to give me lectures about copping out, after what you've done, after the game you played with my head and Benedict Howards?" And immediately he was sorry.

'Cause she's right, in her own dumb way, he thought. That cocksucker Howards! Sara never was in his league, who is, he uses people, and then tosses 'em away like a snotty Kleenex; did it to Sara, do it to me I give him the chance, do it to the whole fucking country. That's where it's at, all right, Howards dealing a bummer to the whole dumb country, and old Jack Barron dealing his power-junk for him on living-colour junior high school street corners. That's exactly where it's at, Barron, and you can't con yourself otherwise.

"I deserved—"

"No you didn't Sara," Barron said, and drew her asexually to him, hugged her tight, sucking up her plain human warmth, hoping she was getting the same off him 'cause god knows she needs it I need it we all need it, need a little human warmth, little flesh-reality, with a freak-out monster like Benedict Howards running amok, shooting up the world with his lousy paranoid junk. "You hit me a little too close to home, is all. Bravery you're talking about, courage is all, and right now that's just a word, too..."

Yeah, courage, cheap commodity, when you're a punk Baby Bolshevik smart-ass kid and you got nothing to lose you can lay yourself on the line just for the surge. But with a pad like this, four mill a year, and immortality, and Christ knows what else on the line... throw all that away for a bunch of fucking words, *words*, is all, for two hundred and thirty million slob-loser cowards who wouldn't risk ten cents for Jack Barron? My life on the line, immortal life, and Howards with Christ knows what up his sleeve to pound me to a pulp, and for what, a chance to pin a tin hero-medal on my chest and give me a fancy kamikaze funeral? You're asking too much, Sara, I'm no hero, just a cat happened to get stuck in a position where it's all on his back, sick-joke of Kismet, is all. All I can do is just try to come out of this trip with as much as I can, hurting as few people as possible; that's the name of the game, game of life, is all.

"Promise you just one thing, Sara," he said. "I don't play Bennie's game or anyone else's but my own. We're gonna get ourselves immortality, and we're gonna keep our skins whole in the process—that's the prime order of business. But if I get a chance to stomp Howards without losing any of my own flesh, I'll do it. Bet your sweet ass I'll do it! I hate that motherfucker more than you do—he's trying to use me, and worse, he's got the gall to try and use my woman against me. We're gonna come out on top, you better believe it, and if we do in Bennie on the side, that's gravy. But just gravy."

"Jack..."

He felt warmth in her voice again, but behind it still the thin edge of that crazy Baby Bolshevik berserker determination, and for some reason he found himself digging it this time, digging his simple good-hearted chick, with her cunt-felt black and white silly-ass ideals should be protected, not stomped on, and in any decent world would be. But we're all stuck in *this* world, and here, Sara, baby, there be tigers.

"Know something else?" he asked, feeling mind-circuit connections with his body begin to open, juices flowing into channels of think-feel integration, the skin-on-skin woman-warmth reality against him. "In about five minutes, I think I'll ball you senseless like you never been fucked before. Whatever else you are or aren't, you're good inside, chick, and you deserve it."

We all deserve it.

Gongingonging—gong! gong! gong!

"Ummph ..." Jack Barron grunted, waking up in the disorienting darkness, a weight heavy against his chest. "What the..."

Gong! Gong! Gong!

Uuuh, he thought fuzzily, goddamned vidphone. He half-sat-up against the bedstead, Sara's head sliding down his bare chest into his lap, made the connection, stopping the gonging that had been pounding behind his ears like a headache commercial. What the hell time is it? he wondered. What stupid bastard's waking me up at this time of night?

Grumbling, still trying to shake the sleep out of his head, Barron saw that Sara was still asleep, fumbled the vidphone down onto the bed beside him, turned the custom volume-control knob down to the lowest setting, and squinted sourly at the face glowing up greyly at him from the vidphone screen, wanly phosphorescent in the darkness: long dark hair over a man's thin-boned face. (Something familiar about this silly schmuck calling me up in the middle of the night, how the hell did he get my unlisted number...?)

"Hello, Jack," a gravelly whisper from the vidphone said as Barron sleepily tried to place the face. (I know this cat, but who in hell is he?) "Brad Donner. Remember?" the vidphone image said.

Donner... Brad Donner... Barron thought. Berkeley or Los Angeles or someplace, old Baby Bolshevik type I haven't seen in years... Yeah, LA, just before I got the show, friend of Harold Spence, some kind of brown-nosing brat-lawyer always talking about running for Congress or something... Jesus Christ, every prick I ever talked to in person thinks he can bug me any time he feels like it...

"You know what time it is, Donner?" Barron snarled, then lowered his voice, remembering Sara's sleeping against his lap and, boy, what a night, am I sore! "'Cause I sure don't. Must be four or five in the morning. Where'd you learn your manners, in the Gestapo?"

"Yeah, Jack," Donner said. (Stop calling me Jack, you brownnosed mother!) "I know it's a bad hour, but I had to get to you right away. Got your number from Spence in LA, you remember, Harry was a big buddy of yours in those days?"

"Nobody's my buddy at *this* hour," Barron said. "If you're asking me some favour you sure picked a stupid time to do it, Donner."

"No favour, Jack," Donner said. "I've been working here in Washington as public relations counsellor to Ted Hennering these three years, anyway till he was killed..."

"Bully for you, Donner," Barron grumbled. Figures that this putz with all his SJC bullshit would end up as flack for a lox like Hennering! Now with Hennering dead, I'm supposed to get him another job—at four a.m.? Jesus—

"I just got woke up myself," Donner said, "by Ted's widow Madge. She's all shook, Jack, been scared out of her head since Ted was killed. Came over to my place, woke me up, said she had to talk to you right away, and I think you'd better listen, after the hell you just gave Benedict Howards. Mrs Hennering?" Donner's face was replaced by what once must've been an old-fashioned 'handsome matron' in her fifties, thick grey hair in semi-disarray, prim little lips trembling, and wild frantic eyes staring up from the vidphone screen. What's going on? Barron thought, coming full awake. *Madge Hennering?*

"Mr Barron..." Madge Hennering said in a voice that seemed accustomed to be being snotty-patrician-calm but was now edged with shrill frenzy. "Thank God! Thank God! I didn't know where to turn, what to do, who to go to, who I could possibly trust after they... after Ted... And then I saw your programme, the things you said about Benedict Howards, and I knew you, were one man I could trust, one man who *couldn't* be involved with that murdering... You'll believe me, won't you, Mr Barron? You've got to believe me, you've got to tell the country how my husband died ..."

"Take it easy, Mrs Hennering," Barron said soothingly, slipping half-mechanically into *Bug Jack Barron* cool vidphone-circuit consciousness. "I know how you must feel, that terrible accident, but try to—"

"Accident!" Madge Hennering screamed, loud enough even at minimum vidphone audio to make Sara stir in his lap. "It was no accident. *My husband was murdered.* I'm sure he was murdered. There must've been a bomb on his plane. Benedict Howards had him killed."

"What?" Barron grunted. She's gibbering, he thought. Hennering was Bennie's stooge all the way; nobody lost more when he died than Howards. This poor old bat's gone round the bend, I gotta be a shrink too, at four in the a.m.?

"Don't you think that's a matter for the police?" he said. "Assuming, of course, that it's true." Get the hell off my aching back, lady!

"But I can't go to the police," she said. "There's no evidence. Howards planned it that way. There's nothing left of Ted or his plane... nothing..." She began to sob, then with an effort Barron could not help admiring, set her jaw, said, icy-calm: "I'm sorry. It's just that I was the only witness, and I've got no evidence to back it up, and I just don't know what to do."

"Look," Barron said wearily, "I realise it's bad taste to talk politics at a time like this, but I guess I have to. Howards had no reason in the world to kill your husband, Mrs Hennering. Your husband was a co-sponsor of the Foundation's Freezer Bill, and it was an open secret that Howards was backing him for President. To be blunt, your husband was Howards' stoo—er, *ally*. Howards had nothing to gain by killing him and everything to lose. Surely you know that."

"I'm no fool, Mr Barron. But the day before Ted died he had a long phone conversation with Benedict Howards. I only heard part of it, but they argued and called each other terrible things, *terrible* things. Ted told Howards he was through with him, would have no part of the Foundation anymore, said Howards was a filthy monster. I've never seen Ted so furious. He told Howards that he was going to publicly withdraw support from the Freezer Utility Bill, make a statement to the press about something awful he had found out the Foundation was doing. And Howards said, 'No one backs out on Benedict Howards, Hennering. Cross me, and I'll squash you like a bug.' Those were his exact words. And then Ted said something terribly obscene, and hung up. When I asked Ted what it was all about, he got mad at me, but he really seemed terribly frightened—and I'd never seen my husband really scared before. Ted refused to tell me anything, said it was too dangerous for me to know, he didn't... didn't want my life to be in danger. And then he flew back home to talk with the Governor, but... but he never got there. Howards had him killed—I *know* he had him killed."

Crazy paranoid bullshit! Barron thought. Bet your ass Hennering was involved in forty-seven slimy deals with the Foundation, went from State Senator to Congressman to Senator on Bennie's bread, anybody with brains enough to read the funny papers knows that. Real touching lady, old college try to make your husband a dead hero instead of Bennie's late stooge, Democrat front-man for Foundation muscle. Deathbed repentance yet, and just before he's conveniently blown to kingdom come. Ted Hennering, Noble Martyr, Yeah, sure, after a hundred million people saw him two weeks ago gibbering like... like...

Jesus H Christ! Was *that* why Hennering was so uptight? Shit, it *does* figure! Hennering was killed on Thursday night, which means he could've had it out with Howards either on Wednesday or Thursday, like she says, would've known whatever was supposed to have turned him off the Foundation when he was on *Bug Jack Barron*. Would sure explain why he was so out of it...

"You do believe me, don't you Mr Barron?" Madge Hennering said. "Everyone in Washington says you're an enemy of Benedict Howards. You'll want to use this against him, you'll want to put me on your programme and help me tell the country how my husband died, won't you? And not just to save Ted's reputation. Mr Barron, I was married to Ted for twenty-one years. I really knew him, I know he wasn't a great man, and I know he did cooperate with Howards, but he wasn't a bad man or a coward. He found out something about the Foundation for Human Immortality that infuriated him, sickened him, something so terrible he feared for his life, and for mine, just because he knew it.

"I don't know much about politics, but murdering a United States Senator is something that even a man like Benedict Howards wouldn't risk doing unless... unless he felt he couldn't afford not to. I don't know what this is all about, but something terrible has to be going on for Howards to resort to political assassination. A lunatic with a gun is one thing, but this... this is something out of European history books... the Borgias... Ted, oh, Ted!" and she began to shake, sob convulsively, convincing Barron that at least the woman wasn't trying to put him on.

But cold-blooded political assassination, he thought, that's gotta be pure paranoia. So maybe Hennering did find out something rank enough to turn him off the Foundation (but what the fuck could be rank enough to make a phony like Hennering get enough religion to throw away Howards' backing for the Presidential nomination?), maybe he did have a fight with Howards, and maybe Bennie did threaten him (how many times has Howards given me that squash-you-like-a-bug schtick?). But blowing up aeroplanes, the whole Borgia bit... pure coincidence, is all. This hysterical chick adds up one and one and gets three, is all.

Donner replaced Madge Hennering on the vidphone screen. "Well, Jack," he said, "what're you going to do? Should I have her call in Wednesday? This is big, scary—"

"Yeah, it's scary all right," Barron said. "What scares me is the thought of the lawsuit Howards could slap on everyone in sight if that woman gets on the air and accuses him of murder without a scrap of evidence. You're supposed to be a lawyer? Don't even know libel when it's screaming in your face! Not only could Howards sue, but the FCC would have me off the air quicker than you could say 'yellow journalism.' Forget it Donner, I may be crazy, but I'm not out of my mind."

"But, Jack—"

"And don't call me Jack!" Barron snapped loudly. "In fact, don't bother to call me at all." And he broke the connection as Sara's eyes finally blinked half open.

"Uh... whazzat...?" she grunted.

"Go back to sleep, baby," said Barron. "Just a crank call, is all. Just a couple screwballs."

Yeah, he thought, just a pair of nuts. Bennie may be a little flakey, but he's not about to go around killing people; he's got too much to lose, his precious immortal life in the electric chair.

Nevertheless, his back against the bedstead began to itch faintly.

12

JEEZ MAN, what's the matter with you, Jack Barron thought as they rolled the final commercial. Real stinkeroo tonight. So acid's legal under Strip City SJC jurisdiction, but maybe illegal under Greg Morris' California State Law, so Morris has his Attorney General demand access to the Strip City Narcotics Licensing Bureau records, to make Woody Kaplan look like either a criminal or a stoolie, and the mayor of Freakoutsville says 'nyet.' Big fucking deal. Should've suggested the state-fuzz bust into the Strip City offices, grab the records on a state writ, then the hippy cops could bust 'em for breaking and entering under local law, and the state cops bust the local fuzz for interfering with state police, and you'd have all the cops in the County of Los Angeles arresting each other on street corners, good for laughs, at least. Which is about all the last 45 minutes could've been good for.

But I even blew that, just can't keep my mind on that kind of crap, not with the *real* action that's going on. Madge Hennering run over by a truck! Hit-and-run by a Hertz rental with the plates removed, impossible to trace, try to tell yourself *that* wasn't a pro job! Try to kid yourself you don't know who bought the hit, Barron... Man, oh, man, would I like to get Bennie on the line now and hit him with *that!* Yeah, and what would he hit me with, a safe falling off the Empire State Building, or a lawsuit and the FCC and the kitchen sink...?

'Course it all *could* be coincidence, or the Hennering clan could have other enemies she didn't talk about. Yeah, sure, and the Mars Expedition's gonna find out Mars is made of red cheese. What the hell am I mixed up in anyway?

Snap out of it man, you've got a show to run, gotta try and pull *something*, out of tonight's fiasco. And the promptboard said '60 seconds.'

"Hey Vince," Barron said over the intercom circuit, "we got any real kook calls come into the monkey block tonight?"

Gelardi's face was sour and worried behind the control-booth glass (Vince smells the egg we're laying too), but he grinned wanly as he said, "You kidding? This is still *Bug Jack Barron,* just barely maybe, but we still got every freako in the country calling in." And the promptboard flashed '30 seconds.'

"Okay," Barron said, "give me the screwiest call you got, don't even tell me what it is. My head's just not on straight tonight, and I want something'll really blow my mind, get some action going. But no politics, for chrissakes, I want a real Little Old Lady from Pasadena type, good, clean, All-American kook."

"Have *I* got a kook for *you,*" Gelardi said in a thick Yiddish accent as the

144

promptboard flashed 'On the Air.'

Looks like he meant it, Barron thought as the monitor screen split down the middle; on the left hand side the grey on grey image of a wasted Negro face, uncombed semi-nappy hair, black on black jaw-stubble shadow, over a fancy five-hundred-dollar gold-filigree-collared sportjac half unbuttoned revealing a torn old T-shirt, semifocused watery eyes staring across the monitor at his living-colour image in an obviously advanced state of alcoholic stupefaction.

"This is *Bug Jack Barron*, and you're on the air," Barron began, coming alive with old-fashioned freak-show anticipation, remembering that Los Angeles Birch-grill Peeping-Tom dock-and-hotseat show where the whole thing started when he turned around the third degree light and rubber hose of old Joe Swyne—and, Joe, baby, wherever you are, this looks like one that would've been right down your twisted little alley.

"Name's Henry George Franklin," a rheumy basso said, and behind his head the screen showed vague slat-shack outlines beyond the rococo shape of the most gigantic pseudo-Arabic TV-stereo console the world had ever seen. "Y' can call me Frank, ol' Jack Barron, jus' call me Frank."

"Okay, Frank," said Barron, "and you can just call me Jack. And now that we're on a first-name basis, let's hear what's bugging you." Come on, come on, freak out already, got about twelve minutes to turn tonight's turkey into instant Salvador Dali. And Vince, anticipating, split the screen in a crazy jagged diagonal, with Henry George Franklin above Barron like a custard pie about to be thrown.

"Well, y'see, ol' Jack, it's just like this," Henry George Franklin began, waving a horny finger in front of his wet lips, "yeah, just about 'zactly like this. Fella like ol' Frank down here in Mississippi, sharecropping little ol' cotton farm, he's got t' have him a woman, right? I mean, poor or no poor, mouth to feed or not, woman she comes in mighty handy, fixing supper and breakfast and givin' him a little pleasure inbetween. I mean, you can afford her or not, don't matter, no matter how poor you are, woman she hauls her own freight."

"Apparently you meet a better class of chick than I do," Barron said dryly. "Maybe I oughta drop down and look around. But I hope you haven't called just to discuss your love life. Interesting as I'm sure it must be, we can both get in big trouble if it gets *too* interesting."

"Ain't had no love life—'cept a night in Evers every week or so for seven years, ol' Jack," Franklin said. "Not since the old lady kicked off sticking me with a daughter. Thas what I mean, see? Don't seem like a fair trade, do it, woman for a daughter? Daughter eats almost as much as a woman, but it's like keeping one of them there parakeets, just eats and jabbers and don't do nothin'. Means y'can't even afford another woman, not regular like. So it just makes good sense, you stuck with a useless mouth to feed, somebody makes a real nice offer, sensible man's gotta take it and sell her."

"Huh?" grunted Barron. "I think one of us has had one too many. Sounded like you were saying something about selling your daughter."

"Well, sure. Ain't that what I called you about in the first place, ol' Jack...?" Franklin said fuzzily. "Didn't I tell y'all? Maybe I didn't. Thas what's bugging me, I mean me being a rich man now I kinda miss the little critter, now that I can afford her. I want y'all to help me get her back. Seems to me that buying someone's daughter, that might just not be legal. Thing to do is maybe find her and make the police get her back. Ain't had no doings with the police before... not from *that* side of things, if you know what I mean. Thought ol' Jack Barron was the man to get to help me."

"You... ah... sold your daughter?" Barron asked as the promptboard flashed '8 minutes,' and Vince inverted the diagonally-split screen showing wry, cynical Jack Barron now uppermost. Boy, this cat's loaded! Even money he never had a daughter. But what's the schtick, why did Vince feed me this lush?

"Hey don't look at me that way!" Henry George Franklin said indignantly. "Not like I sold her to some pimp or something. That fancy-looking shade fella, he said they were gonna take real good care of her, feed her nothing but the best, dress her nice and fancy, and give her a college education. Seemed like I would just be a bad papa I didn't let her have all them shade-type advantages—and besides, that shade fella he gave me five hundred big ones in United States money."

Could be he's on the level? Barron wondered. One of those illegal adoption rackets? But don't they usually go after infants? Not seven-year-olds, not seven-year-old *Negroes*. What he say, five hundred dollars? Going price on a nice WASP baby on the black market can't be much more than that, how can any adoption ring make a profit paying five hundred bucks for some seven-year-old Negro—and what was that about a college education?

"Five hundred dollars *is* a lot of money," Barron said. "Still I—"

"Five hundred?" Franklin yelled. "Hey, what kind of man you think I am—sell my own flesh and blood for five hundred dollars? I said five hundred *big* ones, ol' Jack. Five hundred thousand dollars."

"You're... you're trying to tell us that someone bought your daughter for *five hundred thousand dollars?*" Barron said archly as the promptboard flashed '5 minutes.' "Nothing personal, Mr Franklin, but why would anyone want your daughter, or anyone else's for that matter, bad enough to shell out five hundred thousand dollars?"

"Why you askin' me?" Franklin said. "You the big, smart, expensive shade, ol' Jack, you tell me. How should I know why some fancy shade's crazy enough to hand me $500,000 in hundred dollar bills, whole satchelful of money, for my worthless daughter? You gotta understand I was dirt-poor at the time. I never saw so much money in my whole life, never expect to again. Sure, I figured the shade was crazy, but that money was the real thing, and when a crazy man hands you a satchelful of money, who's gonna stop and say, 'Hey, you actin' crazy, man giving me all this nice money?' You just gotta hope he stays crazy long enough to give you the money and forget your address."

Something (too loaded to make up a story like that, too defensive, got past the whole monkey block, dig that sportjac he's wearing, and that crazy jukebox of a TV-stereo must've cost at least a thousand dollars) told Barron that Henry George Franklin, raving though he was, wasn't lying. Some lunatic bought this cat's daughter for a satchelful of money, whether it came to exactly five hundred thou or not, and this load of garbage was far gone enough at the time to take it. Some Tennessee Williams screwball-millionaire-colonel type cracker's running around in his Confederate-Grey longjohns... who knows, maybe he just never conceded the 13th Amendment and bought this jerk's daughter and sold her to some adoption ring at a big loss just so he could tell himself he was keeping the darkie slave trade alive? And this Franklin cat is so rank, now he's trying to double-cross the Mad Cunnel and keep the bread too! Real American Gothic; poor old Joe would cream in his pants over this one, just his bag.

"This cat you say bought your daughter," Barron said as Vince gave Franklin three-quarters screen, "what was he like?"

"Like...? Why, he was just this fancy-dressed shade with a satchelful of money, and, anyway, y'know all shades look alike No, wait a minute, ol' Jack, y'know even though he was dressed real rich-like, I kinda got the feeling he was some kind of what-you-call-it, like one of them English butlers...?"

"You mean a flunky," Barron suggested as the promptboard flashed '3 minutes.'

"Yeah, thas it, a *flunky*. I mean, he didn't hand over that satchel like it was his own money... I don't care if you old Rockefeller himself, you got to feel something, make some sign, handing over five hundred thousand bucks worth of your own money... No, I guess he was just some kind of fancy messenger boy."

"The question is, a messenger boy for *who*?" Barron said, wondering who could be doing something like that for what? Strictly from old comic books and TV shows—gotta be either Fu Manchu or Dr Sivana behind it... Or, more likely, some slimy old pervert with a lech for tender young... *blech!* How the hell did I end up with a call like this? Go tell a crazy wop to blow your mind!

"Just what did this man say he wanted your daughter for?" And the promptboard mercifully flashed '2 minutes.'

"Something about what he call a *social experiment*," Franklin said. "Used a lot of ten-dollar words I just didn't understand, ol' Jack. Some kinda...

genics or something. Something about heredity and 'vironment and random samples… taking poor black kids and growin' 'em up with rich white kids, like they was born rich, y'know, send 'em both to the same schools, send 'em both to college, give 'em both what that shade called equivalent childhood environments and see who comes out ahead.

"This shade said it was supposed to prove black kids were as smart as shade kids, what he called *herently* or somethin'. So I figured how could I refuse, what with doin' something fine for Tessie—that's m'daughter—doin' my part for black people, like Governor Greene down here's always saying, and a whole satchelful of money, y'know…"

Barron tapped his left foot-button three times, and Vince gave him the winding-up-for-the-sign-off three-quarters screen as the promptboard flashed '90 seconds.' Maybe not a Mad Cunnel, he thought. Maybe some crazy black shrink got ahold of big bread somehow, decided he had a mission to prove Negroes as good as whites? Vince really goofed this time, something crazy going on, but strictly garden-variety lunacy, *National Enquirer* stuff and lousy television. Well, I suppose you can't be brilliant every week.

"And that's all you know, Mr Franklin?" Barron asked. "You sold your daughter for $500,000 to a flunky working for some kook you've never seen, supposedly to take part in some half-assed social experiment?" Barron paused, trying to time the ending, waiting for the '60 seconds' signal, at which Vince would give him full screen, and—

"Hey, wait a minute!" Franklin shouted. "Hey, I want her back, you gotta get her back! Look, ol' Jack, I know I did wrong, an' I wanna get her back. (The '60 seconds' signal flashed across the promptboard, but Vince couldn't cut Franklin out in the middle of a freakout, look real bad, Barron knew, gotta cut him off somehow.) Thas why I called in the first place, that shade musta been crazy—I don't want my daughter with some crazy nut, not now when I got the money to feed her. Hey, you gotta—"

"I'm afraid our time is about up," Barron finally squeezed in, signalling to Vince to bleed down Franklin's audio.

"Yeah, but, hey, what about Tessie, ol' Jack?" Franklin's waning voice said as the promptboard flashed '30 seconds,' and Barron saw that his drunk was edging over from lightly-maudlin to guilty-belligerent, and thanked whatever gods there be that the timing was so right. "I didn't mean to do it… fact is, I had been maybe hitting the corn a little at the time, I didn't know what I was doing. Yeah, thas it, I was mentally incompetent can't hold no man what's mentally incompetent to no—"

Vince, maybe figuring that Franklin was about to utter The Word, cut his audio entirely and gave Barron full screen.

"Our time's up, Mr Franklin," said Barron (thank god!), "but we'll be right here at the same old stand next week, Area Code 212 969-6969, and you can call in again then, and have the same chance as every man, woman, and child in the United States (in a pig's ass!) to... *Bug Jack Barron.*"

And at long last, the promptboard flashed 'Off the Air.' Barron thumbed the intercom switch, his instant impulse was to scream at crazy wop Vince wincing behind the safety of the control-booth glass like a cocker spaniel just shit on the rug and knows it.

But Gelardi beat him to the punch: "Hey, I'm sorry, Jack. He was real funny all the way through the monkey block till he got on the air. Sounded like some crazy spade gibbering about the revival of the slave trade. Last time I feed you any kind of drunk, Scout's honour. Hey... you don't think he was on the level, do you?"

Aw, what the fuck, Barron thought, so Vince blew one. My fault as much as his, my head just wasn't there this week. "Who gives a shit?" he said tiredly. "Let the *National Enquirer* and the Mississippi fuzz worry about it. Forget it, Vince, let's all go home and get stoned. Lousy show, is all, we got a right to goof once in a while."

Yeah, a real stinker all around, Barron thought. And you damned well know why; sixty minutes of pure mickeymouse on top of two real nitty-gritty shows on the Foundation, and that's where the big-league action's really at right now. And you can't touch that now with a fork.

And as he got up, the seat of his pants soaked with sweat from the hotseat, Jack Barron experienced a strange sense of loss, remembering the adrenaline surge of his mortal duel with Howards against the background of this week's trivia created a weird nostalgia for the taste of playing the big game for the big stakes, a game that was already played out.

Time like this, Barron thought, I wonder why I dig this business in the first place. Maybe there's a bigger kick somewhere than being a star?

"Don't say it, Sara, for chrissakes, don't say it. I know, I know, I laid a dinosaur egg tonight," Jack Barron said, opening up the front of his sportjac, flopping down flush on the carpet next to Sara's chair, fumbling in his pocket and pulling out a pack of Acapulco Golds, sticking a joint in his mouth, lighting it, sucking in the smoke, exhaling, all while Sara stared at him blankly. "Thousand-year-old Chinese rotten dinosaur egg with green mould on it, is all."

"I thought that Strip City bit was pretty interesting," she said with what he recognised as dumb, infuriating sincerity. "That freako you had on at the end, though—"

"Don't mention that man's name," Barron said. "I know what you're gonna say, and I don't wanna hear it, tonight's show was strictly from old Joe Sw—"

"Hey, I wasn't going to say anything at all. What's the matter with you, Jack?"

Yeah, what *is* the matter with you, man? Barron thought. She's only trying to make you feel good, and you come down on her with paranoid stomping boots. Come on, man, you've done bad shows before, dozens of 'em, never got you this uptight before. Cool it, for chrissakes!

He got to his knees, reached up, pulled Sara's face down to him, kissed her tongue on tongue, held it for a *pro forma* moment, but couldn't get interested. Shit! he thought. My head's been out in left field ever since I found out someone killed Madge Hennering. Someone... *yeah, sure.* Someone name of Benedict Howards got my name on his piece of paper, thinks he owns my bod, and maybe he's right. Kills Hennering because the lox found out some fucking Foundation secret scared him shitless, scared Howards shitless... and what scares Howards shitless...?

Jesus H Christ! Been staring me in the face all along! Only thing that scared Bennie was me finding out what his immortality treatment was... That's gotta be what Hennering found out, what they killed him for! And that cocksucker Howards is practically twisting my arm to make me take the treatment!

Barron flopped down on the floor again, took another drag. There it is, he thought, Rome to which all roads lead. Howards' willing to risk killing a goddamned *Senator* over it, he's so scared someone will find out. But... but then, why does he want me to take the treatment? Don't make sense, if he's so uptight about keeping it secret. Why? Why? What the fuck's going on?

"What's wrong Jack?" Sara asked. "You look like you're about to turn purple... and that kiss was about as sexy as a bowl of raw chicken livers."

"I don't know, baby (can't tell her Howards is going around murdering people, just uptight her), I just smell something bad in the air, nothing personal intended."

"Couldn't be that you're pissed at yourself for just screwing around tonight when you really wanted to go after Howards again?" she asked, half-knowingly, half-hopefully.

"That too," Barron muttered. "But not for your gung-ho Baby Bolshevik reasons. Cutting up Bennie was good television, last week's rating was the best in three years, goddamn hard act to follow. And Woody Kaplan's insanity and some gibbering drunk's the kind of crap that went out with old Joe Swyne. Boring is all, when you've played in the big leagues there's not much kick in being a hero in the bushes. Yeah, that's all it is, a letdown from two real winners..."

"You're sure you really mean that?" she asked, and he saw what she was fishing for; shit, all I need is another round of that cop-out crap on top of—

The vidphone began to chime.

Barron got up slowly, letting it chime—a nasty premonition that it was Luke with more bullshit, more Jack-you-fucking-cop-out-you, more waving of the Baby Bolshevik let's-you-and-him-fight-bloody shirt—finally reached the vidphone, made the connection and felt a weird adrenaline-thrill punch pulsing into his brain as the old familiar black and white image of Benedict Howards looked out of the vidphone screen at him with crackling paranoid eyes.

"Kill it, Barron. Sit on it, I warn you!" Howards said, his voice shrill-edged and threatening.

"Sit on—(*what?*, Barron was about to say, stopped himself, realising something was really uptighting Bennie, best way to find out what is to make like you know, he seems to think I know, let him know I don't, maybe he'll clam)—it? Why, *whatever* do you mean? Far as I know, there's nothing to sit on." And the last with a number one dirty smile.

"No more games," said Howards. "No more screwing around, you're working for *me* now, and you jump when I say frog, and don't you forget it. Or else—"

"Or else *what*, Bennie?" Barron drawled, knowing on one level that in the game Bennie was playing it's the Big Or Else, is all; on another level unable to take seriously the whole cops-and-wops hit-man scene. "What do you think you *can* do? I got *your* name on paper too, remember? I got Greene and Morris anxious to jump into my corner in case you get too feisty with me. I got *Bug Jack Barron*—and I got immortality legally free and clear any time I want it. You couldn't afford to have me sue you for breach of *that* contract, and we both know it. Time you got it through your fat little head you can't *own* Jack Barron… or you're gonna get hurt, Howards, hurt real bad."

And Barron saw Benedict (five-hundred-billion-dollar power of life-over-death Senatorial-assassin immortal) Howards fighting for self-control, forcing a sickening rictus that was almost a smile, actually eating crow.

"Look Barron, so we don't like each other. Know why? 'Cause we're too much alike, that's why. Two strong men, and neither of us has ever been number two to anyone. We both want it all, and we both want it on our own terms—and that's the only way to fly. Well, we just can't both be number one, and isn't that what we're really fighting about? But it's stupid, Barron, pig-headed stupid. In the long run we're both on the same side, right? I mean the real long run, million-year long run, we both got the same thing to lose.

"Let me show you, you and your wife fly out to Colorado, let me make you immortal like me. Then you'll taste how much we both got to lose every time you breathe. Make a different man of you, Barron, make you more than a man, take it from the only man who knows first-hand. Jack Barron immortal'd have to see he's on the same side as Benedict Howards immortal—us against them, life eternal against the fading black circle, and, believe me, that's all that counts, everything else is shit for the birds."

He really means it, Barron realised, and maybe he's right. But you know he's sure he'd be *numero uno* in that set-up for some reason... and Ted Hennering died because he found out what the immortality treatment was. Found out and had his choice of being Bennie's flunky and maybe President, or risking his life—and a phony cop-out like Hennering told Howards to get stuffed. And Bennie killed him. And he wants me in that position, thinks he can somehow get me there by making me immortal...

"I'm still passing," Barron said. "I just don't trust you." And he felt the adrenaline-surge of the smell of danger, took a quick drag of pot on top of it, picking up on the kick of being back in the big league again, playing for life-and-death stakes, and said: "And I know a few things you don't know I know, Howards. And I'm not gonna tell you what they are, gonna let you sweat a little, it's good for the soul."

He saw fear and anger fight each other in Howards' eyes, knew he was biting flesh, turned and saw Sara's eyes shining with that berserker Berkeley fire drinking him in, found himself digging the pure my-man my-hero heat she was giving off for him from Berkeley attic Meridian streets his chick all the way beside him, felt ten years younger than tonight's lousy-turkey of a show, full of piss and vinegar and good pot and an old line from a childhood book *(The Dying Earth,* wasn't it?) drummed like a chord inside him: 'Danger goes with *me.'*

"I'm warning you, Barron," Howards said, his eyes now crocodile-cold, "you put that Franklin lunatic on the air again, and you've had it—you've *really* had it. Benedict Howards plays for all the marbles, and he plays for keeps."

Franklin? That crazy sot? *That's* what's uptighting him? Don't make sense, what's that kook got to do with Howards?

"Don't tell me how to run my show," Barron said. "Maybe I'll do another show on Franklin, or a piece of a show, depends on the next Brackett Count (if I got the stomach to look at it after this week's fiasco)."

"I'm telling you, and I won't tell you again, don't put Franklin on the air again!" Howards shouted.

Just what *I* said! Barron thought. Maybe I was wrong? Maybe hottest Foundation show of all's tied into raving nut Henry George Franklin? Bennie sure thinks so. But how?

Barron smiled nastily. "You know, the more you tell me not to, the more I think it'd make a good show. You and me and Franklin and a hundred million people, nice and cosy. How's it grab you, Bennie?" (Hey, why in hell am I doing this? he wondered, feeling his unknown belly calling his shots.)

"You can push me *too* far," Howards said. "Push me too far, and no matter who you are you get fed to the fishes. Even—"

"Even a United States Senator?" Barron suggested. "Even, oh, say, someone like for instance, Ted Hennering...?"

Even on the vidphone screen, Barron could see Howards go pale. Paydirt! How's it feel to play patty-cake with a murderer? A kick, is all! He fingered the Acapulco Gold in his hand. What they putting in these things these days?

"You..." Howards stammered. "I'm warning you for the last time, Barron, lay, off the Franklin thing, or no one'll ever warn you about anything again."

Jack Barron felt something snap within him. Nobody threatens Jack Barron like that and gets away with it! Think I never spit in death's eye, Bennie? You should've been in Meridian, whole fucking mob with blood in their beady little eyes, me and Luke and Sara and a couple dozen others against a thousand rednecks, death on the hoof, and I faced 'em down 'cause I know the secret you don't—murder's a coward's game, is all, and deep inside murderers know it, you just gotta let 'em know *you* know it; never run from a wild animal, I read somewhere. Cop-out maybe, bullshit artist maybe, but Jack Barron doesn't run from any man!

"You can take your silly-ass threats," Barron said, feeling the words like hot lava bubble out of his throat, "and you can write 'em on broken Coke bottles and shove it up your ass! Threaten me, and you won't be worrying about your precious immortal life much longer, you'll be too busy wishing you were never born. Know what I'm gonna do, Bennie? I'm gonna fly down to Mississippi and have a long man to man talk with Mr Henry George Franklin, and, who knows, when I'm through, maybe I'll do two shows or ten or a hundred on him—and there's not a fucking thing you can do about it! I'm sick of you, Howards! I'm sick of listening to you play big man 'cause you're not a big man, you're the kind of thing that crawls out from under wet rocks, coward, is all, kind of coward I eat for breakfast, and you'll be pissing in your pants scared shitless till the day you die if you live a million years. You bug me, Bennie, know that, *you bug me*. And you haven't even got a taste yet of what happens when you really bug Jack Barron."

"I'll kill—"

"Aw go stick your tongue out at babies!" Barron shouted. "Maybe you'll have better luck there, 'cause you don't scare me, Howards. And I'm tired of looking at your ugly face!" And he broke the connection.

And wondered in the next moment just what the hell his big mouth had got him into—and why.

"Do you really mean it this time?" Sara asked, her eyes wide as saucers.

"Bet your sweet ass I mean it!" Barron snapped, surprised that his anger was still mounting, not cooling, "I'm tired of listening to that motherfucker threaten me, treat me like some fucking flunky! Who the hell does he think he is, five hundred billion or no five hundred billion, immortality or no immortality, telling me how to run my show run my life? Maybe I shouldn't tell you this, but you're in this too, you got a right to know what

I'm playing around with. I'm pretty sure Howards had Ted Hennering murdered, 'cause the good Senator tried to cross him. *That's* the kind of man you want me to go after—sure you wouldn't rather have a nice safe cop-out in your bed now?"

"Are *you* afraid of him?" Sara asked quietly.

Who knows? Barron thought. Way I feel right now, I'm too pissed to be scared of anything. And he felt the blood singing the berserker Berkeley Jack-and-Sara battle-song behind his ears, and man, oh, man, it felt good, like a hard-on of the mind.

"No, I'm not afraid of him. He packs a big switchblade sure but Bennie's nothing but a punk, fifty-year-old five-hundred-billion dollar immortal *punk*. Punk, is all! You never saw me back down from no punk. Maybe I should be scared, shit, maybe I *am*, but I'm sure as hell not gonna *act* scared."

"Then I'm not scared either," she said with a pure girlish grin, and hugged him to her, He kissed her, hot, wet, tongue on tongue hard, felt the juices rising in him. Jeez, it feels good, he thought, my woman in my arms the night before the battle, haven't felt like this in ten thousand years.

"Eat drink and make Mary," he muttered into her ear, "for tomorrow we die..." *That ain't so fucking funny.*

"What're you gonna do now?" she asked, pulling away half-playfully to arm's length.

"Gonna play arpeggios on your quivering bod," he said.

"But first, I'm gonna call Luke, have him locate Mr Henry George Franklin for me, then hop a plane right on down to Mississippi, just like I told Howards. Be gone only a day or two, and if anyone asks, you don't know where I am. I want this to be strictly between you and me and Luke and old Henry George."

"And Benedict Howards," Sara said. "Be careful, Jack, please be careful."

"I'm glad the bastard knows I'm going," said Barron. "Show him I know he's bluffing. Come on, baby, don't worry about me, it's all on Luke's turf, remember? I'm supposed to be the 'black shade' down there, or so they tell me. I'll keep out of dark alleys. Bennie won't dare try anything with a guest of the Governor."

13

EVERS, MISSISSIPPI, Jack Barron thought as the plane's wheels contacted the runway. Jeez, it's been a long time since I was down here, Luke's original inauguration as Boy Governor (wasn't it?), all those familiar faces from Berkeley and New York and Los Angeles—every Baby Bolshevik with the black skin entrance-fee zoomed in on Evers like narco-fuzz on a junk party when Mississippi finally went black. Only there *wasn't* no Evers then, that's right, was part of Luke's original platform: 'A New Capital for the New Mississippi.'

Yeah, just like any other Banana Republic, hundred million bucks to build a fancy new Capital, and five years later Luke's yelling for Federal subsidy of the state budget, Mississippi's so broke, and fat chance of *that!* Bread and circuses, is how the SJC took over Mississippi—long on circuses, that is, and short on bread. Way it'll stay too, unless...

Watch it, Barron! he told himself as the plane taxied toward the spanking-new gull-winged airport terminal (everything in Evers wasn't made out of old tin packing crates Coke sign garbage was strictly World's Fair stuff). Don't even think about that kind of crap down here, with Luke close enough to play with your live-in-person head. Got enough to handle with Howards & Co. without playing Napoleon.

As the plane approached the terminal building, Barron saw a funky-looking crowd milling around between the planes and the building; maybe a couple thousand ragged-looking Evers-slumtype down-and-out Negroes waving dozens of signs he couldn't quite make out, TV cameras clustered around a late-model Cad limousine, gaggle of reporters and photographer... But the screwy thing was that in the wan, grey, morning overcast every man and woman in the crowd was wearing dark sunglasses.

The plane rolled to a stop, the main door opened as an old-fashioned debarkation ramp was wheeled up for some reason, then there was some kind of commotion at the door between a stewardess and someone outside. Two Mississippi State Policemen, dressed and swaggering like every redneck Southern cop Barron had ever been but black as the proverbial ace of spades, stepped into the plane and sauntered heavily down the aisle, obviously digging the uptighting effect they were having on the white passengers, stopped in front of his seat.

"Mr Barron," the taller one said with gross formality, "please come with us."

"Hey, what is this," Barron said, "some kind of bust? You crazy? You know who I am? Wait till Governor Greene—"

The shorter cop laughed fraternally. "Don't get uptight, man (obviously an import, Barron thought)," he said. "The bossman knows all about it. No bust, just the old red carpet treatment for the Black Shade."

Oh, no! Barron thought as he got to his feet and followed the cops down the aisle past grumbling passengers who obviously were being held on the plane till he debarked. He couldn't have! Not on twelve hours notice! Not even Luke could've set it up that fast... not unless he was all ready and waiting, just in case. Rastus, you conniving son of a bitch! Limousine, cops, crowd, TV cameras... No, no, this can't be happening! Jesus H Christ!

But the moment he stepped out onto the ramp in the cool morning air, flashbulbs began to blind him and the motley crowd began what was patently a carefully-rehearsed chant:

"Bug Jack Barron! Bug Jack Barron! Bug Jack Barron!" Squinting against the intermittent scintillance of the flashbulbs, Barron could now make out the signs the crowd was waving—full-colour posters of himself with the kinesthop-under-blackwash background he used on the show screaming '*Bug Jack Barron*' in red slash lettering; black and white photos of himself with 'Jack Barron' in white letters across the top and 'the Black Shade' in black letters across the bottom; white placards with oval featureless white head-outlines wearing opaque black sunglasses and no lettering at all he couldn't figure out.

"Bug Jack Barron! Bug Jack Barron! Bug Jack Barron!"

As he trotted down the ramp he saw Luke waiting for him at the bottom in a gaggle of flunkies. Luke wore a big button in each lapel—and he was also wearing shades. All his flunkies were wearing shades too, dark shades, black—

"She-*yit*," Barron groaned as he reached the bottom of the ramp. *Black Shades. The Black Shade!* That slick motherfucker!

"Welcome to the New Mississippi," Luke said with a great shit-eating smirk as Barron stood nose to nose with him in a sea of flashbulbs, read the buttons on each lapel: 'Bug Jack Barron' in red letters over blue kinesthop pattern (so that's where those buttons in the Village came from after all) in the left lapel, and in the right, the black on white head-outline wearing black glasses, but this time with the legend 'The Black Shade.'

"You mother—"

"Cool it, man, you're on the air," Luke whispered as he reached into a pocket, pulled out a pair of... *black shades,* and before Barron could make a move to stop him, jammed the sunglasses on his head, grinned, draped an arm over his shoulders as flashbulbs popped like manic fireflies and hot TV lights bathed the whole silly scene. And the crowd, on cue, began to chant: 'the *Black* Shade! The *Black* Shade!'

Then someone shoved a microphone between him and Luke, and Barron felt forced to smile back, mumble, "I'm glad to be here"; had the urge to kick Luke smack in the balls. Smart-ass black bastard! Why did I tell him in advance I was coming, should've snuck into this loony bin wearing a goddamn false beard. This crap'll be spread all over the country, and I can't stop it, friends like these, who needs enemies?

And now Luke was making a goddamn speech, his arm still draped around Barron's shoulders: "It's not often we see a shade down here we can welcome as a true brother, the black man in this country doesn't have many white brothers. But this cat standing here with me's not really a white man even if he is a shade. He's a Founding Father of the Social Justice Coalition, paid his dues in the most dangerous battles of the Civil Rights Movement, my oldest and closest personal friend, the man everyone in America, black or white, looks to every Wednesday night to give a voice to those who have no voice, a friend to those who have no friend, a real soul brother. He's not black, but he's not white either; he's a zebra—black with white stripes, white with black stripes, you pays your money, and you takes your choice. Fellow Mississippians, The Black Shade—*Jack Barron!*"

"Show biz all the way, eh Luke?" Barron muttered, sotto voce.

Greene kicked his ankle. "Come on, schmuck, don't screw me up," he whispered under the ragged roar of the crowd. "When's the last time you got an intro like *that*? Make nice, Claude, come on, don't make us both look like idiots. You can kick me in the belly later."

Now what? Barron wondered. Tell 'em all to get stuffed, cool all this crap once and for all before it gets started? But he felt the old-friend weight of Luke's arm across his shoulders, (Can't knife my old buddy even if he deserves it. Some buddy you are, Luke.) looked out over the crowd, pale black ghost-shapes through the dark glasses, saw mouths open for real yelling for every pain of being dirt-poor-black in white man's country, saw *déjà vu* crowds in Meridian, Selma, a hundred sullen Southern towns yelling in anguish surrounded by rednecks dogs cops prods hoses, Luke behind him, Sara's worshipful eyes on him in streets of danger, remembered the warmth of close to the blood Baby Bolshevik black and white together and all that jazz, marches, laying his life on the line every time he opened his mouth, felt the heat coming off this big-league real live Governor's arm around his shoulders crowd so thick you could cut it, crying anguish, chanting put-on Madison Avenue hope, sold-out black losers, always sold out, conned, cheated, used, fed, to the fishes, and whatever foetid game Luke's playing with all this... shit *they* really mean it, not a game to these poor fuckers, it's the real nitty-gritty, and how can I give 'em one more kick in the balls when even *Luke's* using 'em?

"The Black Shade! The Black Shade!"

"Thank you... thank you," Barron said into the mike some black hand was holding under his chin, heard his voice in tinny reverberation, hidden behind his shades like a TV screen interface shield, almost like a session of *Bug Jack Barron*.

"Don't really know what to say. I never expected anything like this (giving Luke a real *hard* kick on his smart-ass ankle), and I don't really understand it. I mean, I'm not a candidate for anything, like certain other cats got their arm around my shoulder."

He flashed his best one-of-the-boys smile. "All I can really say is that all those signs say 'Jack Barron, the Black Shade' is the nicest thing anyone ever said about me. Even if it's not really true, it's something to live up to, not just for me, but for the whole country. That's where it *should* be at, everywhere in the United States—black shades and white Negroes, Americans, all of us, is all, and none of us, black or white, should ever even have to think about it. That's the America we all want, and I guess a black shade is what you're stuck with till we get it, until this country has grown up enough to become a zebra—and I hate to contradict the Governor here, but that's a *no*-colour animal with black *and* white stripes."

"Snap them galluses!" Luke whispered into his ear as the crowd broke into cheers. "Still the same old Jack Barron underneath all that mung. Knew I could count on you."

Son of a bitch, Barron thought, should've told 'em all where it's *really* at. Should've told 'em how they were being used, how you using me to play with their heads, Luke. Yeah, (he admitted sourly to himself as the crowd continued to cheer, waving signs flashing flashbulbs kinesthop buttons national TV coverage hot white spotlight on the sound of his name on desperate lips getting to him, turning him on in spite of himself, turning on Berkeley Baby Bolshevik Jack-and-Sara other crowds other times memories of blood rushing behind his ears, the sound of his voice made flesh—and won't this hype the ratings) and use them on my head, too.

"You can count on me to give you a good, swift, on-camera boot in the testes, you don't get me out of here and do it fast," Barron said tautly, half-aware (admit it, man, it *does* get to you) he was also threatening himself.

Luke laughed an infuriating knowing laugh, like two buddies meeting again on the street outside after a trip to a low-class whorehouse. His arm still resting on Barron's shoulder, he led him to the limousine whistling 'Hail to the Chief' in hideous offkey, shaking his head from side to side.

Aw, take it and stick it, Barron thought as a flunky opened the car door. But for some quixotic reason he didn't take off the shades till he was inside.

"All right Lothar, what's the big idea?" Jack Barron said as the car began to roll, scaled off in the rear compartment of the air-conditioned limousine with Luke like a rolling *Bug Jack Barron* studio through the streets of Evers—knocked-together packing-crate slums immediately outside the World's Fair Gothic airport like some unreal Rio hillside TV documentary *favela*, antiseptic and safe behind the electric-circuit insulated monitor-screens of the car's sealed windows.

Luke measured him with his big, cool, snide eyes. "The *Big* Idea is all," he said. "I already told you, didn't I? I'm gonna play with your head till you agree to run for President. Simple as that, Clive. We need you, and we're gonna get you."

"Just like that?" Barron said, pissed, but at the same time admiring Luke's unabashed amoral honesty. "Fact that I got no qualifications to be President, that don't mean squat to you?"

"I said we need you to run for President," Luke said as the car continued to pass through some of the ghastliest slums Barron had ever seen: crazy-quilt shacks of old greyed wood and tin Coke signs windowed randomly in mad Dali patterns; mountains of uncanned garbage in the sidewalkless streets dull-eyed black World War II Dondi street urchins liquid lounging street hoods hopeless fourteen-year-old whores junkies nodding on heaps of rusting metal, made Harlem, Watts, Bedford-Stuyvesant, look like Scarsdale. Scars*ville*, Barron thought. Huge purple cancer-scar across the fifty-dollar-pants-hidden backside of America. Stag-film of despair-pornography across the TV screen car windows, living-colour image documentary losers.

"We need a candidate, a man who can win," Luke was saying as Barron dug him with his ears while image-faces of hollow hope grey hands waving as the vip car went by, 'Bug Jack Barron' and 'Black Shade' buttons pinned on rags seared through the window-glass interface into the back of his eyes. "And that's you, man. Don't tell me you have no eyes to run. I saw you out there, saw you sucking it up, way you rapped it out right off the top of your head just like in the old days, same old Jack Barron. Getting the taste of it back, aren't you, Jack?" And Luke stared at him with knowing, sardonic, laughing pusher eyes.

That's what you are, Luke, Barron thought, pusher is all. Power-junk dealer'd hook his own grandmother to feed his monkey. That's a big power-monkey on your back, Luke, fucking gorilla's bigger than you are.

"Not the taste, Luke," he said, "just the smell. Nobody can smell out junk better than a reformed junkie, but you're not gonna get me to taste it, not again, not ever. 'Come on, man, let's just split a friendly little bag for old time's sake, you won't get hooked, and this one's for free.' I spent too many years beating my brains out in the political junk bag. Yeah, there's a real surge in seeing people with your name pinned on 'em hanging on your words, real big charge, but it's never enough, you gotta have more and more and more and that power-monkey gets bigger and bigger till there's nothing left of *you*. And you forget why you got started in the first place. You stop caring, stop feeling, stop really trying to help people, start using 'em... I'll take show biz over politics any time—nice white-collar job keeps your hands clean."

Now the car turned into a wider street, main drag of Evers slum Lenox Avenue disaster of all the world, hock shops open air butchers' fly-coated meat in electric-green dresses wasted angry men shuffling outside endless makeshift bars, and a crowd coalesced and disintegrated in waves on the boredom-choked street as the car passed by, yelling waving sunglasses, kinesthop flashes from *Bug Jack Barron* buttons, and a guttural animal sound shaking through the car's windows—*Black* Shade! *Black* Shade!—fading through the rear window like a bow-wave passing to sullen ugly boredom as the big Cadillac passed and left them behind.

"Look out there," Luke said, "look at those people screaming your name. They want you, Jack, *you*. Thousands of 'em, millions of 'em, and they're looking to you, they want you to lead them, and all you have to do is say the word."

And Barron heard the envy behind Luke's voice. *His* people, Barron thought, but he knows they're not enough, not strong enough, not enough of 'em to ride alone to the Big Time. They've taken him as far as a black man can go. The monkey keeps getting bigger, but there's no way to get more junk to feed him, is there Luke? Shade connection's what you need, good old Jack Barron, the power-junkie's friend.

Ahead of the car, as if behind an invisible Gardol shield against tooth decay, the slum ended, and way away over a sanitised empty grass lawn Barron saw a soaring cluster of real Space Age buildings—the Capital, the Governor's Mansion, office buildings—the Capital, the Governor's Mansion, office buildings for carpetbagging black Baby Bolshevik parasites—the clean, sharp shapes of made-it: a polyethylene-wrapped Promised Land shimmering just across the invisible Jordan, Jordan River ten thousand miles wide twice as deep as time.

From deep inside him, the words erupted, from the sullen streets of a hundred Southern towns, Jack and Sara close to the blood streets in Berkeley dreams of self-anointed knighthood, Boy Wonder savage-innocence speaking through ten years of electric circuit insulation with the voice of the man:

"*You* look out there, Luke! Take a real good look for a change! Look in front of you and dig all those fancy buildings cost Christ knows how much, dig that fucking cave of the winds Governor's Mansion, rent-paid plantation house, Massah Luke, and all them fancy outbuildings. Feel that two-hundred-dollar suit you're wearing, taste the word 'Governor' in your mouth, clock this car and your uniformed flunkies, and everyone calls you 'Governor' or maybe 'Bwana' wherever you go. Got it made, don't you, you and your boys. King of the Mountain—Kingfish, is all."

He half-shoved Greene around, pointing his face out the rear window at the festering neo-African slums quickly falling behind.

"When's the last time you walked those streets without a bodyguard?"

Barron said. "*I'm* the cat that forgot what he was? You were out there with me, Luke, remember? Or don't you have the balls to remember anymore? That's what those fancy buildings come from, big shiny toys built on nothing more than a pile of shit! But you don't have to smell the shit anymore, do you? Take a couple drags of that old power-junk, you don't even have to know it's there. But it *is* there, it'll always be there, and shit always stinks like shit. Look at those buildings in front of you, and look at that cesspool behind you, and, baby, you're digging exactly where the politics bag is at—nice shiny false-front hot-air fairy castles built on nothing more than a pile of shit. Clock it sometime when the wind changes—you're fat and happy in your plantation house only because those poor bastards are stuck in their dungheap. *Politics!* You can tie it in fancy ribbons, but you can't hide the smell."

Greene turned to him and Barron felt remorse and shame sugar-coating years of unfaced gut-anger, felt himself go out to this man, black man is where it's at, was his friend had stood beside him in streets of danger, balled Sara before he had and made him like it, butting his poor black head against white stone walls ten million years thick, knowing he was a *nigger*, always knowing there was a line beyond which he could never pass, knowing he was a power-junkie, knowing what he was and how it had been done to him and why, and still a man, is all, a man, as Lukas Greene smiled a brittle-bitter-but-triumphant smile and said: "This is the man who said the worst moment in the world is when you decide to sell out and no one's buying?"

"What's that supposed to mean?"

"What's it mean?" Greene snapped. "It means you're full of shit and we both know it! Any man could sit there knowing he had nothing to gain from it and say a thing like that to a friend, and knowing damn well that I know you're right, that everything I've ever done down here is pissing into a hurricane. . . that's a man I'd follow, a man I *did* follow once, a man every black man in America'd follow, and we both know it. Damn it, Jack, you *are* the closest thing to a black shade going. Goddamn it, why won't you admit it? You're a hero down here, a hero in the Village and Harlem and Strip City, in every fucking ghetto in the country, because you're the one cat that crawled up from the gutter to the big time without copping out, with your brains and your mouth and not on a ladder of dead bodies. That's your image, man, you made it, and whether it's true or not, don't mean squat because people want to believe it, and you dig having them believe it—and the name of *that* game, Claude, is *politics.*"

Thinking of his name in triplicate on Benedict Howards' paper, Barron said, "That, Rastus, is what I call horseshit. If I'm the Hero of the People, it sure don't say very much for the People... *Hell,* I'm tired of all this. I came down here to talk to that Franklin cat, not debate the ethical structure of the Universe. You located him?"

"Got his address and phone number. I'll send a car for him. He lives pretty close to town. You'll stay at my digs, natch, you can talk to him in private there."

Barron clocked the shiny Government Buildings looming before him, then looked back out the rear window at the sprawling black pustule of shantytown Evers festering behind.

Gotta walk the street again, he thought. Don't know why, but I gotta do it. Show Luke, Sara, Howards, Franklin too, show 'em all. That's where the real show is, back there in the shithole, out there in the audience, nitty-gritty Brackett Audience Count estimated hundred million people are out there in the gutter... Jack Barron returns to the People. Sara'd cream in her pants, and why now?

"No, man," he said. "I'm just not up to doing the Bwana schtick. I'm gonna meet the cat on his own turf. I see him out *there*."

14

NIGHT STREETS. Yeah, night streets of Harlem, Watts, Fulton, Bedford-Stuyvesant, East-East Village, Evers all the same, hot heavy crowded and sullen with odours of greasy cooking dirt drunk-piss pot junk and cheap whore-perfume; oil-on-steel sounds of quiet, too quiet in shantytown side-streets, the hollow frenzy of Saturday night (it's always Saturday night) on King Street, Evers' main drag. The Street, The Street running down Lenox Avenue to Bedford to Fulton to King Street, night on The Street same in any city with interchangeable parts of mass-produced Black America like cheapjack copies of the real thing turned out by Japanese sweatshops; whores junkies jds bars Lenox Avenue strip joints Fulton jazz cellars Bedford hockshops furtive street-light pushers winos. King Street miasma, a Desolation Row of daisy-chain memories coast to coast made Jack Barron feel like a pale white predator moving on his toes down the black jungle trail of King Street—the Shade, the Man, hunter and the hunted.

Bet your ass there's no 'Black Shades' out *here*, Barron thought, feeling a thousand liquid Negro eyes on the back of his neck clocking the lone shade moving down *their* street, *their* turf—hey, what's that shade doin' here, he the Man? (Every shade moving down Bedford, Lenox, Fulton, King, The Street marked as The Man by the grey tin badge of his skin.) But ain't that what you really are betting, Barron, your living-colour ass is all, out here in the nitty gritty, black nitty gritty, where the word came from in the first place?

Hey, what you doing here, White Boy? street signs junkies sloe-eyed black women forward-panther-sloping bucks polishing their cool-eyed gaze like New York PRs honing up their switchblades seemed to ask. Go walk this street, and tell yourself America don't have a race problem—Civil Rights is all, wars and whores on Poverty is all, never had no race problem here man, not in the good old USA. Slavery maybe, lynchings maybe, riots maybe, endemic small-scale revolution maybe, wouldn't want one to marry my sister maybe, degenerate black motherfuckers maybe, send 'em all back to the jungle maybe, but them's all *social* problems, see, we got no *race* problem in Land of the Free, Home of the Brave.

Send 'em back to the jungle, yeah! Barron thought wryly. Somebody say send 'em *back*? Walk in Harlem, Fulton, Evers, man, and you stop worrying about sending people back to the jungle, too uptight watching the *jungle* come back to people.

Course there's something to be said for the jungle, Barron thought, clocking the alive, desperate faces, jazz of the streets moving nice and easy in a liquid sulky beat, sensual relief of a junkie making his score, smirking mating-dance bridal-bargain between a tall thin cat and a little A-head-eyed whore. It's nitty and it's gritty and it's all here you happen to be black, in Strip City, the Village, H-A, you happen to be cool. But if you're a square old shade with no jungle inside you at all, never walked down MacDougal at 5 a.m., never from door to East Side Puerto Rican door, never felt the heat, never saw The Man out there waiting—then, baby, when you hear those tom-toms wailing from Evers Harlem East Village tribal jungles, better pour another stinger, rub on the old citronella, and fit a new clip in your carbine, 'cause the natives are restless tonight.

That why you're trotting down this here jungle trail to meet Franklin in *The Clearing* instead of playing Big Bwana and summoning the cat to the District Officer Governor's Mansion gin and tonic carefully guarded by loyal askari? So you got no eyes to play Bwana—Tarzan of the Jungle's the name of the game.

Yeah, maybe. Maybe it's all a crock of shit, but maybe you gotta give that jungle inside a little transfusion once in a while, score on a street corner, fight in a bar, see the wrong end of a knife, keep the old juices flowing. All them Bwanas out there, they don't, except every ten years or so—and then they call it a war.

Up the block was an opaque-windowed barfront, green-paint-on-dirty-glass palm fronds under a tinfoil moon in a dead-black sky, green grime-subdued neon sign flashing '*The Clearing.*' And outside maybe twenty bucks goofing, cats too down and out not to get bounced from inside. Right outside the doorway like an honour guard of junkies—native kraal and Mr Henry George Franklin waiting for him inside.

Look dangerous, man, Barron told himself, feeling old remembered instincts hunching him forward in his funky black Jacket, picking up neon flickerings in the pits of his hardened, tense-muscled eyes. Way you gotta play it on this ground, no black shades here—just Us and The Man.

Feeling the tension-interface before him bulging inward against the clot of black men guarding the door, eyes straight ahead never looking to the side to acknowledge the sullen-stare question the back of his neck knew was there—Hey what you doin' here, you shade mother you?—Barron threaded through them, neither intruding on turf nor giving ground. And like a bubble bursting through layers of oily tropical waters, was through, and inside.

A big barn of a room (scars patterning the flaky-paint ceiling where the barroom, amoeba-like, had absorbed shops or apartments by knocking down walls) sunk down a half-flight from the entrance, down three stairs into the cellar, huge slash-pop green poster-fronds painted halfway up the dim grimy-white walls like chartreuse flame in the junkie-funky fluorescent light that turned the sea of black faces to ashy washed-out blue-grey.

The far side of the room was a long bar with a black plastic bartop over some phony ersatz wood; no bar stools, only beertaps visible, and behind the bar no bottles, no mirror, just a crude phallic mural of warriors black and pagan around a tribal fire. Not a mirror in the entire room.

Below him, the floor of the bar somehow reminded Barron of the New York Stock Exchange: a sea of tables, no more than three or four chairs to each, more people milling about in the aisles than seated, black brothers with beer bottles and shot glasses quoting the latest market averages runner-to-runner: schmeck down three-quarters, pussy up a half, drunk-rolling unchanged, desperation up all the way in strictly a bullish market.

Barron stood above the tangle trying to spot Franklin before stepping down into *The Clearing,* the turf, choked with invisibly bruised black bodies, gut-knowing he had better show a non-Man reason for being there real quick. Sullen eyes began to turn upward, measuring him as he stood there like so much meat—*one* spade? Hard-up junkie? Flush dumb john out for a piece of black tail? *The Man?* Is this shade mother *The Man?* Down here in black man's country, where *The Man's* a nigger? Federal heat? Barron felt the paranoia rising, a thousand eyes sharpening their knives... gotta make a move *quick!*

"Hey, ol' Jack Barron—" a hoarse barroom shout from a two-man table at the far corner where the bar met the wall. Barron saw Henry George Franklin, alone with a bottle and two glasses, blearing at him through the thick blue smoke, waving a vague hand from a fawn-coloured sportjac sleeve. "Hey, ol' Jack, over here!"

Barron felt an electric thrill as he sensed his name flashing like a running mouse through the crowd. No shouts, no mumbling, just a sudden series of dampening drops in the general noise level jumping around the room like a silence-ghost, leaving knots of black men, dark-skinned women, staring up at him in its wake; then a general turning toward him, a couple of shouts, a quick tension-moment when nobody moved that came as fast as it went. And then a tall, willowy, New-York-street-face Negro standing just below him flashed him an ironic, brother-hippy smile, pulled a pair of black shades out of a jacket pocket and put them on.

And the man next to him did likewise. And the man next to him. In waves. In spreading circles. Then a rustle of glass and clothing and plastic and three-quarters of the people in the room were wearing black shades, staring up at him with obsidian plastic-framed sightless eyes as if waiting for some countersign while the moment continued to hang.

More of Luke's mind-fuck games? Barron wondered. Guy that started it a plant? Luke's having me followed? Or... or could it be real?

He fished into his jacket pocket (did I put them there on purpose?), pulled out the pair of black sunglasses Greene had given him, put them on, stepped down to the floor of the bar room.

And abruptly the wheeling and dealing resumed, and it was like Jack

Barron wasn't there, like he was invisible, like he was black as the best of them—the ultimate compliment, but cool and distant as the top of Mount Everest. Like he was… a black shade. And he knew dead-certain Luke hadn't engineered this one; it was too cool, too choreographed, too underplayed, too *yeah*, to be anything but a gut-reaction. The Black Shade…

Barron made his way across the crowded barroom with no more than a nod or two in his direction, a smile here and there (cool, real cool, from the womb of cool)—to the table where Henry George Franklin nodded to him, poured him a shot of Jack Daniels even as he sat down.

Barron fingered the drink, then sipped it as he studied Franklin's seamy, puffed face, stubble on the verge of becoming a beard, liver-brown bloodshot eyes, yellowed teeth in a slack wet mouth, and stinking like a brewery: face of Brackett Count estimated hundred million losers behind the glass interface of the black shades.

"Y' came, ol' shade Jack Barron," Franklin said half-affrontedly, "now ain't that a bitch! Big important shade TV star in a place like this."

"I've been thrown out of crummier holes flat on my ass," Barron said, one-of-the-boys-wise, tossing down the drink half for the flash half for the gesture.

Franklin studied him thoughtfully, his eyes no less opaque than the shades Barron still was wearing, finally said: "Maybe jus' have," and poured each of them another drink.

"Yessir," he said, "good ol' Jack Daniels. No more corn out of Mason jars for ol' Henry George… nossir, nothin' but bottled-in-bond for me and my fancy shade guest. Yeah, ol' Jack, five hundred thousand dollars, that buys a lot of good whiskey and bad women…" And he bolted down another drink.

"Let's talk about that money, Henry," Barron said, noticing strange hostile looks flickering across the faces of men who happened to glance sideways at the table, dirty looks seemed directed at Franklin the Negro, instead of Barron the shade. "The man who gave it to you must've given you some name."

"Suppose he did," Franklin muttered, pouring yet another drink. "Don't rightly remember, and besides, ol' Jack, who cares? Like I say, he was just some crazy rich man's fancy shade messenger-boy, wouldn't be using his real name, now would he? Not for goin' around buying people's kids. That's gotta be some kinda crime, don't it?"

"Did it ever occur to you that it might be a crime to *sell* your daughter?" Barron asked.

"Look, ol' Jack, let's talk man to man, okay?" Franklin said, waving a maudlin thumb in Barron's face. "Y' got jus' two kinds of people, lotsa different names, maybe, but only two kinds of people—them as got somethin' to lose, and them as got nothin' to lose. Shade what can go around handing out satchelfulls of money, that's gotta be someone's got *somethin'* to lose, got reason to worry 'bout legal or not legal, 'cause he plays it cool and The Man's on his side, unless he does something real stupid. But a dirt-poor nigger with nothin' but a crumbly ol' shack, few acres of no-good land he don't even own and a seven-year-old daughter t' feed, he got nothin' but nothin' to lose, why should he care 'bout *legal?* Law's against him day he's born till the day he dies, 'cause he's black, 'cause he's poor, 'cause he's been in and out of jail a few times for having too much to drink, gettin' in a couple fights, stealin' a little here and there to keep his belly from growling... When you broke, you take chances."

"So you sold your own flesh and blood just like that," Barron said. "Like you were a fucking slave trader, is all! I don't understand you, Franklin, and I don't know if I want to."

Franklin bolted down his drink, poured another, stared into the brown liquid, said: "Black shade they call you, tha's a good one... 'cause there jus' ain't no such thing. *Jus' like that,* the man says. Ain't no jus' like that, either. Try being black, try havin' nothin' at all for forty-three years, try living on Food Stamps and tinned peanut butter, savin' up enough money in a month to get drunk one night to forget you is nothin' got nothin' never'll have nothin', and knowing that little girl eats up half what money you got never gonna be nothin' better than you, dirt-poor nigger maybe married off in a few years to another dirt-poor nigger and off your back, you lucky, and then some crazy shade drives up to your place when you had a little corn to begin with, feeds you a whole bottle of whiskey, then throws a satchelful of hundred dollar bills at you and all he wants is..." Franklin began to shake, sobbed once, downed the drink, poured another, and drank that too.

"Look, Mr Barron," he said, "I told you everything I know. Maybe I'm not a good man maybe I'm a bad man—piece of shit I sometimes think. But I want her back! Don't want some crazy shade to have her! All right, all right, I did wrong, did real wrong, couldn't help myself. I want her back! Y'gotta help me, man. I'll give back the money if I gotta, but I want her back... I ain't much, but I'm her poppa. She ain't much, but she's all I got. Y'gotta help me get her back."

"Okay, okay," Jack Barron said as Franklin's watery, bloodshot, livery eyes pinned him, eyes of a man who'd done wrong and knew it, but didn't quite know why, guarded eyes of a man who didn't see himself as a criminal or a louse but a loser, congenital black-skin-predestined loser, stupid, ignorant mark taken in some con game based, as they all were, on his desperation, on the difference between being a spade and being a shade, eyes that accused Barron, himself, his daughter, the child-buyer, the nature of the universe, saying: 'It's not my fault I'm a shit, it's what *you* made me, all of you, it's what I've been born.'

"I'm on your side," Barron said. "Yeah, comes nitty-gritty time, gotta be on your side whether I like it or not. I don't know what I can do, but whatever it is I'll do it, right now, tonight. Okay? Show you what happens when you bug Jack Barron. We're gonna go straight to the Governor's Mansion and I'll have Luke Greene put every fuzz in the state on it, run you through the files on every kook in the country. Come on, let's split."

Henry George Franklin stared at him in stupefied, disbelieving awe. "You mean it, man! You really *mean* it? Ol' Jack, you ain't jus' putting me on, you gonna take me up there to see the *Governor*, top nigger what runs the whole state? You gonna tell *him* what to do?"

"Bet your ass I'm gonna tell him what to do!" Barron told him. (Fucking Luke owes me plenty for not shafting him today, let him do what he's paid for, for a change, give him less time to mess with my head.) "Bigger men than Governors are gonna do what I say when I get back to New York."

Abruptly, he remembered what had really dragged him to Mississippi was not Franklin at all, was Benedict Howards. First time in nearly a month I've gone a whole day without thinking of that fucker. But there's the stink of Bennie all over this, he half-threatened to do me in over it, scared shitless I'd find out something from this cat. But what? He's just a poor dumb fucker don't know his ass from his elbow. Makes no sense. Not unless…

"You okay, man," Franklin said as he got up from the table. "Y'know that, ol' Jack, you're pretty fuckin' all right for a shade TV star… Who knows maybe you got black blood back there somewhere, maybe you *are* a black shade?"

Outside, King Street had passed over the midnight line: people coming from more than going to, junkies either fixed or in the deep shakes, quick-throw whorehouses past their peaks, winos far gone or sleeping it off in pools of vomit, paddy wagons raking up the fallen human leaves, a London-fog of pot-smoke rancid grease spilt beer drunken piss settling down on the buildings, gutters, alleyway in a funky-spent film.

Beside him, Henry George Franklin was stone-silent, like a hunched-forward wino who had made the price, passed through the flash, and was now out of it whether busted in the tank or pissing in his pants blotto in an alley; he had done his thing for the night and till the bleary dawn came entrusted his fate to the hands of the gods. And Barron, picking up on the wasted roach-end mood thought: throw the whole damn thing in Luke's lap and forget it. What else is there to do?

He stared up the street looking for a cab—nothing in sight but a paddy wagon, couple trucks, and two funky old '70s cars. New York reflexes, Barron began walking up the street, some reason you never get a cab in the ass-end of nowhere just standing around, and besides, on a street like this, gotta keep moving, is all. Franklin trailed after him a glassy-eyed zombie.

Half a block up King Street, Barron got a flash. Something was out of tune, blowing a cold wind down the back of his neck. It made him break his stride, twist around to look behind him—

Like a sudden slap in the face, an unreal firecracker-backfire sound, a hard metal bee buzzed by his ear, and a sharding scream of tin as a garbage can between him and the wall of a nearby building exploded in a flash of metal, grey slop and wet orange peels.

Barron dove to the sidewalk face forward, arms covering his head rolled behind a parked car as another shot split the air around a low sickening moan saw Henry George Franklin clutch at his belly as he folded; then a third bullet smashed Franklin's skull, flipped him backward to the sidewalk like a bloody ruined doll.

Across the street people were shouting as they ran in both directions from the mouth of an alley, and he saw a man resting the barrel of some kind of snub-nosed assassin-rifle on the lid of a rusty garbage can behind which he crouched.

A smoke-flash from the rifle, and a bullet exploded through two layers of car-window, ricocheting off the wall behind him and blowing the tyre by his leg with a soft cush of air as it sprayed him with glass. Another backfire-sound, and the car body shook twice against his cheek as a bullet tore through the double metal walls of the far door, then spent itself in the door against which he huddled.

Down the street two cops were running toward the alley from the paddy wagon, and the siren sounded as the paddy wagon began to back jaggedly up King Street.

A clatter of metal as the gunman fled up the alley, kicking over the garbage can.

Barron got to his feet, both pants-knees torn and the flesh beneath abraded and bleeding lightly. He was shaking. Five shots in as many seconds—the first five bullets he had ever faced.

A yard or two away lay Henry George Franklin, blood pooling on his stomach, his smashed face mercifully hidden by a clot of amorphous red. Barron retched once, turned away, saw one of the cops racing across the street toward him, and, in a flash of adrenaline, the reality of the moment penetrated the time-delay circuit to his head.

First shot was for *me! Me! Déjà vu* gunshots cowboys Indians racing up the hill at Iwo Jima Eliot Ness Zapruder film capgun-marching soldiers Oswald folding Viet Nam-headline war-images echoed in his mind... but the blood on the sidewalk in gallons and quarts was the same stuff in nicks on his own face cut shaving, same as the light redness on his skinned slightly-burning knees, pieces of Henry George Franklin white slivers of skull in sickening red wetness was same stuff inside him, just as sticky-soft vulnerable bag of pulsing slimy organs was him, kept him alive.

Dead... I could be dead, laying there a lump of decomposing meat, no difference except he missed me. And he didn't mean to miss me, first shot was at my head, and after he got Franklin he went after me again, the motherfucker tried to kill me, *really tried to make me dead*. Some son of a bitch wanted me dead!

How's *that* for your nitty-gritty street-reality, smart-ass? Some Oswald-Ruby-Sirhan loony whips out a—

Image of man resting a gun on a garbage can flashed on the playback screen of his mind, zoomed in on the gun, a cool piece of lightweight, high-powered, purposeful steel. High-powered, rapid-fire, no mail-order .22 no Manlicher-Carcano. A pro gun.

And a pro job.

Bang! Bang! Bang! Five shots just like that, first one right on the old button, if I hadn't moved off-rhythm, next two right into Franklin, and then right into the car. A hit-man contract job for sure!

"You all right?" The cop had reached him, taken one quick look at the ruined body, then ignored it like the rest of the ugly refuse littering the street. The cop's square face like any other cop's face, hardly noticed it was black.

"Nothing broken..." Barron muttered, his thoughts elsewhere, back in the apartment, Benedict Howards saying, "Don't talk to Franklin, or else—" Howards scared shitless, Hennering's plane exploding, his widow smashed by the wheels of a rented truck. ...Or else ...or else...

Only three people knew I was coming down here time enough to arrange a hit, he realised thickly, Sara. Luke. And Howards. No one else. Howards killed Franklin like he killed Hennering, tried to kill me. Had to be Howards!

The Foundation bought Tessie Franklin. The flash seemed to come from nowhere, but in the after-image wake of the gestalt-inspiration the train of logic behind it stood out hard and clear:

Howards is the only man in the world could've contracted for the hit in time. Howards wanted me dead, wanted Franklin dead, something he was scared enough of coming out in public to kill me for, kill Franklin for, and the only thing that made Franklin any different from twenty million other losers was he'd sold his kid. So if Bennie wanted Franklin shut up, Bennie's outfit *had* to have bought the kid...

And if Bennie bought Tessie Franklin, that'd sure as shit be reason enough to make double sure I didn't find out, and if I did I wouldn't get it on the air. Hit-man maybe really did his job after all, maybe only supposed to scare me. Anyway, Franklin's dead, I got nothing live to put on the air...

"Hey," said the cop, "ain't you Jack Barron? Sure, I see your show every week."

"Uh..." Barron grunted, lost in convolutions of snake-dancing logic, remembering the first bullet right at his head, two more college tries after

Franklin was dead... No doubt about it, that cocksucker Howards wanted me dead, Franklin or no Franklin, and that don't make sense with the only cat I could do a show around dead, unless...

Unless there are other people who'd sold their kids to the Foundation walking around loose.

"Yeah, I'm Jack Barron," he said, coming out of it fighting, "and I'm staying with Governor Greene. How about getting me a lift back to the Governor's Mansion *muy pronto?* Got a whole lot of checking to do."

"You got any idea who wanted to kill you, Mr Barron?" the cop said.

Barron hesitated. No thanks, he thought, this is between Bennie and me. Too many tangles, in too deep—immortality, three murders and my name on a murderer's paper, the show, national politics, and Christ knows what else, all balled up in a writhing glob like a mob scene at a convention of spastic octopuses, too many waves to risk ringing in any dumb local fuzz.

Yeah, and something else too, admit it Barron, something maybe only the Sicilian in Vince'd understand. Vendetta's the name of the game, Bennie, just a two-handed game of Russian roulette for all the marbles between you and me. Your boy blew the opening move, and now it's my turn, Howards, don't walk past any dark alleys. I'll nail your ass to the wall or know the reason why! Nobody takes free pot-shots at Jack Barron and gets away whole.

"Haven't the faintest idea, officer," he said. "Far as I know, I haven't got a real enemy in the world."

15

WONDERS OF MODERN SCIENCE, Jack Barron thought as he turned the rented car off the access road and back onto the highway to Evers. As the car picked up speed he glanced at the thin Manila folder beside him on the leatherette seat.

Take school-attendance records and birth certificates for the last fifteen years and put 'em into the old computer for a cross-correlation, and you get all the kids who should be in school but ain't; you feed 'em back into the computer and run 'em off against death-records, out-of-state-transfer records, for the same fifteen years, and you get maybe a couple thousand kids truant from school, alive, and in the state for more than a month; and you whittle that down against hospital and loony-bin records, and down again by running a cross-correlation with parental destitution, and after a final shuffle for a fifty-mile-from-Evers radius you get four names, four little visits, four nitty-grittys out of the whole fucking state. Simple as that.

Four names, four Negro children, ages seven to ten, with parents either on the edge of broke or on some kind of welfare. Four kids that disappeared from the face of the earth.

Four visits to four crummy slat shacks. Four new cars outside four traditional Southern niggertown shitholes, ranging from a Buick to an honest-to-Christ Rolls. Four crazy fairy tales: another 'Educational Foundation' schtick, one kid supposedly visiting relatives for six months, a none-of-your-fucking business, and that incredible dumb motherfucker actually believed his kid is now the adopted heir to the kingdom in some non-existent black African state. And four satchelfulls of untraceable cash money left by four different high-class shades.

No doubt about it, Barron thought as he moved over into the left-hand lane, whoever's doing it is flush as hell. Plenty of cash and a mighty smart operation, five tries and five sales and in situations all carefully selected to make the fewest possible government paper-waves. Adds up to someone with private access to a mighty expensive computer, rich enough to buy an expert on the Mississippi State Records filing system—or even to buy a top man on the inside. At an average of five hundred thou a kid, that's two-and-a-half million right there, not to mention what it takes to buy the computer or the computer time, at least five flunkies, grease to get hold of government records… millions of dollars just to make off with five kids!

How could it be anyone else *but* that crazy fucker Howards?

And why did he kill Hennering who didn't know a thing about this? Or did he? Hennering found out the Foundation was buying kids so Howards killed him…? Millions of dollars and dangerous murders just to get hold of children supercool-like? Bennie just ain't the frustrated father type. Only one thing could make Bennie act like such a paranoid spender—immortality, his life, gotta know his hide's somehow at stake. But why risk his precious immortal life over…?

"Schmuck," Barron grunted aloud. Sure, that's gotta be it only thing that would make Bennie risk murder-death-sentence is covering up prior murders, and the only thing would make him risk murder in the first place is his goddamned immortality. Jeez, it figures… he must've used those kids like guinea pigs to develop that immortality treatment, whatever it is, and *that's* why he gets so uptight anytime anyone gets near the subject. And that's why it was worth three murders to keep it cool!

For the first time in years that he could remember, Barron felt a flash of pure feral anger, a selfless, uncalculated anger that served no cause but its own. Murdering children to buy his own rotten immortal life! Murdering Hennering and his wife and Franklin to keep it quiet! Buying a Congress and maybe a President soon to cool it, to stand on a pile of bodies on the neck of the whole country for paranoid nightmare million years! Yeah, and buying *me* to ram it down their throats—sell snuffing out lives in Frankenstein laboratories for the secret of life eternal for the fat-cat few to Brackett Audience Count estimated-hundred-million suckers!

"And if you don't, Barron, I just hire a hit-man to kill you too…!"

Barron slammed the accelerator to the floorboards in a spasm of fury, held it there, and fought the car *mano a mano* as it screamed down the highway like a scalded cat.

Everybody's got his price he thought and immortality buys anyone, eh, Bennie? Think you know it all? But that's 'cause you're shit, Howards, pure shit clean through. Don't dig that there are men aren't like you, men you can push just a little too far. Well you pushed, you motherfucker, and you're gonna find out the hard way what happens when you push Jack Barron too far. Immortality… sure, what's done is done, can't bring back those kids paid for it with their lives by throwing it away. But my way, Bennie, not yours—over your dead body, is all. Try to, make me a murderer like you, Bennie, okay you made it, so now I'm a killer, but the corpse is gonna be your own!

His hands on the wheel seemingly sensing every crack in the pavement as the car tore down the highway, Barron felt a strange *déjà vu* Berkeley attic Jack-and-Sara exhilaration, realised it was nothing but hate had made the Baby Bolshevik bag go round. Yeah, just where it was at, we hated everything that wasn't the way we wanted it to be. Our strength and our weakness—we knew just how to react, black versus white, to everything. Anything wasn't totally right was totally wrong, and you could hate it, had to hate it knowing Us Anointed were on the Side of the Angels, everything against us was on the side of wrong. Not to hate, we called a cop-out.

Never trust anyone past thirty—'cause when a boy becomes a man he stops seeing that hate-line between right and wrong, and if you stay in the Movement then, you're an opportunistic phony, a fucking *politician...* a hag-ridden Lukas Greene.

There's your definition of politics, grown men playing kid games, hate-games, to get same simple kicks I get off *Bug Jack Barron*, living-colour, man-up-front, self-image is all. And that's cool. But the real difference between show biz and politics is nothing fancier than *hate.* Think you could understand that, Luke? You're the cop-out, not me, playing the politics-hate game, dead Berkeley-game you can't even feel.

Yeah, but there's something about hate that comes on like junk thinking about it, you know it's a loser, but oh how good that dirty old surge feels! Gives you something certain to build your whole schmear around—go get what you want, and feel it in your gut. Pure dumb groove to nail Benedict Howards' head to the old barn door...

Driving the car at a reckless speed which demanded full physical commitment, the wheel alive and deadly in his hands as the flat land flashed by, Barron grooved on the heady feel of life-and-death riding on his reflexes, his consciousness not trapped in a point behind his eyes but diffused through his hands and through prosthetic metal linkages to the car body and wheels.

Through electric circuit feedback loops, he anticipated the parallel kick of total *total* commitment reaching out through satellite-network-vidphone senses to the coast-to-coast hundred-million Beckett Count audience, to Luke, Morris, SJC, Republicans hot for his bod, all integrated by amplified-power circuitry into his electronically-extended *Bug Jack Barron* being, alive in a new way, jaw to jaw with death (with Howards as with the highway), in total war of total commitment for total revenge, and immortality, the most total of stakes.

I'll do you a show, Howards, you'll never believe. I'll chop you to pieces, and be alive and immortal when you're nothing but a lingering bad taste in a hundred million mouths, fried to a crisp in the electric chair, you Frankenstein axe-murderer you!

He eased off the throttle as he felt the heat of the moment pass through him leaving a wash of post-adrenaline warmth behind. You're out of your mind, you know that, man? Only schmucks and Sicilians hate like that...

Yeah, he thought, clinging to the memory of total hate, but a cool head should know how to use even his own glands.

"My mammy told me about these here Smoke-Filled Rooms, but this is getting ridiculous," Lukas Greene said. The smoke level in the conference room, air-conditioned though it was, was beginning to get rather impressive as Sherwood Kaplan lit another of those godawful mentholated filter-tipped ('they get you high and they keep you kool') Kools Supremes, and Deke Masterson rolled another Bull Durham (where in hell they still making that stuff, Greene wondered) tobacco cigarette, and Morris' cigar smouldered wetly in the cut-glass ashtray opposite Greene, at what in his mind was the foot of the square table, like the green rotten cock of a decomposing corpse.

Now *that*, thought Greene, is what we call in the trade symbolism—the GOP is indeed a slowly-decomposing corpse, and green or no, Greg Morris is certainly a rotten prick. But at least a rotten prick I got in the old bag.

"I zuppose you are all vundering vhy I zummoned you here tonight?" Greene said in a thick Lugosi accent. Morris scowled at him primly, but he didn't count now—Kaplan and Masterson were the real targets for tonight—and Woody's petulant, ageing-cherub face cracked a faggoty false smile. But Deke was still a pudgy-faced black sphinx.

"Cut the crap, Luke," Masterson said in that cultivatedly gravelly voice of his. "You dragged us here to sell us on Jack Barron we all know that. Where in hell is your so-called Black Shade?"

"Jack'll be down any minute," Greene said, "but you've got it ass-forward, Deke, the problem isn't selling you on Jack, but selling Jack on running. Try and remember that when he gets here."

"What is this shit?" Kaplan said with ill-concealed jealousy. "Running Jack for President's crazy enough, and playing footsie with *that* (he pointed the Kool at Morris, ostentatiously wrinkled his nose, but Morris, pro all the way, put him down the way you put down Woody the best, by ignoring him), makes it lunacy in spades and now you're telling us that that goddamned phony's gotta be treated like some fucking virgin prima donna?"

"Let's get right down to the uglies," Greene said, "so we don't end up washing our dirty linen when Jack's here. President or no President, you and Deke have one very good reason to play ball with me, and Governor Morris already knows *who* that reason is..."

"Russ Deacon," Masterson said as if it were a dirty word.

Kaplan grimaced. And Greene thought, yeah, poor old Russ gotta be the boy that gets the shaft. Deke and Russ been at each other's throats since they been in Congress over whether the State SJC Chairman should be black or white, Deke's boy or Russ's, whether Harlem or the Village should run the New York SJC show, and up till now, with all our New York shade money men in Russ's corner, Deke hasn't had a prayer of throwing Russ out, and, oh, how he knows it.

"That's right our soul-brother, Representative Russell Deacon," Greene said. "Now you know I got nothing personal against Russ at all, but I want Barron for President, and the two of you, added to what I've already got lined up, can swing all the votes I need on the National Council, so if I gotta deliver Russ's head on a silver platter to get 'em, it's Deacon for dessert."

"I'm listening," said Kaplan. "But how do you expect to get Deacon out of my way?"

"I can't," said Greene. "That's just the point: I can't, but Jack Barron can. Look, Woody, Deacon's got the Village, and the way things are set up now, that means the New York SJC. You got Strip City, and except for some noise from the Bay, that means the California SJC. A Mexican stand-off. But with Deacon out of the way you'd be the Grand High Poobah of Hip, just like you always wanted. You'd control all the East Coast hippy action and California besides."

"What's the point?" add Masterson. "This is a broken record. Why knife each other in front of the good Governor of California?"

Greene smiled as Morris sat there silently with amused contempt on his broad face. Which is cool, Greene thought.

"Okay, in words of one syllable," Greene said. "The three of us want three different things. If we play ball with each other, we all get 'em. Deke, with Woody in control of the Village SJC instead of Deacon, the New York SJC'd be your baby 'cause he's off in Strip City running that show, and with a blackstate SJC, that cuts the floor right out from under Malcolm Shabazz and his back-to-Africa phonies been bugging you in the bargain. You can afford Woody as hippy-faction leader 'cause he's three thousand miles away and he's got no eyes to run New York, better him than Deacon, right? And Woody, it's no skin off your teeth to have Deke run New York so long as there's only one Grand High Poobah of the Hippies. And me, well, you know how thick I am with Jack, he wins, I'm the black power behind the Shade House throne. (Morris smirked. That's cool, Greene thought, let him.) So those are the stakes. Now, ask yourself, fellas, guess who's a bigger magic name in the Village than Russell Deacon?"

"Jack Barron..." Kaplan said slowly. "In his own half-assed way..."

"Yeah, but you're looking at the other half of his ass," Greene said, smiling smugly. "Jack couldn't care less about party politics, in the infighting I'd just work his head. And our friend Governor Morris couldn't care less about what goes on inside the SJC. So it'd be no sweat to use Jack to squeeze out Deacon, once he's the titular head of a coalition. Dig?"

Masterson smiled. "You got a point," he said. "Okay, let's say I'm with you, provided Barron convinces me he'll play ball."

"That's where I'm at too," Kaplan said. "Hey... you don't think Jack could actually *win*?"

Watch it! Greene thought. This is the kicker. They know who'd be running the SJC if Jack actually won; play dumb, let 'em think you're just a kamikaze schmuck they're getting the best of. "Who knows?" he said. "I think it's worth a try, with the Republicans on our team... Sure, it's still a long shot, but it's the best chance us chilluns will ever have. We gotta try it, way I see it, isn't that right, Morris?"

"You know what I think of you and your kind, Greene," Morris said, "and you know how fond I am of Barron. But it's either Barron or some Democratic stooge Benedict Howards picks. With the Foundation against him, Teddy the Pretender hasn't got a real chance. Call it a truce, gentlemen, till we kick the Democrats out. After that, I'm sure the... best party will win."

"That's the nitty-gritty," Greene said. "That's why we need Barron, just his running would shake things up, win or lose, bust up that Democratic-Foundation cabal if nothing else. But for chrissakes, remember Jack's playing Reluctant Dragon, and where his head's at it just could be real. Play it cool when he gets here—and remember, *we've* got to sell *him*."

Well that's it, Greene thought, all set up and waiting; waiting for fucking Jack who started it all in that attic, and now the chicken's come home to roost.

Greene tasted twin pangs in the heavy waiting silence: bitterness and hope. Whatever happened now, it would be the climax of his whole career, the moment of truth; he had ridden the SJC as far as he could go.

Far as any *nigger* can go, he thought. Hand-pick your own shade front-man, your own bosom-buddy, *shade* buddy, of course. Jack wins, you're President-by-proxy; Jack's lost the taste for nitty-gritty politics. A nice clean shade candidate-image to front for me, is all. Not like you're using him, man, you don't have to, he doesn't want to get his... *lily white* hands dirty and anyway, he *is* on our side; Founding Father and all that bullshit. He wins, he'll only be too glad to suck up the glory and let me do the dirty work.

President-by-proxy, black power behind the lily-white throne—face it, you nigger you, that's precisely as far as any black man can go. And wouldn't you know it'd all depend on convincing some cat like Jack Barron's got it all for the taking he oughta take it? Way the world is, number one nigger in the country still gotta make it riding the back of some shade. Even a 'Black Shade.' (Ain't *that* one a bitch!) All riding on what crazy Jack does in the next few minutes.

And don't put yourself on, man, even you could never tell which way Jack Barron's head would go.

So we're gonna do *that* schtick again, Jack Barron thought as he entered the conference room and recognised the three men seated around the table with Luke, recognised who they were, what they were, where they were at, and what they wanted from him. Bugged at Luke though he was, some instinct told him to cool it, play with their minds, now that the whole crazy Presidential schtick was a potential component in the electric circuit of power-confrontation, along with bought children immortality power of life against death, power of Brackett Count estimated hundred million people, that he was beginning to wire around Benedict Howards. And the easiest cats to use are cats think they're using *you*.

Before Luke could go into his spiel, Barron crossed the room in three long strides, sticking an Acapulco Gold in his mouth as he moved, lit it as he sat down on the edge of the table beside Luke's chair, smiled his best number one brat-smile, blew a cloud of sweet uptighting pot-smoke in the general direction of Gregory Morris, and with heavy knowing cynicism said: "Gee, fellas, a surprise party just for little old me? I forgot it was my birthday. On the other hand, who knows, maybe I threw this little... Electoral College smoker for *you?*" And he shot a quick knowing look at Luke for the benefit of the others.

Luke's face went totally blank for a second, Masterson went tense, and that psychopathic prick Woody Kaplan almost laughed as he clocked his late arch-enemy Gregory Morris half-rolling his eyes as if, to say 'Fucking smart-ass Jack Barron,' and Barron knew that he had pulled the rug out from under Luke, from under whatever this grotesque cabal had been hatching, that he was now in the good old upper-right screen quadrant catbird-seat, was now his show all the way, strictly show biz all the way, and these cats got no more on the ball in the flesh than on the vidphone.

"Shall we skip the traditional bullshit, gentlemen, and get right down to the nitty-gritty?" Barron said. "You're here to sell me on running for President on an SJC-Republican coalition ticket; I know it, and now you know I know, so just make your pitch without waltzing me around the block, 'cause it's been a hard day's night."

Poor fucking Luke! Barron thought as he sensed Greene's head trying to catch up to his. And he clocked Governor Gregory Morris of California, Mayor Sherwood Kaplan of Strip City, US Representative Deke Masterson, so-called movers and shapers, all completely off-balance, not knowing what was coming off next, and it came to him in a laughing flash just what a total shuck the whole Great Man bag was.

Dig: four cats in a smoke-filled room with star of television and groin-kneeing Jack Barron got the power to run me for President they say the word and Bennie Howards can buy the whole lot of 'em out of petty cash, and he's nothing but a prick with five hundred billion dollars I can think immelmanns around with my head tied behind my back. Thing is, it's all show biz, is all, politics is nothing more than show biz with no class, and these high-powered vips are men just like me, only a little dumber. All a game of *Bug Jack Barron* and even without a promptboard, they don't have a chance 'cause they're dead serious and I'm playing it strictly for show.

Kaplan, maybe because of the envy-thing that went way, way back, recovered first. "Haven't changed at all, have you, Jack? But don't kid yourself, the game's not the same. This is for all the marbles."

"All *your* marbles, maybe," Barron said, "but not all mine, and you better believe it, all of you, 'cause you're just wasting your time thinking I'll jump through hoops and say 'Yes, Massah' just for the chance to be your front-man. You got *your* fish to fry and I got mine. We can use the same fire, that's groovy, but otherwise—later."

"All right, so we'll play by your rules," Masterson said. "Let's lay it right on the line. I don't know what you want, but what I want is Russ Deacon's head on a pike. And Woody wants the same. You can deliver that, we got enough votes on the National Council to put you over."

So that's it, Barron thought, yeah, it figures, poor Russ. Yeah, poor old Russ who'd be here playing the same dirty game, Luke thought he held the right cards. It ain't power that corrupts, it's the changes you put your head through getting it. Woody, Masterson, Morris, Luke, Howards—five different bags, but it don't matter, because the same monkey's working all five heads. Power-junkies, is all.

Barron took a deep drag on the Acapulco Gold. "You mean to tell me you're not really a band of patriots gathered together in Holy Council to pick a Moses to lead the Children of Israel out of the Wilderness? Come on, fellas, don't destroy my innocent, childlike illusions."

"Before you get so high you start to gibber," Morris said, speaking like the wise old toad for the first time, "maybe you should just shut your big mouth for a change and listen. I couldn't care less about the crap that goes on inside the SJC—it's got all the charm and grace of a Chinese Communist Party Central Committee meeting—and it really doesn't matter that you're a neo-Bolshevik punk, because I think we really understand each other, Barron. We don't like each other, but what counts is that we've got common enemies. Like Benedict Howards, or, who knows, maybe even Teddy the Pretender. We're wasting our time trying to con each other. You interested in making a deal, or not?"

Something to be said for a cat who's a swine and doesn't care who knows it, Barron thought. Better an unselfconscious GOP Fat Cat than these three fucking cop-out Heroes of the Underdog. And to think that the SJC was *my* baby! How's *that* for a case for legalised abortion?

"Sure, I'm interested in making a deal," he said. "Question is, what kind of deal? What's in it for you, and what's in it for me?"

"You sure going through changes, aren't you, Jack?" Luke said, trying to regain control. "So, as long as you seem to be playing Boss Tweed tonight, let's just riff it out in words of one syllable. We can all walk out of here with an agreement that you'll be the coalition candidate for President on a common anti-Howards platform if you can convince Deke and Woody to throw in. Morris and I and all the southern votes on the National Council are already committed and the Republican vips are ready to go along the moment they're guaranteed an SJC nomination. Woody and Deke *will* throw in, if they're assured that Jack Barron, as head of the SJC national ticket, will put the screws on Russ Deacon. That's the nitty-gritty, Claude—you willing to let us use your fan club in the Village against Deacon, you can be

President of the United States."

"With you as Vice-President," Barron said on sudden impulse, clocking Morris blanching at the thought of a Baby Bolshevik nigger on his precious Republican ticket. (Better see just how far you'll go, Morris.) "What's about it, Morris, are you *that* hot for my bod? I don't even think about running without Luke on both tickets. Will you ram *that* down your party's throat?"

"Hey, wait a minute—" Luke began.

"Cool it," Barron snapped. "You got me into this, Luke, and I'm dragging you in after me whether you like it or not. What about it, Morris, you still in the game?"

"If I accept Greene," Morris said, fingering his cigar, "that means we get to pick the Secretaries of State, Defence, Transportation, Labor and Commerce, a majority on the FTC, the NLRB and the FCC when appointments come up, the first two vacancies on the Supreme Court, the head of the Bureau of the Budget, the Chairman of the Joint Chiefs of Staff and the Attorney-General, and no questions asked. Ask your SJC friends if *they're* still in the game."

Barron cocked his head at Luke, was not surprised but wished he could've been as Greene said, "You're faded," and Masterson and Kaplan nodded in instantly-calculated agreement. Politics! Politicians! Where's the difference between my boys and Morris? Junkies'd sell their own mothers to a Saudi Arabian slaver, you wave the shit under their noses hard enough...

"What about Deacon?" Masterson asked coldly.

"What the fuck do I care about Deacon," Barron answered with measured cavalierness. "You want a candidate, right, not another politician. You're up to the ears in politicians, and they're all losers. You just want me to front for you, right? So I let you cats handle the politics, you want to use my name against Deacon, that's cool, but don't expect me to do your dirty work for you."

"Gentlemen," Luke said with a big shit-eating smile, "I think we're in business. Now the question would seem to be how and when we announce our—"

"Not so fast," Barron said. "Now that we've all got together on what I can do for *you*, the question before us is what are *you* gonna do for *me*?"

"You flipped?" Luke said. "We're gonna make you President Of the United States!"

"You'll excuse me if I don't go into ecstasy," Barron said dryly. "But for openers, you're just gonna make me a Presidential *candidate,* is all, and just between us chickens, I don't think I have a Chinaman's chance of winning. I don't think anyone except Bennie Howards' handpicked Democrat has a prayer, not unless Teddy pulls off a bona fide miracle at the Convention. And if Teddy gets the nomination, we've had it. There's no way to tie *him* to Howards, because the only way he can get the nomination is over

Bennie's dead body. But even that's not the main point. I don't have eyes for running, and I have even less eyes for *being* President. I find the whole thing a king-sized drag, fellas. Believe it or not, I'm in a bigger game elsewhere, and the only reason I'd consider running is because I need *your* backing in that game, Morris. I need you to keep Bennie Howards off my back. That's *my* price."

"Just what's this 'bigger game' you're talking about?" Morris said, and his eyes betrayed him, betrayed smug assurance that he could certainly control a Jack Barron who didn't even want to be President in the first place, and isn't *that* cool? And Luke and the boys were getting the same happy look.

"That's none of your business at the moment," Barron said. "It's all still up in the air right now. If I end up not needing your muscle, wild horses couldn't get me to run, and if I do need you, don't worry, the whole country will know why. It's all riding on the next show. Let's just say that if I get into a war with Howards, I want your fat cats to see to it that I don't hurt for sponsors, that Bennie can't lean hard enough on the network to make 'em drop me, and that the FCC situation will likewise be cooled.

"You see the only reason I'd run is if I need you to save my ass, because I don't think I'd win, and that means I gotta make sure I don't blow *Bug Jack Barron*. I want insurance because, ladies and gentlemen, whether you dig it or not, that show is where I'm at, where I want to be at, and I don't intend to blow it for no one or nothing. That's show biz, boys."

"*Show biz!*" Luke snapped. "We're talking about the Presidency of the United States, and you come on with *show biz!*"

Barron smiled wolfishly. "I was in your shoes, I'd be mighty happy to hear me talk that way," he said. (Might as well lay it right on the line, spell it out in black and white for these pricks.) "I mean, why are you so hot for my bod in the first place? Because I'm show biz, is all. Dig: *being* President and *running* for President are two entirely different bags. Cats who would be best at *being* President lay turkey eggs as candidates. Or am I wrong, and did Stevenson beat Eisenhower? You know I'm right, or Morris anyway wouldn't touch me with a fork. I don't have eyes for being President, and I don't have any qualifications either, that's politics, which is just not my bag. How groovy for you guys if you should happen to elect me—it'd all be your show after Election Day, and you can fight it out among your own sweet selves who runs it, far as I'm concerned it's horseshit either way. *But* if I need that GOP muscle to keep me in show biz, I'd hold my nose and be the best fucking *candidate* you could get from central casting, and you better believe it. Running for office in the good old USA is show biz all the way. Remember Ike? Remember Reagan? Remember JFK? Don't know show biz, but whether you know it or not, it's your stock in trade. Well, what about it, Morris, you back my play if I back yours?"

They all look like they just fell down a rabbit hole, Barron thought, not even bothering to hide his smug bad-boy satisfaction. One thing'll always knock power-junkies back on their asses—talk straight to the monkey and avoid the middle men, among themselves they don't dare admit what they are, so they're out of their class when they come up against someone who's got no reason to pretend the Emperor isn't swishing around in the altogether.

And that, he suddenly realised, is why a lox like Howards, who really isn't very big in the smarts department, can buy and sell them like used cars. He's no smarter than they are, he's just a bigger swine but with no front to worry about. He's a power-junkie too, but he's also the biggest dealer in town. And every junkie knows he had better bark when his Man says dog. Which is also why I drive Bennie up walls: he knows I'm one cat not hooked on the shit he peddles.

"All right," Morris finally said. "I think you're nuts, but why not? If you do run, we've got to keep you on the air anyway—and you've got to sink your fangs into Howards. You've got a deal, Barron."

Beside him, Barron felt Luke sigh with triumphant relief. Sorry about that, chief, he thought, and said, "No deal yet. You guys got some mighty fancy competition—like Benedict Howards. I know where you stand now, but before I jump I want to see what Bennie thinks he has to offer."

"What can Howards possibly offer you that's bigger than the Presidency?" Morris said.

Barron laughed. "Believe me," he said, "you wouldn't believe me if I told you. I'm not so sure I believe it myself. Tune in next Wednesday, though, and you'll find out. I guarantee that if I decide to play your game all your questions will be answered. You'll see the hottest live TV show since Ruby shot Oswald."

16

"AND TELL US in twenty-five words or less what you did on your vacation, Miss Westerfeld," Jack Barron said, peeling off his sportjac and shirt, kicking off his shoes, and punching a stud on the nearest wall console which slid the glass patio doors open. The chill New York morning air, clean and clear at twenty-three stories up (at least at this hour) began to wake him out of his plane ride semi-sleep stupor, and he walked barechested out on the patio, with Sara in a bleary interrupted-sleep bathrobe following him outside, shivering.

"All I asked is what happened in Evers," she complained in not-unjustified wounded tones.

Barron shrugged, grimaced, hugged her to him as much to warm himself as her. "The whole scam would make about three one-hour specials," he said, "but at least I'll give you the flash. I land at the airport. Luke has a whole fucking circus set up for my benefit, Ye-Olde-Presidential-Trial-Balloon schtick, as much to work on my head as on the press. After I shake that, I talk to this Franklin, find out someone really did buy his kid, find at least four other kids were probably bought by the same someone, put one and one together and come up with Bennie Howards, then back to Luke's plantation where he's got Morris, Woody Kaplan, and Deke Masterson all lined up to play the Smoke-Filled-Room number. I messed with their minds for a while, hopped a plane, and here I am, live in person. Satisfied?"

"There's something you're not telling me," she said firmly. "You look like... like something terrible has happened. Like... Jack, for chrissakes, tell me the truth!"

Barron looked out over the morning-clear East River-Brooklyn skyline, like a goddamn postcard-picture against the Technicolor blue sky. And in about two hours, he thought, the air'd be filled with about a trillion tons of muck and filth, the river'll stink like a sewer, all those smokestacks already starting to stoke up wonder what they make in all those goddamn factories over there, shit, probably, is all. And what did that cat say? "It is perfectly obvious why Man was created. Human beings are the most efficient organisms in all of Earth's evolutionary history for converting food into shit." And, man, am I on a bummer! So tell the little lady, man, they try again, she may be in the line of fire.

"Benedict Howards tried to have me killed," he said quietly. He felt the muscles of her arms tighten around him, and she pressed her cheek against his naked goosefleshed chest. "Didn't come very close, though," he lied. "I dunno, maybe he was just trying to scare me off. Gunsel in the street, strictly Dodge City. Got that poor bastard Franklin, though. Howards really

183

wanted to shut him up."

"But why?" Sara said. "After all the trouble he went to to get you on his side?"

"Now there's the $64,000 question. Think I figured out part of it. Howards killed Hennering because he found out something about the immortality schtick that scared him shitless enough to blow the whistle. Howards killed Franklin because he was afraid I'd find out the Foundation was buying children, and he tried to kill me, or at least scare me off, because he was afraid I'd put it on the air. Can only mean that Howards' boys used those poor kids as human guinea pigs to develop the immortality treatment; and some of 'em must've died in the lab, 'cause the only thing that Bennie would risk being tried for murder for is covering up another murder, and the only thing he'd risk killing for in the first place is immortality."

"What do we do now?" she asked, and her eyes staring up at him were pool-deep tunnels into his own gut into angers from the past into hard metal bee passing his ear Franklin in a pool of blood stretching from Berkeley attic to Evers street to four (five) cop-outs in a nice air-conditioned room in Luke's plantation house divvying up dreams of desperation and playing power-junkie games 'No one crosses Benedict Howards' and the cool professional assassin rifle on the garbage can sharding behind him orange peels and muck flying like a smashed junkie's skull and hard metal bee passing his ear 'the *Black* Shade! The *Black* Shade!'—and you know damn well what you want to do, Barron!

He smiled a bad-boy smile at her and asked, secretly rhetorical, knowing almost word for word what he would get back but wanting to hear his old close-to-the-blood self speak through Sara's lips: "What do *you* want us to do?"

"Isn't that all you need?" she asked. "Howards a murderer, and even if you couldn't prove it you could put the parents of those kids he bought on the air, and then get Howards... But that's your line of evil, you know just how to destroy the Foundation you almost did it twice. And we could be careful, not let anyone get at us to... to... I'm not afraid."

"I wonder if Madge Hennering said that too," Barron said, but it was only a *pro-forma* cop-out and he knew it even as he said it. Got Bennie's ass against the wall now for sure, he thought, and he's not fucking around with Ted Hennering now, he's playing chicken with Jack Barron, and I wrote that book. You set up your insurance already, didn't you? What the fuck *can* Bennie do? Can't get you off the air, not with that GOP Fat Cat action from Morris... should be able to keep away from hit-men you know are there. The fucker tried to kill you, you gonna let him get away with *that*?

"No, goddamnit, you're right for once, Sara, Bennie's not gonna get away with *this*. Not murder. Not sitting on top the whole country on a pile of dead bodies for the next million years, not a cat tries to kill Jack Barron and gets off whole! Yeah, no sweat to kill his Freezer Bill, and with the kind of stink I can hang on Howards, he'll never be able to hold onto enough Democrats to block the Pretender... Sure I can do him in. And I will. Only..."

Only maybe the stakes are just too big for you to afford revenge, he thought. Across the river, smoke reached into a blue sky that went up and up and up till it became a cold, clear, black nothingness that went on and on in all directions as far as... as far as forever. And that's a big thing to blow, *forever*. That's more hero than any sane man can be. Jesus H himself'd have to think twice. Big deal, he died to save us, but he had an angle, he died knowing he had forever made ('but if you black, when you go, you don't come back'). How big a Baby Bolshevik would he have been if he knew he was blowing the Big All, immortality, on that dirty old Cross?

"Sure," Barron said, "it sounds groovy when you riff it out like that. Makes you forget the one thing Bennie does have going—I do him in, we kiss immortality good-bye. You really ready for that, Sara?"

And this time her eyes were only a question; there was no answer anyone could give. But, he thought, there *is* that piece of paper.

"Sara," he said, "are you ready to play the big game for all the marbles, today, right now?"

"What do you mean?"

"I mean I call Bennie right now, tell him we're on our way to Colorado, we want that immortality treatment now, and once we get it—then we've got it all! Yeah! That's his only edge, and once he blows it, we've got him. You ready? You ready for immortality *now*?"

"But... but how do you know he won't just kill us?"

"Wonders of Modern Science plus a little pure nastiness," Barron said. "I'll carry a miniphone and get him to spill the beans to me, fuck with his mind till he's gibbering, and—"

"What's a... miniphone?"

"Huh...? Oh, that's a new Bell Labs gizmo, personal portable phone not on the general market yet, strictly for vips. Transmits directly into the phone system's satellite-ground-relay circuit, so you can use it from anywhere, just like making a call from an ordinary vidphone.

"I can set up a conference vidphone hookup, one or two phones here, couple at the office, and have the miniphone feed into the circuit with recorders on all the phones to get everything Bennie and I say on tape thousands of miles away, with instructions to Vince to mail copies to Luke, the FBI, Morris, maybe the AP, if anything happens to me. All I gotta do is get Bennie to incriminate himself when he thinks we're alone, and he won't be able to touch us no matter what."

"You really mean it this time, don't you?" she said. "I can hear the real Jack Barron talking now..." And her arms around him, her lips half-open, eyes that reflected bottomless depths of naked pleasure were eating him up in

Berkeley sheets Meridian streets Acapulco-tropical-night-sounds bottomless feral worshipping hunger sucking him to her flashing images of Berkeley SJC attic streets-of-danger the feel of his own blood surging hot through his arteries with Sara beside him, always beside him with that manic turn-on hunger screaming "Go! Go! Go!"

Yeah, a free hard-on in every bag of power-junk, and a free bag with every hard-on, Baby Bolshevik bullshit and you know it, but man, oh, man, feel that dirty old surge! Yeah, we felt everything all over in those days, it was just us kids against all the crap in the world, and wasn't that groovy, and shit we were more or less right. And then along came magic age thirty and we all got hungry for a piece of the action, and before we knew it, it was all just use me and I'll use you politics, and them that stayed had the monkey on their backs, like Luke... didn't *want* the monkey, just didn't dig power-junk hooks everyone who makes that scene, sooner or later, like it or not. And that's what I saw when I got out. I wasn't the cop-out, they were, or as much as me anyway, and show biz was the only thing could keep the monkey off my back. Yeah, everyone sells everyone else down the river sooner or later, was luck, is all, I found show biz or I'd still be doing it too. And letting Bennie cool things'd be selling everyone down the river in one big forever lump, biggest cop-out of all time...

"Seems like I don't have much choice." Jack Barron said.

Like cherries coming up on a slot machine, he saw that old familiar delicious Pavlovian reflex-arc close behind the windows of her eyes in a sizzle of hero-worshipping sparks, and she moved her mouth down his chest, licking and biting, leaving a trail of sweet juices, as her hands undid and dropped his pants with that old weirdly-masculine efficiency. She dropped to her knees, free hair bobbing, hands undulating over him, mouth moving against then around him in one sinuous fluid movement as her rolling tongue and warm pulsing lips sucked him in ...

She paused in mid-beat, stared wide-eyed up at him across the flesh of his stomach as if it were the marble of some heroic statue; then her eyes mercifully closed as her nails bit the roundnesses of his ass, hands stuffing him into her mouth like a big bite of sweet melon. She grunted once softly as she picked up on the beat, faster and faster and faster in an asymptotic rhythm, kneading and clawing and sucking faster and faster and faster...

Faster, faster-faster-faster-faster fasterfasterfaster—and he slumped forward, half-limp over her as pleasure-waves inside him crested and crested-crested-crested-crested-crested-crested crestedcrestedcrested in on-rushing rhythmic explosive series till they dopplered merged peak-to-peak in a continuous timeless flash... and he sighed a great air-release groan and exploded through her tension released in a synapse white-out reversal, paused, then cupped her face in his hands, lifted her up to him and kissed her softly on her moist, love-bruised lips.

And the breeze from the river was warm and soothing, filling him with a calm as wide as it was deep. Ah, it's all such a shuck, the whole damn hurricane, when you stand at the centre, none of it's real. And anyone's at the centre if he sits up and looks. Got as much going for us as the next cat, just gotta be *me*. Peel the biggest vip going down till he's mother-naked, and all you get is a man who deep inside, won't believe what he is. *Mano a mano,* you got enough going for you to stand up to anyone, you're looking down from where all those big-league politician cats look, and no wonder they don't talk about it, it's all just a shuck, none of those pricks got any more business telling the whole fucking country what to do than you have. You know it, and they don't, is all. That's where show biz is at—the only way to get that old surge without getting hooked on the junk, and without doing anyone in along the way. Politics! Statecraft! Horseshit! All you need to get into the big game is a little bit of muscle and a lot of bluff.

And one hell of a strong stomach.

No, no, too easy, thought Benedict Howards, too easy a victory over forces of the fading-black-circle Jack Barron smart-ass up-nose down-throat servant-of-death.

Howards whirled his swivel chair around like a spastic marionette, and like a Hollywood backdrop wilderness the mountains facing the northwest quadrant of the Rocky Mountain Freezer Complex Administration Building spread themselves out before him, a view carefully unspoiled by buildings. But it was no backdrop, it was ten thousand acres of the Rocky Mountains, an amoeboid estate rippling across uninhabited, impassable mountains. And next week, when all the sales were final, the few roads leading in from the outside world would be cut, and I'll be safe in the middle of ten thousand acres of impassable wilderness, the only airport on it mine, he thought, no way for anyone to get within fifty miles of the Complex unless I say so. I'll be safe in here, safe for the next million years.

Twenty million dollars. That prick Yarborough thinks I'm crazy, paying twenty million dollars for ten thousand acres in the ass-end of nowhere. Three-score-and-ten fool! Amortised over the next million years, that's just twenty bucks a year, and that's mighty cheap life insurance, when you can afford to take that real long view.

Nothing looks the same when you can figure on a million years. Five hundred million getting the Freezer Bill through Congress, a hundred million to buy a President every four years, and, if you can't buy him, for ten million you can hire a pro to kill *anyone*... Teddy Hennering, and, yes, Teddy the Pretender too, it ever comes down to it.

You can do literally *anything* if you've got working capital and can amortise the cost over a million years. Save money too on all those smart-ass tax lawyers; cheaper to buy a new law when you got what it takes to make it stand a million years.

So screw you, Jack Barron, whatever bush-league crap you're up to, coming out here like this—walking right in for the treatment after I been chasing you for a month, after you gotta know I hired that dumb prick who missed you. Don't matter what you think you're up to, what counts is you're *here*. Yeah, smart-ass, you and your woman are right here where I want you, and until I say so, there's no way you can get out. And you don't leave here till you have the treatment, and once you do, you're in it with me—in it in ways you can't even dream of now... More than your life on the line, it's the next million years.

Yeah, no way you could ever trust three-score-and-ten Jack Barron, but immortal Jack Barron'll be in the bag for certain. For *dead* certain, dead like rotting in six feet of maggots fading black vultures laughing over your flesh for ten thousand years of tube up nose down throat life leaking away in plastic vulturebeak bottles simpering nurses bedpans of maggots clashes of metal drooling in mud laughing images of eviscerated niggers picaninny eyes rolling in cancerous bloody cotton fading fading fading in ruined balls shrivelling rotting...

"Mr Barron is here," the plastic-secretary-voice of the intercom said.

Howards whirled the chair around, blinked his eyes once, and was back. Watch that stuff, he told himself. Couple days, it'll all be over, Barron in the bag, and everything safe from fading black faces of eviscerated picaninny eyes rolling in—

The door opened, and into the room walked Jack Barron. There was something hard and round and black behind his big, electric-dangerous eyes, like a fading black circle vortex reaching out as he stepped across the room. His eyes never leaving Howards, he sat down in the chair by the desk, stuck his feet up on it, lit up one of those damn Acapulco Golds dope-fiend cigarettes, and said: "Save the heart-attack, Bennie, this is the straight schmear, just between you and me. I know *everything*, Bennie, *everything*. I got you pinned to the wall, and I got a mighty good reason to nail you, best reason in the world, and we both know what it is."

He knows! thought Howards. He knows fading black circle of eviscerated—no, no, he can't know *that*. It's gotta be another smart-ass bluff.

"I don't know what game you're playing now, Barron," he said, "but whatever it is, and whatever you want, it won't work. You're on my ground now, and this'll be the last time you'll dare to forget it."

"You wouldn't be threatening me, would you?" Barron asked, with that snotty phoney innocence. "It doesn't pay to threaten me. Haven't you learned that? Apparently not. Thought you could handle me the same way you did Hennering, didn't you? But you can see it didn't work."

So he found out about that coward Hennering, and he knows it was me bought that dumb Mississippi hit—and he thinks he can use it! Could that be all it is, not fading cancerous balls of bloody cotton picaninny circle of assassins plastic vulture beaks up nose, down—Get hold of yourself, man! There's no way he can know. And even if he does, he's here, and you've got him. And he soothed himself by stroking the guard-call button hidden under the lip of the desk.

"What did you come here for anyway?" Howards said.

"Just what I said on the phone, Sara's in your outer office, and we both want the immortality treatment. We're exercising our legal option under the contract, and we want the treatment now. Any objections?"

Howards found himself almost laughing. The idiot's here to somehow force me into doing exactly what I want him to—and after he kept refusing to do it. But that doesn't make sense!

"No objections," Howards said a bit uncertainly. "You play ball with Benedict Howards, you'll see a deal's a deal."

"Groovy. I've got no objections now because I know the big secret, found it out in Mississippi. Five kids bought for about two-and-a-half million dollars, and then someone tries to kill me to keep me from finding out, and there's only one logical conclusion since you're the only man knew I was going to be there long enough in advance to contract out a hit."

He knows! He knows! Someone talked! Palacci? One of the doctors? Yarborough, Bruce, Hennering (no, Hennering's dead!)? Some son of a bitch talked, sold out to the fading black circle of eviscerated death maggots up nose down throat, some cocksucker sold out a million years... or is he just bluffing again? Does he know it all, or just faking? Got to find out...

"You can't be this stupid, Barron," Howards said. "You said yourself you knew I killed Hennering. (Give it away, admit it, see if he twitches... No! No! Howards thought as Barron smiled placidly, not moving a muscle, that much he really did know.) So why did you come here? You know I'd have the balls to kill you if I killed Hennering, a goddamn Senator. What makes you think I'll make you immortal now, when I could kill you a lot easier than I killed that prick Hennering, and a lot cheaper too?" And under the desk, he touched his thumb to the guard-call button.

Barron reached into his sportjac pocket (a gun? Howards thought wildly in a moment of pure panic), and put what looked like a small transistor radio with two speaker-grids down on the desk. One of those new Bell miniphones, Howards thought.

"That's why," said Jack Barron. "Recognise it, don't you? It's one of those new miniphones that feed directly into the phone-satellite circuit, and it's been picking up every word you said, feeding it directly back to New York to three separate vidphone recorders. And before you can even think about making a move, there'll be five separate copies of the tape sent to five different mailing services with orders to send 'em to Luke Greene, Gregory

Morris, the FBI, the AP, and the Colorado fuzz—unless I'm back in New York on Tuesday to stop 'em. *Murder*, Howards, you've admitted to murder, and it's all on tape to be shouted from the rooftops by your own voice, if anything happens to me... or even if I don't like the way you smile."

Benedict Howards sighed a sigh of naked relief. You prick, you've trapped yourself, he thought, thinking anything could matter once you came here. Murder! What a joke, murder. Thinking to threaten me with electric chair death sentence your own funeral, Barron! He *doesn't* know, doesn't know the only thing that matters. By tomorrow I'll have the same weapon, electric chair death sentence to use on immortal Jack Barron any time he thinks of crossing me. *Murder*! You're too much, Barron, and to think you had me going, fading black circle of eviscerated niggers trap you too, and tie you to me, immortal murderers both of us, with a million years to lose... and he walked right into it. All that smart-ass conniving led him right here to me.

"Well, Howards, the game's over, give!" Barron said. "Let's hear all the nice juicy details on your immortality treatment, and don't bother to tell me what lab techniques you used to develop it, that I already know."

Howards smiled as he pressed home the button. So that's it, he knows about eviscerated fading black nigger children from black scum would sell their own flesh got no right to live, and he thinks we just used 'em for expensive guinea pigs. No sense in telling him now he's wrong, Wait till after the operation. Let him feel how he's hooked when he wakes up immortal. Won't have to tell him who's boss then, he'll tell himself.

"Don't worry, Barron," he said, "you'll have your answer soon enough. But not until you can understand what it really means."

"I warn you, Howards, you'll tell me everything now or—"

And then two uniformed guards, pistols drawn, burst in.

Barron got to his feet wheeling, blanched for a moment as he stared into the barrels of the guns. But by the time he had turned his back on the guards to leer at Howards, that fucking smart-ass smirk was back. But the joke was on him!

"Won't work, Bennie. I know you're bluffing. Go ahead, have your shaved apes shoot me right now, I dare you. And those tapes go straight to—"

"Shoot you, Barron?" Benedict Howards smiled triumphantly. "Why would I do that? You're much too valuable alive and immortal. These gentlemen will simply escort you to the hospital, wouldn't want you to get lost. You guys pick up that woman in the outer office too, on the way outside. You'll both have the operation and be back safe and sound in New York on Tuesday, just as you planned, but with one minor modification—you'll be more than ready to take orders from *me*."

"You're crazy," Barron said. "But who cares, I've still got you where I want you, no matter what you think. So we play your game till I leave here. Why not, I've got nothing to lose and everything to gain. But why the guns? You can tell your creeps to put 'em away, they don't need 'em."

"Just a precaution," Howards said. "When you're guarding a million years it pays to take precautions. But don't worry, when you wake up immortal you'll know just what I mean."

Know what it means to wake up each morning, breathe the air, know it's forever so long as you own ten thousand acres safe from assassins, Congressmen, President, Freezer Utility Bill holding back the fading black circle, safe, safe behind impregnable walls of power, safe forever in cool closed rooms in impassable mountains, know what's to lose when you're immortal, know that you lose what I lose if you don't play ball...

Know what it means to be my flunky all the way, Barron: power of my word eternal life or death eternal in six feet of maggots eviscerated niggers with plastic beaks up nose down throat laughing for a million lost years just my shut mouth between you and the fading black circle, way it's your shut mouth between death and me and it'll be shut forever, those discs *both* our electric chair dead flesh shrivelled balls death sentence, in it together for the next million years—just you and me.

And the fading black circle of maggot arms holding us together, always there to hold back with ten thousand acres of impassable mountains, Congress, President, silence... But always there waiting with plastic tubes maggot-filled bedpans of life's fluids leaking away... But you'll never get me, none of you—not Benedict Howards, not fading black circle electric-chair assassins eviscerated rolling-eyed niggers you'll never be strong enough to take it away, not ever, never... never... Never! Never! Hold back the fading black circle with life-against-death power! Never! Never! Never let them take Forever away!

He saw that Barron was looking at him in bewilderment, and behind it there was confusion, fear, and disgust. Christ, what do I look like? I've gotta control it, take it easy, the long view, million-year insurance amortisation! Yeah, yeah, get hold of yourself, it's all right, no fading black circle of cancerous picaninnies electric-chair death sentence ever's gonna be able to take it away...

But he heard his own voice sound like an alien thing, pale and croaking, as he shrieked: "Get him over to the hospital! Take him away! Take him away!"

Never! Never! They'll never make *me* die! Fading black circle... you always lose never win... I'll kill you! Kill you! I'll never die!

17

GUNS and a long white corridor green mountains looming over ether-smelling sheets... lemon-coloured ceiling... soft sunlight shadows becoming bright-blue fluorescent operating-theatre glare lying warm and weak on a soft pillow... the guns of the guards lifting him onto the stretcher-table... pentathol-needle of drowsy indifference... wheeling the table past looming cool mountains... cold white robes of the cold white doctors... nurses burbling machines... impersonal steel of scalpels blued by harsh fluorescent lighting... cotton swab in the warm comfortable bed with the shadowed mountains on the ceiling... smell of hospital mingling with the smell of fir trees... the needle dripping sleep in the pit of his arm... And behind him he sensed another table's vibrations, wheeling into the blue-white operating theatre behind him (Sara?) on the shore of the consciousnessless sea unable-not-wanting to move... the white robes... blue-scalpel machinery of the operating theatre blurring to white sheets, lemon-coloured ceiling, cool green mountains... anaesthesia-euphoria of awakening-weakness... smell of ether to pine needles, lemon-coloured doctors...

Then (when?) the blurring became a memory of a moment past—and Jack Barron was awake, fully conscious, aware in retrospect of an interminable sojourn on the interface between sleep and wakefulness, images of the preoperative past moulding with the postoperative indefinite present as if that unrememberable moment of crossover had been prolonged ten thousand years. But now he was finally awake all the way, and he was:

Lying in bed, his head on a warm white pillow, his unfocused eyes staring up at a lemon-yellow ceiling, and to his left was a full-length door-window looking out past buildings on the Rocky Mountains, and the smell of pine drifted in past the heat-curtain shimmer that kept out the cool mountain breeze.

Jeez, he thought, what day is it? How long have I been out? No calendar in the plain white-walled room, only the bed and a small hospital table, not even a clock. And if they used Deep Sleep recovery, which they probably did, no way of telling how long I've been out.

Confused memories swam into focus. Those cats with the guns took me to the operating... No wait, they took me to *this* room, put me on a stretcher-table, gave me a needle, and I was already half out when they wheeled me into the operating room, and then they wheeled someone else in after me—must've been Sara—last thing I remember. Sara must be immortal now too.

Immortal...? Don't feet any different, at least I don't think I do. Tuning in on his body Barron felt a slight soreness in the muscles of his stomach, a barely noticeable kink in his back, felt kind of comfortably weak and drowsy, like lying in bed the morning after a hard night. Nothing different, really, I still feel like *me,* is all.

Is *anything* different?

Barron strained his mind trying to remember just exactly how his body had always felt, not something you're really aware of unless you're real tired or sick. My imagination, just looking for it, or *do* I feel just a little different? Hard to tell. I don't feel sick. A little weak from the operation, maybe, whatever it was, but no X-Ray-vision Superman powers, that's for sure. Weak, yeah, but it's a funny kind of weak, feels almost too good, like when I get up I could go run a mile... or is thinking maybe I'm immortal just playing games with my head?

Immortal... Shit, how do you know you're immortal till you've lived a couple hundred years? No reason to suddenly feel different. Thing is, I suppose, you just keep feeling the same, young and healthy and strong the way you started, when you turn forty, fifty, seventy, a hundred... What feels different, I guess, is you don't *ever* feel different, forty, a hundred, two hundred years, and you still feel the same, and that can't feel different till after it *hasn't* happened.

Immortality—no reason to feel any different, they could tell you it was just your appendix out, and you'd never even know.

Hey, *am* I immortal, or could the whole thing be a shuck? How the hell can I know, got only Bennie's word for it. Could be they just faked it to cool me, I'd never know, can't trust Bennie, and *that's* for sure. Well, it doesn't make any difference, win or lose, *that* game's played out. Either way, when I get back to New York, Bennie's had it. Next show I'll *really* do him in... got those discs safe and sound to make sure I get out of here alive, immortal or not, and maybe...

Why not? Get Bennie on the line, then play the tape on the air... What can he do? Sue me for libel, when it's his own voice libelling itself? Dunno, better cheek first with lawyers—discs can be edited, faked; they're not evidence in court. Does that mean I'd have to prove another way he's a murderer, or else he'd have a libel case? Unless I can con him with the discs into confessing on the air... Shouldn't be too hard to do. Seems like he's finally flipped all the way, the way his eyes looked... maybe I *could* pull it off. It'd sure be nice and tidy, but dangerous as hell if I couldn't bluff him. Better think about that, and get some good legal advice... maybe GOP lawyers...?

The door opened, and a dark man in a white tunic, obviously a doctor, peered inside, said: "Ah! Mr Howards, he's awake. He's come out of it."

And Benedict Howards followed the doctor as he stepped inside.

"Well, Palacci," Howards said, "go examine him. Tell me if it took."

"No need to, Mr Howards," the doctor replied. "If he's alive and awake now, it took. The only danger was that the antibody suppressants might not work and his body would develop an allergic reaction to the grafts. That *does* happen, you know, in about two cases out of a hundred. But if it had happened he'd be running a high fever, probably be in a deep coma. In fact, by now he'd most likely be dead. It's all right, he's immortal and well, just like the woman."

"Sara!" Barron shouted, feeling a stab of guilt that he had forgotten. "Sara's all right?"

"Better than all right," said Howards, and his eyes were still mad and gleaming the way they had been in his office… *how* many days ago? "She's immortal now, just like you. And like me. How does it feel, Barron? How does it feel to wake up immortal, smell that pine in the air, and know you'll never have to die? So long as you cooperate, of course."

"I don't feel anything, Howards," Barron said guardedly. "I don't feel any different at all. How do I know you didn't just open me up and close me, or just drop me in a Deep Sleep chamber for… how long has it been? What day is this, anyway?"

"It's Monday," the doctor said. "You've been—"

Benedict Howards raised his hand, cut the doctor off. "I'll do the talking," he said. "When can he get up, Palacci? There's a few things I want Mr Barron to see. Time he knew for certain, *dead* certain, who's boss."

"With forty hours of Deep Sleep recovery, he could get up right now. Strictly speaking, it's not really a major operation. We don't have to plant the grafts very deep."

"Well, then go get him his clothes," Howards said. "Mr Barron and I have a few things to talk over in private."

As the doctor left, closing the door behind him, Barron propped himself up against the bedstead. He felt surprisingly strong and much more in control of the situation than he did flat on his back.

"All right, Howards," he said, "so prove I'm immortal. I'll admit I have no idea how it should feel, but it seems to me all I've got is your word for it, and all your word and thirty cents'll get me is a ride on the subway. Just remember those discs. You gotta keep me happy to keep me cool, and you gotta keep me cool just to stay alive, and you better not forget it."

"Sure, you and your smart-ass discs…" Howards smirked. "When you get back to New York, you'll mail all the copies to me and we'll have a nice little bonfire."

Barron smiled. He's really flipped for sure. "What planet you say you're from, Bennie? You prove you really delivered, and I just might let you off—just maybe, depends how I feel. But those discs are the property of yours truly, and I think I'll just keep 'em around to keep you—you should pardon the expression—honest. The penalty for murder is death in the chair, and you better keep that in mind."

"I'll try to keep it in mind, Barron," Howards said. (But his paranoid loony eyes were laughing. Laughing!) "And I think you'd do well to remember it too. And you *are* immortal, and I *will* prove it. I'm gonna show you everything, give you a guided, tour of the whole operation. You're gonna find out just how you were made immortal, and believe me, that'll prove to you that I really delivered."

"You're gibbering, Howards. How'll that prove anything?" Howards laughed, and in the chill certainty behind his paranoid eyes Barron got a flash of mortal dread, knowing for certain, dead certain, that Benedict Howards was now sure he had everything in the bag.

"All in good time," Howards said. "You'll see. You'll see what my percentage was in making you immortal all along. Maybe those discs do put my life in your hands, but your own immortality is what gives *you* to *me*. All the way, Barron, I own you now, you're *my* flunky now, and you'll never be able to forget it. But wait till your clothes get here, then you'll see. Oh, man, will you see!"

"You see, Barron, what they tell me, it's all in the glands," Benedict Howards said as the elevator finally stopped, down in what Jack Barron figured had to be a deep subcellar of the hospital.

Wouldn't be surprised to see a Frankenstein Monster slimy-stone passageway, he thought, as the elevator door slid open and anticlimactically revealed an ordinary white-walled, windowless, fluorescent-lit hospital corridor.

"Endocrine balance, that's what they call it, endocrine balance ..." Howards continued babbling as the two guards, with their pistols conspicuous but holstered led them out of the elevator and down the hall. Apparently the guards already had their orders, since Howards hadn't spoken a word to them after they had left the hospital room, just kept babbling a lot of stuff about hormones and glands.

Barron was hardly listening. Howards' abstracted, glazed eyes, the way he kept talking a blue streak, turning his head here, there, here, like a frightened bird, convinced him that Bennie was way round the bend. And, he thought, all this fucking medical jargon he obviously only half understands...

But that, Barron suddenly realised, *that's* the kicker. If it were all a shuck, he wouldn't know all this stuff unless he had memorised a whole set-spiel just to put me on, and then he'd be way smoother, Bennie's not show biz enough to pull a con *this* subtle off. Which means...

It's for real; at least it's possible. *Immortality.* Maybe I really got it, he's *not* putting me on? Immortal! I don't feel any different, but why should I, I'm young and I'm healthy, and if it's true, I'll *never* feel different, not now, not in half a million years.

Or will I? he wondered. Bennie's sure different, more paranoid by the minute since this whole thing started. But maybe the whole Foundation schtick was a paranoid bag for openers, and the more money Bennie's got, the longer he's got to live, the more he's got to be scared shitless to lose. Which puts him exactly where I want him.

But then why's he so fucking sure he's got me where he wants me?

All this screwing around... Then it flashed like cold fire through him: Howards' been dying to make me immortal all along. And now I've been had? But how? He can't touch me now, and I can walk all over him. The treatment... yeah, he got uptight every time I tried to find out what the fuck it was, and now he's telling me and I'm not listening! And whatever it is, pretty safe bet it's really been done to me. Listen, you prick, for chrissakes listen, isn't this what you played all those games to hear?

"Man's as old as his glands," Howards was saying. "You could keep the hormone balance you had as a kid, you'd never stop growing... No, that's wrong, I think... or... but that's not important. Point is, you're no older than your glands. Up to a point, a kid's glands keep his body from ageing, something about anabolism exceeding catabolism, whatever that means. Anyway, whatever it means, the moment it reverses you start to age, start dying, fading black... Way they explained it, normally a human being's either growing or ageing, never inbetween, depending on the balance of his glands. It's like a clock at midnight between one tick and the next it's a different day, one tick you're growing, next tick you're ageing. You keep growing, sooner or later it kills you, they told me, but I don't really understand why... But anyway, the moment your glands pass over that line, sometime in your teens, they say, you start to die. You see, Barron? You see? Immortality's all in the tick."

"Tick, schmick," Barron finally said. "What're you gibbering about?"

"You're pretty dumb, Barron, can't you see it? If it's exactly twelve o'clock Tuesday night and you stop the clock right on the moment it stops being Tuesday, and before it can start being Wednesday you're caught inbetween. Not growing, not ageing. That smart-ass Palacci calls it 'Homeostatic Endocrine Balance.' Stop that gland 'clock' right between ticks and keep it there, balanced between growing and ageing, and that's immortality. That's what we've got, way to take all the glands and keep 'em balanced what they call homeostatically forever. Forever! We got glands that'll stay young forever, Barron. That's why we'll never die."

Makes a kind of screwy sense, Barron admitted, fishing in his memory for two terms of Berkeley biology. "Anabolism and catabolism equal metabolism," the meaningless phrase from some old gypsheet popped into his mind, But what the fuck did it mean? Lessee, metabolism's like a biological checking account: anabolism is growth, catabolism's decay—or the other way around? Anyway, in a kid, growth exceeds decay, so the account's solvent. And in an adult it's vice versa and you're overdrawn, so you start to die. Yeah, but if you were just even, and could keep it that way, like Howards says, you'd be immortal! That all immortality is, tuning up the old glands in the shop the way they tune the Jag's engine? But how do they do it?

"I think I dig now, Bennie," he said. "Just out of curiosity, how do your boys do it—I mean, tinker with all those glands?"

Howards leered at him, and the cold words he spoke were somehow totally obscene: "Hard radiation and lots of it. An overload of radiation kept up for two days."

Barron went cold. Radiation—a witch-word, like cancer. Overload of radiation for two days! But that means—

Howards laughed. "Take it easy, Barron, you're not gonna die. I'm not dead, am I, and we've both had the same treatment. My boys found out something about some special kind of radiation in big killing doses, it freezes the balance of the glands in this Homeostatic Endocrine Balance thing, if you catch 'em young enough…"

"But all that radiation, what's it do to your body?"

Howards grimaced, his eyes seemed to glaze over as if he were running some dirty movie on the screen in his head; he muttered something crazy about niggers, then seemed to snap out of it as the guards halted outside a plain steel door.

"I never seen it, but they say it's pretty awful," Howards said. "Flesh starts to rot and fall off and the whole body breaks out in a million little cancers… but the glands are okay, if the quacks time it right. Better than—"

"You crazy fucker!" Barron howled, half-lunged at Howards, then stopped as the guards whipped out their pistols.

"Don't foam at the mouth, Barron, no one said you were irradiated." Howards said, caressing the knob of the steel door. He laughed. "I'll show you why we're both all right, be all right forever, and why I've got you right where I want you. I said you had glands that'll stay young, keep you young forever…" Howards' eyes were black pits of feral paranoid madness as he turned the doorknob and said, "… but when did I ever say they were yours?" And opened the door.

Beyond the door was what at first glance looked to be a pretty ordinary hospital ward: A long, narrow room, with a central aisle dividing two rows of about a dozen beds each, headboards set flush against either wall. At the far end of the room was a large complex of consoles facing a small desk behind which a white-smocked man sat, apparently monitoring them. To the right of the desk was another door.

But it was the occupants of the beds that made the room a chamber of grotesquerie, filling Barron with a disbelieving nauseous dread.

Two dozen beds, in each of them a young child, none younger than six, none older than about ten, and more than half of them black. All were being fed intravenously, but the tubes feeding the needles taped in their armpits led not to drip-bottles but to a master-tube that ran along each wall and back to the complex of consoles at the rear of the room. A similar arrangement emptied the catheters that snaked out from under each set of bedclothes. Each child had electrodes taped to head and chest, the wires converging in trunk-line cables that ran along either wall to the monitor consoles. There was no sound as they entered the ward, not a head turned, not a muscle moved; the kids were all in deep comas.

The ages... the preponderance of Negroes... Christ on a Harley! Barron thought. These gotta be the poor kids the Foundation bought!

"Neat, eh?" Howards said. "I mean, when you think what a mess it could be, a whole roomful of squalling brats, and the personnel it'd take to take care of 'em... In the short run, all this equipment's real expensive, but when you think of what it saves on food and salaries and trouble and amortise it out... well, even in the medium run it saves an awful lot of money."

"What the fuck are you doing to these poor kids?" Barron said. "What's wrong with 'em, why are they all out cold?"

"*Wrong with 'em?*" Howards said neutrally, but with some kind of terrible mania leaking out of his eyes. "Nothing's wrong with 'em, they're all perfect physical specimens, or you can bet your ass we wouldn't be blowing the money it takes to keep 'em here. We don't do anything to them here, this is just our nursery. The whole process is perfectly painless for the kids. From beginning to end they don't feel a thing. What do you think I am, some kind of sadist? We just keep 'em out and quiet and feed 'em on glucose till they're ready for processing. Saves time and mess and money this way—one man at the instruments there can run the whole show."

Can't be happening, Barron told himself as Howards led him and the guards down the aisle. But he knew damn well it was. A death-stench of madness so thick you could cut it as they walked past the rows of sleeping children plugged into tubes and wires like some hideous circuitry—and that's all he sees, fucking production line, is all. Production of *what*? Bennie's gone totally round the bend, and when I get him on the show I'll tear him to pieces, then tear the pieces to pieces... He's stark staring mad!

Yet he found himself listening in dread fascination, unable to think past Howards' words as Bennie babbled on like some damn production manager conducting a guided tour of a refrigerator factory:

"Of course this is just a pilot plant... If we could solve the problem of safe revival from the Freezers we wouldn't need all this crap—just irradiate 'em as soon as we get 'em and drop 'em in Freezers, then thaw 'em out when we need 'em, save a lot of money. We're working on it, but they tell me that's still years away, so we gotta make do. Keeping 'em alive after the radiation's the real bind. What with the radiation disease and cancer, none of 'em last more than a couple of weeks. So the timing's real tricky, keeping a dozen or so always ready. Damn, if they'd only figure out how to keep glands viable in the Freezers we could get rid of all this mess."

As they reached the door at the far end of the ward, the man behind the desk looked away from his dials briefly as Howards said: "Don't pay any attention to us. I'm just giving the guided tour to our very first client."

Then he turned to Barron, his eyes unreadable beacons of madness, and said, "Still, a pretty neat set-up for a pilot plant, eh, Barron?"

Barron felt the flood of unbearable sensory-data finally getting through to where he lived. *Murder.* Some kind of crazy mass-murder! He's killing these kids, killing 'em slow, gotta be totally nuts to show me all this. What's he think I am... gotta know I'm gonna nail him to the wall...

"What the fuck is this?" Barron shouted. (And seeing a window in the door before him opaqued with ripples like a toilet window, he moved toward it.) "And what the hell's behind this door?"

Swift as a cat Howards was between him and the door, his eyes wide with terror. "You don't want to look in there," he said, his voice frenzied and shrill. "Take my word, you don't want to see. That's the post-radiation ward... cancer... rotten flesh... falling apart... It's ugly, Barron, they tell me it's real ugly. I've never been in there, I don't want to see. Doctors, they're used to that kind of stuff... But we'd both be sick if you opened that door."

"What are you doing? WHAT THE FUCK ARE YOU DOING?"

"Stop raving, Barron, haven't you guessed? With enough of the right radiation, kids' glands can be retarded just enough so they stay in this Homeostatic Endocrine Balance, keep the body the way it is, never ageing, forever. Immortality, but with two big catches. First, it only works with children under twelve, so that'd mean no immortality for grown men—for us. And it wouldn't work anyway, 'cause the radiation we gotta use to balance the glands is a fatal dose. Big joke, eh? Got a way to make kids immortal, only the treatment kills 'em—the operation was successful but the patient died.

"But the *glands* don't die, Barron. After they're irradiated they're still perfect and balanced to keep a man alive forever. The radiation doesn't kill the glands at all, all they need is a healthy new body to keep 'em alive, and they'll keep that body young and alive forever. Just a simple transplant operation, and with the stuff they got today, transplants almost always take. They don't even have to put the glands where they'd be in a normal body, just a package in the gut and another in the back, not even a major operation—duck soup for my quacks. See what I meant? We got glands that'll keep us alive forever now, but that doesn't mean they gotta be *ours.*"

Snakes undulating slug-slime oozing all over his skin, Barron felt mindless urge to tear it all away, rip himself apart with his fingernails, tear out the soft green pulsing globs of flesh dripping stolen life-juices of Forever, death-junk drip-dripping eternally into his veins... Images of sleeping faces of mountains of Evers slum children Franklin's smashed face hard metal bee by his car gutted bodies exploding garbage can slime rivers of blood thick like slime in which he was drowning! drowning! in slime in bodies of niggers crawling all over him maggots inside him all burned unforgettable tracers of anguish through the quivering meat of his brain.

"You fucking crazy axe-murderer!" he screamed. "You monster! You got no right to be alive! And you won't be, Bennie, I swear, one way or another I'll kill you! Got those discs… I'll get you even if you kill me right here right now! Go ahead, have your apes shoot me right now! You better! Kill me! Kill me! Either way, I'll kill you! You fucking—"

And with an animal growl, he lunged at Howards, felt the tips of his fingers just touch the scaly dry skin of Howards' throat—and the guards grabbed him, one to each arm, snapped his arms behind his shoulder blades in a vicious double hammerlock.

"Murder?" Howards whined. "What do you mean, murder? So the two of us are alive, and two of them are dead… How long would they have lived, at most a century, and then, either way, those kids'd be the same place—dead. So it costs two lifetimes to give us two million lifetimes, don't you see, life comes out ahead on the deal a million to one. That's not murder, that's the opposite, pushing back the fading black circle, pushing it back, back, back, opening, not closing the fading black circle of death, pushing it back a million years! What do you mean, murder, it's life, man, it's *life*. Not to do it, *that's* murder… murdering yourself, throwing yourself to the fading black circle, six feet of eviscerated nigger maggots ten million years of vultures laughing with plastic beaks up nose down throat fading black circle of death and murder…"

As Howards screamed at him, eyes rolling in pure terror inches away, face to face, hate to hate, Barron felt himself turning cold—the cold logic of light years of electric-circuit—insulation distance, the kinaesthetic horror of the things sewn into his body becoming phosphor-dot images of death on the screen of his mind. He scrabbled for purchase and found it in the reflexive satellite-network interface forming between his consciousness and the phosphor-dot mosaic-image of madness in Benedict Howards' eyes.

Cool it, he told himself, you're kick-'em-in-the-ass Jack Barron, and you're alive. And knowingly, he conned himself, sucking up the vidphone-TV-screen-interface anaesthetic reality, forced himself cold.

Gotta stop him, kill him, finish him, is all. Got the muscle to do it, got murder discs, *Bug Jack Barron* hundred million Brackett Count pipeline, GOP insurance; you got him cold.

But glands in your body like green slime crocodiles dripping blood of murdered babies to keep you alive…!

He saw that Howards too had retreated to a more bearable level of reality. "So you see, I got you right where I want you after all. Murder, yeah, legally it's murder, and it's gonna take some doing before I can change the law. Before we change the law—'cause you're in just as deep as I am, Barron. Your contract... I'll bet you didn't read *all* the fine print, the part where you agree to accept full legal liability for any results of the treatment. Thought that was just to cover us in case you died?

"That contract was drawn up by some mighty high-priced lawyers. It's iron-clad, and it's a signed legal admission to accessory to murder in any court in the country. It's a confession, and if you blow the whistle on me, I'll buy twenty witnesses who'll swear you knew all about the treatment when you signed it. We're in this together, Barron. You want to stay alive, you take your orders from me."

A blind berserker flash erupted through Barron: Ruined bodies soft slimy gland-slugs drip-dripping their eternal vampire-slime filling his veins with the blood of broken babies crocodile mouth of Howards' madness chewing gobbets of cancer forever, so long as he was alive, so long as Howards was surrounded by guns by five hundred billion dollars by Freezer Bill by bought President (bought with *what*?), Congress, safe forever, immortal vampire monster going on and on and on...

"You really think that matters. Howards?" he howled. "Think that'll save you? With... with... (scrunching his body in anguish) these *things* inside me, you so sure I want to live? I'll get you, Howards, there's not a thing you can do about it. I'll get you even if it does cost me my life."

"Not just *your* life," said Benedict Howards. "You don't like immortality, okay, you got a right to be crazy. Who cares? You feel rotten, want to die, that's your business. But if finding out did this to you, what'll it do to your wife?"

"Sara—"

"You've got a short memory, Barron. Your wife signed the same contract too—makes her an accessory to murder just like you. There's any murder trial, it'll be a triple trial, she's in it with us And she never knew what was coming off, did she? *You* got her into it, and if you don't play ball it'll be *you* killing her. Don't hand me any crap about murder. You're a murderer too Barron, whichever way you turn."

"You... You've told her...?"

"Do I really look that dumb?" Howards said. "You're a lunatic, who knows what you might do, even with your own life on the line. But Miss Sara Westerfeld, or Mrs Jack Barron—whichever the hell it is—we know what *she's* like, don't we? Of course I haven't told her. Why should I, that's my final insurance. I don't tell her a thing, so long as you play ball. That's how I *know* I've got you. And I do have you now, don't I, Barron? Come on, say it, I want to hear you say it."

Shit, Barron thought, he *does* have me. He knows it, I know it, he knows I know... I'm trapped! Can't tell Sara, she'd... worse than leave me, she'd freak out altogether. Gotta… gotta … *what?* What the fuck can I do?

"All right, Howards, for the moment we'll play it your way."

"For the moment! That's good, that's real good, Barron. *For the moment.* For the next million years! And you know something, friend? Sooner or later you're gonna thank me, you'll see what I mean. You can't help wanting to stay alive, can you? Immortal… fifty years or so, and you'll understand it's worth *anything* to be immortal, anything… eviscerated nigger bodies in heaps of… You'll thank me, Barron. You're immortal, you're more than a man, your life's worth a million of theirs. Give it time. You'll learn to like it, my guarantee."

And from Howards' mad eyes Barron sucked a fear, a mortal fear the like of which, he had never felt before: fear that Howards might be right, fear that in fifty or a hundred or a thousand years the things inside him would rot him to a gutted hulk, fear that someday he might stare into those paranoid monstrous eyes and see—*himself.*

18

NO WAY OUT, such a goddamn neat trap, Jack Barron thought as he paced the patio under the grey, overcast New York sky, feeling the damp chill of the lull between down-pours through the upturned collar of his sportjac. The setting sun painted the cloud layer with ugly smears of dirty purple, and the waning rush-hour street noises seemed to have been made more savage by the wet black mulch (compounded of rain and good old New York filth) that covered the sidewalks, streets, cars, people scurrying buglike in the onrushing dusk twenty-three stories below.

Tuesday night. Yeah, soon it'll be night, and then morning, then dusk again, and then 8:00 p.m. Eastern Daylight Time. And then... what, man, then what? What the fuck you gonna do? What *can* you do?

Inside, Sara was playing one of the scratchy old Dylan albums she had brought up from her pad, and the grating old ricky-ticky voice from the simple funky past mocked him with a random moment of worn-out irony:

> *"I wish I could give Brother Bill his big thrill,*
> *I would tie him in chains at the top of the hill,*
> *Then send out for some pillars and Cecil B De Mille...*

Poor old Dylan should be alive now, get a charge out of how close to the nitty-gritty he comes twenty years later. Poor paranoid bastard was just a little too early for *real* Paranoiasville, is all. Knew then where it's at now, and wouldn't it be cool if it could be that simple, the good old Samson-smash schtick, get in that studio chained to the satellite network and bring the whole fucking schmear down around everybody's ears.

And you could do it as easy as playing the discs, riffing on Bennie and giving that hundred million Brackett Count audience the straight scam on slimy green glands drip-dripping the vampire life-blood of broken babies forever and ever into your veins, and how they got there, who put 'em there and why, tear 'em out bleeding and dripping and throw them in the faces of a hundred million dumb slobs and let 'em see just what a fucking hero their kick-'em-in-the-ass Black Shade Jack Barron really is, foam at the mouth and rip Howards and his Foundation and all his flunkies to little bloody pieces... All you gotta do is reach out and push, and all those stone walls come smashing down, pounding everything to pieces, you got the balls to stand there screaming and do yourself in, do Sara in...

Barron winced as it came to him that the name of the song Sara was playing was *Tombstone Blues*. And that's where it's at, *exactly* where it's at.

Howards may be crazy as a bedbug, but he sure knows where *one* thing is at, and who knows, maybe he's right, maybe only one thing *does* matter—life, is all, just staying alive. Comes nitty-gritty time, no man's got the choice'll do the kamikaze schtick. Sara... yeah, Sara in there, stoned silly on adrenaline since we got back from Colorado, thinking now we got it all made, immortal and together forever, and tomorrow night is Judgement Day for Bennie Howards, with Baby Bolshevik back-to-the-people Jack Barron ready to bring the Apocalypse and we march arm and arm into the sunrise, Battle Hymn of the Hail to the Chief Republic coming on in the background as we fade in on Forever.

Sara... Sure, con yourself into believing it's all for Sara; wasn't for Sara, you'd kamikaze right into Howards, right into accessory to murder and banzai for the Emperor, live a thousand years.

Sure you would. A thousand years... a million years, throw it all away. Sure you would. Wasn't for Sara, you'd kill yourself dead to take Howards with you. Sure you would. The fuck you would!

Dead... dead... Barron rolled the word around his mind, squeezed it like a lemon for the acid juice of gut-reality. *Dead... death...* No one ever came back to give you the straight scam on how it felt. Maybe someday they'll thaw someone out of the Freezers and then you'll know what it's like to be dead before you die. But no slot for murderers in the Freezers, no flash-freeze straight from the electric chair sizzle—'If you black, when you go you don't come back.' The Black Shade... Yeah, there's another side to Luke's Madison Avenue mickeymouse slogan, like dead, like death, like a million years of everything shot to shit or a million years of nothing. *Sure you would.* It's all for Sara, old Jack Barron's not afraid to die. The fuck he isn't!

Tombstone Blues...

Yeah, you got class, Barron, you make the hero scene, you do it up brown; throw away more than thirty, forty years, throw away a million years forever, and who knows, maybe a hundred years from now, there'll be losers huddling in some fucking attic thinking what a noble cat old Jack Barron was (remember him?) and a lot of good it'll do you when you're dead. The fucking Black Shade...

"But if you black, when you go you don't come back."

That what they see when they see a shade? Pale white papier-mâché mask over black reality black colour of death black colour of Forever black colour of emptiness black colour of loser black colour of the jungle inside black babies black pit of black blood feeding a pale white forever-vampire?

That's the nitty-gritty choice—white or black, winner or loser, alive or dead, and no ground between. Stand alive forever on a pile of dead bodies—or be one of the bodies, that's where it's all at.

Wasn't for Sara, you'd be on the side of the losers, side of corpses dead forever and you with them forever you're the fucking Black Shade, aren't you? Sure you are! Sure you would!

And like a sewer leaking grey blood-muck it began to rain again, a dirty grey New York uptight rain straight from special effects.

Before him, the city was a dirty wash of colourless grey on grey, and in the living room behind him Sara had turned on the colour organ and it was scintillating the room with colours... music... the homey orange glow of the firepit over the rich red carpeting and wood-panelled walls... Sara, bouncing about, alive and innocent and immortal... The living-colour science-fiction California of the mind *he* had created twenty-three stories above the grey New York murk, and he had to let the rain hit him, fat and wet and dirty, for long grey minutes before it bugged him to give him the balls to go inside.

The living room was rank with the taste of Forever. He could taste it in the thickness of the carpeting the ersatz phoenix-flame of the firepit the jang of steel guitar over harmonica-wheeze over the squeaking-door voice of Dylan (*dead* Dylan), the drumroll of the rain on the skylight facets flashing with random colour organ patters the sweet funk of potsmoke in the air the wall of electronic gizmos in living-colour satellite-network reality-contact with the whole wide universe, listen to the smell of Forever flashing! Life!

Life... Life was orange wood smell flames searing steak juices trickling down potsmoke music colour blue colour red colour emerald clinking off the glass skylight facets, was harmonica riffs honking the night, was every tension-feel of every muscle moving as he walked across the carpet giving under his weight, was air going in-out-in bringing the smell of rain of flame of pot of the woman-musk of Sara, was the taste of his tongue in his mouth, was everything happening every moment in the electric universe inside him, was the surge of his own blood in his arteries—and life was Sara.

White skin he could feel with his eyes taste with his nose, rounded naked-ness framed in an open black velvet robe lying with legs unselfconsciously bare and open on the orange-furred couch, moving her loose blonde hair in delayed afterbeat to the rhythm of the music, waving a half-smoked Acapulco Gold (getting ashes on the rug again, dammit!), the piebald flashes from the colour organ ricocheting off the skylight facets and caressing her flesh with a thousand scintillating fingers of lovely-obscene stroking light, and on her face an open smile of feral child-happiness child-innocent of babies torn apart slug-green glands drip-dripping behind big brown nipples of pleasure screams of dying black faces behind—cool it, man, cool it!

Like the best image-Sara ever fucking twenty-six-year-old image-Jack Barron stage centre on the monitor of his mind, she was there and perfect, breasts still tight-skinned massive softnesses smooth skin of Berkeley Acapulco LA nights hair freely flowing, there in his pad, in his California-wet-dream controlled reality, would always be there, young soft gonad-vision forever, alive forever, his forever, Sara forever... And beneath the soft smooth nakednesses, slug-green trails of black baby-blood drip-dripping drip-dripping drip-dripping...

"Jack! You're sopping."

She bounced to her feet, breasts moving nice and easy hide-and-peek like puppy-noses with the tensual black velvet robe as she walked barefoot across the carpet in long overstrides toward him and he moved real cool-like toward her, kicking off damp slippers (the fuck with the rug!), tossing aside the sportjac, and then letting her playful fingers take off the damp shirt as he functionally dropped his pants, kicked them away, and they stood lightly touching each other in robe and jockey shorts.

Eye to eye, pool-deep eyes of Berkeley-past-New York-present not merged into a forever-future, eyes that had won, had won him on her back-in-the-old-Berkeley-bag terms, had won immortality like a free lollipop to lick forever, forever hers, forever free, no piper to pay, woman's eyes shining, that had won every wet-dream of the girl, all in those hungry eat-me eyes—and it was all a lie.

All a shuck, and tomorrow night she'll know, know for sure where her big hero is at when I start doing riffs on Bennie's Freezing competition instead of giving him the knife she's expecting. No way of keeping *that* from her, but at least she doesn't ever have to know about slimy slug-green baby glands drip-dripping inside her.

He dropped his gaze from her innocent accusing eyes, rested his attention on the tactile shape of her neutral crotch-reality body, breasts hanging free and easy in the open robe over the kettledrum of her belly with its off-centre mole a second navel leading his eyes to the haircurled triangle-parting of her smooth-skin curving full woman thighs, all so tactually hyperreal, like the massive sculptured reality of a Michelangelo realer-than-real living-marble statue and, if he played Bennie's game, just as eternal.

"Jack..." She smiled, sighed, misinterpreting the sweep of his eyes, let the cool black velvet robe slither off her shoulders as she wriggled her arms out of the sleeves, breasts bobbing, then half-threw, half let herself fall against him, soft breasts against his self-felt hardness, image-contrast man-woman interface, with his consciousness living on the line between as he felt the full woman-strength of her arms contracted around his ribcage, strong, young, fiercely-tender woman-arms, young and strong and smooth like... like a healthy female animal, like young, like strong, like healthy, like forever.

She giggled against his chest, hooked her naked leg behind his knee, pulled back against the joint with her leg as she shoved her body-weight forward, and toppled him like a puppy over on his back, the warm rug-fur on his naked skin an electric charge erotic contrast with the smooth cool of the velvet robe he had half fallen on. He took the fall lightly, pulling her mock-fiercely down on top of him, dug the kick of the hard real woman-muscles of her shoulders beneath the skin-patina of softness on his fingertips as she moved, round on round, belly to belly against him.

She pulled off his shorts, and now they were naked against each other, primal Sara pure flesh-taste of rounded masses moving against him in slow funky rhythm, and he reached out with both hands and smoothed her sweet wicked ass real and round and warm legs contracting froglike up and around him, opening herself to him, coaxing him in hair-on-hair teasing as her mouth moved up his chest in a quicksilver trail of hard little biting kisses up his neck across his jaw, and he caught a glimpse of white wet pearled teeth and pink tongue-tip, closed his eyes, hips picking up on her slow-building pelvic rhythm as their mouths met.

Mouth to open mouth, tasting her breath in the warm wet soul-deep cave, and like an eruption of massive world-filling wet life-flesh her tongue poured itself into his mouth, filling it, engulfing it, overwhelming him with wet-on-wet sly man-woman role-reversal pleasure, filling his world with a huge, blind, wet-writhing organism, an amorphous damp creature with a will of its own like a blind pulsing thing from deep inside body-secrets, like a thing of glandular sentience from deep inside life's secret juices overflowing drip-dripping wet huge alive and pulsing, drip-dripping alien life-juices into his mouth, moving and mocking and filling his cheeks with pulsing naked flesh-secret, heavy syrup drip-dripping like green slug-slime tongue-gland warm-blood wetness from carcinoma-ridden bodies of broken babies, choking, drowning him in stolen life-juices, cloying over-sweet immortality-honey from black children sleeping the long slide to Forever, catheters glucose-needles meeting in obscene trunk-line tube of death down his throat, her heavy huge rolling gland-organism-tongue choking him, choking him, choking him, retch-reflexes building against his will toward a gut-heaving spasm of broken black babies glands wet and writhing-tongue life-warm blood-filled blind organism, stolen life-juices filling his mouth in horrid pelvic rhythm—

In a mindless spasm-reaction, he pushed her mouth away as the retch wracked through him in a mercifully-dampening anti-climax, and she lay inert atop him, confused eyes bleeding as he stared at her like a cornered animal, trapped and panting.

"Jack...? Wha...? You..."

She stared down at him with wounded, stunned eyes as he felt the membranes of his cheeks singe-contract like an alum wither-reaction, his tongue a lump of dead shoeleather in his own mouth.

I just can't cut it, he realised. Can't live with the taste of my woman the taste of slug-green glands, tasting the stolen life-juices inside her every time I touch her. I gotta tell her, or we'll be lumps of dirty meat to each other forever, living a lie forever, lost to each other forever. Gotta tell her, is all, no matter what happens.

"Truth between us, Sara," he said "I... there's something I've just gotta tell you."

She stretched against him, cupped his cheeks in hands that felt like damp leather. "What's with you? I've never seen you like this... When I kissed you it was like kissing a... (Her body twitched against him.) And you got... *sick*, didn't you? I felt it."

"It's not *you*, Sara. I swear it's not *you*, baby. It's me, the whole fucking world, Benedict Howards..."

"*Benedict Howards?* What in hell does making love to me have to do with Benedict Howards?" !

Barron grimaced. How the fuck do I say it: see, it's like this, baby, you're a murderer, dig? Got stolen glands inside you, just like me, life-juices of broken babies oozing so bloody thick I taste it when I kiss you?

"Sara—oh, what the fuck!" he snarled, feeling a hopeless spasm of futility, a get-it-over-with, riff-it-out, retch-reaction. "There just isn't any easy way to tell you. We're murderers, Sara, we're both *murderers*. Yeah, we got immortality inside us—but you know what it looks like? Looks like slimy green glands—ever see a gland?—all green and wet and dripping ugly slimy stuff, but it keeps you alive, and us it keeps alive forever, *glands* is all, and you live forever. But they're not *our* glands, Sara, we stole 'em. Stole 'em from children, dead, broken children..."

And his body writhed in a gooseflesh spasm.

Her eyes seemed to draw back light-years distant; he felt her body go limp, her hands fall like dead flounders to his chest as she muttered, "What are you talking about?"

"What Howards did to us," he said, "the immortality treatment. It's a gland-transplant, is all. They irradiate glands to keep 'em in perfect balance, and then they keep your body from ageing, forever, something they call Homeostatic Endocrine balance. But not *our* glands, dig? *Children's* glands. It only works on children's glands. That's why Howards killed Hennering—he found out the Foundation is buying the children, soaking them in hard radiation to balance their endocrine system, then transplanting their glands to make adults immortal."

"But... but the children, what does... losing their glands do to the children?"

"What the fuck's the matter with you?" Barron shouted, the vibration bouncing her bare breasts against him. "Haven't you heard a word I've said? It *kills* them, Sara, it *kills* them! If the radiation hasn't killed them first, the transplant operation kills them, and they just throw away the bodies like so much garbage. Because you and I are alive and immortal, two kids Howards bought for the purpose are dead. *It's murder*, I'm trying to tell you, pure, simple murder!"

He felt-saw her cringe in a foetal-spasm, shoulders hunching away from his chest knees upward along his thighs, like paper wilting in a fire. Her jaw went slack, the depths of her eyes seemed to take a discontinuous jump backward like a quick-cut reverse-zoom camera image "Murder... murder... murder..." She mouthed the word over and over, chewing it to two meaningless gibberish syllables.

Barron grabbed her cheeks in both hands, shook her. Her body relaxed, but her eyes were still way out there, light-years away, buried in electric-circuit insulation, and when she spoke it was like a message from a spacecraft commander, cold and detached, from somewhere north of Pluto.

"Inside of us? Children's glands? Children? Cutting apart children? Cutting open living children, tearing out pieces of living flesh and sewing them inside of me? Children?"

"Please, Sara, for chrissakes, don't freak out now," Barron said stridently, feeling strident as he said it, but not knowing what to say, what to do. "Imagine how I feel—knowing Bennie tricked me, outsmarted me, made me *ask* to be made immortal, made me fight for it, connive for it, go through a million changes, and then I finally get it, win it, for you and me, and when I wake up, I find out... find out inside of me—"

"You didn't know?" she said, pouncing like a cornered cat. "He tricked you into it? You didn't know what it was, and you woke up, and *then* he told you?"

"What the fuck do you think I am?" Barron shouted. "You think I'd let him do a thing like that if I knew? Think I'd let them cut apart some poor kid so I could live forever? What do you think I am, a goddamn monster?"

"*He* did it to us," Sara whispered shrilly, eyes filming to a blank flatness. "*He* did it, that monster Howards, with his money and his frozen bodies and his murderers and his dirty lizard eyes seeing right through you, measuring your price like a piece of meat. ...We never had a chance, no one has a chance, Howards can make anyone do anything, trick him or kill him or force him or buy him. No one can stop him. He'll go on and on and on forever, buying children, chopping them up, owning them, owning us, everybody, forever, always that lizard and his cold white..."

"Sara! Sara! For chrissakes!"

Suddenly she grabbed the flesh of his chest, fingers convulsed into talons, digging in, bruising cruelly. "You've got to stop him, Jack! You've got to stop him! We can't live with ourselves, we can't live with each other, can't stand being alive with murdered things in our bodies till you stop him! You've got to be able to stop him!"

Wanting to shout yes! Yes! yes!, Barron instead found himself confronting the same old cold reality. Kamikaze's the only way to stop Bennie, take us down to the electric chair with him... To die, to be dead rotting in maggots, tasting nothing, hearing nothing, seeing nothing, feeling nothing, being nothing... throw away being young and together for a million years. A million years of broken babies' slug-green glands drip-dripping stolen life-juices inside us...

"I can't! I can't!" he cried. "Bennie was too smart for me. Those contracts we signed prove us accessories to murder, evidence that'll stand up in any court. You understand what that means? It means *we're* murderers, is all. I blow the whistle on Bennie, he blows it on us, and we all waltz to the electric chair together. *Dead.* I knife Bennie, we die. You know what dead means? Know what we'd be throwing away?"

"It's not fair!" she shouted. "We haven't done anything! We're not really murderers, we're victims, just like the children. We didn't know."

"*Nazis?*" Barron said in a bitter mock-Prussian accent. "Ve vasn't Nazis, ve vas all in der Resistance, all of us, all eighty million of us Chermans. Ve didn't know, ve vas chust following orders. Jawohl, Mein Herr, chust following orders! Yeah, baby, go tell it to the judge—see how far you get when Bennie trots out twenty paid witnesses say we knew exactly what the treatment was when we got into it. He's got us, Sara, there's not a thing we can do and live to tell about it."

"But you've *got* to do something. We can't let him go on like this! There's gotta be a way to stop him!"

"Only one way to stop him," Barron said, "and that's the old kamikaze schtick. You ready for that? You ready to die—now, when we can stay alive for the next million years? You got the balls to make yourself *die*?"

"No," she said simply, but there were volumes of torture in her eyes.

"Well, neither have I," he said, and felt his consciousness withdrawing to the safety of electric-circuit phosphor-dot ersatz reality.

"It's just not right... it's just not fair..." she muttered, and he felt her skin shrinking away, and her eyes were as opaque and unreadable as stainless-steel mirrors.

"Right, schmight," he said, her body now a dead weight of cold, unreal flesh pressing obscenely against him. "It's where it's at, is all. And we're stuck with it."

And suddenly the air in the room was cold gooseflesh on his naked skin. And they got up and dressed without saying a word to each other. Like strangers.

19

SARA WESTERFELD dropped the cap, then sat down on the couch facing the dusk lights of Brooklyn to wait for the acid to hit. Supposed to be seven hundred mikes, she thought, but it's been laying around since I moved in with Jack, never even thought about taking it until... until...

Her body shivered, even though it was June-evening warm. Too warm, in fact, sticky-warm like heavy flowing molasses under her skin, like crawling wetness-things inside her body... She got up, went to the nearest wall console, threw a switch, and the glass patio-doors glided shut. She turned the thermostat to 70, the humidity control to medium dry, and the airconditioning unit began pumping in cool dry air through the circular series of vents around the base of the domed ceiling.

She walked to the communications-complex wall, put the surf-sound on continuous replay cycle, keyed the colour organ down toward blues and greens, sat down on the couch again, and stared out at the duskscape across the river. It was like a painted mural now, the glass interface of the patio-doors separating it from the swirling blue-and-green surf-sound Big Sur-pine reality within.

Sara strained against her own mind, testing the swirl of colours and surf-sound melding, trying to feel it, trying to make the LSD hit. A good way to have a bummer, she cautioned herself, so uptight trying to make it hit... Why'd I drop acid in the first place, now, with Jack going on the air soon, with lizardman Howards safe in his bone-white lair of power and bleeding things inside me cut from dead children...

A black chill went through her (the acid starting to hit?) as she remembered how mindlessly she had turned to the LSD, almost as if the acid were taking *her* instead of she the acid, like a thing waiting to be born or to die within her, a thing with which her conscious mind had no contact at all reaching out through the reflex-arc of her arm, directly, bypassing conscious volition, reaching out to grasp the acid key to its release, a thing with reasons and shapes of its own that might or might not be those of what she thought of as Sara, a blind captain leading the ship of self on an unknown voyage into the dark sea within, and she knew that the acid was hitting.

A visceral fear began to grip her as the Sara within mocked her, reminded her that there were reasons and compulsions to take acid at any given time and some of them could be evil.

Evil... the word had an archaic medieval sound-shape to it, black bishop's robes swirling, Marquis De Sade dark things from murky European history books... Evil... something ominous and serpent-edged in the knife-shape of the word, dreadful and slimy, but somehow outdated, ... Evil... a word with bone-white crocodile-teeth, like the smile of Benedict Howards from his bone-white temple of death-god power... Evil... wet green things under moist rocks in blue-green moonlight, sucking lifejuices from corpses... corpses of babies bleeding and broken... Evil... Evil... The blues and greens swirled reptilian-fashion across the snake-house glass of the domed ceiling like octopus tentacles, and the sound of the surf was a sea-thing sigh from the bowels of a bottomless black ocean, and across the sky outside the dark closed in... Evil... It was cool and dry in the room, like a lizard's skin... Evil...

Evil... there was a primeval oldness in the word, inevitable and eternal like the dawn-musk of swamps... Evil...

And there's an oldness in Benedict Howards, she thought, a sick evil oldness as if he's living his life backward, as if the shadow of a million-year future of power-fear-sweat-stinking madness has already made him something not-human, dead in ways no man's ever been dead before, dead from a million years of hoarded, fermented oldness, a withered vampire living on blood like a frightened cancer, dead but undying.

Immortality.

"Kiss me, and you'll live forever. You'll be a frog, but you'll live forever." A grotesque vision of green plastic swam before her eyes, a kit-model she had seen in some Berkeley apartment geological ages ago—a comic-hideous, slime-dripping, cross-eyed disaster of a green plastic giant frog, sitting on a green plastic lily-pad from a Walt Disney swamp with tiny dwarf-frogs beside it leaping like frantic tadpoles at the placard the frog-monster held aloft, proclaiming: "Kiss me, and you'll live forever. You'll be a frog, but you'll live forever."

And the frog-face began to change as the surf sounds poured over it like a great black tide of evil. The comic cross-eyes became lizard-eyes, cold, black and reptilian, the eyes of Benedict Howards; and the goofy grin became a crocodile-leer, a sharp, bone-white lizard-man smile, hungry, totally ruthless and totally knowing. The figures leaping up in worship at the placard were green plastic human beings in a great thronging crowd, a pile of live writhing bodies pillaring to the sky, fighting each other to leap eagerly through the great crocodile-jaws that chewed them to green plastic frog-flesh pieces, green slime fluid drooling past the bone-white teeth, and, above it all, way above it all, holding his placard like a sceptre against the shattered sky, black lizard-eyes gaping like holes into the final darkness, Benedict Howards, his crocodile-mouth a vast cavern, and a river of human beings pouring down it, leaping like flames at the sly, knowing sign they worshipped: "Kiss me, and you'll live forever. You'll be a frog, but you'll live forever."

The sign of immortality.

That, she thought, that's Howards' immortality. And oh, oh, have we kissed the frog, with his wet green lips like pulsing gland tissue; lizard-lips running all over our bodies like a dirty old pervert; inside, outside, kissing, sucking, drooling baby-blood spit, green monster-slime of immortality...

She shuddered, trying to throw off the vision, stared through the glass doors at the darkening sky over the city as the surf-sounds flowed around her like the eternal moaning of everything everywhere struggling in grim mortal anguish as blue and green sinuous colour organ shadows played at the corners of her vision like a sea of frog-green tentacles—and abruptly the interface between the green swamp-reality of miasmic evil engulfing her and the flat mural-reality of the cityscape beyond the glass doors inverted, and she was no longer on the inside looking out but on the outside looking in.

The undulating blue-green light writhing behind her like a forest of tentacles the roar of the surf like the sigh of some great beached and expiring sea animal, seemed to press her against the glass reality-interface like a bubble being forced up by decay-gas pressure from the depths of an oily green swamp pool. She felt the weight, the pressure of the whole room pushing behind her as if the blind green monsters that lurked in the most unknowable pits in the ass-end of her mind were bubbling up from the depths and elbowing her consciousness out of her own skull.

She moaned, pressed against the glass, keyed the door-switch frantically; but when the doors finally slid open, she found herself caught in the reality-interface itself: the bile-green mists of madness the surf-sound sucking behind her becoming an unreal nightmare she now knew was just an acid bummer; but before her, the moist wind from the dark million-light city seemed to be blowing in off a sea-coast jungle that felt as if it might go on forever. Realer than real, there was a vacuum out there, a hole opening onto infinity into which she could fall up and up forever, up and up and up till she might drown in the sea of herself and be lost forever.

Yet she felt the siren-song of that bottomless nothingness calling to her, calling, promising... and she *had* to look, had to walk the shore of that infinite black sea—and she stepped out onto the patio.

And again reality went through changes.

It was like stepping out into a Tibetan monastery perched atop some ascetic mountain. She felt the interface between her personality and the Universe take a quantum-jump outward, as if an inner telescope had suddenly switched over to a higher power. As she stepped through the doorway she felt the ceiling explode away in shards, like a satellite-shield ejecting, leaving her naked to the bare black marches of infinity that began at the edges of her being and ballooned outward forever.

And far below her, a shimmering arabesque carpet of lights and street sounds, the electric city coruscated like a continuous sheet of incandescent protoplasm, rippling in kinesthop patterns from Brooklyn glowing on the horizon to the base of the concrete mountain on which she stood like a remote eye tipping the pseudopod of a continent-wide human amoeba contemplating its own piebald vastness.

With the surf-sound sighing behind her, Sara walked to the parapet, leaned over, and it seemed as if she stood on the interface, *was* the interface between that living, human, upward-reaching organism of lights and the black depths of infinity that yawned above her.

Immortality—was electric-light slime reaching for the stars, and she stood poised on the brink, balanced on the razor-edge between life and death, the flickering and the eternal, the human and the immortal, sanity and the holy madness that was realer than sanity, more cogent, a path to oneness with the timeless infinite that could be hers if she had the courage to cast off her moorings to the shores of self and trust her fate to that all-forgiving sea.

She half-turned as if to look behind her, and the blue-green sinuousness of the sighing chamber inside was a foul mocking reminder of the slime-things dripping stolen secretions of dead children within her that had brought her to this dark place.

And now the surf-sound seemed to be coming from below her like a vast invisible sea, its breakers cresting against the concrete parapet against which she found herself leaning vertiginously, calling to her with the wordless voice of forever to cast herself upon its buoying waters and be carried away... away... Away from the mocking lizard-face of Benedict Howards, with his cold reptilian eyes leering out at her from bone-white lair of death... Away even, it promised, from the monstrosities oozing murder... within her... away... away... away...

On a stone pedestal a few yards from her, rested an extension vidphone. The dead grey screen seemed to leap out at her. Jack! Jack! Oh, Jack...

JACK JACK JACK... The shape of his name was a hard-edged shimmer before her, and she found her hand dialling his office vidphone number. JACK JACK JACK...

"Sara..." Jack's face was a tiny moon of bone-white phosphor on the vidphone screen. "What the hell is it, you know I'm going on the air in half an hour."

Even on the tiny soft-focus vidphone screen, his wild curling hair and those deep inward eyes crackled phosphorescent electricity into the darkness around her.

"What are you going to do on the show tonight?" she asked. But the *she* that said the words seemed to be existing a beat ahead of her in time, and Sara knew what she was saying only after the words had left her mouth.

"Come on, baby, you know damn well what the score is," Jack said. "Bennie Howards calls the shots tonight."

"You can't do it," she found herself saying, and again it was as if the pressures of the words were moulding her tongue and lips and cheeks into the necessary configurations—she wasn't saying them, they were saying themselves. "You've got to stop Howards. No matter what, it costs, you've got to stop him."

Jack's face twisted into a withdrawing scowl. "It's bad enough, for chrissakes!" he said. "Get off my back, will you, Sara!"

Get off my back... get off my back... The words were one more accusation. I *am* on his back, she thought. He's doing it to protect me.

"I won't let you do it," she heard the strangely reverberating sound of her own voice say. "You're doing it for me, and I won't let you, it's not right. I won't let Benedict Howards own you just so I can stay alive. I won't let you do it to yourself."

"Spare me the martyr-schtick, will you, things are shitty enough as it is," he said, and she could sense that it was close to an exit-line, that he was handling her the way he would some vip on *Bug Jack Barron.* "Don't put yourself on, it wouldn't make any difference if I was in this alone. I don't want to die, is all. Why is that so fucking hard for you to understand?"

He's lying, she thought, he's lying for me, and I love him for it. *But I can't let him do it.*

"You're doing it for me," her mechanical inner voice was saying. "I know you are, and I know you're lying about it for me too. And I'm not going to let you do it, Jack, I'm just not going to let you do it."

"What in hell is this?" he said, and his voice seemed tinny and unreal yet somehow amplified realer than real over the vidphone circuit. "Delusions of grandeur? Look, baby, you know how I feel about you, but don't get any funny ideas... nobody works my head, not even you."

"Not even Benedict Howards?"

Even on the tiny vidphone screen she could see the words that she hadn't meant to say, that someone else within her had said, biting home cruelly across Jack's face. "Not even Howards—circumstances, is all. But that's not letting Bennie work my head, that's just living in reality. Oughta try it sometime, Sara."

Sara looked out over the living carpet of light that was the city, the great anguished body of humanity of which she was but an insignificant part, and the blackness above and below seemed to be calling to her with the surf-sound of the timeless sea from the buoying depths of forever; calling, promising forgiveness, and a way out... the only way out...

"Didn't you ever think," she mumbled, "that there are things better than reality, cleaner, purer, where no one can touch you with death or the blood of children oozing inside you or anything that's rotten and dirty and evil..."

"Goddamn it," Jack snarled, "you're stoned out of your mind! You're freaked out on acid. Get hold of yourself, Sara, ride it out baby... Jesus H Christ, how could you be so dumb, what a time to drop acid! With all this shit going on, you *knew* you had to have a bummer. Why the hell did you do it?"

Standing there, with Jack's image a grey on white ghost from a million miles away and a thousand years ago on the vidphone screen, she herself wondered why. A bummer, sure, she had known deep down it would have to be a bummer. But how could *anything* be worse than reality, worse than torn fragments of murdered children sewn inside her, inside Jack, and Benedict Howards going on and on forever? With or without acid, it was all a bummer, a bummer that would go on and on and on forever, with no way to ever come down, a freakout she could never wait out... unless...

She lifted the vidphone off the pedestal and set it on the parapet lip, the screen now at her chest-level, and Jack's face was a black and white spectre looking back at her with blind, uncomprehending eyes. I've got to make him understand... he's got to understand.

"Please, Jack, you've *got* to understand..." The words gushed out of her in a self-propelled torrent. "There's no way out, not in what you call reality, it's a trap, and there's no way out for either of us except... except death, except turning ourselves off and sleeping dreamless innocent dreams forever... Reality... Don't you see, the only answer is something greater than reality, purer, cleaner, infinite, something to give yourself to, something that can wash it all away, something to merge yourself with, something infinite to be one with—"

"Spare me the parlour Buddhism, will you?" Jack said. "I wish you could hear yourself, I mean I wish *you* could hear yourself baby, 'cause your head's just not there. You're gibbering, and you're starting to scare me. Take it easy, Sara, and for chrissakes do what I tell you. Go inside, sit down on the couch, put on some happy music, and wait it out. You're stoned. *Remember* you're stoned. It's just a bum trip, is all. You'll be all right when the acid wears off. Whatever happens inside your head, remember it won't last forever, you'll come down. *Remember, you'll come down.*"

"Come down!" she found herself screaming at him. "I'll never come down! It's not the acid, it's me. Dead children's glands inside of me, that's not the acid, Benedict Howards, that's not the acid, what I'm doing to you, that's not the acid... It's me, me, *me*, and it stinks!"

"Sara! You haven't done anything to me, I've done it to you..."

She studied his face, and even on the black and white unreality of the vidphone screen, the man, the essence that was Jack, JACK BARRON, leaped out at her from the darkness through layers and layers of phosphorescent reality, pulsing image-waves of his face on the pillow blue and stubbly on the vidphone with Luke naked beside her in the Berkeley attic her knight in soft-flesh armour brave beside her the Black Shade they call him his tongue inside her the taste of his body, wave after wave of JACK BARRON images flashed from the vidphone screen through her, merging and dancing on the back wall of her mind. Overlapping, flashing, reversing, contradicting in a cresting-wave pattern, the sum of the images forming an essence that coalesced like a standing-wave formed from the flux, an essence that shone with an unwavering light—an essence that was pure *Jack*.

And the Jack that she saw dwarfed and flickering on the tiny vidphone screen before her seemed an anguished denial of the greater Jack that blazed across the screen in her mind. *That* was the real Jack Barron, a Jack Barron who could never cop out just because he was Jack. No matter what he did, *that* Jack was still JACK BARRON (in flaming capital letters). And how many times was I sure that Jack was wrong and he turned out to be right? JACK BARRON... a creature bigger in every way than herself, and hadn't she always known it, even when she hadn't known she knew, wasn't it why she loved him? Bigger than herself... bigger than anyone, not her Jack, but *Jack's Sara*, how could she ever be anything else? Or want to be.

And that's what I'm taking from him because he loves me, because he can't see me die—I'm taking away JACK. And if he loses Jack, I lose Jack, the world loses Jack—because I love him and he loves me. It's not right!

"Jack... Jack... I love you, I'm sorry, I can't help it, I love you!"

"I love you too, Sara," he said quietly, soothingly, and she felt that marvellous gyroscopic sense of tenderness, and she loved him for it and hated herself for his loving her. I'm destroying him...

"I know you do, and I'm sorry... I'm sorry you love me and I love you. It's destroying you, Jack, it's making you something less than what you were meant to be. I can't let that happen... I *won't* let it happen!"

Won't let it happen! The thought filled her mind. I *can't* let it happen. Got to save Jack... save him from lizardman Howards... dead things in my body... got to save him from *me*. From me!

And as she stared out over the endless lights of the amoeboid city spreading out below her like the throng before the Mount, she knew who really stood at the summit of that mountain, who they all looked to, who could do it, could bust it all wide open, destroy the Foundation Black Shade Social Justice President of the United States. Luke was right, it was Jack—Jack all the way, and a whole nation riding with him, and me, only *me* bringing him down.

I'm all that's stopping him from being JACK, the Jack that everyone needs. He loves me, he'll always love me, he'll never leave me, and as long as I live I'll never be able to leave him, we're too deep into each other. As long as I live...

With a sudden, mindless leap she found herself crouched on the narrow concrete parapet beside the vidphone, staring at his image only inches from her face, muscles tensed smoothly like a cat gathering to spring.

"Sara! What the fuck are you doing?" Jack shouted, and she sensed him fighting fear for control and knew he would win. He would always win. "You're stoned!" he snarled, and the harshness in his voice was a purposeful slap across the face. "Remember you're stoned, and get the hell off there... but do it slow and easy, don't get shook, first put one leg on the ground, then put all your weight on it before you step down... Sara! Come on! Snap out of it!"

"I love you Jack," she said to his tiny distant image. "I love you, and I know you'd always love me. That's why I've got to do it. You've got to be free—free of me so you can really be Jack Barron, free to see what you are and what you've always been and what you've got to do. You've got to be free! And so long as I'm alive you'll never be free. I'm doing it because I love you, because you love me. Good-bye, Jack... Remember, only because I loved you...."

She straightened her legs convulsively, and stood waveringly upright on the narrow parapet as the vidphone beside her feet shouted: "Don't do it, Sara, God, don't do it I You're stoned out of your mind! You don't know what you're doing! For chrissakes, don't jump! Don't jump!"

But the voice that called to her was mechanical and tiny and seemed to be coming from another world, a black and white unreal vidphone world encapsulated in the meaningless thing by her foot, where she couldn't even see it; a voice drowned out by the surf-roar that cloaked her shoulders with sighing green tentacles, the foetid wet breath of torn babies within her green tentacles of light crawling up her back from within pushing her forward with an avalanche of dead children a million maggots writhing under her skin. And before her, above her, below her, all around her was the soothing black velvet nothingness of an infinite ocean, buoying like pillows to an endless, dreamless sleep, pure and clean and safe forever from pain and remorse and dead bodies of broken babies, calling, calling, calling, "Give yourself to me."

"Sara!"

Jack's voice was a fading cry from a world already abandoned, the memory fading, an unreal nightmare world of frog-green tentacles broken babies dripping slime under her skin the bone-white crocodile-smile of Benedict Howards on his green plastic lily-pad on a pile of dead bodies, forever and ever, and Jack chained to him by a thousand links, and each one of them her body...

For him! For him!

The taste of Jack at last free at last Jack all Jack was a delicious orgasmic spasm through the muscles of her legs ("Sara! Sara!" she heard him scream), and she too was free—free as a bird, with the air whistling through the pinions of her hair, weightless, buoyed, her consciousness expanding outward in rippling waves that merged with the blackness in streamers of mist till all that was left of what was hers alone was a blazing word-shape-smell-taste that whited out every sensory-synapse:

JACK and stars spinning across her retinas JACK and
the skin of her face pulled drum-tight JACK free
fall nausea JACK mass rushing up JACK screams
below JACK fear JACK acid freak-out, JACK
for you JACK I'm afraid JACK help me
JACK no no JACK don't want JACK
death JACK forever JACK no
JACK no JACK no JACK no
JACK no JACK no no
JACK flash of blind
-ing pain
JAC—
●

●

20

Sara
No! it ca-
n't have happen-
ed. Sara you're not
Sara dead no! not dead
not down there on the sidewalk
in a puddle of— Sara! Sara! no no no,
You can't be dead! Can't be dead! No! No! Sara!
Sara you crazy bitch, how could you do a thing like this to me!

How could you do a thing like this to me… The foulness, the utter selfish foulness of the thought brought Jack Barron's mind back into reality from the point of anaesthetic blackout into which it had retreated like a whipped dog howling.

The vidphone screen before him showed a crazy slash of black sky over a section of the concrete parapet off which—

He reached out, snapped off the vidphone, and in the same motion fumbled an Acapulco Gold out of the pack on his desk. He jammed it into his mouth, lit it with the table-lighter, and sucked the smoke in-out-in-out-in-out in savage compulsive pants.

How could you do a thing like this to me—oh, Barron, you shit you! How could you do it to *her*? You bastard! You heartless motherfucker! Sara! Sara! You… you…

He flagellated himself with images of her eyes: pool-deep eyes before she blew him wide and shiny my hero little girl eyes naked beside him in Berkeley attic cold eyes boring through him shouting cop-out! the day they broke up eyes glazing and opaqueing to stainless steel mirrors as their flesh crawled from each other the last night (last night! last night there ever was between them and a night spent as strangers!) poor lost phosphor-dot eyes like windows into grey on grey blind acid jungle inside naked and writhing, and I could see it building and building like runaway cancer, and all I could do was gibber into the fucking phone while her eyes grew crazier and crazier as she was sucked deeper and deeper into the acid freakout nightmare, eyes from the nowhere non-reality of LSD insanity, and all I could do was watch on the phone while she jumped; poor crazy lost eyes, and I couldn't do a fucking thing but watch her jump!

SaraSaraSara… No Sara any more, never, no Sara Sara Sara Sara Sara-shaped hole against the sky of his night that would never be filled, not in a million years, and he *had* a million years, dammit, a million years to be without her, a million years to watch her jump, million years to know he killed her—

Bullshit, man! he thought. Stop trying to con yourself... Guilty, maybe you should feel it, but you don't. You didn't kill her, damn it, it was the acid, was nothing you did or could've done, was Sara freaking out into her own crazy bag again, doing it to save me, make me free to be the fucking Baby Bolshevik hero I never was... to save me... From what, from living? From caring? From giving a shit about what happens next? Sara... Sara... I didn't kill you, you killed me!... killed the best things inside me, is all. Tore out my flesh-and-blood guts, replaced with electronic circuitry, can't even make myself cry knowing you're dead. Was nothing I did that killed you, Sara, was what I *was*. Murderer... vampire off babies... not even , that, was it Sara?

Was fucking cop-out, is all! Was seeing my bod owned by that fucker Howards, body not even my own, with slug-green pieces of immortality-slime drip-dripping inside me, was seeing me selling out to Bennie... You didn't kill me, and I didn't kill you, we were both dead already, died when we couldn't stand to touch each other last night, that motherfucker Howards killed us both. Killed us both by making us immortal, now ain't that a pisser?

Sara... I can't cry for you Sara, don't have any tears left in me. But... I can kill for you, baby, kill that fucker Howards! Oh, yeah, I can kill for you, all right! Can hate, all right! Maybe you were right in your own dumb way, 'cause you're gonna get what you wanted, you and those hundred million dumb bastards out there.

Yeah, I'll do a show like no one's ever seen! They want their fucking hero, I'll give him to them on a silver platter, see how they like it! Let the stupid bastards out there see where it's really at for once in their lives—how's *that* for a television first?

The vidphone began to chime. Barron made the connection, and Vince Gelardi's face appeared on the screen, ashen, stunned, and Barron knew that he knew even before Vince muttered: "Jack... the police just called... Sara..."

"I saw it all happen, Vince," he said quickly, determined to spare Vince the agony of telling him. "Don't say anything. Don't even tell me how sorry you are. I know... I know..."

"Jack... I hate to have to bring it up but we go on the air in nine minutes. I'm trying to get through to the network brass so we can run an old show, so you don't have to—"

"Forget it!" Barron snapped. "I'm gonna do the show tonight, gonna do it for Sara! Show biz, baby... the show must go on, and words from the same picture..."

"Jack you don't have to—"

"But I do, man! More than any show in the history of this whole dumb business, *this* one's gotta go on! See you in the studio, Vince—but thanks anyway."

"Jack," Vince Gelardi said over the intercom circuit, his face grey and lifeless, all too real to come off real in the network-reality world behind the control booth glass, "look, you don't have to go on the air. I checked with the powers that be, and I got the okay to run one of last month's shows if you... I mean..."

Jack Barron sat down in the white chair behind the blackwash-over-kinesthop background, clocked the cameraman (cameraman he never noticed during the show) staring ashen-faced at him, saw that the promptboard was live and showed '3 minutes,' and somehow he could sense the disaster-aura reaching all the way to the monkey block behind the control room.

And it bugged him. Fucking network brass coming on like they really care how I feel with Sara. Sara... Yeah, sure, all they want to know is does it mean a fiasco if I go on the air with her body not yet cold, where's that crazy Barron's head at now, Gelardi, think he can go on the air, Jeez, if we do a rerun unannounced now, after the stuff he's been rapping out these past few weeks... Oh, my aching Brackett Count!

But that, Barron thought, is show biz. The show must go on, there's no business like show business, and like that. But *why* must the show go on? No big secret, it don't go on, that audience out there might get the idea that there was only a human being like them behind that image, and that would screw up the ratings. Which is enough reason in this business to do *anything*.

Yet Barron felt pissed that the whole damn crew was preparing its ulcers for a massive disaster. The show must go on—bullshit, sure, just a dumb-ass game, but what the hell isn't? This show's gonna go on, all right, and the brass won't believe the ratings 'cause this is kamikaze night, and they're gonna get the Big All, the topper to end all toppers, the greatest show on earth: Two living-colour stars of stage, screen, and gutter politics going at each other for blood.

"Snap out of it, Vince!" Barron said, cracking his voice like a whip for control. "I'm going on the air, and this is gonna be a show like no one's ever seen. Stick with me, baby, keep me on the air no matter what I do, believe me, I know what I'm doing, and if you cut me off, and the network doesn't back you up, you're fired."

"Hey, man..." Vince crooned in a wounded tone of voice as the promptboard flashed '2 minutes.' "It's *your* show, Jack..."

"Sorry, Vince, I didn't mean to threaten you, I just gotta be sure you're on my side and I stay on the air no matter what, and to hell with the network and the FCC," Barron said. "There's a thing I gotta do that's bigger than the show, and I have to know you won't try to stop me. It's nitty-gritty time, buddy: who you working for, the network or me?"

"Where was I eight years ago?" Gelardi said, still hurting. "You're the best in the business, you *are* this show. It's your baby, not the network's and not mine. You didn't have to ask—you know I work for you."

"Okay, then hang on to your hat. Get me Bennie Howards on the line—and don't worry, I guarantee he'll go on," Barron said as the promptboard flashed '90 seconds.'

"Calling *out* first?"

"That's the way we play it tonight. A television first—I bug me."

Gelardi shrugged, and a ghost of the old crazy-wop smile came back. "Who you want in back-up and safety?" the old Gelardi said. Good old one-track Vince!

"No back-up or safety tonight, just me and Howards— *mano a mano*."

Gelardi shot him a funny, scared look, then a wan grin, and went to the phones as the promptboard flashed '30 seconds.' As he waited, Barron stared at the grey-green glass face of the monitor. With his guts so damn empty—a musty cavern haunted by unreal ghosts—there was something hypnotic about it; he felt the vacuum within reach out for the waiting vacuum in the cathode-ray tube, meet, merge, form a reality-to-reality tunnel across the nonspace of the studio, as if there were nothing real in the whole Universe but himself and that screen and the circuit connecting them. Even the network that logic said connected him with a hundred million other screen-realities didn't seem to exist, just him and the tube.

The monitor screen came to living-colour life, a phosphor-dot image straight to the backs of his eyes: his own name 'BUG JACK BARRON' in red Yankee-go-home letters, with the bar-room voice behind it.

"Bugged?"

Then the montage of anger-sounds, and the voice again:

"Then go *bug Jack Barron*!"

And then he was staring at his own face, a living-colour mirror-reality that moved when he moved, the eyes shadowed, the mouth grim and heavy. He backed off a bit from what he felt, saw the face on the screen become less tense, less savage, responding to his mind like a remote-controlled puppet.

As they rolled the first Acapulco Golds commercial he pulled himself away from that vertiginous rapport with the screen, saw that the promptboard said 'Howards on Line'—and it was like a nerve in his own body reporting back on the readiness of his fist. Indeed, it was hard for him to feel the interface of his own body—his consciousness seemed as much in the promptboard and the monitor as in his own flesh. He was the room, was the studio set-up, the monkey block-control-booth-studio gestalt. It was part of him, and he of it.

And everything else—memories of Sara, slug-things inside him, all he had ever been—was locked away, reflex-encapsulated, unreal. Though he felt the mechanism activating and knew it for what it was—electric-circuit-anaesthesia—he was grateful for it, knowing that his gut wouldn't have to feel what was going to happen, living-colour kick-'em-in-the-ass image-Jack Barron was back in the catbird-seat and knew what to do.

His face was back on the monitor screen. "This is *Bug Jack Barron*," he said, feeling the flesh of his mouth move, seeing it duplicated in the image before him, cell by phosphor-dot-image cell, "and tonight we're gonna do a show that's a little different. You've been bugging me out there for years, folks, using me as your voice to get to the vips. Well this is worm-turning night, folks, tonight we play the old switcheroo. Tonight *I'm* bugged, tonight it's my gripe, tonight I'm out for blood on my own."

And in a weird leap of perspective, he seemed to be moving the image-lips on the screen directly, a brain-to-phosphor-dot electronic-flash reflex-arc circuit, as he said: "Tonight *Jack Barron* bugs *himself.*"

He made the face on the screen an unreadable devilmask (let Bennie sweat, don't tip him off till he's too far in, blow his mind naked on camera!), said: "Tonight we're gonna find out a few things about cryogenic Freezing that nobody knows. Seems like we haven't been able to do two shows in a row without mentioning the Foundation for Human Immortality lately, and those of you out there who think it's just a coincidence got a few shocks coming. Lot of people got a few shocks coming. So stick around for the fun and games—you're gonna see how the old fur flies when Jack Barron bugs himself."

Lowering his head to shadow his eyes, he caught kinesthop flashes off the backdrop, turning the image on the screen sly and threatening as he said: "And we won't wait to get down to the nitty-gritty either, friends. I've got Mr Benedict Howards right on the line."

Signalling Vince to give him three-quarters screen, he made the connection on the number one vidphone and Benedict Howards' face appeared in the lower left-hand corner of the monitor screen, a pale grey on grey vidphone phantom, enveloped by Barron's living-colour hyperreal image. You're on my turf tonight, Bennie, he thought, and so am I, all the way this time, and you're gonna get a flash of what paranoia can really be...

"This is *Bug Jack Barron*, Mr Howards, and tonight we're going all the way for the straight poop on... (he purposefully paused, smirked a private, threatening smile, watched Howards freeze in terror, then threw him the change-up, fat, hanging curve)... the Freezer Utility Bill."

And watched Howards' face melt to jello, every tense muscle relaxing in flaccid momentary relief, leaving Bennie wide-open for the primrose path schtick, he'll think I'm playing ball till I pull the reversal, and he'll be stuck before he can hang up the phone.

"Good," Howards said awkwardly. "It's about time all this crap about the

Foundation for Human Immortality was cleared up."

Barron smiled, tapped his left foot button twice, and Vince gave Howards half screen. "Don't worry about that, Mr Howards," he said. "By the end of the show it'll all be... *cleared up.*" And again Howards tensed as he picked up on the emphasis of the last words. Sweat, you bastard, sweat, Barron thought And it's only beginning...

"So let's talk about this Freezer Utility Bill," Barron said, saw that once again he was putting Howards through changes tension-release-tension-release, bounce him back and forth like a ping pong ball. "Now basically, this bill would grant the Foundation for Human Immortality a Freezing Monopoly, right? No other outfit could legally Freeze corpses, the Foundation would have the whole field to itself... a law unto itself..."

"Hardly," Howards said, picking up on the cue they had arranged in Colorado. "Cryogenic Freezing would become a public utility like the phone system or electric power—a monopoly, sure, because some services just have to be monopolies to function, but a monopoly strictly regulated by the Federal Government in the public interest." Beautiful, just like you think we arranged, Bennie—but now it's time for another change of pace.

"Well now that sounds pretty reasonable to me, don't you think so out there?" Barron said, and Howards' image on the screen smiled an inside I-got-you-bought smile across at his image. Barron made the electronic puppet-mask smile an earnest-flunky smile back, and for a weird moment he felt his consciousness slur over to the screen, and it was almost as if he were facing Howards flesh-to-flesh.

"Don't see how anyone could object to that," Barron said. "But it seems to me you could say that real simple-like. So why's your bill in so much trouble, Mr Howards, why all the static in Congress? Know what I think your trouble is, Mr Howards?"

"Suppose you tell me, Barron," Howards said guardedly. Yeah, that seemed like a harmless lead-in, Bennie, but you know it wasn't in your little script. And he foot-signalled Vince to give him a commercial in five minutes. Timing here had to be just right.

"Why, I think it's just screwed-up semantics, is all," Barron said, so sweetly innocent that Howards knew he was being sarcastic, and fear crept into his image-eyes, but it was all too subtle, inside stuff, for the audience to pick up on it yet, Barron knew. Which abruptly reminded him that there *was* a hundred-million Brackett Count audience digging the whole scene, out there on the other side of the screen.

"What do you mean by that?" Howards snapped, and Barron recognised it as a slipping of control.

He smiled blandly. "Your bill's in trouble 'cause it's badly written, is all. So long and complicated for something that's supposed to be so straightforward and simple... all those funny little clauses, twisty and turny like a snake.

Pretty hard to figure out what it all means."

He pulled a blank sheaf of papers out of a pocket. (The old Joe McCarthy schtick.) "Tell you what," he said, waving the papers across the monitor screen at Howards' now-uptight image, "why don't we clear it all up right now, straight from the horse's mouth, you can explain the confusing parts to a hundred million Americans, right now, Mr Howards, and who knows, then maybe your simple little bill'll go right through. Soon as we hack away all the confusing underbrush, dig?"

He put a razor in the last word, signalled to Vince to give him three-quarters screen, and zingo, Howards was a scared little twerp cowering below him in the hotseat. He suddenly realised that to the hundred million people on the other side of the screen, what they saw there was reality, reality that was realer than real because a whole country was sharing the direct sensory experience; it was history taking place right before their eyes, albeit non-event history that existed only on the screen. A strange chill went through him as for the first time he got a full gut-reality flash of the unprecedented power wielded by his image on the screen.

And like an internal neural time-sense circuit, the promptboard told him: '4 minutes.'

He hardened that image to a mask of inquisitor-iron, yet spoke blandly, innocently, creating a gestalt of impending dread in the contrast. "Now lessee... this bill would set up a five-member regulating commission, appointed and holding office at 'the pleasure of the President'. That's a funny set-up, isn't it? Seems like the commission would be totally controlled by the President if he could hire and fire commissioners whenever he pleased..."

"Freezing's a very delicate problem," Howards said defensively, like a boy caught with his hand in the old cookie jar. "If the commissioners had fixed terms, they might make mistakes that couldn't be corrected for years. And in this case, time means human life."

"And, of course, the Foundation for Human Immortality is very concerned with... *human life*," Barron said as the promptboard flashed '3 minutes.' "Now there's another bit of funny language in here The part that gives the Freezing Commission full power to 'regulate, oversee, and pass on the appropriateness of all current operations of the Foundation for Human Immortality and any further operations in the area of life-extension as the Foundation may in the future undertake.' If you translate that into English, it seems to mean that the commission would operate independent of Congress, in effect making its own law in the area of... life-extension."

"Well... ah, doesn't that answer your first question?" Howards said shrewdly, trying to tread water. "Congress just moves too slowly. Say... say we developed an immortality treatment; it could be years before Congress approved it, and in the meantime people would be dying who didn't have to die. A commission could act at once. Sure, that's a lot of power to entrust to appointed officials—and that's why the President must be able to hire and fire commissioners at will, to keep the commission responsive to... public opinion. It may seem complicated, but it's all very necessary."

It sure as shit is, Barron thought. That's where the whole schmear's at—the bill's a license for the Foundation to do anything, so long as the President plays ball. And Bennie figures on owning the next President, and he can do it too, and if not this time, then the next time round. One thing he's got plenty of is *time*. Gets his bill through, and his flunky in the White House, he can have... killing children made legal somehow, or have his tame commission insist he's not doing it. Time to show the fucker the razor inside.

"In other words, Howards, you and the President'll run the whole show, The Foundation will control all freezing and... *life extension,* and only the President, comes nitty-gritty, can tell you what you can and can't do."

Howards' image glared at him like a rat in a trap, and the paranoia within began to leak out through his eyes.

"The President..." Howards practically gibbered, "What's wrong with that? Don't you—"

"I wonder if it's smart to trust all that to one man, even the President," Barron said as the promptboard flashed '2 minutes.' "I mean, one man, even a President, could be bought. With all your money, and maybe... *something more?"*

"You're crazy, Barron!" Howards shrieked, blowing all cool, his eyes becoming really rabid. "You're slandering the President of the United States!"

"Who, me?" said Barron, signalling Vince to cut Howards' audio, and give Howards three-quarters screen. "Why, I'm a regular pussycat, I wouldn't slander anyone. I'm talking about a hypothetical President in a hypothetical situation, so all I gotta worry about is a hypothetical lawsuit, right?" Howards' face was a mute backdrop of paranoia surrounding his on the monitor screen.

"So let's just take a farfetched blue-sky hypothetical situation," he said, foot-signalling to Vince to give Howards full screen. "Let's say the Foundation for Human Immortality finally develops an immortality treatment..."

A feral twitch of pure terror spasmed Howards' face for the hundred-million Brackett Count audience to see, as Barron called for full screen for himself and the promptboard flashed '90 seconds.'

"Let's say our little story takes place after the next Presidential election, and let's just say the President is the Foundation's man, without naming names. That sound so impossible to you out there, I mean, the Foundation has *only* five hundred billion bucks to work with, and if they have immortality to peddle... well, that'd make a mighty fancy bribe..."

His face on the screen burned dots of living-colour phosphor into him in a feedback of power; he felt the direct satellite-network connection with the backs of a hundred million brains, all of them hanging on his words, sucking up image from that glass tit, and knowing that he was about to say something dangerously big. Yessiree, folks, step right up and see the Greatest Show on Earth, see the peep-show of history in the making, live, no time-delay, and how's *that* for show biz?

"Let's say… purely for the sake of argument, of course," Barron said slowly as the promptboard flashed '60 seconds,' "that our hypothetical immortality treatment involves a little kicker, though. Let's say… well, everyone knows what a dirty mind I have, so let's just say it involves some kind of organ transplant technique which makes the recipient immortal, but, unfortunately, kills the donor. Very tricky and expensive, dig, because somehow they gotta get victims. In other words, to make one winner immortal, the Foundation's gotta kill one loser. I believe the legal profession has a technical term for that… I think they call it *murder*."

Just enough time to set Bennie up, Barron thought as the promptboard flashed '30 seconds.' He let a ray of the hate he felt inside him play on his image, a flash to a hundred-million Brackett Count slobs that maybe it all wasn't just hot air.

"Now see where that's at? Just a *hypothetical* situation, folks," he said, sneering his image-lips slightly, giving the word 'hypothetical' a sardonic intonation. "But hypothetically, if the Freezer Bill is passed as it stands, if the Foundation for Human Immortality can elect itself a President, and if they had a *hypothetical* immortality treatment that involved murder, then *hypothetically* the Foundation for Human Immortality could damn well commit murder and get away with it…"

He paused, filled three full seconds of air time with dead silence, till he was damn sure all of 'em would know exactly what he was saying (and a special dig for Bennie Howards):

"*Hypothetically*…" he drawled, and the word was just a shade off being a bald accusation. "Of course, the Foundation's hot to get the bill passed, and *that's not hypothetical*, and a lot of people who should know say there was hanky-panky between the Foundation and a certain potential Presidential candidate who died under… *questionable* circumstance, and that's not *hypothetical*, and one and one *have* been known to add up to two. And we'll see just how *hypothetical* the rest of it is—if Mr Benedict Howards has the guts to stay on the line—after this word from our unquestionably non-hypothetical sponsor."

"What the fuck are you *doing*?" Vince Gelardi said over the intercom circuit the moment they had the commercial rolling, his face tense and drawn, but a kind of manic elation that Barron could sense peeked through it. "The phones are going crazy, and Howards is gibbering, I mean literally gibbering, man! Stuff about killing you, and eviscerated niggers, and black circles... makes no sense. He's flipped, he's all the way round the bend, Jack. Christ knows what he'll say if we put him back on the air."

Caught up in the smell of combat, Barron found himself saying, with the old *Bug Jack Barron* relish: "This is not *Bug Jesus H*, Vince, it's *Bug Jack Barron*, and Christ doesn't have to know what Howards is gonna say so long as I do, dig? Keep him on the line, and feed him right to me as soon as we're back on the air."

Vince winced through the control-booth glass as the promptboard flashed '60 seconds,' said nervously: "You're right on the edge as it is. You let a lunatic babble on the air, a lunatic like Bennie Howards, who knows where half the bodies in the country are buried, and we could have a lawsuit that—"

"It's my show," Barron said sharply. "But... maybe you got a point. (Can I keep Howards from doing me in, really pull it off?) Tell you what, when I'm talking, give me three-quarters screen and kill Howards' audio. When I throw the ball to Bennie, give *him* three-quarters, let him rave for a couple seconds, then quick-cut back to me at three-quarters and kill his audio again. We play it back and forth like that, and he won't be able to get more than a couple words in edgewise, dig?"

"Ah, that's the dirty old Jack Barron we all know and love," Gelardi said as the promptboard flashed '30 seconds.'

As the last seconds of the Chevy commercial rolled, on the monitor screen, Jack Barron got another flash of the total power he wielded over that screen, the power of an artificial phosphor-dot pattern that went straight from his mind through the satellite-network circuit to a hundred million brains, the power of a reality-illusion that wasn't even real. Life and death, he thought, just Bennie and me, and the poor bastard doesn't have a prayer. No matter how high the cards he holds in reality are, he still wouldn't have a chance on my turf, 'cause on those hundred million screens, he says only what I let him say, he *is* only what I let him be, it's *my* reality, it's like he was stuck inside my head.

And he finally understood fully where Luke and Morris were at. It didn't matter that he would be a joke as President, what the flesh and blood man in the studio is doesn't matter at all—the only thing that matters is what a hundred million schmucks see on the screen, *that's* what's really real, image is all, because when it comes to what's happening in That Big World Out There, image is all the poor fuckers ever get to see.

Oh, what a shuck! he thought as the promptboard flashed 'On the Air,' and he stared at his own electric face, the eyes sinister pits of power, strictly from holding his head slightly downturned to catch kinesthop flashes from the backdrop behind him. I can do *anything* on that fucking screen, anything—no one's in my league in *this* brand of reality, no matter who the hell they are in the flesh-and-blood private-reality that nobody sees. What happens on the screen is just my word made flesh, I make all the rules, control every damn phosphor-dot the whole country sees. Why couldn't it make me President, or anything else—shit, they haven't elected a *man* President since Truman, they elect an image, is all, and who's bigger league in the image-racket than me?

And the unreal black and white face of Benedict Howards in the lower-left quadrant was nothing less than pathetic; Howards didn't even have the beginnings of a chance, because what the whole country was seeing wasn't Benedict Howards, but Benedict Howards as edited and rewritten by Jack Barron.

"All right," said Barron, feeling unfairly, obscenely confident, "let's get back to our fairy story and see just how *hypothetical it* really is. A while back on this show we discussed immortality research, didn't we, Mr Howards? (Howards began to, shout something soundlessly on the screen, and Barron thought of Sara, felt a savage elation at the total paranoid frustration Howards must be going through, knowing it was his life going down the drain and not a damn thing he could do about it, not even scream.) You said then you didn't have an immortality treatment… What if I say you have? What if I say I have proof? (Watch those libel laws, man!) What do you say to *that*, Benedict Howards? Go ahead, I dare you, deny you have an immortality treatment, right here, right now, in front of a hundred million witnesses!"

Barron's face was a triple-size full-colour monster surrounding the mute image of Benedict Howards. As the images inverted, Barron realised what was about to happen even as—

Howards' eyes glazed over, and crazy tension-lines from every coarse, open, black-and-white-exaggerated pore seemed to radiate paranoid fury as the devil-mask of his face filled three-quarters of the screen, and as Vince cut in his audio, he was screaming:

"…you, Barron! I'll kill you! You—" Howards suddenly blanched as the fact that he was on the air penetrated the red mist.

"It's a lie!" he managed to shout somewhat less shrilly. "It's a goddamn lie!" But every fear-line in his face shouted that it wasn't. "There's no immortality treatment, I swear there isn't, only the fading black circle, against it, we're against it on the side of life, we don't eviscerate picka—" Howards' whole face shook as he realised what he had started to say, and he cut himself off even as Gelardi killed his audio and gave Barron back three-quarters screen.

Jeez, doesn't matter *what* he says, Barron realised. All I gotta do is blow my own riff and just let 'em see it bounce off his face…

"Stop gibbering, Howards!" he said coldly. "Makes you feel any better, why, then, well talk about the other end of our little hypothesis. Let's just suppose, hypothetically, *if you insist*, that there *is* an immortality treatment that involves, oh, say a gland-transplant operation that requires the glands of young children, that involves cutting them apart, *murdering them* for their glands..." He paused. Howards was screaming mutely again on his quarter of the screen like an impotent bug impaled on a pin. Squirm, you bastard, squirm! Had any brains, you'd hang up the phone, but you can't, can you? I got you in too deep now.

"Dig?" Barron said. "If there was such a treatment, and it did involve murder, that would sure explain a lot of funny things, wouldn't it folks? Would explain why Mr Howards is so hot to get his Freezer Utility Bill passed, get himself a nice commission, with his Foundation answerable only to that commission, and the commission controlled completely by the President... Especially if the President we elect is answerable only to *him*. What about it, Mr Howards, doesn't that make sense?"

Gelardi inverted the images, and Howards' stricken face once more dominated the screen. "You—" he began to shout. And then Barron could all but see a shade pulling down behind his desperate eyes, a shade of silence, his only possible retreat.

"Okay," said Barron as the images reverted, "so Mr Howards doesn't care for... hypothetical situations. So let's talk about hard facts. Let's talk about Presidential candidates. (Watch them libel laws!) Now I'm only repeating what I read in the papers—but a lot of people thought that the late Senator Theodore Hennering had the inside track to the Democratic nomination, and things being what they are, that meant the inside track to the Presidency. Before his... *unfortunate accident.* Tell us, Mr Howards, were you a Hennering man—or was Hennering a Foundation man?"

Howards came out fighting this time as his audio came on and the images on the screen inverted: "That's libel, Barron, and you know it!" But before he could get in another word, Vince flashed him back into the silent Coventry of the lower-left quadrant hotseat.

"Libelling *who*? Now there's a good question," Barron said. "You or Hennering? Anyway, I'm not libelling anyone, just asking a question. Fact: Hennering was a sponsor and the Senate floor leader for the Freezer Utility Bill. Fact: Hennering's Presidential balloon had mighty big bread behind it. I gotta watch those libel laws, folks, so you'll have to add it up all by yourselves—one and one makes... Got it, folks? 'Cause here comes some more *hypothetical* stuff. Let's say that a Foundation which the libel laws prevent me from naming has bought itself a Presidential candidate who the libel laws prevent me from naming got a lot of muscle behind a certain bill—which the libel laws prevent me from naming because they've got a beep! Beep! treatment that amounts to murder, and let's say that our unnameable Senator from Illinois *doesn't know* about this treatment. Are you with me so far, out there? Ain't it wonderful, living in a free country where you can... *hypothesise* anything you want so long as you don't name names?

Even when you all know what names to put into the blank spaces."

He paused and clocked how Howards' face had become a pasty mask, how he didn't even seem to be paying attention, knowing for sure it was all over now.

"Let's go one step further. Let's say that our unnameable Senator finds out about this here... *treatment*. Let's say he doesn't like it one bit. Let's say he calls up the unnameable head of the unnameable foundation and tells him precisely where he can stuff his unnameable treatment. Let's say our Senator tells him he's gonna oppose his own bill, blow the whistle on our hypothetical foundation on the floor of the Senate. That means our hypothetical foundation head's gonna be tried for murder, unless... unless something happens to close our Senator's mouth. Tell us, Mr Howards—just *hypothetically*, of course—if *you* were the head of our hypothetical foundation and this Senator's big mouth was your ticket to the electric chair, what would *you* do?"

"I'll sue you!" Howards' voice shouted as Vince switched the images and cut in his audio. "Sue you for libel! I'll get you, Barron! Send you to the chair! I'll—"

Gelardi hustled him back into the lower-left quadrant hotseat like a sergeant-at-arms, and Barron felt the moment hang in the air. Nitty-gritty time, he thought. All I gotta do is spring it; I've got him set up for the kill. Kill myself with him maybe, with that contract as a signed confession, me and Sara—Sara! SaraSaraSara... No more Sara... He felt slug-green things drip-dripping the stolen life-juices of broken babies within him, and in a flash of pure, blessed berserker rage knew that it had to be get Bennie first, and try to save himself later.

"Now let's get back to what's laughingly known as the real world," Barron said. "Fact: Senator Theodore Hennering was killed in a mid-air plane explosion which conveniently destroyed any evidence there might be of murder, hypothetical or otherwise. Fact: A few weeks later, Hennering's widow just happens to get herself run over by a hit-and-run rented truck. What do you say to that, Mr Howards?"

Vince flashed Howards to three-quarters screen just long enough for him to mutter, "How should I know? Coincidence—" before he was cut off again, and Barron was back at three-quarters screen.

Here comes a tricky part, Barron thought. If I can get him to admit it, at least I'm off the libel hook.

"And another fact that nobody knows: Madge Hennering called me before she was killed, told me that Benedict Howards had threatened to kill her husband shortly before he died, *just* before he died, because Hennering had found out something about the Foundation that was terrible enough to make him switch sides. And that's not libel either, friends," Barron lied, "because I can prove it. I have the whole conversation on tape."

"It's a lie!" Howards screamed, as Vince flashed him on, then off. "Lie! Goddamn fading black circle lie! Lie!"

"Watch that Bennie," Barron said, giving his puppetmask on the screen an ironic smile, "you're calling me a liar, and that's libel, and I can prove it with the tape."

Barron paused, knowing what the next link in the chain had to be. Gotta come right out and accuse him of murdering Hennering, and that *is* libel any way you slice it without legal evidence which I ain't got unless he gives it to me—and he won't unless I climb out on that limb. Okay, smart-ass, this is the *real* nitty-gritty, the razor inside—go! go! go!

"Last week I flew down to Mississippi to talk to a man who claimed—you saw it here folks—that someone had bought his daughter for $500,000," Barron said, still playing footsie with the libel laws. "Now, if some foundation needed children for an immortality transplant operation... get the picture, folks? Three people, and only three people knew I was going down there: Governor Lukas Greene, a very old friend; the woman I loved, and—Mr Benedict Howards. Someone shot the man I went down there to talk to, a real pro job, and he almost got me too. One of those three people had Henry George Franklin killed and tried to kill me. Who do you think it was, my friend, my wife, or...?"

Barron paused again, half for the effect, half hesitating at the bank of an abysmal Rubicon, knowing the total mortal danger his next words had to bring. Howards' inset face on the monitor screen was ashen but strangely calm, knowing what was coming, knowing he couldn't save himself, but also knowing that the power to destroy was mutual, was also his. Fuck you, Bennie! Barron thought. Banzai for the Emperor, live a thousand years! Yeah, a *thousand years*...

"Or Benedict Howards, who bought that man's child to cold-bloodedly vivisect in his Colorado labs, Benedict Howards, who is immortal with the glands of a murdered child sewn into his rotten hide, Benedict Howards, who murdered Theodore Hennering and his wife and Henry George Franklin, Benedict Howards, who tried to kill me. After all, *Mr* Howards, murder's cheaper by the dozen, isn't it? You can only fry once."

And he foot-signalled Vince to cut in Howards' audio and give him the full screen treatment. Moment of truth, Barron thought as the image of Benedict Howards ballooned on the screen like a bloated bladder. I'm wide open for a libel suit unless Bennie's far gone enough to cover my bet. He let Howards' silent face eat up three or four seconds of dead airtime, and behind his eyes Barron could sense a straining interface between blind paranoid rage and shrewd vestiges of the amoral coldness that had built the Foundation, had made this ruthless fucker immortal, let him gut children on a goddamn assembly-line and then bitch about the cost.

Two sides of the same coin, Barron realised. Paranoia either way, is all. A cool paranoiac uses his head coldly and ruthlessly to do in everyone in sight 'cause he *knows* everyone's out to get him, and when a cat like that finally freaks out, he's gonna be shrieking and screaming at everything in sight. Gotta push him over that line!

"How does it feel, Howards?" he said, speaking from his own gut, washing the words over Howards' full screen image like the black-wash-over-moiré-patterns behind his own head. "How's it feel to have the stolen glands of some dead kid inside you, crawling around under your skin like spastic slugs oozing slime all over your body twitching and itching—feel 'em?—like they were slowly eating you alive always eating eating eating but never finished eating you up inside for a million—"

"Stop it! Stop it!" Howards screamed, his face filling the screen with a mask of feral terror, his eyes rolling like dervishes, his mouth slack and wet like that of a man in a trance. "Don't let them kill me! Fading black circle of eviscerated niggers tubes of slime up my nose down my throat choking me... Don't let them kill me! Nobody kills Benedict Howards! Buy 'em own 'em kill 'em Senators, President, fading black circle... I don't want to die! Please! Please! Don't let them—"

Zingo! Vince chickened out finally; Howards' face was off screen, his audio dead, and Barron's face filled the entire screen.

Fuck! Barron almost muttered aloud. What a time to get squeamish! What—Suddenly, came a gut-flash that nearly knocked Barron out of his chair! Bennie's *totally* freaked out! Doesn't know what he's saying. Maybe I can do more than get him to admit he killed Hennering, get him to admit on the air he conned me, I didn't know about the treatment beforehand. The truth! Maybe he's crazy enough so I can get him to tell the truth. But I gotta lay it *all* on the line, take away even his doomsday machine weapon, pull out all the stops, throw it all in their fat little laps out there, my life, everything. How's that for a television first—the *fucking truth!*

"Tell them, Howards," he said, "tell the whole damn country what you're putting over on them. Tell them about Teddy Hennering, tell them about the Foundation for Human Immortality, tell them about immortality from the inside. Tell 'em what it feels like to be a murderer."

He paused, tapped his left foot-button once—and nothing happened. Behind the control booth glass, Gelardi shook his head 'no'. Barron tapped the foot-button again; again Gelardi shook his head. Barron slammed his foot against the floor. Vince groaned silently then capitulated, and Howards' face filled three-quarters of the screen.

"You tell 'em, or I'll tell 'em," Barron said, tapping his right foot-button twice for a commercial in two minutes, almost grinned as Vince brought his hands together in a mock prayer of thanks.

"Barron, listen, it's not too late, Barron," Howards whined, and the rage was gone from his face, whited-out by a craven feral fear. "Not too late to stop the fading black circle closing in closing in. ... I won't tell, I swear I won't tell. We can live forever, Barron, you and me, never have to die, young and strong, smell the air in the morning, it's not too late, I swear it, you and me and your wife..."

Barron signalled to keep the screen split as is, said softly, measuredly, letting something harder than sorrow and colder than anger gleam in his image's eyes: "My wife is dead, Howards. She jumped twenty-three stories, *twenty-three stories*. Suicide... but not from where I sit. From where I sit, you killed her sure as if you pushed her. Afraid now, Bennie? Can you guess where my head is at?"

Incredibly, the total fear on Benedict Howards' face took a quantum jump, it was more than terror now, it was abysmal paranoid despair. And all he could do was mutter, "No... no... no... no... no..." like some obscene million-year-old infant, trembling wet lips of incredible age forming a baby's drool. He knew.

Barron signalled for and got full screen and solo audio as the promptboard flashed '90 seconds.' "Let's talk about why my wife died," he said, his voice and face purposely composed into an artfully-ill-concealed ersatz calm that was far more wrenching than any histrionics could ever be.

"My wife died because Benedict Howards made her immortal," he said. "He made her immortal, and it killed her, now ain't that a bitch? She couldn't live with herself after she found out... Sara wasn't the only one her immortality killed. There was someone else she never saw who died so she could be immortal—a poor kid whose body was irradiated by the Foundation till it was one living cancer, so they could cut out his very special glands and sew them into my wife. And make her live forever.

"But she won't live forever, she's dead; she killed herself because she couldn't stand living knowing what had been done to her. I loved that woman, so you'll pardon my thinking it wasn't just guilt. She told me why, just before she jumped. She knew that he would get away with it, live forever, kill forever, buy or kill anyone that stood in his way unless... unless someone was desperate enough or dumb enough or didn't care enough about living to scream from the mountaintops what he was doing. Sara Westerfeld died to make me do just what I'm doing now. She died for *you*! How does *that* grab you, suckers?"

Barron felt himself cloaked in the crystal mist of legend: the studio, the monitor, the figures behind the control booth glass were things that couldn't possibly exist. The things he had said were things that were *never* said in public, not in front of a hundred million people. What was happening did not ever happen in front of cameras, you could watch the glass tit forever and not see anything like this.

But it *was* happening, he was making it happen, and it was the easiest thing in the world. History, he thought, I'm making fucking history—and it's nothing but show biz, is all. Moving images around and making myth...

He foot-signalled and got Howards back at one-quarter screen, with his audio back on. But Bennie was as stiff and mute as a still photo.

"Go ahead, Howards," he said, "now's your big chance, tell 'em the rest. Tell 'em why you made Sara Westerfeld immortal, tell 'em who else you made immortal. Go ahead, time to hit back, isn't it?"

Howards remained silent, didn't even seem to hear, as the promptboard flashed '30 seconds.' His empty eyes looked off into the dreadful landscape within. Barron knew he had him sick and bleeding—set him up right, and after the commercial, he'd start to shriek.

"All right," Barron said with razors in his voice, "I'll tell 'em!" He reached into a pocket, pulled out the same blank papers he had used before.

"See this, folks? This is a Freeze Contract, a very special Freeze Contract. It entitles the client to have the Foundation for Human Immortality make him immortal..."

He paused, waved the paper at the camera like a bloody shirt.

"This is *my* contract," he said.

And the promptboard flashed 'Off the Air.'

The commercial rolled, and behind the glass of the control booth Barron could see the confusion, the deathwatch smell, and Vince's face seemed ten years older as he stared through the glass and then spoke into the intercom circuit:

"Jack what are you—"

"Keep me on the air, Vince," Barron said.

"What in hell is going on? Do you realise what you're *doing?*"

Do I realise what I'm doing! Barron thought. Did I ever realise what I was doing before tonight?

"Just keep me on the air, Vince," Barron said, "and make damn sure Howards stays on the phone."

Gelardi hesitated, and Barron could read the pain on his face as he said: "The network brass is screaming. You've laid them open to the biggest libel suit in history. They're ordering me to keep you off the air. I'm sorry..."

"This is *my* show, Vince," Barron shouted, "and you can tell those fuckers to get stuffed! You can also tell them that every word I've said is true, and the *only* way they can avoid a libel suit is to keep me on the air and let me prove it."

"That's pretty dirty pool," Gelardi said as the promptboard flashed '60 seconds.'

"It's a pretty dirty world, Vince," Barron said, and he broke the intercom connection.

How's this for the old power-junk, Barron thought. Benedict Howards totally raving out of his mind, and I've got him trapped on my turf where

I make all the rules, can change 'em anytime I want. Howards, with all his power, with his dirty fingers in every Democratic pie, I can do more than save myself—that's no real sweat now—I can kick the whole cabal that runs the country to pieces, throw the next election so wide open *anyone* might win. Right here, right now, live!

A dream, yeah, a Jack-and-Sara dream, just me standing at the focus of everything and kicking the whole rotten schmear apart. Dream made reality—I got the monster that knows where all the bodies are buried (shit, who you think buried them in the first place!) right where I want him, ready to pick him apart...

Sara! Sara! If only you were here to see the show now, baby! *Bug Jack Barron* goes down, it'll go down with a bang that'll take the whole sorry mess with it. Sara... Sara... it's the only way I know how to cry for you.

He stared at the meaningless commercial on the monitor as the prompt-board flashed '30 seconds,' and knew that in half a minute his image, a reality that was realer than real, would burn into a hundred million eyes as if they were in the room with him.

No, they would be sucked in deeper than that, they would be in his head, behind his eyes, seeing and hearing only what he wanted them to, nothing more and not a phosphor-dot less.

And in a strange reversal of perspective, he saw that if they all were a part of him, the image-Jack Barron was also a part of them. What he had always avoided had come at him from where he least expected it—*Bug Jack Barron*, like it or not, was power, terrible, unprecedented power, and with it came the unavoidable choice that had faced every power-junkie since time began: to have the sheer gall to fake being something greater than a man, or cop-out on the millions who had poured a part of themselves into your image and be something less.

And as the promptboard flashed 'On the Air,' Jack Barron knew there was only one way he could play it. Been called a lot of things, he thought, but *humble* was never one of them!

On the screen, the pack of Acapulco Golds fades out and is replaced by a face, an expanded vidphone grey, fuzzy, somehow bloated. There is something inhuman about the eyes, a too-bright rodent emptiness and the mouth is trembling, the lips beaded with spittle.

Over this close-up of Benedict Howards, a voice, controlled, unwavering, yet with an undertone of suppressed agony that gives it total conviction, the voice of Jack Barron:

"Surprise! Surprise! We're back on the air, and in case you tuned in late, the man you're looking at is Benedict Howards. The man you're looking at thought he could buy anyone in the United States, me included, and you know something—he was *right*."

The black and white face on the screen seems to shout something soundlessly at this, as if the words will not come, and then suddenly it is gone and the face of Jack Barron, in close-up, fills the screen. His sandy hair is a tangle as if the pregnancy of the moment has forbidden him to comb it; his eyes seem huge, leaping out of the screen from deeply-shadowed pits, and somehow he looks older and younger all at once.

"Think *you* couldn't be bought, out there?" he says, and the words are bitter, knowing, yet also somehow ironically forgiving. "Pretty sure of that, aren't you? So was I, baby, so was I. But what if the man that was buying was Benedict Howards, and the coin he was paying for your bod was eternal life? You so sure now? Really? Then think about what it's like to be dead. You say you can't? Of course you can't, 'cause you can't *nothing* when you're dead. Think about that, because you're *all* going to die, gonna be *nothing*—dead. Unless Benedict Howards thinks he has a good reason to give you eternal life. And he thought he had a good reason to buy me—so he bought, and I sold. No excuses, friends, I just didn't want to die. Would you? So now I'm immortal, with the glands of a dead child sewn inside my hide. How's that grab you? You hate me—or is that twinge in your gut just envy? But before you make up your mind..."

Now the left half of the screen is filled with the face of Benedict Howards, a grey spectre of menacing madness that Jack Barron pins with his big green eyes as he says: "Go ahead, Howards, tell them the rest."

"Rest...?" Benedict Howards mumbles like a lost little boy. "What rest? Isn't any rest, just fading black circle life leaking away in plastic tubes eviscerated niggers... you're killing me, Barron, throwing me to the black circle of death closing in choking me choking me... you're killing me! Rest...? Rest...?"

Jack Barron's sky-blue sportjac and yellow shirt, his sandy hair and wounded eyes, seem like an oasis of embattled humanity beside the grey grey madness that radiates from the left half of the screen, as unreal and preternatural as a grainy newsreel of Adolf Hitler.

"You forgot your little kicker, didn't you Bennie?" Barron says. "Back in Colorado, folks, Bennie told me I'd never have the b—, ah, *cojones* to do what I'm doing now. Remember Bennie? Remember the contract? Remember the special clause you wrote in just for this occasion? Remember what you said you'd do?"

Howards' face seems to expand like a grey balloon, and it fills the entire screen and he begins to babble, his voice dopplering upward in pitch as the words pour out faster and faster: "I'll get you Barron, swear I'll get you for this, you murderer you killer on the side of the fading black circle closing in, you killed me, Barron, get you kill you like you're killing me..."

Jack Barron's living-colour image appears in the lower-left-hand quadrant, a frail, vivid splotch of fleshy humanity, threatened by yet somehow more cogent than the grey newsreel monster surrounding him, a contrast that makes you proud to be a man.

"Got your name on the contract in black and white," Howards babbles shrilly, "a legal confession in any court in the country. Murder! Yeah, he's a murderer, accessory to murder, I can prove it, got his name on the contract accepting legal liability for the results of the immortality treatment—if it's murder, sends me to the chair, you fry with me, Barron; you're a murderer too!" Coming from the grey unreal monster, the words are unreal, and there is a blessed relief of tension when the images reverse and Barron's flesh-and-blood face fills three-quarters of the screen, and Howards' black and white newspaper photo face appears tiny in the lower-left quarter of the screen, as if a more natural order has been restored.

"*Too?* I'm a murderer too?" Barron says, and every syllable seems to carry a total conviction, coming as it does from a *man*, not an image.

"You are! You know you are I can prove it, you're a murderer too!" the little newsreel figure says.

Jack Barron turns from the thing below him, stares out from the with pain and fury written in those huge green eyes. Those wounded *human* eyes.

"I'm a murderer too," he says. "You heard the man, folks, *too*. I'm a murderer *too*. Didn't I tell you I sold out to Howards? He made me immortal, and to get that I signed a contract that made me legally liable for every result of that treatment, including a charge of murder. Yeah, murder, because the Foundation's been buying children, killing them and transplanting their glands, and I've got pieces of some poor dead kid sewn inside me. So I'm a murderer too."

The image of Benedict Howards winks out, and the face of Jack Barron fills the entire screen. And as it does, something seems to happen to that hard-edged face. It goes soft, vulnerably soft, and the big eyes seem to become wet and shiny, guilty, self-accusing—a face that makes you want to comfort the hurt soul behind it, a face that in its pain bears the mark of unquestionable wrenching truth.

And when Barron speaks, his voice is quiet, subdued, without an iota of guile in it:

"I'm going to ask something of you out there that I've never asked before. I've got no right to do it, but I'm going to ask you to believe something just because I say it's true. I didn't know. I really didn't know that my immortality meant killing a child until I woke up in a hospital bed and Benedict Howards told me.

"Look, I'm no little tin saint, and we all know it. I admit I wanted to live forever bad enough to sell out to Benedict Howards, and you've got every right to hate me for that. But murdering children is something I would never stomach under any circumstances for any reason, and that's all I'm asking you to believe. Proof? Howards has all the proof on *his* side, the signed contract and the best witnesses money can buy to say that I knew what I was doing. And you'd better believe it, money can buy plenty. The only proof I've got that I'm telling the truth is that I'm right here in front of you, laying my life in your hands and saying it, telling you the whole truth because I couldn't live with myself otherwise, and to hell with what happens to me. It's all up to you out there. I ask you to believe that I'm telling the truth."

Silence, three full seconds of dead silence that seem to crawl on forever, as the face of Jack Barron stares out from the screen, the eyes like a pair of open wounds, windows into the soul within, hurt eyes, strangely humble eyes, and yet with a certain open defiance, a guileless defiance with no defences but the truth. And in that very open and defenceless defiance, the certainty of the truth behind an unbearable moment of human reality leaping out from the flat phosphor-dot pattern of the screen...

And then suddenly the moment passes, and a certain hardness returns to Barron's face (but a hardness made poignant by the knowledge of the softness behind it), and purposefulness comes back into his eyes.

"Only one more thing to tell you, friends," he says, "and then you'll have the whole ugly truth. Now you know what Bennie did for me; the question is, what was I supposed to do for *him?*" The grainy grey face of Benedict Howards appears in the lower-left quarter of the screen, and now Barron is not a victim but an inquisitor as he stares down at him.

"What about it Howards?" Barron says. "Do you tell them or do I? Go ahead, tell them! Tell 'em how you've been buying up children, tell 'em how many Congressmen you got in your hip pocket, tell 'em your plans for the next Democratic convention. And tell 'em what you wanted me for, tell 'em what I was supposed to do for you."

Howards' face expands to fill three-quarters of the screen, with Barron in the upper right-hand corner, his eyes flaying the grey image like whips.

"No! No!" Howards screams. "You got it all wrong, don't understand, no one understands, gotta push the fading black circle back forever... Life is all I want, I'm on the side of life against death! Senators, Congressmen, Governors, President—gotta be on the side of *life*, not the side of the fading black circle closing in eviscerated niggers vultures' beaks up nose down throat choking away life in tubes and bottles—"

Howards is suddenly compressed into the lower left-hand corner of the screen, screaming silently as Jack Barron ignores him, stares straight out from the screen, says:

"That's where it's at, folks. All I was supposed to do is lie to you. Tell enough lies to get that Freezer Bill passed, and then help Bennie elect his tame President—and guess which party he has bought? I may stink to high heaven with Foundation BO, but half the Democrats in Congress stink worse than I do. I can't name names, but just maybe now some of 'em'll have the guts poor Ted Hennering had and stand up and be counted. And if they don't... well, just read a list of the Congressmen who support the Foundation Bill. Can't sue the Congressional Record for libel!"

Now Howards' face fills the entire screen, his eyes glazed and rolling, little flecks of spittle spraying from his trembling lips as Barron's voice-over begins to almost chant: "You're a dead man, Bennie. Dead... dead... dead. You're gonna fry till you die. Till they kill you dead. Dead... dead... dead..."

"*Nooooooo!*" Howards screams. "I'll get you get you all kill you buy you own you destroy you forces of the fading black circle nobody kills Benedict Howards, Senators, Governors, Congressmen, kill 'em all own 'em all kill... Nobody kills Benedict Howards! Nobody, never, young and strong and..."

Howards' mad eyes stare straight out from the screen, and his screaming becomes harsh, clipped, savage. "Barron! Barron! I'll get you, Barron! Kill you! Kill you! Kill!"

From nowhere, a great grey fist suddenly fills the entire screen—and then the whole screen goes dead, a scintillating field of speckled grey and white static and over it an electric serpent hiss.

Just the dead screen and the hissing static for a beat, then the grey field of random electric impulses is pushed up into the upper-right-hand corner as if by the hand of Jack Barron, who fills the rest of the screen in a head-and-shoulders shot, pointing to the square of hissing nothingness (like the random non-being of the grave) with his eyes.

"You, out there, you suckers, you!" he shouts. "Look at the thing you made! We all made Benedict Howards, we always make our Benedict Howards, because there'll always be men who know the Big Secret: *we can all be bought.* Who wants to die? Who wants to live in a rat-trap? Who wants to eat garbage? They know it, and they suck on it—politicians! Power-junkies, giving you just enough to keep you bought with Welfare and Medicare and Niggercare and nice-sounding lies; crumbs from the table, is all! Just enough to cool it, and not a crumb more. Hold your noses and take a good look around you for a change—we've got a thousand little Benedict Howards calling themselves Governors, Congressmen, Senators, Presidents. And the only difference between them and Howards is that they're not in his league, they're pikers. What are you gonna do about it? Sit on your fat asses like you always have? Or maybe go out and get yours—anyone with a kid can get a nice piece of change for his bod. A lot more than thirty pieces of silver. Well, suckers, had enough? Or are you gonna let it go on and on and on till you die? Just remember, though, when you die *now*, baby, you die *alone.*"

Barron pauses, and almost laughs the old inside-joke laugh as he says the next words with the old endearing bad-boy shrug: "I'm afraid you're gonna have to wait some more to get your licks folks—till after this word from our palpitating sponsor."

Epilogue

NEVER... NEVER... never... never kill me, Barron! No no no no no one kills Benedict Howards, Your Honour! Buy you, Your Honour, kill you own you with the power of life against death, Your Honour... make you immortal, Your Honour... Barron's on the side of the fading black circle, Your Honour... I'm innocent, on the side of life, Your Honour... No one kills Benedict Howards, Your Honour! No one! Young and strong and healthy soft-skinned women in air-cooled circles of power Los Angeles, Dallas, Vegas, New York, Washington, forever, Your Honour...

Benedict Howards paced the small room endlessly; planning, scheming, mumbling threats to himself. It was a pretty bare room, not quite what he was accustomed to, but not really very much like a prison cell either. Yeah, he thought, maybe those goddamn lawyers knew what they were doing after all.

"My client is obviously mentally incapable of standing trial at this time."

See, Barron, even you couldn't do it! Nobody can do it, nobody kills Benedict Howards! Young and strong and healthy for the next million years! Forever! No electric chair, no prison, just a nice public sanitarium commitment until those goddamn expensive lawyers figure out a way to get me off scott-free. And they will, they said they would, promised me they would! They got all the time in the world to get me off, got a million years ('... paranoid delusions...'), got enough time to breed me lawyers ('... semi-hallucinatory state...'), yeah, breed whole new races of the bastards ('... incapable of standing trial... is to be confined in a hospital for the criminally insane until such time as he may be deemed mentally competent to stand trial...'), controlled mutation whole new races of purebred lawyers can kill that murder indictment and then I can get out of here, when it's safe.

Benedict Howards insane! What a joke! Joke on Jack Barron, Senators, Congressmen, President, Your Honour. You prick, Your Honour, I didn't even have to buy you, Your Honour, you could've lived forever, Your Honour, but you cretin you, you did just what my lawyers wanted you to, put me here where the fading-black-circle electric chair can't get at me, never get at me, while my Miners hold it back, push it back, keep it back for a million years.

All they gotta do is quash that murder indictment, and the next day I walk right out of here, 'cause I'm not crazy, Benedict Howards is the sanest man in the world, saner than a man, better than a man, immortal like a god...

Howards paced the room, thinking: I paid good money for worse rooms than this in cold dry Panhandle days when I couldn't afford better, not a bad deal, the dumb sap government pays the rent on this joint while I sit it out, while they quash the indictment... Then I can stop faking it and get myself declared sane again, easiest thing in the world, 'cause I'm the sanest man in the world... nobody's ever been as sane as me...

Yeah, not such a bad room, pretty good view, the bed isn't bad, and they even bring me my meals, breakfast, lunch, dinner in bed any time I want it. Even got... even got... even got...

Howards froze. Mustn't think about it! Can't think about it! Think about it, and it turns itself on! Barron! That fucker Barron, he can turn it on from the inside, the bastard! Any time he wants to he can turn it on from the inside, any time I forget not to think about it, he can turn it on... from in inside... don't about it... don't...

But Benedict Howards knew that it was too late. He *had* thought about it, about the television set built into the wall, high up where he couldn't get at it, couldn't smash the leering smart-ass fading black circle of Jack Barron watching him, always watching him, immortal just like me, be there forever, always watching! Watching! Watching! Watching!

He found his eyes moving upward to watch the face on the television screen; he had to watch, had to stay on guard, that fucker Barron was always watching him! And Barron's immortal, I made him immortal, can't get rid of him, and he's on the side of the fading black circle, gotta watch him, don't dare turn my back...

Benedict Howards shook his fist at the television screen, the screen they had sworn they were cutting out of the hospital circuit the first time he had tried to climb the wall to smash it. But they lied! They lied!

"Damn you, Barron! I'll get you, kill you, buy you! You hear that, Barron, I own you! Own you down to your toes!"

But the smirking phosphorescent face burning itself from the glass into the back of his eyes said nothing, just smiled that damn smart-ass smile, the deep, shadowed eye-hollows black, black, black, shimmering, circling, face of the fading black circle closing in, fading circle of death...

Howards staggered backward, felt the edge of the bed cut into the small of his back, fell backward onto it, feeling tube up nose down throat choking him his life leaking away in phosphor dot plastic bottles, and Jack Barron's face laughing smart-ass doctors nurses fading black circle life leaking away tube up nose down throat forever...

"Noooooooo!" Howards screamed and screamed and screamed. "I'm dying I'm dying I'm dying..."

Footsteps outside, the man with the needle again, needle of sleep, of blackness, needle of dreams of the fading black circle closing in, darkness closing in, face of Jack Barron, life leaking away forever... forever...

"I'm not crazy!" Howards screamed. "I'm not! I'm not! I'm dying... I don't wanna die, don't wanna, don't wanna... Don't let it kill me! Don't let him kill me!"

Lukas Greene pushed the vidphone across his desk, rubbed his eyes. Malcolm running too, he thought. What's that make, four... or five? Everybody wants to get into the act! As the Chinese like to say when the shit hits the fan, "We are living in interesting times."

Hard to figure what's gonna spring next. When Jack torpedoed Howards all the shit in the country hit the fan. Teddy the Pretender locking up the 'regular' Democratic nomination, if there is such a thing any more... And the old 'Foundation Democrats' read out of the party and running their own candidate... Democrats jumping to the SJC... maverick Republicans bolting the coalition and running *their* independence candidate ...now Malcolm Shabazz running, and even old Withers making noises again. Still, with Jack on an SJC-Republican coalition ticket we probably have the inside track.

But it's sure become a bookie's nightmare! Yeah, we're living in interesting times. But at least we got as much chance as anyone to come out on top when the Great Unwashed finally puts Humpty-Dumpty together again.

Greene sighed. President Jack Barron, he thought, and vice-president Lukas Greene... Well, stop crying, you nigger you, you knew that was the way it had to be. Jack up front, and you number two shit-colour brown, black is more like it, you maybe get to go as far as any nigger can.

The Black Shade, oh, what a laugh, you white nigger you, as if there could be a black shade any more than there could be a white nigger! Who knows, Greene thought, maybe that's why I started that one in the first place. If there really could be a black shade, then maybe there could somehow be a white nigger... in a White House, someday, somehow... Can't kid yourself now, baby, this is nitty-gritty time, and if the SJC finally gets its President, it's gonna be Jack, not you, white, not black.

Come on, he told himself, snap out of it, man! Remember why you got into this racket in the first place, you felt it in your belly then. Remember how it was? Only lost that gut-feel when you got your little piece of the action. Well, that's over now, it's a whole new hand of cards, and who knows, maybe now we got some aces.

And without Jack, we'd still be nowhere. Whatever Jack gets, he deserves it, he paid his dues, the poor fucker, with him immortal, and Sara dead, the only immortal except for Howards squirreled away in some loony-bin somewhere. Don't envy Jack Barron, man! Maybe now he *is* like a black shade in the way that counts, like black is being a stranger in someone else's land. Like alone... And who's more alone now than Jack?

Greene shivered at the thought of the man who was his friend, who might still be alive when he was dust a million years, unless they found a new way to immortality in time. But until then, who can be as alone as Jack, who can see what he sees, feel what he feels...?

Look him in the eye and call him friend...!

Jack Barron finished the Acapulco Gold, hesitating at the door of his outer office. Come on, man, you gotta stop brooding and play 'em one day at a time already. Can't keep playing this *Weltschmertz* schtick for the next ten thousand years...

But so many things I want to forget that never should be forgotten. Sara... won't forget Sara ever...

Oh yeah? *Ever*... The word had a whole new meaning, like everything else when you looked at it through new eyes. Eyes that would *always* be new, young eyes going through changes every morning like a kid who knows he's got his whole life ahead of him, always ahead of him, and what will I be like in a thousand years?

A thousand years alone...

No, that's old-style thinking, just the short view. Someday they'll lick immortality for everyone without murder, now that the slobs can taste it coming, with a Public Freezer Bill already on the President's desk and hara-kiri for him not to sign it, and with all that public pressure... In the long run, everyone'll make it to where I stand, and in the meantime I can sit it out alone, got all the time in the world. In the meantime...

In the meantime, looks like I'm stuck in the politics bag till after the election—had to play along with Morris to keep the show. And anyway, admit it, man, it's kinda fun.

Forty-seven different Presidential candidates all running around like chickens with their heads cut off, sure to, shake things up, just what the country needs. And who knows, I might even win—and then the good old US of A is *really* gonna get a boot in the ass. But not the one Luke and his boys are figuring on...

What a joke on Luke, he thought, he'll piss in his pants! 'Social Justice'—hope I do win just so that dumb fucker Morris can clock what Jack Barron's brand of Social Justice is. *Nitty-gritty* Social Justice, is all, once we get a Negro in the White House, even by the back door, nothing'll ever be the same.

Politics! Politicians! Such schmucks, they got no sense of humour at all. Think they got themselves an image that can win, and a puppet they think they can screw around behind the scenes with after the election.

Boy, if I *do* win, is everyone gonna shit bricks after the Inauguration! When good old Jack Barron resigns the Presidency in favour of Vice-President Lukas Greene. *Black* Vice-President Lukas Greene!

That'd teach the pricks to play the image game with the world's champ. A nice juicy custard pie in the face of the whole country, just what it needs, four years of a black President, and who knows, they might end up liking it enough to make it eight the hard way.

In the meantime...

He opened the door, stepped into the outer office, and stood by Carrie

Donaldson's desk. Carrie looked up at him with guarded eyes. "Mr Barron?" she said.

Well, why not? thought Jack Barron. You got wounds, but they'll heal, and anyway, you owe this chick something. And she's a mighty fine lay, remember?

"Let's go have some lunch, Carrie," he said. "I'm gonna take the afternoon off, so you're off duty too. Want to take it off with me?"

"Does that sound the way I think it sounds ... Jack?"

Barron laughed. It felt good. "It does, so long as you keep calling me Jack," he said.

"*Jack* ..." she said, taking his hand. And they left the office together.

Just another chick? Barron wondered. Or something more? Well, who cares how it'll turn out, a one-night stand or a week or a year or a hundred years, what's it matter how long?

Suddenly it didn't seem very important to know just how anything would turn out, or what would happen in the next minute, or the next year, or the next century. It wasn't even such a hang-up anymore that he hadn't learned how to remember Sara without hurting. It had finally got through to him that he had plenty of time to heal even the deepest of his wounds, play any game he wanted to any number of times, become anything he wanted to be and then change his mind. Time enough for anything...

Like all the time in the world.

Afterword

Michael Moorcock

AUGUST, 1967. Milford, Pennsylvania. Damon Knight's Gothic manse. (A ringer for the *Pyscho* house.) I'm attending a writers' conference, my first and last writers' workshop. I'm representing *New Worlds* and what will be called (never by us) the 'New Wave'. Knight (who, as a paperback editor, has published several Ballard originals, as well as work by me, Disch and other ambitious writers of the day) is publishing many of the same writers in his *Orbit* anthology series. Judith Merrill, anthologist and critic, is our greatest publicist in the USA, championing Ballard in particular. *New Worlds* is already publishing such outstanding US writers as Thomas M Disch, John Sladek, Pamela Zoline, Roger Zelazny, James Sallis and Kit Reed alongside UK writers like Brian Aldiss, BJ Bayley, DM Thomas, George MacBeth, JG Ballard and Langdon Jones. Soon we'll see the first work of M John Harrison, Gene Wolfe and others. A great fusion of talent, the first real flowering of what we've been working for. We're all very excited. Talking night after night with high verbals like Jim Sallis, Chip Delany, Harlan Ellison, Judith Merrill and Tom Disch saves a lot of money on speed but doesn't necessarily improve your judgement. The days grow crazier. Spinrad and Ellison are in a brawl at the local diner. Ellison, who did his best with it, comes back cursing Spinrad for letting the gigantic trucker pummel him into the ground. Spinrad points out reasonably that Harlan picked the fight and he was ready to call help if it looked like Harlan was going to get killed. After all, Harlan handled himself well enough in his famous Pacific Dining Car parking lot fist fight with Frank Sinatra.

Ellison's in his own Golden Age, riding high and boiling with attitude, turning out lippy eloquent hits like *Repent, Harlequin, Said the Ticktock Man*. He and the equally height-challenged Spinrad make natural comrades, full of the kind of mouth that made Warner Brothers gangsters the only kind you ever wanted to be. Can't keep it shut. Cagney and Tracey. Always in trouble. (Leigh Brackett once laughed when I suggested the snappy villain in her Elliott Gould *Long Goodbye* was based on her friend Harlan. It could easily have been, she said.) The stately, amiable Disch has completed his *Camp Concentration* as our best serial yet and I'm wondering how we'll possibly equal it. Jerry Cornelius has been appearing in *New Worlds* for about two years. Ballard's been publishing his 'condensed novels', beginning with *The Assassination Weapon*, for about a year. At *New Worlds* parties William Burroughs and Arthur C Clarke enjoy glasses of orange juice, politely disdaining all drugs, neither man too happy with this zesty new rock and roll which makes it hard to hear the others' substantial drone. In London that strange cross-fertilisation between the new sf writers, beat and pulp literature, poetry, music, French cinema and pop art painting is becoming identified as some sort of rough and ready movement. Voices of common experience.

Spinrad's brought bits of his new novel along to Milford. Previously he's best known for a pulpish hard-boiled sci-fi caper called *The Men in the Jungle*, which showed his promise. But the new novel seems light-years ahead of anything else I've read of his. It's called *Bug Jack Barron* and is about media manipulation of the public, about politics in the near future. A subject dear to my heart. And written in ambitious language, inspired by the same possibilities of expression demonstraied by Burroughs, who learned to take the jack-hammer thrust of pulp prose and turn it into a sophisticated literary method.

Where mainstream writers still struggle to reproduce the careful, unambitious sentences of Kingsley Amis, the Frenchified retrospective tone of Durrell's *Alexandrian Quartet*, the dull authority and over-familiar rhythms of the orthodox American novel of manners, or fall back utterly on pastiche, *New Worlds* writers have kicked all that aside and are finding and making instruments to do a job, rather than reproduce a riff.

That's how it was in the summer of '67.

Ballard, drawing on his own medical education, his work as a scientific journalist, his relish for the rhythms and resonances of techno-prose, had found one brilliant solution to the problems we talked about. We had just run another—Sladek's classic *Masterson and the Clerks*. We had recently introduced the graphic work of MC Escher to the anglophone public. Aldiss had begun his *Acid Head War* stories (superior to their revised book versions), composer Langdon Jones had found his own approach which would culminate in his powerful cycle *The Eye of the Lens* and Barry Bayley, idiosyncratic as ever, was producing the extraordinary stories (Burroughsian geometries?) which would become *The Knights of the Limits*.

That first time I met him, Spinrad had written what was far and away his best work to date and couldn't believe that it wasn't being enthusiastically celebrated, rather than rejected, by its commissioning publisher.

Several of us were familiar with this pattern. My own *Final Programme* dismayed the first publishers to see it and took a couple of years to come out from an independent publisher, only to be censored in its US edition! Ballard's *Atrocity Exhibition* was pulped by its first US publisher, Aldiss's *Hand-Reared Boy* was dumped by its publisher at proof-stage while his regular publisher, Faber, firmly refused to publish *Report on Probability A*. *Camp Concentration* was also turned down by its commissioning publisher. We got condescending letters. Mervyn Peake's original publisher refused to reprint the *Gormenghast* books because they insisted (following Amis's dismissal of the sequence) there was no market and it took Penguin Books, Langdon Jones, Maeve Peake, Anthony Burgess and a few others to pressure them into republishing the classic we know.

Time after time we'd come upon that mixture of narrow snobbery and illiterate prejudice which continues to make the average corporate publisher a kind of goalie between writers and their public. While much of that work from the '60s might seem pretty ordinary today, *New Worlds* scarcely featured a story or serial which didn't involved its author and publisher in some kind of trouble.

I went back to London with Spinrad's manuscript and promptly succumbed to bed where I read it and was enchanted. He was using ambitious language, the language of the modern streets. The prose had a vigorous eloquence, a swaggering vulgarity, drawing on Burroughs, Brooklyn and Los Angeles for its inspiration as well as its metaphors. I was so keen on the book that I truncated Brian Aldiss's serial (just about to appear in book form by then and needing no further support) and started doing the copy for the next issue's cover. It seemed to me that we were about to make another quantum jump.

That same issue (178 December 67/January 68) carried one of Ballard's earliest advertisements (*Does The Angle Between Two Walls Have A Happy Ending*), Aldiss's acid streaming *Auto-Ancestral Fracture*, Sladek, acid about McLuhan, Emshwiller's non-verbal account of his own movies. It had Disch's cold heroin comedy *Linda & Daniel & Spike* and Giles Gordon's *The Line-up on the Shore*. The critic and polemicist Christopher Finch contributed a piece on the state of British avante garde art, discussing Paolozzi, Richard Hamilton and Peter Blake, among others. There were articles on the future of fiction, illustrations by Paolozzi from his *As Is When* series. Pretty much a typical issue for the times.

GET SET FOR THE BEST THING THAT EVER HAPPENED TO YOU, says the shoutline for the opening of Spinrad's serial. IT'S BUG JACK BARRON TIME. And off we went.

Straight into a lot of very time-consuming idiocy with WH Smith and Britain's other monolithic distributor/retailer Menzies. In fact Menzies took the trouble to phone their rival and tip them off to the kind of dangerous filth they were selling. I soon discovered, to my surprise, since they were by then perfectly happy to sell and distribute soft porn, that we had been banned. We'd been banned in South Africa and elsewhere, but why here? They could be prosecuted, they said, for libel or obscenity or something and they couldn't take any chances.

We went to see them.

Following the usual lunatic logic of these situations, the man representing the magazine arm of WH Smith was Mr Baron. He wasn't much like Jack Barron. He favoured muddy brown clothing. He was very vague about what the law could do to them, but he was very certain that *Bug Jack Barron* was 'deliberately disgusting' and he wasn't a man at one with himself when he contemplated (from the next issue by now awaiting distribution) Langdon Jones's *Eye of the Lens*, in which a character has a discussion with Christ on the Cross. That, he declared, with certainty, was blasphemy and blasphemy *was* against the law.

And so, after some time down the establishment rabbit hole, I came up for air with the message that Smiths and Menzies were refusing to distribute us. Unless, they said, we cut our serial, *Bug Jack Barron*, forthwith. Part of *New Worlds'* policy was that we only survived by selling through normal newsagents. We had no desire to become a 'little magazine'. Our economics, though real-world, were very fragile. There was never any question about cutting the serial, but it looked as if our chances of staying afloat were pretty small. Especially since our distributor was, without permission already destroying the offending issues.

Then, for some reason, the press came to our support in a big way. The publicity forced Smiths to reconsider their strategy, if nothing else. The subject matter and general thrust of *Bug Jack Barron* and the fact that Smiths were hugely unpopular with journalists at that time, meant that we got a great deal of publicity, most of which was sympathetic. Some wasn't. The right-wing press loathed the very notion of the Arts Council (who had given us a small grant) and were only too happy to leap on one of these 'state-funded' publications. *The Daily Express* phoned me at home to ask if I'd let my kids read such filth and I replied that they were showing no interest so far but I'd be very grateful if they'd read anything.

A Question was asked about us in the House of Commons. Why was the government funding this foulness? To her credit that principled old socialist battleship Jenny Lynn, then Minister for the Arts, got up and defended us. But I don't think she thought much of the language, either. She'd checked with Lord Goodman, then Chairman of the Arts Council, who'd said it was all right, he'd looked on our masthead and we had Eduardo Paolozzi as our aeronautics advisor.

We were getting more respectable. A few years earlier, during an argument over William Burroughs's novels (the famous *Ugh!* Correspondence in the *TLS*), Edith Sitwell had accused me of trying to nail her nose to a lavatory seat. An image which has never left me.

The News of the World report caused a football team in Manchester to go into a newsagents and buy eleven copies. Probably to their intense disappointment. Oddly, for a publication frequently described as pornographic by the press, we just didn't seem to turn the punters on. This caused a lot of head-scratching at West End Central. As so often happened with the underground papers like *IT* and *Frendz*, the authorities were only used to dealing with commercial pornographers with whom they usually had some sort of understanding, not people who published from aggressive idealistic motives, intending to say in public what was said and done in private.

More recently God's Cop Anderton's jolly bobbies had a very similar problem in Manchester with the irrepressible David Britton, author of *Lord Horror*, whom they had to prosecute and jail by various back door methods, scarcely realising that his sojourns in Strangeways and other prisons were meat and drink to him. They fueled him up. They made him go after them all the harder. The average coppers know how to give a nod and a wink to a sleazy porn-dealer and keep everything in balance (often getting a bit of free filth from the merchant in return) but idealism defeats them. They have no language for dealing with it. It makes coppers, magistrates and judges deeply irritable. As a result it turns them a bit vindictive. Self-righteous and profoundly unimaginative, they recognise in those satires only their own dark bigotry, their hatred of creative popular intellectualism, and are as happy as any know-nothing thug to turn on it with clubs and guns and burn the evidence of its existence. Those jackboots are only a shade or two away from our faces at any given time...

Tired of the familiar hypocrisies and the empty moralising of the middle-class, bored with the sententious orthodoxy of the official Left, suspicious of the motives of big business, especially the arms trade, hearing the first intimations of a very noisy uncontrollable cyberspace, a virtual universe of spin and image manipulation, understanding how popular media can become a sinister instrument of public brainwashing, how easily the culture of consumerism buys and sells our representatives, thirty years before these notions started to drift into the consciousness of the chattering classes, Spinrad put his finger on the pulse of his times. Which, as it turns out, aren't so very different from these times.

Spinrad's future may seem to be part of our past, but his message is if anything more important than the message of *1984* and a lot more relevant to us than *2001*. Alternative future or alternate past? Does it matter? The message is what drives *Bug Jack Barron*. Its observations are what fuel its anger, its impatient dynamic, while the language of the real world is what inspires its edgy, funny, streetwise idiom. Spinrad was riding high on the times, high on his own language, high on the buzz he followed from New York, to Los Angeles, to London and to Paris (where he eventually settled). One of the most politically engaged writers of his generation, he can no more write a non-political book than Ballard could write a space opera.

For thirty years Spinrad has been a prophet only intermittently honoured in the anglophone world. Now at last, with one of his most passionate and entertaining pieces of polemic back in print, you can

see why they love him in the country that welcomed so many of his
great predecessors, Hemmingway, Fitzgerald, Joyce, Hammett and
William Burroughs amongst them, long before they were recognised
at home.

Bugged?

Time to Bug Jack Barron...

Michael Moorcock,
Circle Squared Ranch,
Lost Pines, Texas,
April 1999

OTHER BOOKS OF INTEREST FROM THE OVERLOOK PRESS

THE ARABIAN NIGHTMARE
Robert Irwin   1-58567-217-3 *Paper* $14.95

A BED OF EARTH
Tanith Lee   1-58567-455-9 *Paper* $14.95

BENDING THE LANDSCAPE
VOLUME I: SCIENCE FICTION
Edited by Nicola Griffith and Stephen Pagel
0-87951-732-8 *Paper* $16.95

BENDING THE LANDSCAPE
VOLUME II:HORROR
Edited by Nicola Griffith and Stephen Pagel
1-58567-372-2 *Paper* $15.95

BENDING THE LANDSCAPE
VOLUME III: FANTASY
Edited by Nicola Griffith and Stephen Pagel
1-58567-576-8 *Paper* $15.95

THE BOOK OF THE DAMNED:
Tanith Lee   0-87951-697-6 *Paper* $15.95

THE BOOK OF THE BEAST
Tanith Lee   0-87951-698-4 *Paper* $15.95

THE BOOK OF THE DEAD
Tanith Lee   0-87951-798-0 *Paper* $15.95

THE BOOK OF THE MAD
Tanith Lee   0-87951-799-9 *Paper* $15.95

BUG JACK BARRON
Norman Spinrad
1-58567-585-7 *Paper* $14.95

CITIES IN FLIGHT
James Blish   1-58567-602-2 *Paper* $16.95

THE COMPLETE RODERICK
John Sladek   1-58567-587-3 *Paper* $17.95

THE DARNESS THAT COMES BEFORE
R. Scott Bakker   1-58567-559-8 *Cloth* $25.95

THE WARRIOR PROPHET
R. Scott Bakker   1-58567-560-1 *Cloth* $25.95

FACES UNDER WATER
Tanith Lee   1-58567-245-9 *Paper* $14.95

THE GORMENGHAST NOVELS
Mervyn Peake   0-87951-628-3 *Paper* $28.95

**GREAT TALES OF JEWISH FANTASY
AND THE OCCULT**
Joachim Neugroschel
0-87951-782-4 *Paper* $23.95

ISLANDIA
Austin Tappan Wright
1-58567-148-7 *Paper* $21.95

THE MABINOGION TETRALOGY
Evangeline Walton
1-58567-504-4 *Paper* $24.95

MORTAL SUNS
Tanith Lee   1-58567-207-6 *Cloth* $26.95

PRAYER-CUSHIONS OF THE FLESH
Robert Irwin   1-58567-220-3 *Cloth* $22.95

SAINT FIRE
Tanith Lee   1-58567-425-7 *Paper* $14.95

SHARDIK
Richard Adams
1-58567-182-7 *Paper* $21.95

VENUS PRESERVED
Tanith Lee   1-58567-653-5 *Paper* $14.95

**WHAT IF OUR WORLD IS THEIR
HEAVEN? The Final Conversations of
Philip K. Dick**
Gwen Lee and Elaine Sauter
1-58567-378-1 *Paper* $14.95

Check our website for new titles

THE OVERLOOK PRESS
WOODSTOCK & NEW YORK
www.overlookpress.com